A CRUMBLE OF WALLS
BOOK 4 OF THE KIN OF KINGS SERIES

Copyright 2016 by B.T. Narro
Cover and Map by Beatriz Garrido:
@beatrize_garrido

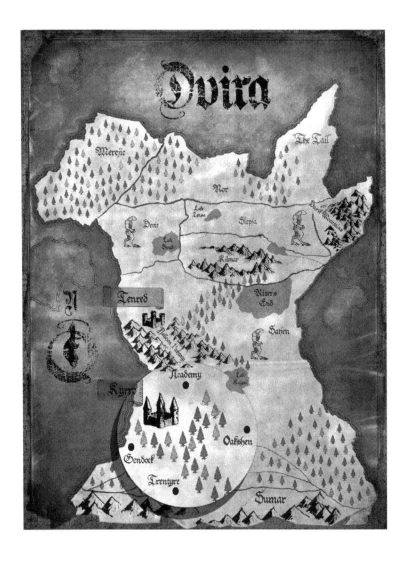

CHAPTER ONE

Sanya read the mysterious note left on her pillow enough times to memorize it. *"I know who you are, S. Come to the dungeons at midnight. Follow the torches once you're there. If you don't show up, I will notify Tauwin."*

"S," it said. Whoever wrote it did seem to know her. *"Midnight. The empty dungeons."* He or she, probably he, wanted to lure her to a place they wouldn't be seen by others in the castle. He would either threaten her further or attempt to harm her. She was confident she could handle either, but waiting for midnight proved to be difficult as she paced around her apartment in the castle. She'd never been patient.

For hours, her mind had raced with panicked thoughts that she might be forced to kill this person or leave the castle for good. Now it was finally time to find out. She hurried down the quiet halls as best she could with her loose black robes getting in the way of her feet.

Escaping the secret room with the hidden weapon of death had shredded her last concealing outfit, but Ulric had given her new robes of black silk that didn't grate against her skin like the cheap linen she had before. It wasn't much of a gift from a man so rich, but she'd never received something so expensive and would cherish it as if he'd sewn it himself.

Her silver mask had not been damaged. It would continue to hide her face as it had before, but she feared that whoever left the note had recognized her from the way she moved about the castle. She could think of only one person who knew her that well and was observant enough to figure her out. Tauwin's mother, Kithala. But Kithala was one of the few people Sanya couldn't bring herself to kill.

She wished, instead, that it was a psychic who awaited her, someone who'd spent enough time around her when she was engaged to Tauwin to recognize her energy again now that she'd returned to the castle. Someone like that might want money or something else of value. She could handle such a request by taking care of him quietly.

Her opportunity to steal control of Kyrro from Tauwin was as dead as her mother, Lori. Sanya would stay at Ulric's side, eventually proving that she deserved to be one of his most trusted advisors. Soon the war would be over, and Ulric would take control from Tauwin.

She didn't know Ulric's full plan. She hoped she could formulate one with him that would allow her to have the honor of executing Tauwin. He needed to pay for the damage he'd done to her and all of Kyrro.

And I do as well.

Damn her guilt.

She wondered how long it would take, once the war was over, for Kyrro to return to its former glory. She supposed it depended on how the war ended. If Tauwin remained king, the people would continue to be hungry and unruly. She couldn't imagine them any less volatile than ocean waves in a stormy sea, with the castle a sturdy ship struggling to stay afloat. Would it sink or would the waves calm? It would be one terrible storm.

Could Ulric be behind this note? He was a cunning man, but devious plots involving threatening notes didn't seem his style, especially when Sanya was the target. She'd felt his energy after she'd escaped from the room containing the weapon. He genuinely cared for her.

That weapon. She didn't have to ask Ulric if he'd removed it yet. She still felt it there in the bowels of the castle, creating a sour taste deep in her throat and a throb in her chest. She felt weakened by that dark energy. It was too close, even when she was in her quarters high above.

In the short time since the weapon had nearly killed her, she'd suffered frequent bouts of terror. Her whole body would tremble, then a fire would ignite in her stomach. After rushing to the nearest lavatory to relieve herself, she would calm her speeding heart in private, where she was able to remove her stifling mask.

Sanya continued to follow the torches, reaching out with psyche to sense for life. Shadows lurked in every corner. The squeaks of rats echoed around her. She was not afraid. She was *not* afraid.

Eventually she came to a circle on the ground made by chalk. "Stand here and wait" was written within.

She took her place and strained her mind to feel for energy in the same way she might strain her ears to listen for footsteps.

She detected someone's energy behind the wall to her left. She tried to read the energy, connect to it, but through the wall the task was like trying to make out words in the dark.

A muffled voice called out. "Sanya, who else knows

how you conceal yourself in this castle?"

She didn't answer as she tried to recognize the voice. It seemed to belong to a man, though it could've been a woman distorting her voice to sound like one.

Whoever it was had to be a psychic. That was the only way he could tell she was standing on the other side of the wall in this narrow hallway. She put her hands against the stone to search for a hidden doorway like the one that had opened to the chamber containing the weapon.

"Answer me, or Tauwin finds out who you are," the voice threatened.

"Who are you?" she asked to buy herself more time to search.

"Answer the question!"

Definitely a man.

She searched almost all the wall near her and found nothing. "If you answer a question of mine," she said, "I will answer you. Why did you summon me down here?"

She didn't hear him as she ran down the hall, took a left, ran down another hall, then took another left. She felt the wall for anywhere that had give and finally found it. Level with her knees, one part of the stone sank into the wall as she pushed. She turned the heavy wall enough to fit through, though the sheer blackness ahead made her stop. She went back to fetch a torch.

"You will stop and get back in the circle!" yelled the voice, "or I will kill you."

No you won't.

In his panic, the man wasn't able to keep his voice low enough to disguise it anymore. She recognized the sound of Yeso's tenor even before she brought the torch within the room. Of course it was him. She should've known. The Elf was loyal to Ulric to a fault, guarding him like an aggressive dog unable to tell friend from foe. He probably saw Sanya as a threat to his position or to his *master.*

"I know it's you, Yeso," she called from the gap in the wall. "Come out here."

She felt his energy for signs of aggression. There was a bit of anger, but mostly he was embarrassed.

He slinked out and faced her. She took off her mask to show she was unafraid.

"Why the note?" she demanded.

"Ulric needed to test your loyalty."

She could feel it was a lie, but she didn't call him on it. "How is this supposed to test my loyalty?"

"We needed to see what you would do to keep yourself from being caught, and whether you would come to us for help."

He keeps saying "we" and "us," but all of this was his decision. So Ulric knew nothing of this clandestine meeting.

"You still don't trust me."

"I don't, but I know why Ulric does. He can't sense what I can." Yeso patted his closed fist against his chest. "I can feel you're hiding something. At first I thought it was your ability to manipulate bastial energy, but even after that came out, I still felt you wanting something. What is it?"

"I want only to be allowed to live in the castle and serve Ulric by giving counsel." She changed her energy to hide her lie. "And of course I want Tauwin dead. Then I can live freely." *So long as you and everyone who wants vengeance on me is dead.* She couldn't think about that predicament right now.

"You'll be left alone when you've proven your loyalty and worth."

"You're such an irritation. How am I to prove those things?"

"You were to be ordered to leave the castle without telling Ulric. Just disappear. I was to threaten you once more with telling Tauwin of your identity if you disobeyed. Ulric and I needed to see how much trouble you might cause if your goal was threatened. Now—"

"Stop lying." She couldn't contain her irritation any longer. "This was solely your idea. You want me gone and thought this way would be a cleaner method than killing me. Afterward, you planned to tell Ulric I ran off because someone figured out who I was."

Yeso's face normally was put together nicely until times like these, when anger flared his nostrils and tightened his mouth. "Ulric needs something from you. I was going to tell you what it is once you'd proven your loyalty."

"Just take me to him."

"He's sleeping."

"In the morning, then."

"He'll be too busy tomorrow to deal with you. You must tell me what he needs to know."

She was surprised to find Yeso was telling the truth, at least as he saw it. She doubted Ulric would've bluntly said, "I'm too busy to deal with Sanya."

"Ulric is certain Tauwin will send an assassin for him soon," the Elf continued, his face contorting as if in pain.

"We need to be certain who he will send." Yeso looked hard into her eyes. "Who is it?"

Finally. A task that only she could help them with that didn't involve a threat to her life.

She should've figured Tauwin would send an assassin sooner or later. Then she could've had an answer ready for Yeso. Now she was forced to think quickly as he stared impatiently.

She thought of the least trustworthy people to Ulric first, Stanmar and Cheot, who had both shown a penchant for betrayal. Cheot had betrayed the first king, James Kerr, by allowing Tauwin to storm into the castle with his army. But Stanmar was more dangerous, because while Cheot was satisfied to be Tauwin's most trusted councilman, the army commander would do anything to increase his power. If he thought Tauwin would win this battle of the Takarys, Stanmar would switch sides again. But would he do something as foolish as sneaking into Ulric's room and stabbing him as he slept? No, and neither would Cheot.

Both men might send someone else, though, on Tauwin's behalf. No, the young king was foolish at times, but not foolish enough to surrender such a decision to anyone else. He would select the assassin himself.

"You don't know the answer," Yeso said.

"Give me a moment. You want the right person, don't you?" He didn't reply to her rhetorical question. "Then don't rush me."

Tauwin would pick someone he trusted wholeheartedly. That limited his choices to his psychics and his family. His mother would never take on such a task, and Sanya doubted Tauwin had any aunts, uncles, or cousins who would kill another Takary. That meant it had to be a psychic.

Bliss. If she were still alive, she'd be the prime suspect. Memories of that annoyingly beautiful young woman ground away at Sanya's mind. She had made so many mistakes. Too many were decisions based on what she'd felt in her heart instead of her head. She'd known it was wrong to bring back her mother from the dead, especially when Nick, Alex, and others had to die for Sanya to accomplish it. But she'd stayed true to her goal no matter the cost, and now there was no chance of redemption.

But there was also little left to lose.

Whoever she named as Tauwin's assassin would certainly be killed, yet Sanya couldn't summon any sympathy. His psychics were strange and unemotional, doing nothing more than detecting lies. Sanya imagined the type of people who wanted to live like that as having little joy.

Then again, how happy was she? Her life had become one grab for power after another. What had her ambition brought her besides heartache and guilt? *Why do my thoughts always sink into hopelessness? And at the worst times.*

"The assassin is the psychic who Rockbreak nearly killed," Sanya finally informed Yeso. "Tauwin would assume this man will want vengeance for the embarrassment Ulric caused him, and killing Ulric would prove to Tauwin and to the psychic himself that he's more capable than Ulric made him seem."

"Good, I agree. You will kill him tomorrow."

What?

Yeso folded his arms. "This is a demand from Ulric."

"How do I know you're not lying again?" she asked, already knowing he was.

"That this comes from Ulric?" Yeso acted surprised and confused. "Why would I lie about that?"

"Because you've admitted you want me gone. I'm likely to fail and be executed. I know nothing of assassinations."

Yeso squinted as if in concentration. He suddenly reached up and grabbed her head. An invasion of psyche tore through her mind. She'd put up a wall between the energy her body produced and what she'd let Yeso read, but it crumbled under the weight of his power. She was completely vulnerable.

"Say it again!" Yeso yelled through his teeth as he dug his fingers into her scalp. She grabbed his wrist and struggled to stay on her knees as agony overwhelmed her.

She could easily break the bastial energy around them, then take the knife concealed in her robe and end Yeso right now. But how would she explain it to Ulric? She couldn't hope to kill Yeso without getting blood on her robe, and the castle staff was sure to find traces even if she laundered the silk herself.

"Again!" Yeso repeated. "Tell me you know nothing of assassinations. Lie to me again!"

The bastard Elf must've felt something in her energy she'd failed to mask. She fell to her knees as pain sapped her strength. It felt as if every muscle was twisting to the point of tearing.

He reached in her robe and found her knife. He

clicked his tongue as if disappointed as he discarded it, then searched her for more weapons.

"You can die from pain," he said. "Your heart can stop. Your body gives up, knowing that death is the only relief."

She grunted in anger. Even without the dagger, she could kill him. She wanted to get her hands on his head as he did hers. She would slam it against the wall until he stopped moving. She just had to break the energy. It was as easy as snapping her fingers, but what would become of her after the Elf was dead?

She would have to run.

I might have to anyway if I agree to carry out the assassination, but I'll definitely have to flee if I kill Yeso.

She reached up and grabbed Yeso's wrists, but she hadn't the strength to push him away.

"Say it!" he demanded.

"I *know* about assassinations," she admitted.

He smiled smugly as he let the spell come to a blissful end. Sanya sprawled on the cold stone as her chest heaved. She felt as if she'd been released from a coffin.

"You can keep your secrets so long as you do what you're told," he said. "But if you go against me—and I know you're smart enough to understand what I mean by that—the two of us will have a *conversation* with Ulric, and he will hear the truth about your past. Much more than I heard tonight."

He plans to pain me again in front of Ulric. The important question was whether Yeso would do it even if she killed the psychic whose name she hadn't cared to learn. She was glad for that now, as it seemed that murdering him would be her best option.

"You don't seem to care if the man I kill turns out to be innocent," she said.

"Neither do you."

He left her panting on the floor, but not before kicking her dagger back to her.

Anger roiled in her chest. She sat up and grabbed her weapon by its hilt. It took all of her restraint not to chase Yeso down and plunge her blade into his chest.

CHAPTER TWO

Freezing rain sapped all the heat from Basen's body. There were two endless lines of people, and Basen and his father stood between them. Abith put himself at the front of one, while Terren crouched at the head of the other, reaching for his sword slowly with all eyes upon him.

"Don't, Terren," Basen whispered, realizing he was in a dream yet unable to wake up.

The Academy headmaster didn't listen as his fingers crept over the hilt of his sword. He charged Abith.

"Stop!" Basen yelled, but the rain beating down was too loud for him to be heard. Abith grinned. He would kill Terren in front of everyone and enjoy it.

The Redfield bell rang out as the two men clashed swords. For a breath, everyone was still.

"Battle!" Terren screamed.

"Battle!" Abith mimicked.

Everyone ran toward the ringing and disappeared. Basen tried to follow, but something kept him from moving. A tight grip on his wrist.

"Come on, Father," Basen pleaded. "The bell is ringing."

It continued to beckon them toward battle, but Henry wouldn't let go.

Basen turned to find it was Fatholl holding him, the Elf's grip stronger than tree roots clinging to the soil.

Basen gasped and struggled to get free. The bell was

calling to him. He needed to fight.

He fell out of bed and hit the floor, the dream dispersing like a cloud of steam. He groaned as he slowly pushed himself up, then heard the sound.

Ding! Ding! Ding!

The Redfield bell! He wasn't dreaming. He shook his head and slapped his cheek to dispel the grogginess as he stumbled toward the door.

"My pants," he grumbled, then stopped to tug them on one leg at a time. "Dammit, why do they have to attack while I'm sleeping?"

The bell continued to ring as thunder rattled the windows. Basen got his pants up and his belt tightened, then checked to make sure his wand and sword were secure in their sheaths. There was little point of fighting without a weapon, but a shirt he could forgo.

Now fully awake, he rushed out into the hall between his and Annah's rooms. She was just opening her door as he reached the front of their shared house at the Academy.

"You must be insane!" she yelled after him.

"No time," he replied, figuring she must mean his lack of a shirt.

He threw open the door and stepped out. Screaming wind seemed to blow right through him as freezing rain hit his back. His breath was forced out in a loud and sudden curse that nearly shocked him as much as the blast of cold. All the heat was gone from his body in an instant, the shivers attacking so violently that he bit his tongue and tasted blood.

By the time he turned to retrieve a covering, Annah

was there with his cloak.

"Thanks." He secured it around his neck and held it shut as he ran against the wind. He and Annah headed south with the other students emerging from their houses.

It felt like a longer run than usual as Basen wondered whether this would be his final battle. Annah seemed so small as she hunched against the cold. Basen had to remind himself that she wouldn't need protection. Being a psychic, she was probably more capable than he was.

From the darkness ahead came screams of warnings. There was a powerful crash that shook the ground and startled him into grabbing Annah to pull her behind the nearest student home.

A rumble followed, like a castle collapsing...*like a wall falling*, he realized. They were running again before it ceased, Annah squeezing his hand in obvious terror.

He recognized Terren's voice ahead of them. "Move back! Move back!"

Through the haze of darkness and rain, Basen caught sight of hundreds being herded toward him.

"Stay back and await orders!" Terren yelled.

Everyone flinched with the second crash. The sound was like a mountain collapsing, mud exploding out from the darkness ahead and raining down on them. Basen could think of only one thing that could cause such destruction. Catapults.

He'd heard his father speaking about weapons of war yesterday, but Henry had made it seem as if they had more time to prepare.

Perhaps it's just one catapult. That would explain the

delay between each attack.

Basen joined the mages in shining light at the southern wall ahead. There was a gaping hole directly in front of them, but that seemed to be the only breach so far.

*****

By the time Terren organized most of the Academy, Abith and his followers from Tenred had finally arrived to help. Abith angrily told Terren they hadn't known which wall to go to, but the headmaster gave no reply. Instead, he shouted, "Henry, are you ready?"

It was surprising to hear Terren yelling to Basen's father, as Basen hadn't seen him here yet. He joined the many mages in aiming light toward his father's responding voice but still couldn't locate him.

"Ready, Terren!"

Everyone stood away from the wall to avoid being crushed by hurled boulders, back where the student houses and classrooms blocked Basen's view in all directions. He figured the rest of his allies were gathered in the paths between buildings and waiting for the inevitable charge, but he needed to see them to know for sure.

Why hadn't the headmaster announced how many soldiers were preparing to invade the Academy? Was the number likely to be disheartening?

They needed courage. Stanmar's recruitment trick last

evening had left spirits low, but not Basen's. He yearned to fight, determined to end this damn war.

He climbed up the side of the nearest mage classroom by jumping to grab the awning, getting his forearms up, then pulling the rest of his body over. It was a short jump from the awning to reach the top, and soon he was all the way up where he could see the rest of the Academy's army.

Basen couldn't find Henry, though he recognized his father's troops by their ugly gray uniforms. Whether it was because of Terren's or Henry's order, they were gathered near the open gate and looked to be lined up in columns as if to charge out of the Academy. Basen had seen the entirety of his father's troops yesterday; there weren't more than a thousand. Why would they go alone?

Terren was busy giving orders to the Academy's instructors, who organized the students still arriving, but he hadn't taken the time to explain the plan to Basen and the others already there. Basen checked behind him, using his wand to cast light. All seemed to be chemists glancing up at him. They would wait there in safety to help the injured. He caught sight of a beautiful face that stirred his heart. Alabell showed him just a shadow of her usual bright smile as she approached.

"What do you see?" she asked.

He turned and tried with his light to pierce the darkness at the breach of the wall, but it was no use. He wouldn't catch sight of the enemy until they came dashing through.

"Nothing," Basen said, "except my father preparing to

charge with his troops."

"They'll be massacred," she said softly. "I'm sorry. I shouldn't have said that."

"No, it's true." *Then why am I about to climb off this building and join them?*

He got down and took one last look at Alabell in case it would be his last. She moved her wet auburn hair out of her eyes. Every time she looked at him, he could feel her understanding. She might be the only one who'd truly known him since he'd arrived at the Academy, and that included his father. But that didn't make Basen love Henry any less. He would fight at his side no matter the circumstance.

"Basen, be careful!" she yelled after him.

The only way to Henry was past Terren, and as Basen expected, the headmaster called out for him to stop.

"It's my father," Basen shouted back, knowing he needed no other reason.

Just then, Cleve emerged from the line of warriors to join Basen.

"Cleve!" Terren yelled to his nephew. "Stay here."

"Henry's troops need re-enforcements," Cleve yelled over his shoulder as he reached Basen's side. "What's the plan?" the warrior asked.

"No idea," Basen replied.

"Dammit. I thought you knew."

"Turn back if you want."

Cleve unstrapped the bow from his back and seemed more comfortable with it in his hands. Basen drew his sword with his dominant left hand and held his wand in his right to show his father he was prepared to engage their enemies in close combat. It was the only way Henry would allow Basen to join the charge.

He and Cleve soon reached Henry's men to hear the end of a question from his father.

"...Every archer paired with a mage?"

Basen looked to Cleve, who nodded back.

"Everyone is, sir," one of Henry's officers confirmed.

"We've done this before," Henry said. "We'll do it again." He'd always been a confident man, often giving Basen the boost he'd needed when he was younger and less sure of his abilities.

"What's the plan?" Basen risked calling out in a much higher voice than normal. He huddled close to the troops around him in hopes his father wouldn't recognize him and force him to return to Terren.

It didn't work. "Basen? Come here."

Somehow, even facing death, Basen was filled with embarrassment as he hurried to the front. It was even worse when a gust of wind blew open his cloak, giving everyone a view of his bare chest.

Henry had no words, only an indifferent look completely absent of pride.

"I didn't have time to grab a shirt," Basen muttered.

Henry took hold of his shoulder and stood close so only Basen could hear. "Listen to my orders out there and be as quick as I know you can be."

Pride swelled in Basen's chest. His father not only would let him fight but believed in him.

However, there was still the matter of not knowing what to do. Before he could ask, one of Henry's officers yelled from atop the wall, "They're about to fire to the west like before!"

Men with shields rushed around Basen to get in front just before Henry gave the order to charge.

Basen started to sprint but soon realized that everyone else was jogging as they approached the gate. He slowed to find Cleve, who towered over his comrades at the middle of this large cluster.

There was another crash—to the left. While it sounded nowhere near Basen, his reflexes forced him to cover his face with his arm. Cleve flinched as well, but they seemed to be the only ones among these seasoned troops who weren't used to the demolishing power of the boulders.

Basen heard more of the wall crumble down, but he would not be intimidated. Courage would be needed for his task.

If only he knew what it was.

The men bearing shields were covered in armor, their steel boots thudding against the wet sod. The only problem was their speed. The steel and bronze might be able to stop a fireball or arrow from killing them, but at this rate, it would take their small army twice as long to reach their enemies. Basen could only hope the darkness of this storm would provide cover until they were close.

Basen heard Cleve request a rag from another archer. Using his cloak to shield the cloth from the rain, Cleve wrapped it around the head of his arrow. Basen realized then what his father hoped to accomplish. The one question that remained was how many men Tauwin had sent to stand in their way.

"I hope you're as good with that bow as you are with

your sword," Basen told Cleve.

"Better."

"Don't lie just to make me feel better."

"I would never do that."

They rushed through the darkness until they encountered an entire army guarding a single catapult. Enemy mages were the first to fire upon them, hurling smoking fireballs that hissed as they exploded just short of the front line.

"Hold here!" Henry ordered. "Light the arrows."

It became a race as Tauwin's archers also hurried to load theirs. But they weren't taking the time to light them first, and soon their arrows began to zip by with a quick yet sharp squeal. The eastern wind was strong and blew most of the arrows to the right, but it was only a matter of time before the enemy archers adjusted.

"The wind—"

"I know," Cleve said.

Basen seemed to be the first mage to get his archer's arrow lit in this downpour. Unfortunately, the fire was bright enough to blind him temporarily. He didn't see how Cleve could aim with a flaming arrow in front of his face.

The warrior took time to stare at the catapult as he raised his flaming arrow up. He somehow ignored the fireballs and arrows coming down around him and striking his comrades. Men screamed as they fell and stumbled into one another. Basen fought the urge to duck and cover his head. How could Cleve appear so calm?

The next sight caused Basen to curse. Cleve didn't

seem to notice the horde of psychic Elves rushing toward them. "You might want to hurry," Basen advised in as calm a voice he could manage, barely refraining from shouting the words and possibly startling Cleve. The other archers had begun firing at the catapult, though the few arrows that struck didn't stick.

Basen gathered energy for a fireball, waiting until Cleve shot so as not to distract him. Finally, Cleve pulled back his string and fired in one smooth draw of his arm. Basen formed and shot a fireball, striking two of the Elves leading the charge. It didn't slow the rest.

Basen looked over their heads at the catapult, hoping to see Cleve's arrow catching it aflame. One lick of fire flickered around the back of it.

The basket! He got the basket! Knowing little about catapults, Basen had no idea what to call its different parts. But if there was one thing he could tell, it was the wooden structure looked weakest in the back, where an enormous bucket could be pulled down for loading and then tossing boulders. The wood there appeared thin, probably to keep it light for the design of the catapult to work.

It didn't burn quickly, but at least it burned. However, Basen's enemies were quickly pulling down the beam to get at the basket. Basen had already gathered enough energy for another fireball. It was a long shot, and he put everything he had behind it.

The front line of Basen's allies yelled in pain as they collapsed. The Elves had their arms out and their faces twisted from the focus of psyche, staying out of range of the attacking swordsmen. Basen heard his father's scream among the others and tore his eyes away from the soaring fireball.

CHAPTER THREE

The wind and rain provided scant protection as enemy archers fired freely. Several men were struck, but none fell out of rank. A mage took an arrow to the shoulder, grunted, then continued to light another of his comrade's arrows.

Basen's fireball finally landed a good distance in front of the catapult. He might've killed one or both of the enemies hit by his explosion, but that didn't matter. The burning basket was extinguished before any damage was done.

More flaming arrows were shot, but every time they hit, the same enemy mage smothered the flame with heavy sartious energy that looked like tiny storm clouds from this great distance.

The woman responsible couldn't have graduated from the Academy, because Alabell had witnessed graduates being dragged out of their homes to be killed when Tauwin took the castle. Those who escaped death had joined up with Henry. So where had this woman come from?

She must've trained in Greenedge specifically to take our territory from us. Anger made Basen fearless as he gathered energy for his next fireball. Out of the corner of his eye, he noticed his father standing tall against a psychic spell. Basen had never spoken to his father about resisting psyche and wondered how Henry was capable.

Gritting his teeth against the pain, Henry screeched,

"Tell Terren to send the reinforcements!"

"Already done!" one of his officers called from somewhere behind Basen.

"Move back while we wait!" Henry yelled.

But it seemed as if their enemies were retreating as well, as they began dragging the catapult away. The psychic Elves looked over their shoulders and then sprinted back toward their army, who continued to fire.

Ally archers changed their targets to the Elves, felling only a few of them. Basen paid them little mind as he moved to the outskirts of his group and condensed all the energy he could gather into a ball. He would have to form and then shoot this fireball even farther than the last, and there was only one way he knew to do that.

The danger of this risky spell was not lost on him as he brought out a thin stream of sartious energy from his wand to catch the bastial energy aflame. He then split his focus, pulling the burning bastial energy toward him and pushing it away at the same time. It was a game of balance, the fireball jittering forward and back as the burning energy fought to break free from the hold of his mind, akin to getting ready to snap a finger.

He propelled it forward as he released his hold and watched the ball of flame soar through the air. At first he thought he might have overshot his mark, but the escaping army had wheeled the catapult just far enough for Basen's fireball to come down and explode on top of it.

Unfortunately, he missed the sartious mage who dove out of the way. She was now back on her feet and heading toward the burning basket.

"Cleve!" Basen said as he rejoined the group. "You

have to shoot—"

"I know."

Cleve already had his string pulled back with an arrow notched. He fired. Basen lost track of the arrow in the darkness and watched the sartious mage as time seemed to slow.

The arrow struck her hard enough to take her off her feet. Two others bent down to help her while everyone else threw mud at the burning basket.

It was too high for them to get a good angle, the flames growing too quickly.

The rain had stopped. *God's mercy, when?* Had Basen been religious, he would've credited divine intervention, but it was just luck.

With the rest of Terren's army quickly approaching, Tauwin's troops running away and leaving behind the catapult, the battle appeared over for now.

"Good shot," Basen told Cleve.

"You as well."

Terren and Henry met amidst their men. "You were right," the headmaster said. "But how did you know?"

"Tauwin's army always uses specific formations for certain battle tactics," Henry answered. "We've seen enough formations to predict what they're going to do."

Terren smiled. "When they return, I'll make sure you have as much time as possible to read their formation."

Henry nodded.

"How did you stand up against the spell?" Basen asked him.

But Abith interrupted as he came up and asked Henry, "How many were there?"

"We're not going after them," Terren said firmly.

Abith gave him an annoyed look before turning back to Henry. "How many did you see, Hiller?"

"That's a very different question than how many there were," Henry replied. "I could've seen a hundred or a thousand, and Terren would still be right. We're not going after them." After staring at a confused Abith for a moment, Henry continued. "I didn't see many, but the night is dark. There's no way to tell how many wait for us to be lured into a trap."

Abith veered back to his group of older troops, who mostly had a nervous look about them.

Basen wanted to ask his father if he had any experiences with such traps during the many battles at Trentyre, but he was still waiting for Henry to answer his first question.

"Let's speak later," Henry told him. "Tomorrow, I will find you."

"All right."

Fatigue caught up with Basen as he neared the Academy and saw the two gaping holes in the southern wall. While the excitement of speaking with his father buoyed his spirit, Basen was frustrated they'd shared precious few words in the hours since their reunion.

He held his cloak closed as he walked around the students, instructors, and all the troops from Tenred and Trentyre. He looked for Alabell among their vast army, all the time wondering how many more troops composed Tauwin's. Basen didn't know why he was reluctant to go back to his student home, where his warm bed awaited, but he wasn't the only one. Everyone paced around aimlessly as if awaiting the next order.

None came, and eventually Basen caught sight of Effie and Cleve walking away from the wall. He started after them in hopes of talking. It seemed like the only way to get his mind to a better place before attempting to sleep again. But as he walked past his father speaking with Terren and Abith about the broken wall, Basen paused to eavesdrop.

"We have plenty we can put to work." Abith's voice sounded more impatient each time Basen heard him speak, as if he'd become tired of his opinion being ignored. "Get the stonemasons to teach them what to do, and the wall should be rebuilt stronger and higher in the next few days."

Basen had seen Abith with other young mages back in Tenred, often looking bored as he waited for them to complete whatever challenge he'd given them. Basen was fortunate he learned quickly, as Abith often told him it was a relief to teach someone with actual talent.

"Sounds like you want to take control of this," Terren said. "So have at it. Do whatever you need to get the wall rebuilt in the next few days."

"That's not what I was saying," Abith argued, but Terren and Henry had walked off.

Basen quickly turned toward Effie and Cleve and pretended he hadn't overheard anything. A bristled Abith was not a man Basen knew how to deal with.

"Basen," Abith called after him. "Come here."

He sighed and marched over.

"I wanted to tell you that you fought well in the Fjallejon Mountains, but you disappeared before I had the chance." He smirked.

Basen was too surprised to speak. Abith only gave compliments when he was in a good mood, which he clearly wasn't now.

"If I'd known you had that kind of potential with a sword," Abith continued, "I would've incorporated it into our lessons."

"And who taught you to sword fight?"

"The same person who taught me how to manipulate energy."

"Yourself?"

Abith chuckled. "God's mercy, no. My father. It's a shame he died before I was skilled enough to be a real challenge to him. He's the only man who could've beaten me in a duel while I was at my best." He surprised Basen by putting a hand on his shoulder. "Keep training with both sword and wand. Perhaps one day you'll be an equal challenge. If not, I at least have a plan for your talent."

He was glad when Abith took his hand off and walked away. Basen wasn't exactly scared of Abith, but there was something about his former instructor that made him nervous.

He hurried off in the same direction Cleve and Effie had gone. Soon he caught up enough to see them stopped behind a student house and pointing at something on the wall. They didn't seem to hear him come up on them.

*****

Cleve's breaths were still sharp from the adrenaline of battle. Effie had taken him away from the wall to speak with him privately. He was worrying about the conversation to come when he realized she was leading him toward Alex's house.

"Look," she said as she pointed to the back of the house where someone had carved "We miss you, Alex" into the wood.

"Did you do this?" Cleve asked.

"No, and that's the point. We're not the only ones who hurt because of what Sanya did."

"Why are you telling me this?"

Effie gave him a cold look from the sides of her eyes. "You've already closed off your emotions. Don't, Cleve. You must remember how that turned out when you did the same after your mother and father died."

He gritted his teeth. "Don't tell me how to—"

"I'm sorry," she interrupted, then gave a long sigh as she shook her head. "I know I shouldn't tell you how to feel. I just don't know how else to explain this to you."

"There's nothing to explain. Everyone who knew Alex misses him." Cleve gestured at the carving. "I didn't need to see this to know that."

"I didn't bring you here to speak to you about Alex. I need to know something else."

"What?"

"Why didn't you do it? Why didn't you...kill her?"

Cleve could easily summon the image of Sanya bloody and dying. He often thought of it when trying to sleep, but it never brought him the comfort he sought.

"Is it only because Reela told you not to?" Effie asked quietly. "I need to know."

"Why?"

"Come on, Cleve. Tell me. Please."

"Are you looking for someone to blame for Sanya still being alive?"

Effie looked down. "Reela told me what happened, and I don't agree with her." The mage gazed up into Cleve's eyes. "I want to know what you plan to do the next time we see her."

Cleve couldn't believe he was about to tell this to Effie. "Killing her won't accomplish anything, except it will keep her from assisting our side in this war."

Effie's mouth twisted in disappointment. "Why do you still defend Reela even though you two aren't...?"

"Aren't what? What did she tell you?"

"She didn't tell me anything, Cleve, but I'm not stupid. I can see what's going on between you. And what isn't."

The two women told each other everything. Reela had to have said something, even if Effie could figure it out on her own.

Someone behind them cleared his throat. Cleve turned to find Basen standing close enough to have overheard.

"Sorry," Basen said, wearing a guilty look. "I should've left or said something earlier, but...I couldn't."

"I'm going to the medical building to visit my sister," Effie announced, then left without waiting to see if anyone wished to go with her.

"Is Gabby all right?" Basen asked Cleve.

"Yes. She's not hurt, just a chemist helping the injured

there."

Cleve crossed his arms for warmth as an awkward moment of silence passed.

"Do you know how many casualties we took?"

"None were killed," Cleve said. "And most of the injured came from our group."

There was another pause before Cleve asked, "Why did you follow us here?"

"I apologize for that. I suppose I wanted a moment with friends before retiring to my room for the night."

Cleve knew he should force a smile and say something supportive, but it seemed easier to fight another battle than that.

"Good night, Basen," he said with a nod.

Cleve traveled home slowly, not wanting to see Reela. Every time he missed Alex, his thoughts turned to Sanya for a moment of anger before eventually shifting to Reela. It was Reela who made him worry the most, because his strife with Sanya would end once she was put down like the savage animal she was. With Reela, however, he saw no way to recapture what they'd lost.

He wondered what Sanya had done to put her mother and Alex to rest somewhere within that black hallway in the castle depths. Cleve got the sense that Sanya had barely escaped with her life, and he wouldn't have fared any better.

He was glad he hadn't killed Sanya while she was weak, for he didn't want her murder on his conscience. Capturing her would've been a good start toward justice, but Reela was right that Kyrro's Allies would've torn her apart as soon as Cleve got her out of the castle.

None of this changed the fact that he still wanted to see her punished for her crimes. It wasn't enough that her terrible choices had led her to misery. Repentance wasn't justice for murder.

However, Reela did have a point that Sanya has been helping their side in this war. *Truly the only reason I didn't go against Reela and kill Sanya.*

Eventually Cleve arrived back at his student home. He walked down the hallway to find Reela standing in the doorway of the room they'd been sharing. He knew what she wanted.

"Have you been waiting long?" he asked.

"Yes, but it's fine."

It didn't sound fine by the tone of her voice. Not wanting to risk brushing against her, Cleve waited until she stepped aside to enter the room. He could move everything out of here in a minute, as all he had were a heavy weapons chest and clothing.

He was too tired to lift the chest and dragged it into the hallway instead. As he got to the door of his old room, however, Micklin opened it from the other side.

"I heard you fought with Hiller's men!" the boy gushed. "Oh, do you need this room? I could share."

Cleve grumbled. "Why'd you come here?"

The boy's face fell. "I wanted to stay in your house. I finally got a chance to ask Terren after the battle and he said there was an open room here. I hope that's all right. Can you tell me what happened when you went past the wall? Did you kill anyone?"

Cleve grumbled again. He was too exhausted for this. He walked around to the other side of his weapons chest and pushed it toward Effie's room. She could share a bed with Reela tonight and move her belongings into Reela's room tomorrow.

"Don't mind him," Reela told Micklin. "He's just tired. You should get to sleep because it'll be a busy day for you tomorrow."

"You don't have to mother me," he told Reela somewhat coldly, to Cleve's surprise, then shut the door. Perhaps Cleve's lack of a response had angered him.

Had Reela heard something about Terren's plan for civilians like Micklin who were unable to fight? Cleve hadn't seen anyone Micklin's age yet, but there had to be more orphaned by the war. *Unless they went back with Stanmar last night.*

"What do you mean it'll be a busy day for him?" Cleve asked her.

"I don't know what he's going to do," Reela whispered, "but I'm sure he'll have a job like everyone else."

A job, not sword fighting. Good. Cleve didn't have time to worry about Micklin. He needed to keep a close eye on Abith's men during the next battle.

"Good night," he muttered to Reela.

"Cleve, wait." She backed into her room and gestured for him to follow.

His pulse quickened. He missed touching her and realized this now with such ferocity that he momentarily forgot why they were fighting.

She pointed at the bed. He yearned to see the look of love in her eyes, craving it more than sleep and food.

But she gave him the dead-eyed stare he'd grown to hate.

"You forgot your pillow."

CHAPTER FOUR

Basen's first morning back at the Academy started off as delightful as he'd anticipated it would be during his time away. Breakfast hours had been extended to give everyone ample time to sleep, and he'd rested well after the short battle. It was a new day, the air fresh and the sun bright in the cloudless sky.

Basen was determined to come up with a solid plan for Fatholl today, no matter if he missed battle training. He'd promised to return to the Elf in a week and had only a few days left. He wasn't about to go without knowing what to expect. Fortunately, he had Annah walking with him to the dining hall. She probably knew more about Krepps and Elves than he could hope to learn in a day.

She appeared not to have slept as well as him, her blue eyes red and swollen as she continued to glance south as if expecting Tauwin's army to come rushing through the broken wall at any moment.

"They'll be back soon," she said. "If you leave, you won't be here to help us defend the Academy."

Last night, she'd begged to know every detail of the battle with the catapult, and he'd made the mistake of telling her that he and Cleve had managed to catch it on fire. Now she had the impression the Academy would lose the next battle if he left to fulfill his promise to Fatholl.

It was sad to see someone as smart and powerful as Annah so easily frightened. He figured it had to do with the years she'd spent fixing her fear with psyche instead of learning to accept it for the harmless feeling it was.

"I overheard Terren speaking with Abith and my father," Basen said, "right after Stanmar recruited our people and left. Terren believes Stanmar will come back today and attempt to recruit more. It means battle won't happen for a while, especially considering that their only catapult is now a pile of ash outside the southern wall."

"Terren doesn't know any of that for certain. They could have more catapults."

"Annah, I'll only be gone a couple of days. I don't want to go, but we can't have the Elves siding against us." *Or sending someone to kill me.* "They did give us the Krepps in armor, after all. Even though the Krepps have been nothing but trouble so far, I'm sure they will be worth the effort in the end. Now I need your help to figure out what Fatholl will make me do. It must be a portal he wants, but for what purpose?"

"I don't know. I can't think right now." She let her head hang. "I didn't sleep well last night."

Basen held back a grumble. He decided to wait until she'd put food in her stomach before pressing her again.

After she took a few bites of hot, generously buttered bread and grinned, he figured the time was right. "If you remember, I was also able to make a portal at the center of the village in Merejic, not just in Fatholl's quarters."

It was from there that he'd transported hundreds of Krepps into the kitchen of Tenred castle while the Elves watched. Now, he wanted to teleport back to the village at night, when he might have a chance to skulk around before Fatholl knew he'd arrived.

"In order to create a portal there, energy had to have

been gathered in that area many times before. It was Fatholl who brought me to that spot after I explained the requirements of a portal. He must've known something else happened there, probably more than just a repetitive use of psyche. Do you know what it was?"

"It's likely to be where Doe and Haemon stood while destroying the Elves and their village. Though, Doe and Haemon weren't standing, I suppose. They slithered. You do know what they were, right?"

"I haven't been living in a cave." Of course Basen had heard of the two monstrous Slugari who had gone against their own kind with an army of Kreppen supporters. What he hadn't heard, however, was that they'd helped destroy the Elven village, causing the Elves to flee to Merejic. He told this to Annah.

"So you don't know about Vithos," she said. It wasn't a question.

"I know he's Reela's half-brother."

"About his past."

"He grew up with the Krepps. What does he have to do with Fatholl?"

"Did you ever think about *why* he grew up with Krepps?"

"I figured they found or took him when he was young—oh, he was in the village when Doe and Haemon attacked with the Krepps."

"Exactly. His history is what you're really asking me about. There was a battle there when he was a baby. It must be why you can make a portal in the center of the village and why Fatholl knew the spot. His ancestors are the Elves who escaped."

One thing was now clear to Basen. The Elves and Krepps shouldn't be getting along as well as it seemed. Perhaps Fatholl wanted to use Basen to get rid of the lizard creatures.

"Do you know if Yeso was with the Elves who attacked us last night?" Annah asked. "He looks similar to Fatholl, from what I've gathered."

No doubt Annah had socialized with the citizens from Oakshen and the capital who'd fled to the Academy. Basen could easily imagine her questioning everyone she came in contact with, pumping them for information about their enemies. He appreciated her efforts but wished she knew how to relax. She seemed more tense each time they spoke.

"I didn't get a good look at any of them," he told her. "I assume Yeso is the one who led the Elves here from Greenedge?"

"Actually, I believe a Takary named Ulric is the one who led the new army here from Greenedge. But it's Yeso who commands the Elves, at least that's what I'm told. They might be here for other reasons than fighting, however. If you're searching for something to use against Fatholl, you might want to find out more about them. Ask Cleve or Reela. They went to Greenedge after the war, you know." She took a few quick bites of food. "Are you going now? I could come with you."

Basen leaned back in his chair, making an effort to relax. "Thank you, Annah, but I plan to finish my breakfast first. Then I'll find Cleve." Basen knew him better than the half-Elven psychic and also knew where Cleve was most likely to be.

By the time Basen had cleaned the last morsel from his plate, it was time for battle training, meaning Annah couldn't go with him. Before they separated, she made him promise to come to her with his plan before he left. He agreed, especially considering that his rudimentary plot involved her.

He wasn't sure if the new recruits would be joining the Academy's soldiers in training yet, or if at all. He would find out later. Annah went to join her fellow psychics while he made his way to Warrior's Field.

His instructor, Penny, would be upset at Basen for missing training, but his time was better spent figuring out Fatholl's plan. He agreed with Annah that there must be something he could use involving the Elves who'd recently arrived from Greenedge. They'd chosen to follow a Takary to war instead of joining Fatholl. There was likely to be strife between the two groups.

A crowd at the center of the enormous field of grass caught his attention. Hoping to find Cleve there, Basen headed toward it. Krepps were clustered on one side of a circle. The humans completing the circle stood farther apart, not pushing to get a spot at the front like the creatures opposite them.

That made it easy for Basen to slip through to the inner rows of the circle, where he not only found Cleve but saw that the large warrior was in the middle of a bout against Rickik, the leader of the Krepps and possibly the biggest of them all. He was a full head taller than Cleve, with arms so massive that Basen doubted Cleve could cut cleanly through them with his bastial steel sword, even if the weapon was made from the sharpest and lightest material in the world.

Fortunately, Basen didn't have to worry about irreparable damage to any of the Krepps he'd worked so hard to bring here, for Cleve and the other warriors were armed with dull training swords of wood. Fortunately for Cleve, so were Rickik and his Krepps.

But neither Cleve nor Rickik wore a protective tunic of boiled leather. Basen had trained with other swordsmen for years and knew there was only one reason someone would forego a tunic. Pride. It was better to train with one and get used to its weight. Although, Basen doubted there was a tunic at the Academy large enough to contain Rickik's chest.

The Krepp fought quickly for his size, swiping his massive sword at Cleve in an endless barrage of attacks. But Cleve was more agile. He seemed to slow time with his ability to duck and dart out of the way.

Eventually he leaned back to avoid the tip of Rickik's wooden sword, then stepped into the Krepp with a thrust of his own. Rickik let go of his weapon to deflect Cleve's attack with his arm, but all the Krepp did was guide the tip into his shoulder instead of his chest. Had it been Cleve's bastial steel sword, it might've gone straight to bone.

"Point!" nearly half the crowd of humans called out, some applauding.

Basen was pleasantly surprised to see the Krepps behaving rather than starting an uproar as Rickik scowled and spat on the grass.

It took two points to win a duel here at the Academy, and Rickik looked as if he wanted to hurt Cleve for the embarrassment the human had caused him. His lizard eyes, yellow and full of fury, had widened to nearly a complete circle. The two holes in the center of his face that made up his nose flared with each quick breath. He exchanged his two-handed sword for a smaller one from one of his Krepps. It was still about the size of Cleve's two-handed sword, but Rickik held it with just one hand and weaved it through the air seamlessly in a show of dexterity.

He muttered something in Kreppen to Cleve. A few of the warriors behind Basen asked what Rickik had said.

"I think he said, 'Humans are weak but quick. Take away their speed and they lose,' " someone answered.

Basen was thankful at least someone knew a smattering of Kreppen. All the Krepps seemed to know at least some common tongue, and a few of them were fluent enough to converse with humans, if they chose to. During their trip back to the Academy, however, the Krepps mostly had kept to themselves, and Basen figured they did the same here. They just wanted to fight and get help to build their own city. Rickik was the only one who wanted more—the bastial steel sword out of Tauwin's dead hands.

Basen hoped the Krepp wouldn't settle for anything less. He did seem to be eyeing the hilt of Cleve's bastial steel sword.

I can understand Cleve worrying about leaving his sword where it might get stolen, but to fight with a training weapon while his bastial steel sword is strapped to his belt seems absurd.

The circle broke as the name "Warrior Sneary" fell off

everyone's lips in a hushed warning. Basen hid behind other students so the approaching instructor wouldn't send him to the mages' training grounds.

Sneary came through and confronted Cleve. "What's happening here?"

"Just a duel."

Sneary took his time regarding Rickik and the Krepps behind him. The instructor seemed to be checking to make sure each had a wooden training sword, his head tilting down toward their waist. Then he turned to the human side of the now messy circle.

He folded his arms and asked Cleve, "Where's your dueling tunic?"

Cleve lifted his hand and a boiled leather tunic spun out from the crowd. He snatched it out of the air and put it on.

Sneary moved back and gestured for them to continue.

Most of the warriors clapped as they reformed the circle. The Krepps hissed and smiled as they seemed to understand Sneary was a leader of the humans and had allowed this to go on.

Rickik gestured with his claws for Cleve to come at him, and Cleve gladly took on the challenge by running and leaping high enough to fill Rickik's eyes with shock.

"God's mercy," Basen muttered as Cleve soared toward Rickik with his knees bent and his sword overhead. It couldn't be pure strength and agility alone that allowed Cleve to reach such heights or give him the stamina to finish three laps around this enormous field before anyone else. Cleve had to be doing *something* else to gain that kind of advantage.

Rickik spun to avoid Cleve and slashed at his back, yet Cleve rolled, giving himself the distance he needed to run and leap again. But he stopped short this time. Rickik was hurrying backward until he realized Cleve was no longer coming for him. The Krepp bared his teeth, obviously embarrassed to be caught moving away from the fight. He charged Cleve.

Basen could only hope this was what Cleve had wanted. Cleve turned his body to assume a stance with his weapon out in front, a tactic usually reserved for one-handed swords. Fortunately, Cleve appeared strong enough to wield his weapon this way as he stepped toward Rickik and kicked with his back foot in an attack that even caught Basen by surprise.

Rickik doubled over, closing his elbows over his injured stomach. Cleve followed with a slash down onto Rickik's shoulder for the victory. It wasn't a hard blow, for Cleve had no reason to injure the leader of the Krepps. In fact, it was probably dangerous to hurt or embarrass any of them, as it might spark another duel, but with real swords.

Basen applauded with the others. For such an honorable man, Cleve certainly seemed to have a lot of tricks. The Krepps refused to look at Rickik as he rejoined them. Many rushed forward to challenge Cleve, which started an argument among them in their throaty language.

"Cleve," Basen said, "I need to speak with you."

"What?" Cleve seemed reluctant to leave the center of the circle, turning toward Basen but looking back at the

Krepps.

"It's important."

"Winner stays." Cleve refused to move.

"Then you might be here all morning, and I don't have time for that. Just give me a few moments. It's about Fatholl."

Finally, Cleve seemed to remember there was more to life than dueling. He approached Basen. "What is it?"

Before Basen could speak, the Krepps had chosen who would fight Cleve next and a large female had her sword pointed at him.

"Now me, human." She was about Cleve's height and looked just as strong and capable. Unlike the other Krepps, she wore a protective tunic. None of the Krepps said a word as they waited for Cleve to accept the challenge. This female had clearly earned respect the same way Sanya had during her brief time at the Academy.

Cleve looked at Basen imploringly. Basen was thankful when Peter stepped out from the crowd and stood tall and strong.

"I will fight," he said.

Given he was about the same size as Cleve, the female Krepp seemed to take no dishonor in accepting the change. Basen watched her stride confidently toward Peter as Basen got down to business with Cleve.

"I need to know what you learned about the Elves during your time in Greenedge."

Cleve raised an eyebrow. "What do you need to know about them?"

"I'm trying to figure out why there's a second group of

Elves here fighting with Ulric and not with Fatholl."

Peter locked swords with the female Krepp. She grinned at him while he struggled to overpower her. Peter grunted as he pushed, sending her back a step. But she appeared to be ready, already drawing back her sword to swipe at Peter's head. He dodged the blow, just barely.

"Why does it matter?" Cleve asked.

"I'm going to see Fatholl soon. Maybe he wants something more from those Elves than whatever he wants from me."

Cleve's brow furrowed, his gaze never leaving the bout. "I don't understand."

He's not listening.

Now that the Krepp had earned Peter's respect, they were circling each other. It seemed the best chance to get an answer out of Cleve, so Basen got straight to the point.

"Have you heard anything about an Elf named Yeso or a group of Elves going against Fatholl?"

"The Elves cast Fatholl out for practicing psyche. They don't allow it."

"Which Elves don't? Obviously not the ones who attacked us last night."

Sneary stepped into the circle and ordered, "Stop. It's time for battle training to begin." He put up his hands when everyone griped. "But we're starting the day with two on two combat," he continued. "Get on your dueling tunics!"

The warriors' groans changed to a quick round of celebration as they laughed and clapped. As the Krepps realized what was about to happen, they joined in.

CHAPTER FIVE

All these men were Basen's size or larger, their collective cheering deep yet harmonious with each other. *These are the Group One warriors*, he realized. *The Academy's best swordsmen, possibly the best of our entire army.* The thought made Basen realized that everyone left to stand against Tauwin was within the school's walls.

Basen wondered whether he would've been placed among these warriors if he'd tested as one instead of a mage on that fateful recruitment day. *Probably not.* He'd been the best swordsmen his age in Tenred, but after watching Cleve and Peter, Basen understood the warriors here were in a different class.

He noticed Nebre standing at the far end of the Krepps, almost within the human side of the circle. Without his human clothing, he was no longer easily recognizable until he opened his mouth. His white teeth gave him away as he seemed to be translating Sneary's message to the other Krepps.

Suddenly the creatures made fists and hissed with wicked grins, a clear sign of excitement. However, a few argued with Nebre, who continued to point toward the pile of thick leather tunics.

Basen was thankful when Sneary selected two men other than Cleve for the first fight. Rickik chose two Krepps to face the men.

"Cleve, which Elves don't allow psyche?" Basen asked as the chaotic bout began.

"All Elves in Greenedge. For centuries, they've lived in a territory called Meritar and have exiled anyone caught using or teaching psyche. Fatholl rebelled because he wanted to use psyche to..." His voice trailed off as the fight drew his attention.

The two warriors announced what their opponents were doing, as if wanting to turn the practice battle into a show. But it was much more than that, Basen soon realized, as one of the men called out "rotating" and came around the Krepp, who turned his bare back toward the warrior's partner. The other warrior took advantage with a stab that drew a screech from the creature.

"Point!" Sneary said. But the Krepp who hadn't taken the hit continued to chase after the man he'd been targeting.

"Stop," Sneary ordered as the human quickly backed away from him. "The point has been claimed. Nebre, tell him!"

Nebre translated, but Rickik interrupted his son to complain to Sneary. "My Krepp no lose, only other Krepp. He fight two humans. No stop."

"When any of your Krepps are struck, the fight is over," Sneary explained.

"Why?" Rickik spat on the grass. "Coward humans, coward rules."

"At the Academy, we discourage our warriors from claiming victory if they let their allies die. The point of the exercise is to learn to fight together, not to sacrifice each other. Do you understand?"

With his scaly forehead crinkled in confusion, Rickik turned to Nebre, who translated. Before he could finish,

Sneary told Nebre, "And explain to Rickik that just because his Krepps are standing near each other while fighting doesn't mean they're fighting together."

While Sneary continued the lesson for Rickik, Basen resumed his prodding. "Cleve, what did Fatholl do with psyche that got him exiled?"

"Greenedge had a dismal future. In a few words, Fatholl made the continent safe again. He wanted the Elves' help but had to force the humans to help him instead." Cleve finally looked at Basen. "He murdered. He killed kings and displaced thousands of men, women, and children. He'll do anything if he believes it will help the world in the end."

"The world, or just the Elves?"

Cleve thought about that for a while. The Krepp who'd been stabbed in the back put on a tunic before the next fight. Many of the Krepps watching did the same. *It won't be long before all of them realize there is no pride in unnecessary injury.*

The fight for the second point was much like the first, ending with the same Krepp taking the blunt wooden sword to his back. He screeched and then stomped toward his ally Krepp in an obvious display of anger, but the other Krepps were quick to intervene.

"Fatholl will do what he thinks is right," Cleve finally answered. "He'll use you in the same way we're using these Krepps."

"He'll think he's using me," Basen corrected. "But I might be able to use him instead."

Cleve looked worried. "How do you expect to do that?"

Basen didn't want to admit he was still figuring that out. "Did he mention anything about another group of Elves having been exiled from Meritar?"

"I don't know anything about another group of Elves." Cleve returned his attention to the duel. "Sorry, I can't help you."

"You have already."

Basen lost Cleve again as the next fight began, but it didn't matter anymore. Basen left Warrior's Field with a smirk because Cleve had given him the answer he'd hoped to hear. If Fatholl had done so much to change Greenedge yet never mentioned anything to Cleve of another group of Elves, there was a good reason they'd remained apart.

They might not know they're on the same continent now.

The library was Basen's next destination. He felt a pang of guilt for not telling Penny why he would be absent, but sometimes it was better to ask for forgiveness than for permission.

He hadn't been to the library since Nick had given him a tour on his first day at the Academy. Although impressed by its size and the number of books, he figured he'd never have time to indulge himself. He'd just discovered portals, not that he'd known it yet. He'd expected to spend every spare moment training.

It was a good thing he had. Being the only one who could make a portal, besides Sanya, it was his responsibility to keep one open long enough for hundreds of Academy forces to go through in case Terren ordered it.

To Basen's surprise, the library was busy this morning.

However, he soon realized none of these people were students but citizens brought here from Oakshen and the capital. These were the brave ones who hadn't left, at least not yet. Stanmar would return to recruit more of them, but the destruction of his catapult certainly would hurt his chances of scaring more people into defecting.

Tauwin's army was not invincible. The sooner everyone in Kyrro learned that, the better the Academy's chances. There were students who'd left last night, and Basen had seen many more considering it from the way they'd moved closer to the wall as Stanmar left. Given another opportunity to leave, many would take it.

The people at the library appeared to be organizing books, not reading them. As Basen looked around the vast hall, he figured he was the only student here, everyone else occupied in battle training. There was no one at the door to greet him, stop him, or even notice him for that matter. He spent a while looking for the librarian.

Finally, one of the women taking books out of a basket and arranging them on a long shelf looked over and stopped.

"Who sent you?"

Sent me?

"Jack Rose," he replied. The master chemist was the only teacher Basen knew who might send someone to the library to fetch a book about Elves and Takarys in Greenedge. "He's looking for more information about Ulric Takary and Yeso the Elf."

"That man…" She shook both her head at Basen as she approached. "He may be brilliant when it comes to potions, but his sharp mind doesn't do him much good keeping track of all the happenings of the day. He came last night, half asleep, and took the book. If he lost it—I don't care if he's the head chemist around here—I'll...*ergh.*" Her hands fisted. "It's the only copy we have! Tell him he has until the end of the day to get it back to me. No pages bent! And tell him to never let it out of his sight and stop forgetting he has it! The dolt."

"I'll certainly tell him all those things." *Sorry Jack, didn't mean to get you in trouble.*

Basen walked out of the library, put his hands on his hips, and sighed. The morning was passing quickly, and he had no idea where Jack would be at this time. He was right to assume the chemist would send him for such a book, but it had nearly cost him his chance of finding out where the book was now. He considered himself lucky that Jack was the kind of man who might borrow a book and then forget, otherwise the librarian would've known Basen was lying.

The masters of each class, like Jack, didn't spend their days instructing, except maybe the master warrior, though Basen had no idea who that was. Perhaps there wasn't one. Being a master was a silly concept anyway, no matter the class. Although Abith was undoubtedly the closest of anyone Basen had met to being considered a master. Basen feared for Terren's safety. During the years Basen had spent under Abith's tutelage, he'd never figured out what to expect from his teacher, and Abith most certainly had a plan to become headmaster.

Basen headed toward Jack's office. If he wasn't there, someone might know where he was. All the instructors had a private home, while many also had an office elsewhere. Nick had told Basen this.

Basen swallowed and paused. He missed his roommate. Alex, too. The pain felt slightly different each time he thought of his fallen friends, though it was usually like a small stone caught between his chest and his throat. This was an ache of regret, he'd come to realize, of wishing he had done more, been smarter, caught Sanya before she'd murdered them. But it was also guilt, for he didn't feel the need to kill Sanya now, unlike Effie. He didn't see how Sanya's death would help unless it was necessary to stop her from killing others.

He felt the same anger toward her that Effie did. Sanya's betrayal made Basen want to wring her neck, but not to the point of death. He would get immense pleasure, however, from hurling her into a prison cell hard enough to slam her into a stone wall before locking the cell door behind her.

More people than usual were bustling around the campus, and the busyness didn't stop when Basen reached the building that housed the instructors' offices. As he walked down the hall and looked for Jack's name next to each open door, Basen had to stay alert to keep from running into people hurrying past him.

It seemed that only chemist instructors had their offices here, because all the citizens rushing around Basen carried something related to their practice. A plant, a beaker, scrolls with edges burned, or books with titles containing phrases that meant nothing to Basen, like "Activated Stages of Energy" and "Beekem's Uncertainty and Risk."

It was easy to forget there was so much more to being a chemist than making potions. Most of the worlds' advances had originated from chemists. Basen was fascinated at how humans could use the energies and elements of nature in new ways. He might've requested lessons if he hadn't been so infatuated with manipulating energy to cast magic. Perhaps it was the word itself. Magic. What little boy didn't want to cast magic?

Jack's office didn't look much different than his kitchen, at least during the time Basen had visited him. It appeared as if a strong wind had scattered anything light enough to be plucked from the table. Basen stood unnoticed in the doorway as Jack practically dove for a scroll underneath the foot of a young man standing in front of his desk.

"Careful where you step! Up. Up."

"Sorry." The young man jumped off. Jack feverishly read through the scroll with his mouth open in concentration.

"Oh, this message is a day old. It's in the wrong place." He rolled it up and tossed it on the floor to one side of his desk, where many other scrolls apparently had been discarded. The young man handed Jack another scroll like the others.

"From Terren," the messenger said, then glanced over his shoulder, spotting Basen.

He gave a faint smile, his eyes telling this young man what a mess he thought this room to be. The young man smiled back in the same way, then turned to face Jack again.

Jack finished reading the scroll and handed it back.

"Tell him I haven't seen Abith today and all of the chemist instructors are to alert me if he comes to them with any requests. In regard to the wall, we have a substance that might adhere the new stone to the old quickly, but it still needs to be tested. Lastly—"

"Excuse me, Mister Rose," the young man interrupted, "but will you write the message? I can't remember—"

"You will remember, and call me Jack. Now repeat everything back to me."

"But...but you haven't finished telling me your message."

"Oh, of course. What was I about to say? Ah. Lastly, tell Terren the psyche-resist serum may be used in dire situations, but it needs testing before it's given to our soldiers."

As the young man recited back the message, Basen wondered more about this potion that might allow him to resist psyche. Soon enough, the messenger hurried off and the room was quiet.

"Aren't you supposed to be in battle training?" Jack barely glanced at Basen as he searched through his desk drawers.

"I needed the morning to do something more important."

That stopped Jack as he put his palms flat on his desk. "And whatever is so important sent you here. What is it?" Jack looked intrigued.

Basen hadn't meant to set himself up in such dramatic fashion. His only option now was to give Jack something worthy of that introduction. "It's about the leader of the Elves...Yeso. I might have a way to stop him, but I need something from you."

"Are you going to make a portal?" Jack nearly whispered it, seemingly holding back excitement. "Yes, whatever you need, of course. Yeso and his psychic Elves must be stopped. How can I help?"

"For now, I just need the book you borrowed from the library. The one about Yeso and Ulric Takary."

Jack grumbled like a disappointed child. "There is no *book* about Yeso and Ulric." He went back to searching his drawers.

Eventually, he seemed to find what he was looking for, bringing out a large book and placing it on Basen's side of the desk. "There are only books about the Elves and Takarys, like this one. It's doubtful you'll find Yeso's name in here. Even if he is mentioned, you'll have to be lucky to come across it."

"I read fast," Basen said as he reached for the book.

But Jack put one hand on top of it. The other went to his chin. "Penny wouldn't send you here for this. And if it was Terren, he would've told me." His voice lowered. "Was it Abith? I know he used to be your instructor. He might confide in you. You can tell us, Basen. You must."

"I haven't spoken to Abith." Seeing that his words did nothing to alleviate the worry on Jack's usually friendly face, Basen continued. "Truthfully, Jack. And if he speaks to me, I'll let you know."

"Then who sent you?"

It seemed like Jack still suspected Abith. It would make sense for Abith to use someone like Basen for a simple request, like retrieving a book that might give Abith insight on their new enemies. Information was power in this political battle between him and Terren.

Basen couldn't blame the chemist or the headmaster for wanting to keep eyes on Abith. In fact, Basen was thankful they were taking his former instructor's presence seriously. What Basen had failed to realize until then, however, was that having a past with Abith meant Basen would have to regain the trust he'd built with his instructors when he'd first come to the Academy bearing his Hiller surname.

Honesty seemed a good way to start.

"I came by my own volition."

Jack frowned. "This is no time for students to be seeking knowledge about Yeso and Ulric. Leave that to us and go back to battle training."

Jack sat and busied himself with one of the many papers on his desk.

"I'm…" The words wouldn't come out. Basen swallowed a lump in his throat as Jack looked up with a furrowed brow. "I'm leaving soon, but I need to know something before I go."

"You're what? Basen, we can't protect you outside these walls. Where are you…" His voice trailed off. "Fatholl, in Merejic."

Basen nodded. He was glad news of his earlier trip there with Cleve and the others had reached Jack. It would make this conversation easier.

"I'll return the book to you as soon as I'm done," Basen said, "and I'll let you know what I've found out. Then you can focus on everything else you're doing."

"You don't have to go to Fatholl. You're safe within these walls. It's only once you leave that you'll be in danger."

Basen resisted the urge to disagree. He'd heard Sanya had snuck in while he was away to leave a note on Reela's bed about the impending attack. If Sanya could find her way in and out of the school, Fatholl certainly could do the same.

"I have to do this," Basen said, "and I believe I can turn this terrible situation with Fatholl into one that benefits us all." He reached for the book. "Give me the chance to prove myself."

CHAPTER SIX

Basen ran out of Jack's office. He drew the gazes of everyone he passed, but he refused to let it bother him. Jack had given him only an hour to return the book. *I have to find somewhere quiet.* He ran up the stairs to the second level, but there was no third stairway to the roof. So much for that plan.

He left the building and looked around for ideas. He wasn't about to sit on the ground and have to deal with anyone who might walk by and wonder aloud what he was doing. He looked up at the Redfield tower, the clock at its top telling him that somehow there were only two hours until midday dining hours. He wanted to be sure of his plan before lunch so he'd have time to speak to the necessary people in the dining hall.

Where could he read in peace? *The Redfield tower,* he realized. Nick had told him there was a way inside. Someone had to ring the bell, after all. Basen headed for it at a sprint. *They probably don't lock the door during wartime to allow the bell ringer to get inside faster.*

He'd guessed right, but there was nowhere he could sit and read, and it was too dark. The only light came from very high above, where the bell hung.

Basen raced up the circular stairway. The tower was the tallest structure at the Academy, and as Basen climbed stair after stair, he began to believe it was taller than even Tenred's enormous castle. He'd made the trek from the lower level of the castle to the top when he was younger, sometimes in a hurry. He didn't recall it fatiguing him like this.

Soon he reached the top and would've lost his breath at the glorious sight if he wasn't already gasping for air. *The view—god's mercy.* It was easy to forget how marvelous the world truly was when he spent most of his life tethered to the ground. The ocean stretched all the way to the horizon. Somewhere farther than Basen could see was Greenedge, the very continent he hoped to learn about from this simple book in his hands.

Kyrro seemed small from here, as he could see almost all of the territory in front of him to the south. Raywhite Forest was looked larger than Basen would've guessed. It stretched diagonally along the center of the territory in the shape of a crooked Y. Its upper corners fit nicely between Gendock to the west and Oakshen to the east, with the capital between both at the top of the Y. Trentyre was the only city that seemed to have no correlation to the shape of the forest, sitting just as close to the even larger southern forest of Kyrro as it did to Raywhite Forest above it. The unsightly land between it and the trees was marred by long trenches that reached all the way to the sea.

He thought of Sanya as he looked to the capital. The castle rose up from the center of the city and made the buildings around it appear insignificant, as if the city had been built for it and nothing else. It *had* been built by order of a Takary, after all. Looking to the north, Basen barely made out a Tenred flag peeking up over the Fjallejon Mountains, but he couldn't see the rest of the castle.

Basen felt free and relaxed and took a few seconds to cherish this moment, as he knew it might be a while before he had the chance again.

He noticed a teenage boy below him wheeling a cart full of training swords straight to the center of Redfield Stadium. The boy stopped and took his time choosing a sword. Then he turned and swung it as if to catch someone surprising him from behind, his attack slow and weak.

It looked as if the boy overestimated his own strength as he tried to get the weapon up again for another strike and ended up stepping on the end of the blade before he could get it off the ground. Still going through the motion of swinging, he tripped himself, stumbled forward for an absurdly long while—he did have good balance—but then finally came down.

As the boy turned to look for a lighter weapon in the cart, Basen recognized him from last evening. *He was the one speaking with Cleve.* He gave his new sword a few test swings, then puffed out his chest as if to show off his prowess to an admiring stadium crowd.

Basen chuckled. He couldn't blame the boy for acting on his fantasy of being a Redfield Champion. Basen might've done the same if he were the boy's age. If it wasn't for the war, he would've looked forward to his classes with Penny and events like the Redfield competition between warriors.

Now that he'd regained his breath enough to focus, Basen sat with the heavy book in his lap and started with the table of contents. "Dammit." The chapters were numbered but not titled. He would have to search each page for anything related to the Takarys and the Elves.

It soon became evident why there were so many pages in this book. It was about the history of Greenedge. The entire history. Basen knew very little about the continent yet soon came to learn that most everyone now lived along the eastern or western border, toward the middle. Dangerous creatures called desmarls had driven everyone to these parts. Most of what he read seemed unimportant to his situation, so he skipped forward to the start of the chapters on the Elves.

He was disappointed to realize this author knew little to nothing about specific Elves. No names or dates.

All Basen gleaned after searching through the earlier chapters was the Elves had always kept to themselves, even though their land bumped up against two territories populated by humans.

There had been multiple wars between kings fighting for territory, and often these kings made generous offers to the Elves in return for their assistance in battle, only to be told forcefully that no human, no matter the circumstance, was to enter Meritar, and no Elves would get involved in human matters.

The middle of the book returned to more human history, ignoring the Elves again. Basen skipped many chapters to get closer to the present. He knew something recent had happened between the Elves and the humans, bringing Cleve and Reela to Greenedge. But what was it?

The book became interesting as he came to the formation of the bastial steel crater. He'd heard it was the only place where bastial steel could be mined, but what he hadn't known was the bastial steel crater had formed naturally after the largest quake known to man caused an explosion powerful enough to destroy a city had it occurred within one. Even more interesting was where it formed: evenly split between the Elves in Meritar and the humans in Goldram, with about half the crater in each territory. This forced the first real interaction between the two races.

A surge of excitement came through Basen as he saw Ulric's name for the first time. *"Ulric Takary took control of Goldram's side of the crater immediately after it formed."* Basen had read earlier that the Takarys already controlled Goldram, so it would make sense for them to claim the crater in their territory. *And they had the army to back up their claim in case anyone challenged them.*

That was exactly what happened. A new war began as the nearby territories fought with Goldram for access to the crater. The Takarys came to the Elves for support, wisely telling them that if Goldram fell, the Elves would also lose access to the bastial steel. But the Elves still refused to get involved.

Basen would've liked to read more about the war, but there wasn't time. He hurried through the account, searching for more about Ulric and the Elves. Finally, the war ended with Goldram winning, yet Ulric's name wasn't mentioned again. There were only a few chapters left, and Basen was beginning to fear he'd have to try a different book or face Fatholl without anything certain to use as leverage.

Then he came across it: Ulric's name and Fatholl's as well. He murmured the words as he read. *"Eventually Ulric Takary had learned enough Elvish to speak with the*

Elves. He was interested in learning more about them because they've survived without leaving Meritar for as long as history has to tell. He imagined that finding out more about their culture could teach him how to improve the life of the citizens in his family's territory. But though he had learned their language and showed a genuine interest, none of the Elves would speak with him.

"Eventually he found out it was fear that kept them from interacting with humans. They didn't fear the humans themselves but the prospect of their own leaders finding out they had revealed Elven secrets. Ulric's determination didn't change, giving many the idea he had more than just an interest in their culture in mind. Ulric had always been secretive, wearing a mask to hide his face and refusing to give a reason why. The men working in his bastial steel crater had little to say about him except that he was always involved in planning something that didn't seem to involve bastial steel.

"Ulric held meetings with Elves openly, one of them being Fatholl, who later became known to everyone in Greenedge. Fatholl's story has been told many times in many different ways, but the facts bear out only a few absolute truths. He was born in Ovira and was forced to come to Greenedge to escape death. He had learned some psyche before arriving and was therefore barred from Meritar, even though he was just a boy. He then spent years training with other Elves who'd been exiled and continued his attempt to return to Meritar. They were never allowed back in the territory, but they did manage to recruit many other Elves with a clear message: It was up to them to save Greenedge because the continent was

slowly being taken over by desmarls, and humans were doing nothing about it."

Basen had read a little about these creatures as he'd skimmed through earlier chapters. They were monstrous beasts thought nearly impossible to kill, and they were the reason all living creatures migrated toward the center of the continent. Instead of banding together to fight them, humans had been fighting each other for space instead.

"Miners in the bastial steel crater reported hearing arguing during the meeting between Ulric and Fatholl. They sounded in disagreement about how to use their power and were never seen meeting again. But one of the Elves who'd been part of Fatholl's group did return later, alone. This Elf, known as Yeso and similar enough in appearance to Fatholl to possibly be related, began to meet frequently with Ulric near enough to the crater for many to see."

As Basen read further, he came across nothing else about Ulric or Yeso.

"No, don't stop there," he said as if the author could hear him.

The next pages transitioned into the beginning of the most recent war in Greenedge, during which Fatholl took complete control. Basen hurried through each page in search of more information, but whatever Ulric and Yeso were doing during this time, it apparently wasn't worthy enough for the author to mention.

Basen had to stop himself a number of times as he read what Fatholl had done, shock forcing him to make sure he'd read the words correctly. By the time he got to the end, he was beginning to think Fatholl was the wrong Elf to try to manipulate. Basen had never heard of anyone like him—the sacrifices he'd made, the sacrifices he'd *forced* other people to make. He'd taken the weight of the world on his shoulders and used it to justify the deaths of countless people.

Basen had every reason to be afraid. Fatholl would use him and discard him without care.

Basen came to the end of the book slightly disappointed in how little had been written about Ulric and Yeso, but he believed he'd learned just enough about the two of them and Fatholl to conclude he was right in his original guess. Fatholl and Yeso didn't work together in Greenedge because they didn't agree on how to use their power. *Yeso clearly agrees with Ulric's choice of war, while Fatholl never has.*

Basen closed the book and thought for a while.

Eventually he whispered, "Yes, exactly. Yes! That's it."

He stood and made a fist in victory. His plan was set. Now it was just a matter of—*god's mercy, what time is it?* People were migrating toward the dining hall, but it couldn't be lunch hours already, could it? He leaned over the stone barrier to attempt to read the clock above him, but he couldn't get a good look without risking falling out. He grabbed the book and rushed down the stairs. *Of course I'm in the one place on campus where I can't see the time.*

He came all the way down and looked up, then cursed. It had been two hours! He muttered curses all the way back to Jack's office, then inwardly raged when the door was closed and locked. He knocked, but nobody answered.

He was thankful for his stamina, because it was a long run to the dining hall. Jack was difficult to find, as he did not sit with other instructors this day, but Basen finally located him in a corner, sitting at the end of one of the long tables. He had papers with him, and the students who shared his table looked to be giving him his space.

"I'm sorry," Basen said as he put the heavy book down on the only clear spot on the table within Jack's reach. "I lost track of time."

"I thought you might," Jack said as he swept the book to him, pushing all the papers to the side. "Which is why I gave you only an hour when you really had two. I just wanted it back before lunch hours were over so I can read after." He went back to writing.

Sneaky. "Well, you won't find anything useful about Yeso or Ulric," Basen whispered as he left quickly, hoping Jack wouldn't hear until it was too late. Otherwise, the master chemist would stop Basen from leaving, and there wasn't time for further delay. He had people to gather.

"Basen!"

Now many tables away, he turned.

Jack stood to say something but then simply nodded, as if he understood Basen would be leaving no matter what.

On his way to Jack's table, Basen had noticed Crea Hiller sitting with Abith. Now they shared hushed words while glancing about suspiciously. They stopped as Basen approached.

"We need to speak," he told Crea.

Crea was the one who'd sent Juliana to Tenred's

prison, where she remained.

Rescuing her was the first part of his plan.

"We should," Crea agreed. "Meet me at house number three hundred fifteen as soon as lunch hours are over."

Three hundred fifteen. He refrained from smirking until he turned around. *Terren put her in a student house.* He supposed it made sense, as it was probably the only vacant place for her. Still, it couldn't have been easy to convince her to accept it. *I wonder where Abith is staying.*

Basen looked back over his shoulder. Crea was considerably older, but was there something romantic there? Basen didn't get that impression, and he was usually quite good at picking up on things like that. Their relationship was probably purely political. *Although Abith might not need her once she loses control over the troops from Tenred.*

Basen crafted the last parts of his plan as he waited in line for food. But a familiar face staring at him interrupted his thoughts. He glanced over to meet the eyes of the man he remembered from his time at the workhouse. The man did not look away, only worsened his scowl.

What in god's world is wrong with him? Basen scowled right back. The man was Basen's father's age, yet much less imposing than Henry. His expression was that of anger, not calculation or threat. It only served to prove what Basen already thought about him from their brief encounters in the workhouse. He was angry, as if he blamed the world for his unhappiness. He'd insult anyone who bothered him, so Basen and Henry had kept their distance.

This man had attempted to kill one of the frightened women trying to leave the Academy yesterday. *If he still holds a grudge because I stopped him—I can't worry about it now.*

Basen got his food and noticed a small space beside Effie at a nearly full table. He stood behind the bench where he hoped to squeeze in.

"Mind if I sit?"

"Basen! Where were you?"

"Move over and I'll tell you."

She scooted to give him room. Every table was crowded like this, thanks to all the new people at the Academy. After the losses the school had suffered, however, a packed dining hall was a good problem to have.

Before he could say a word to Effie, Penny came to stand on the other side of the table.

"Where the bastial hell were you during battle training!"

The entire table of at least a dozen people stopped eating to stare.

"It'll require a long explanation, Mage Penny," he said apologetically. "Instead, let me assure you it's extremely important to this war."

His words did nothing to soften her harsh look. "I don't care how important you think it is—no matter what you're doing! If you miss training again, I will put you in a lower group. I'm thinking at least ten, given your reckless behavior. You can't keep missing training and then expect to know what to do during battle. The Group One mages have to be the most coordinated. You'll get yourself or others killed."

He sympathized with Penny, he really did. But that didn't sway him from his purpose. "I'm sorry. I need to do this."

Her mouth dropped open in horror. "You're going to miss more. On *purpose*?"

He nodded regretfully. "I'll accept the consequences, whatever they are."

She closed her mouth, her jaw muscles bulging. He feared she would humiliate him more before storming off, but instead, she just shook her head and said, "Are you going to be careful?"

The question surprised him too much for him to answer right away. Would he? "Careful" would be to do exactly as Fatholl asked or to stay put and hope he'd be protected here. Instead, he planned not only to poke the beehive but to persuade the queen bee to leave it.

He thought for a moment, unwilling to lie to Penny. As their audience stared and waited, he could only smile apologetically and shrug.

"I'm sorry, Penny. I don't want to lie to you. But I'm doing what I believe to be right."

Penny shook her head. "It's not just my job here to teach students how to improve. I'm to teach them how to stay alive. You're making this very difficult."

With that, she turned on her heel and walked away.

"Bastial hell, Basen," Effie remarked, then chuckled as she spoke with heavy sarcasm, "She's not very happy with you."

He pinned her with a serious look, knowing what he was about to say would otherwise be taken as a joke.

"She's not going to be very happy with you, either."

CHAPTER SEVEN

Basen heard footsteps approaching his door. He was almost done packing for his trip—there wasn't much to take—and opened the door before his father had a chance to knock. He smiled as he hugged Henry, who gave him a firm pat on the back, then leaned back for a good look at his face.

Basen must look tired, possibly even upset. Henry finally had made time for him, but now Basen had to leave.

"How are you able to resist psyche?" he asked, needing to know in case he might have to do so himself. And very soon.

"Training and practice, Basen. Repetition. You'll learn soon. I'll make sure Terren selects you as one of the many to get lessons."

I won't be here. Henry continued before Basen could reply. "I'm sending someone to get Juliana out of prison and bring her to the Academy."

Basen had feared two things about telling his father of her whereabouts. One was that Henry would kill Crea for what she'd done to his wife. The other was that he'd come to a hasty decision about how to free her.

"Whoever you're sending," Basen said, "they won't make it to Tenred. The Fjallejon Mountains have been taken."

"He will go around."

He. Just one man. Basen had been taught from an

early age never to speak back to his father, but everything had changed during their time in the workhouse. Through the pain of Juliana's supposed betrayal and the endless hard work he and his father had endured, Basen had earned Henry's mutual respect.

But it appeared that another shift had happened since then. He could see his father now wearing the same stoic look he used to in the castle, his tone leaving no room for argument.

"If he goes far enough around the mountains so he's not seen," Basen said, "it could take a week to reach Mother."

"One week is not long," Henry replied. "Plus another week to return."

"Unless she's frail from her time in that cage and must travel slowly."

"I've thought of that, but this is the only option."

"How is this man supposed to get Mother out of prison?"

"He has a signed decree from Crea Hiller that Juliana is to be released."

Now this was embarrassing. Basen had never caught his father lying before and didn't know what to say. He'd just spoken to Crea. The awkward conversation had been short but fruitful. Basen really did have a signed decree from Crea, while his father probably had a forgery.

Basen had asked Crea if his father had spoken with her yet, and she'd protested, "You should've waited for me to tell him myself."

"He won't retaliate," Basen had assured her, though he wasn't confident it was true.

"I'm not worried about that! I had a good reason behind that difficult choice."

Yes you are, and no you didn't. "I came here for a signed document from you ordering my mother's release. Let's just get on with this and not speak more about it, all right?"

Crea had looked confused for a moment, then surprised. She'd clearly expected him to ask more of her, probably for her to go to Tenred and retrieve Juliana. It would've been more than fair for Basen or his father to ask, but that didn't mean Crea would do it.

"All right," she'd agreed.

Basen had folded his arms and waited.

Crea had dragged a blank scroll in front of her, dipped her quill in the inkwell and begun to write as Basen waited near the open door.

Neither had spoken until she'd finished and handed it to him.

"I assure you this will be more than enough for the warden to release her."

She'd sounded as if she expected him to *thank* her. She was lucky he didn't run a sword through her black heart.

Why would his father lie now? Basen opted not to find out. Henry had always been direct and sometimes stern to the point of frightening people. He wouldn't hold himself back from telling Crea what he thought of her. Especially not here at the Academy, where she had no power over him like she had in Tenred castle. To lie meant Henry was covering up something else—*an inability to meet with Crea.*

That's it, Basen realized. *He doesn't want to meet with her because he can't treat her in the only way she'll allow people to treat her. He can't play that role anymore.*

Basen wanted to tell his father he needn't worry about that any longer. Crea had been stripped of much of her power. But shouldn't Henry already know that?

God's mercy. "You want to kill her, don't you?"

He expected his father to deny it. He *wanted* his father to deny it. Henry looked like a different man as he met Basen's gaze with a lowered head. His eyes burned with a deep rage Basen hadn't seen since the day of their exile.

"She would've let Juliana rot in prison for years, just for a chance at conquering Kyrro. Your mother has been through *enough.*"

The power of Henry's words could've moved mountains.

"She has," Basen agreed. "Which is why we should get her out as soon as we can. I saw how she lives, Father. She's trapped with a group of ignorant women who have annoyed her to the point of anger. She never gets upset, so you know how miserable she must be for me to have seen her like that. But even through all of her torture, she pleaded with me to leave without her because I might've been in danger. Let's not make her wait any longer."

"I wouldn't want to but..." His father raised his eyebrows. "You mean to go yourself. That's why you're not in battle training. You're preparing to leave imminently!" Henry shook his head. "No. She wouldn't want you to do something so dangerous, and I don't, either. Besides, you can't get there any faster."

"But I can."

"Tell me you're not thinking of going through the pathway." Henry squinted and leaned close. "You've always assumed yourself to be invulnerable. Your mother and I constantly worried we'd hear news of your death after you climbed up some precipice to impress your friends. You're too old and smart to live like that anymore."

"Father, there's no risk. I'm going to make a portal there. I'll get her out *today*."

Henry tilted his head as he took pause. "You mentioned portals yesterday, but I didn't understand what you meant. To what could you be referring?"

Basen patted his father on the shoulder and smiled. "You should be proud. Your son is a portal mage."

But Henry seemed to be in no mood for joy or pride. He took Basen's hand off his shoulder.

"Explain yourself."

"How else to explain it? I can make portals."

Henry appeared annoyed, as if this was a joke.

"I'm serious," Basen said. "You can stay and watch if you'd like."

"You really can make a portal?"

"Yes, to Tenred. Specifically to the kitchen on the first level. I can't make a portal everywhere, only where I've been before, and it has to be a place where bastial energy has been gathered enough times to weaken the invisible walls of our world. Jack Rose can explain it better, if you want. Or you can wait until I return. I don't have time to get into it right now."

Henry's mouth hung open as he looked to be waiting

for the punch line to a joke he cared little about.

"Show me now," he demanded.

"I can't. I need a charged akorell stone for each portal, and I won't waste its stored energy just to prove to you I can make one. I'm not ready to go through the portal yet."

"*You* have an akorell stone?"

"Yes. You remember Alabell? She took the akorell stone from Kyrro's castle when she escaped and later gave it to me."

Deep lines formed in Henry's forehead.

"I can't return with Mother. I can only free her. But I trust that the people coming with me will bring her back to you safely. You'll see her soon enough. I need to go to Merejic after Tenred to fulfill a promise I made to someone very powerful. He's a psychic, Father, so I could use some specific instructions on resisting psyche."

Henry didn't say a word, his confused expression never changing.

Effie came to the open doorway and waved. Basen nodded to her and told his father, "It's time for me to go. So if you have anything to tell me, any advice..."

Behind Effie were Steffen, Annah, Vithos, and Crim the Krepp. The mage had done well getting them here quickly after lunch hours. Basen hadn't even finished packing yet, though he could in another minute.

His father turned to see the party going with Basen, then returned his focus to his son.

Say something, Father!

But Henry still remained silent.

"Effie is one of the strongest mages at the Academy,"

Basen explained. "She's experienced with both bastial and sartious energy. Steffen is the only true battle chemist I know of, skilled with bow and sword, and he's a healer on top of that. Annah is knowledgeable and good with psyche, perhaps the best of the first-years. The three of them will get Juliana back here safely."

Annah bowed low as Henry faced them fully. "It's an honor to meet you, Henry Hiller."

Basen was surprised, and even more so when the others, except for Crim, bowed as low as Annah had. A sight like that would've been common in Tenred, but it was something else to see his father already had garnered such respect here in so short a time.

"I'm not sure if you've had a chance to meet any Krepps," Basen said. "Crim helped us return to the Academy the first time, and it's in his best interest to help again. When we go to Tenred to free Juliana, we'll also be freeing some of his imprisoned Krepps."

"Not my Krepps," Crim grunted. "No Krepp belong to Krepp."

"I can understand why Crim would go," Henry said, "but why would the rest of you choose to do this?" When none gave a response, he looked at Basen. "Did you force Terren to send them?"

"No, Terren doesn't know."

Henry gave Basen a disapproving look before asking again, "Then why?"

"It's not just to get Juliana Hiller out of prison," Steffen replied. He appeared the least uncomfortable about delivering this inevitable news as he moved and gestured more fluidly than Effie and Annah, who looked as stiff as wood. "There's another plan that involves all of us, not just Crim."

"But we *will* bring Juliana back safely," Annah added. "We won't be doing anything dangerous. Our trip won't take more than an additional half day to do what we plan."

"What about you, Vithos?" Henry asked. "Basen didn't mention what you would be doing."

Basen wasn't shocked that Henry knew the name of the most powerful psychic in their army. He and Terren probably had strategized much already. Hopefully this little adventure wouldn't interfere with what they wanted to do.

"I will go with Basen to Merejic," the Elf said in his rough Kreppen accent. "I will return to Elves to make sure *Basen* return."

"And what will Basen be doing there?" His father's gaze bore through his son.

"Surprising that psychic I mentioned" was all Basen would admit. "And to do that, we need to leave now." Fatholl probably wasn't expecting him for a few days. Hopefully this would give Basen a chance to discover Fatholl's plan before being trapped and forced to execute it.

Henry was sure to find holes in this plan—holes Basen already knew about and didn't need reminding. There was no proof his plan would work, but when he had this feeling that something would succeed, it always did.

Basen went to retrieve his akorell stone from his room while Henry and the rest crowded into Annah's room. She was the only one who hadn't packed a bag yet and quickly got to it.

"Did you get enough food?" Basen asked Effie when he made his way in.

She patted her backpack. "Plenty."

"Did you speak with Penny before you left?"

"No, I figured it would be better to miss class than to try to explain. You know how she is about battle training. She thinks it will save us all."

Basen nodded. "What about Alabell?"

Effie looked down. "It was already late by the time everyone had gathered. I figured it would be best to come straight here."

He panicked for a brief moment, moving toward Annah's desk. "I'd better write her a note at least."

As he searched his heart and started to come to the right words, Annah destroyed his concentration by announcing, "I'm done packing."

Damn. He could fill pages with everything he was feeling. Everyone had a reason to fight, and Alabell was Basen's. Tauwin had murdered her family and would kill her, too, if given the chance. This beautiful, caring woman, who brought nothing but good to the world—how could anyone wish to take her away?

He'd wanted Effie to bring her here so he could find some way of telling her how much she meant to him. If Alabell was too busy to come, Effie was at least supposed to say goodbye for him.

Perhaps it was better Alabell wasn't here. If she heard what Basen was doing, she'd want to go with him to Tenred. But the task of bringing Juliana back to the Academy was more dangerous than he'd made it seem to his father. The mountains were most likely guarded, and anything could happen during the weeklong journey back. Enemy troops could return to Lake Kayvol or even venture to Tenred and spot the party returning with Juliana.

If a healer was needed, chances were great someone would die. Steffen seemed like the best option between the chemists, as he had battle experience. Truly, anyone besides Alabell would cause Basen less worry. Hopefully she would understand he didn't doubt her skills. He was trying to protect her.

Penny, on the other hand, probably would react much worse than Alabell when she found out Basen and the others had gone.

"One moment," Basen said, then began to write.

"*Alabell, I wish I'd had time to see you before I left. I'll have to make do with the memory of your smile. Every time I see it, it reminds me of the good in this world. I'll need that kind of strength where I'm going.*"

She deserved so much more than this quick goodbye letter. "Can you bring this to Alabell?" he asked his father. "And this one is for Terren."

Henry took the two scrolls.

Basen pointed at the one for Terren. "That explains the plan. Please inform Alabell of it when she asks."

Henry unrolled it and began to read. Basen drew his wand and readied his mind for the portal.

Henry pushed out his palm. "Wait."

There was nothing Henry could say to dissuade him, but Basen lowered his wand anyway out of respect.

"To resist psyche," Henry said, "you must feel

something stronger than the pain."

"That sounds like one of those things that's harder than one might think."

"It is. Pain is hard to ignore, but fortunately for us, the pain from a psychic is physical, not emotional." He showed Basen a questioning look with his eyebrows raised, silently asking if Basen knew what he was saying.

Yes, Henry was talking about the workhouse. The physical pain of aching muscles and a hungry stomach never compared to agony of their hopelessness. Basen could put his mind there whenever he wanted, remembering the feeling of being trapped in a miserable life all too well. His mother must've felt the same in that horrible prison.

This feeling—this was what he had to recall the next time a psychic had a firm grip on his energy. It gave him the strength he would need, and not just against Fatholl.

But was it stronger than his feelings for Alabell? It didn't seem as if anything could be. Perhaps she was the key to stopping the pain.

"Goodbye for now," Basen told his father.

"For now," Henry agreed with pride in his voice.

Everyone took their place behind Basen as he raised his wand once more. He formed the usual ball of bastial energy, then ripped the energy free from the akorell stone and combined both clusters. He reached deep into the damaged wall of the world and focused his thoughts on the kitchen in Tenred castle.

He broke through the wall as it ripped in every direction, the portal bursting open in front of him.

His father hesitantly stepped toward it as his mouth

dropped open.

Annah was the first one in, then Vithos. Effie and Steffen seemed more nervous as they watched closely, possibly waiting to ensure Annah and Vithos were still whole on the other side.

Basen had practiced holding immense amounts of energy and now felt as if he could keep the portal open without his full concentration. He put his free hand on Effie's back. "It's safe," he said. "You'll just feel dizzy."

She pulled her arms in and jumped into the portal.

Now it was down to Crim and Steffen, both of whom had turned away from the portal as if it might burn them alive.

"Everything I know about portals tells me I shouldn't go in one," Steffen said. "When Effie described it earlier, I figured it would be easier. Now, looking at it, I still don't understand why it won't rip me apart."

"I don't know the reason," Basen admitted. "But I've gone through them enough times to be confident all your limbs will still be attached when you get to the other side. If you look closely, you can see everyone there."

Steffen cautiously stepped sideways toward the portal, using his shoulder like a shield. Annah, Vithos, and Effie looked to be recovering from the vertigo as they found their balance. The tables and counters of Tenred's kitchen were the most clear of the hazy image. What looked to be other people started to appear around the edges, as if a crowd was forming. Their shapes bent as the entire portal rippled like a puddle.

Everyone was supposed to go in before the Krepp to prevent the panic of last time. Basen let out a grunt he'd been holding back, showing Steffen it was no easy task to maintain the portal.

"Oh," Steffen said. "All right I'm going."

But he didn't move.

"I'm going," he repeated.

"Steffen," Basen urged.

The chemist sucked in air through his teeth and covered his face with his arm as he stumbled in. Crim ran in bravely, almost impatiently, right after.

"It's likely you'll see me before they return with Mother," Basen told his father.

"All right, then," Henry replied confidently. "Good luck."

<u>CHAPTER EIGHT</u>

When Tenred's kitchen finally stopped spinning and Basen could stand without assistance, he realized the staff wasn't nearly as alarmed this time. The portal was now closed, and only one Krepp had gone through. This seemed to make all the difference, as the chefs, kitchen cleaners, and servers had paused in their tasks to stare at Basen's party nervously.

"It's all right," he said. "We just came to speak with someone."

He started toward the exit but found he was the only one moving. Even his own party appeared reluctant to follow. They looked at the kitchen staff as if expecting someone to go for one of the many knives on the counters.

Basen cleared his throat and pointed at a pot about to boil over. One of the chefs cursed and lifted it away from the flame as frothy liquid poured over the side.

Finally, people began to return to their work. Basen gestured at his stunned party to follow him as he made his way out.

Crim looked ready to bare his teeth when Annah politely confronted him. "There will be no fighting," she reminded, most likely using psyche to subdue his aggression. "By them or us."

*****

Those they encountered on the way to the prison stared at the Krepp. Basen and Annah assured everyone their party was welcome inside the castle. Of course it was a lie, and anyone who thought so would likely summon a guard.

Basen picked up the pace but made sure not to run, as it most definitely would attract more attention. Guests in Tenred's castle needed to be escorted, and there was no escort with them. But Basen knew where there tended to be more swordsmen, and where there likely would be none.

They reached the warden's office without incident. A guard paced between the warden's closed door and the bolted door to the dungeons. His hand went for the hilt of his sword as soon as he noticed Crim.

Basen quickly put out his hands, holding Crea's decree in one of them. "I'm Basen Hiller, and I have a note from Crea Hiller that is to be shown to the warden."

After standing still for a moment of confusion, the guard let go of the handle of his weapon and approached.

Basen handed off the scroll. The guard took a quick glimpse, then read more closely while peering up at Crim every few seconds.

"Wait here," he said and went to knock on the warden's door. "Basen Hiller is here with a note from the queen that Juliana Hiller is to be released." The guard cleared his throat. "A Krepp is with them. It seems to be behaved."

It took a while for the door to open and the warden to poke his head out and take the scroll from the guard. He likewise didn't read through it without glancing at Crim a few times.

Basen caught a whiff of Crim's musk as the creature stepped close and asked, "He human responsible for battle here?"

That's Crea. But Basen couldn't say that. The Krepps would kill her, or at least try to. A battle would erupt within the walls of the Academy.

Once she and Abith turn against us, that is the time.

"No," Basen lied. "Cleve killed the man responsible when we were here last."

Crim pointed at the warden. "But *he* human who put Krepps in cage."

"That wasn't his choice." The Krepps couldn't be left alone after they'd come into the territory demanding the bodies of their brethren. They would've dug up the entire cemetery, and the citizens of Tenred wouldn't have stood idle. Putting the Krepps in prison actually saved their lives.

"Then who?" Crim asked.

Truthfully, it was probably the warden who'd put them there, but Crim wouldn't understand it was the best decision for everyone.

"No one here," Basen said.

He was glad when the warden signaled for him to approach. But as the rest of the party followed, the warden put out his hand. "Only Basen."

This was a bad sign. If the warden was set to deliver bad news, he was likely to do it out of earshot of Basen's party so they couldn't do any damage, especially the Krepp. Basen needed to remind this man he didn't have the power to refuse them.

"You can speak to all of us, or none of us," Basen said, "and I don't think you want to send us away with nothing."

The guard looked at the warden nervously, who stared at Basen as he mulled his words.

"Explain something to me," the warden said. "As you must remember from before your *exile*, all visitors are to be escorted. You're now a visitor, even with your Hiller name. Yet I see no one here with you. The rest of the castle must not even know of your presence."

"They don't." But they would soon if Basen didn't hurry this along. At least one person had to have gone to fetch the guards upon seeing the Krepp. "The reason there are so few of us is because of an understanding there will not be any fighting. This *is* what you want, isn't it?"

"Of course, but I can't let someone out of prison with just a note that might have Crea's signature on it."

"You know her signature. That's it."

"You know her signature as well." The warden gave him a look as if Basen had been caught stealing. "You could've forged it."

"It's hers," Annah said as she came forward.

"I can't be sure," the warden said.

Basen reminded him, "You've released other prisoners with a lot less than a signed decree like this."

"Yes, but they weren't Juliana Hiller."

Basen turned up his hands. "What does that matter?"

"I received explicit instructions not to release her no matter who came for her."

Crea. She could've warned me so I'd be better

prepared for this stubbornness. He wasn't about to leave without his mother.

"You must be wondering how we've gotten into the castle not once, but twice," Basen said. "The last time, you must've heard that no one saw us enter. It will be the same this time. And it will be the same the next time...and the time after that. We will keep coming back so long as there is a reason for us to return."

He paused for a breath to control his building anger. He needed just the right amount of it in his voice to be threatening yet unemotional.

"This signature from Crea is real, but that shouldn't matter to you anymore. The only thing that should is giving us what we want, or I recommend finding a job that moves you far away from this castle. Because if we have to come back, there will be a battle here that will make the last one look like a simple misunderstanding. Now bring us to my mother, and you'd better bring the key to free the Krepps as well. They're coming back with us, and that's the only way you won't see us again."

There was a moment of sadness as Basen realized how true his words were—how unlikely it was he'd ever return to the castle where he was born. Sometimes he missed the simple life here, and some part of him had always wondered if he could return to it. Only now did he fully realize his childhood was long gone.

"I'll agree if you wait here until I've gathered the necessary men to escort you out," the warden said. "And you will not speak to the prisoners except to notify the Krepps that they'll be leaving. Armored men will bring you all the way to the edge of the territory, and none of you are welcome back. If you're seen within the castle again, we *will* have that battle you mentioned."

The only reason we'd be coming back would be to fight anyway. Unfortunately, a battle against Tenred was likely. There were still men breathing who'd attempted to kill Basen and the others who'd come here before.

"Fine," Basen said.

The warden locked his door and left with the guard. Crim seemed to have understood enough, for he asked no questions.

The warden and his team of guards returned sooner than Basen had anticipated. *They must've already been on the way here.* As they took Basen and his group down into the dungeons, he worried the only reason the warden agreed to cooperate was because he planned to put them in prison just as he had any others who'd caused him or Crea problems.

No, he would have worse problems if he did. Henry would come, and it wouldn't be a peaceful visit. No matter how unemotional he'd been with Basen, Henry had always shown he wanted to protect his son. *He probably blames himself for not getting to the Academy sooner.*

Hopefully, when Basen was done with everything that had caused him to leave the Academy, and his father had seen what he'd accomplished, Henry would finally stop feeling the need to watch over his only son.

Eventually the small army of Tenred guards brought him to his mother's cell. Crim, upon seeing his Krepps in the same "cage" as before, shoved through the guards to get as close as possible. A few men reached for their weapons, stilling Basen's heart. Fortunately, nothing came of it, and Basen moved his hand away from the wand strapped to his belt.

"Basen?" It was his mother's voice.

He smiled happily at her. "Yes. I've come to get you out."

"You have?" She looked at the warden, a man she'd known for many years. He didn't return her glance as he focused on getting the right key into the hole.

"Crea has allowed you to go free," the warden told her, no doubt trying to rid himself of the responsibility for her imprisonment.

Juliana looked as if she didn't trust the situation, hesitantly emerging from the large cell. She kept her hands on the bars as if ready to step back in at any moment and pull them shut.

"What about me?" a woman with a raspy voice asked as she approached. "I'm innocent."

"So am I," others added.

"Only Juliana Hiller," the warden told them, then gestured for his guards to shut the cell door.

"Just because she has a Hiller name," complained one of the dirty women. "That isn't fair."

Basen almost started chuckling. Something good happening to a member of his family because of their Hiller name? Completely absurd.

The indignant feeling was gone in an instant as he embraced his mother and was filled with emotion. He longed to bring her back to the Academy where she'd reunite with Henry. It had been far too long since they'd been a "happy family."

Juliana looked even worse than when Basen had been here last, her black hair crimped and long overdue for a proper wash and comb. She looked thin to the point of weakness, moving slowly as Basen led her out of the suffocating group of armored men.

"Why would Crea let me out?" Juliana whispered.

"I'll explain everything on the way."

"Where are we going?"

"For now, all of us are going to Corin Forest."

The freeing of the many Krepps captured everyone's attention. The creatures had been dueling each other when Basen arrived, but the guards had taken their swords before opening their cell. They celebrated their freedom with an amusing display of dancing to a chorus of grunting and humming. They squatted up and down, jumping off the ground upon rising and throwing out their arms in rhythm to the coarse music.

"What will we be doing in Corin Forest with Krepps?" Juliana asked.

His poor mother; she must be so confused and worried about all of this. He tried to think of the single most important thing he could tell her to ease her mind.

"We're headed back to the Academy, where Henry awaits."

She threw her arms around him and wept.

She would be sad when she found out Basen wouldn't be taking the journey back with them, but she deserved this happiness in the meantime.

CHAPTER NINE

These Krepps were better behaved than the last to come out of Tenred's castle alive. Basen didn't know how long ago they'd come here looking to retrieve their dead, but their time in the dungeons had given them whatever peace they'd needed, as they now left without argument. Annah was the only one of their group who tried speaking with them, asking around if anyone knew common tongue. They didn't.

But Vithos spoke Kreppen better than common tongue, and even though he didn't seem to be liked by any of these Krepps, he took it upon himself to explain why they were walking free now. Hopefully they would choose to stay with Crim and return to the Academy.

Now that guards had escorted them out of the territory, Basen had time to explain to his mother what he would be doing, and more importantly, why they would be separating soon.

"But we will see each other again at the Academy," he assured her at the end.

"Are you sure it's necessary for you to go to Merejic?"

"No, I'm not sure, but whether it's necessary doesn't matter anymore. What I am sure about is it's the best decision."

It had been difficult to explain the progress of the war without giving his mother an idea of how terribly outnumbered they were. Now that they'd discovered the psychic Elves were fighting against them, their chances were even less than they'd presumed. Basen needed to do what he could to improve their odds.

The sun was setting by the time they reached Corin Forest, stars beginning to sprinkle the sky. Learning his lesson from the last time he'd come here with Krepps, Basen had them wait behind with Vithos as they approached the cabin.

"A young man and woman live here," Basen told his mother as he saw her crinkling her brow. "They came from Sumar, not that I know how they got through the mountains. The young man did something to scare away three Krepps last time we were here. I never found out what it was, but Effie has made him sound extremely valuable to the war effort."

"I see."

He could tell she had more questions. He'd already explained the war, the situation at the Academy, Henry coming from Trentyre to join them, Tenred troops forcing their way into this conflict, Basen's brief meetings with Crea, and what he would be doing with Fatholl...yet there was still more. He kept wanting to bring up Sanya. Juliana had known her when she was younger and would be as shocked as everyone at the Academy to find out what Sanya had done. Juliana would blame Sanya's father again, as she always did whenever Sanya had become the topic of conversation at his family's supper table.

"Basen, there's something you're leaving out," Juliana said as they came close to the cabin door. "How were you able to get into the castle *twice*?"

Basen had wanted to bring up his ability to make portals, but that would become the focus of all future conversation, and there wasn't time for a lengthy discussion about it.

Or rather, he wanted to give her an incredible surprise.

"It's the same way I'm going to reach the Elves in Merejic. I'll show you tomorrow."

"Show me?" She took on the same worried expression she'd worn when he was a boy and told her how high he'd climbed.

"Yes, show you."

She would have to learn to trust him completely soon enough.

"Neeko, Shara!" Effie called out as she knocked on the door. "It's Effie and Steffen...and others from the Academy. Can we talk?"

They waited in silence, listening to whispering within the small cabin. Basen expected good news from the two of them. From the brief conversation he'd overheard between Annah and Shara on their previous visit, it seemed as though the young woman wanted to join them but was frightened of getting involved in the war. Hopefully the boredom of cabin life had helped her find courage.

"How many people?" a man's voice asked. Basen figured it to be Neeko, who was the real reason they'd come.

Effie turned and counted quickly. "Five. All of us are allegiant to the Academy. You're safe."

There was another round of whispering. This one went on for quite a while.

The two of them had repaired all the damage the other Krepps had done, including rebuilding the heavy log fence. More apples grew on the nearby tree, and from what Basen could see through the slight opening of the wooden window, the inside of the cabin had been reorganized.

"What about those lizard creatures?" Shara asked.

"Those same lizard creatures aren't with us," Annah explained, "but a smaller, better behaved group is. They're waiting so far back that we can't see them from here. They won't be coming inside your home."

After another moment, the door finally opened. Shara was just as Basen remembered, her black locks bouncing as she quickly surveyed each person in the group. She appeared younger than the man, who had the same determined look on his face that Cleve often wore.

Effie had told Basen that Neeko and Shara were the same age; it was nearly all Effie had a chance to tell him during their quick meal together upon his return to the Academy. That, and that Neeko would be an invaluable asset.

"Come in," Neeko said, moving out of the doorway. His broad shoulders gave him the appearance of a swordsman. As Basen glanced around, he found two blades resting against a wall within the small cabin. Shara had a wand on her belt, obscured by the small sheath that held it. The end of it, possibly all of it, was as blue as a clear sky. Basen wondered if that was a reflection of the type of energy she specialized in, though he'd never heard of blue representing anything known in Kyrro.

Or she just painted it. That seemed more likely, given that she'd acted a little odd upon her first meeting with Annah.

"Hello Shara," Annah said. "I—"

"We met last time," Shara interrupted. "And the one with dark hair was spying behind the trees." She pointed at Basen.

Why did she have to say it like that? He put up his hands. "I didn't want to startle you, so I let Annah speak to you alone."

"I know. Is this your mother?" She smiled as if she enjoyed embarrassing Basen even though they didn't know each other.

Juliana ran her hand through her tangled hair. "Yes, Juliana Hiller. I apologize for my appearance."

"We just got her out of Tenred's dungeons," Basen explained.

"Basen," she whispered. "Now what will they think?" Juliana smiled at Neeko and Shara. "Crea Hiller put me there to keep me from telling her secrets. I assure you I'm no criminal."

Basen had forgotten how easily his mother was humiliated. She always worried he would misbehave in front of the wrong person. It took him years to figure out that she wasn't concerned with how he would appear but rather that she would be judged and found lacking. After he learned this, he made more of an effort to do things like bow, keep his hands clean, and keep his elbows off the table. The hardest had been refraining from making remarks Juliana deemed inappropriate, as hilarious as they might be.

He loved his mother. She was kind and gentle no matter the circumstance, the opposite of Henry. But she often yearned for control over situations and became upset when she couldn't achieve it. Unfortunately, Henry was the same way, and that had led to arguments between them when Basen was younger. Nonetheless, he longed for them to reunite. Everything had become easier since he'd reached adulthood and they'd begun to trust him more, for many of his parents' quarrels had been about the right way to raise him.

"We don't know who Crea Hiller is," Shara said, then widened her eyes and whispered, "but what secrets?"

That brought out a chuckle from everyone except Juliana, who seemed confused as to how these two hadn't heard of one of the more well-known people of Tenred.

"They're from Sumar," Basen explained, guiding the conversation where he knew it needed to go. "They came here to join the Academy, yet they now live in this cabin."

"Come with us," Effie added. "We're going back to the school now."

"But...it didn't seem like a school," Shara said, looking up at Neeko.

He nodded. "More like a fortification for an army."

"It *is* built that way," Basen agreed. "But once you see it from the inside, you'll agree that 'the Academy' is an apt name for it."

"But you're still at war," Neeko said. "And...there are many fighting against you."

How does he know that but not who Crea Hiller is?

Effie turned up her hands. "Which is why we need you."

Neeko and Shara glanced at each other. The sparkle of their eyes showed they each knew what the other was thinking. Basen was sure of it now; they were in love. *Neither of them wants the other to be in danger. But does that mean one might volunteer with the right persuasion? If so, the other certainly will join.*

Shara turned back to the group with a sigh. "We came here having just finished risking our lives in Sumar. Most of you probably know what that feels like, and also what it feels like to have the chance to live without danger."

"Then why did you stay here?" Basen asked. Neeko and Shara seemed a little surprised by the question, perhaps even confused. "If you have no intentions of fighting with the Academy, why'd you stay in Ovira?"

Neeko tapped his fingers against his leg as if the question made him uncomfortable.

"They haven't told us they have no intentions of fighting," Effie said.

"They were about to," Basen countered.

Neeko nodded. "It's true. We don't." He looked to Shara. "Or we didn't."

She stared at him in silence for a moment before turning to Basen. "It's complicated."

"I'm sure it is." Basen wasn't sure how he came to be the one trying the hardest to recruit them. "This war is complicated as well...to an outsider. But to us it's simple. We fight to defend what we believe in. Effie told me you've met Terren—you must've seen what kind of man he is. Tauwin sent someone to assassinate him, and failed. Tauwin sent someone else to take the Academy from him, and failed. Tauwin tried to take all of Kyrro, and—"

"Failed?" Shara interjected.

"So far. He's received help, as have we. Troops from

Tenred have joined us, as have Krepps, and soon we'll have Elves on our side. The outcome of the war does not depend on the two of you joining us, but many lives might. This isn't just a battle about numbers and land, it's about the future of Kyrro."

"How so?" Shara asked.

"The Takarys used to rule Kyrro with a hammer. Keeping control within their family was their utmost priority, as will always be the case."

As he paused, Basen could see he was only making them feel guilty, not changing their minds. He needed another tactic.

"Going to the Academy was the only option I had to change the course of my life," he continued. "Even after everything that's happened to me there, I don't regret my decision. I look at the both of you: young, clearly talented, and with many paths to choose from. You came here from Sumar to join the Academy, only to continue through Kyrro and into this forest when you saw we were at war. Now you remain here, waiting, as if every path that's available to you now will still be available when this war is over. That's not the case. By not coming with us now, you're making the choice to *never* stand with us."

"I don't believe you," Shara said. "They would take Neeko, no matter who controls the school."

"No," Steffen said somewhat shyly as he stepped into the makeshift circle. "Basen's right, Shara. I don't know why I didn't see it this way sooner. The Academy isn't just a place you visit to hone your skills. Before any of us can stay even one night of the three years we'll spend there, we have to agree to defend Kyrro for the rest of our lives.

Not the Academy—*Kyrro*."

Steffen glanced at Effie with a guilty look on his face. "I believe Effie and I were so adamant about you coming back with us that we failed to explain what the school really represents. To join is to agree to defend...well, the king. Ultimately that means we're defending justice. Even though our monarch is dead, we still have to defend what he represented. You can't join the school only to leave when war begins. None of us can. And you can't wait for war to end to join."

Shara's mouth twisted during the heavy silence that followed. "So you're asking us to commit our lives to Kyrro when we've just come to Ovira. We didn't grow up here. Our families don't live here. We know none of the history, nothing about the kings. We haven't even gotten a chance to find out what the weather is like! Does it snow during the winter like in some places in Sumar? We don't even know."

"Not in Kyrro or Tenred," Annah answered. "The weather and resources of the land are some of the reasons Kyrro and Tenred are home to all humans in Ovira."

"That's nice to know," Shara said sarcastically, "but that's not my point. You're asking us to make a commitment before we're ready. We haven't abandoned the Academy. We just haven't joined the war yet. It's like when a man and a woman get together. No one expects them to marry immediately. We aren't ready to marry Kyrro, yet that's what you're asking."

Neeko put his hand on her back, his face without the same annoyance as hers as he spoke to Basen. "We came here expecting a certain kind of life," he explained. "We were looking for more adventure, but not necessarily such danger. Though, we understand what you're saying."

Shara nodded reluctantly. "We do."

"It's almost night," Neeko said. "Give us until the morning to make a decision, all right?"

It sounds like they already have.

"Of course," Effie said.

Neeko and Shara busied themselves getting the cabin ready for everyone to spend the night there. There was only one bed, but an enormous bearskin rug covered most of the floor, and they laid out all the sheets they had to cover the rest. Combined with the blankets Basen's party had packed, it seemed that everyone should be comfortable enough to sleep. So it came as a surprise when Neeko and Shara announced they would be leaving for the night and the bed would be available. They were going to sleep in the forest, most likely so they could discuss privately what to do.

"We should sleep outside," Juliana offered, "so you can stay here."

Both Shara and Neeko put up their hands. "No," Shara said, "we want to be out of the cabin as we consider leaving it for good."

Annah left with them and explained that she needed to tell Vithos and the Krepps what was happening for the night.

There was little risk of enemies finding them in this forest, so the Krepps should be able to sleep safely no matter where they chose to rest. It was fortunate that the night was warm. Mosquitoes would be the worst of their troubles, and that's only if the annoying insects had a taste for them. The creatures did stink, after all.

When Annah returned and everyone was settled, Basen asked Effie lying beside him, "What can Neeko and Shara do that make them so important?"

"Shara is just a mage like me."

"And Neeko?"

"Have you heard of pyforial energy?"

"No."

"Steffen," Effie whispered to her other side.

"What?"

"Help me explain pyforial energy to Basen."

"And anyone else listening," Basen added.

Annah sat up. "Isn't it similar to sartious except that it's clear and holds together better?"

"Yes," Steffen said, his gravelly voice making it sound as if he'd been asleep already.

"You're not making it sound exciting," Effie said. "He can move things with it."

"Oh god's mercy," Basen quipped. "He can move things?"

She slapped his arm playfully. "It's much more than that! He can choke people, too."

Juliana gasped. "Oh, dear."

Effie sat up quickly. "Neeko wouldn't choke anyone who didn't deserve it, Mrs. Hiller."

Did he choke one of the three Krepps going after him? It didn't seem like that would be enough to deter all of them.

"Can he lift people with this energy?" Basen asked. "Can he throw them?"

"I don't think so," Effie said as she lay back down. "Steffen, help me explain. What he can do is amazing, isn't it?"

There was no reply.

"Steffen, wake up."

He snorted, then grumbled, "Yes, amazing."

"The potential of what he can do..." Effie said, but then paused for a long while. "I bet he's learned how to throw knives with the energy."

"Don't many warriors of the Academy also know how to throw knives?" Basen asked. "I thought it's what they learned when the bow was outlawed."

She pushed her knuckles against his shoulder. "All right, I don't know exactly what he's learned to do since we last spoke with him, but we want him to teach others how to manipulate the energy. Maybe one pyorial mage isn't as useful as I first thought, but ten? I'm sure *they* could lift someone."

"Ten archers sounds a lot more intimidating to me. Ten *psychics*. Now they would be worth coming to this cabin for. Even ten skilled swordsmen, or bastial mages. All seem better than ten pyorial mages. Now if Neeko was strong enough to pick someone up and break them in half, or even snap their neck, then—"

"Basen, please!" his mother scolded. "Have you really become this crass in the short time we've been apart?"

Effie and Annah seemed to find that amusing, laughing without reserve.

"Sorry, Mother," Basen mumbled under his breath. He knew she was sensitive to gore, but he hadn't expected to be called out on his "vulgar behavior" during their first night reunited.

"And apologize to Effie and Annah for speaking like that," his mother chided.

Basen felt his cheeks go hot with embarrassment. She'd always treated women gentler than they needed to be treated. Not all were princesses as delicate as ripe peaches.

"I'm sure they don't care if I apologize," he groused.

"Oh, we do," Effie teased. "We care very much."

Annah snickered.

Basen couldn't believe, in the silence that followed, he was actually expected to apologize to them. Was there a portal in this cabin that had sent him into the past? He felt like a child again, but not in a good way. His mother seemed to have that effect on him.

"I'm *sorry* I was crass in front of you, Effie and Annah," he said, unable to keep his insincerity from coming out. "I didn't realize you were so fragile that I could offend your delicate nature with a few descriptive words. I swear to speak only of *flowers, fragrances*, and other *fragile* things in the *future*."

"You forgot *furry* creatures," Effie teased. "And *flowing* dresses."

"And *fanciful, flavorful* meals," Annah added. "We approve of all of these *fascinating* topics."

"*Florid*..." Steffen grumbled, half asleep. "*Florid* something."

When the chemist offered nothing else, Basen concluded the conversation with one last word.

"*Fine*."

CHAPTER TEN

In the morning, Basen led his mother to the stream he knew to be nearby. They'd taken it upon themselves to get water for their group, and he knew Juliana wanted privacy to improve her appearance. She'd borrowed a mirror and comb she'd found in the cabin, and when Basen had noticed them in her hands on the way to the water, she'd pursed her lips and said, "Shara would understand. All women would."

Shara and Neeko hadn't returned by the time Basen left with his mother. Perhaps they hadn't come to a decision. Much had been asked of them, after all. Joining the Academy had been an easy choice for Basen, though he hadn't had the same freedom they enjoyed.

Freedom—he'd felt less of it since rescuing his mother.

He loved her; he did. He was so glad for her to be out of confinement and on her way back to Henry. Now if only he could figure out why she was treating him as if he'd gotten younger instead of older since they'd last seen each other.

"How has the Academy been?" she asked him.

"I haven't spent as much time there as I've wanted because of the war, but so far it's been pleasant."

"What else has taken you away from school besides rescuing me?" She stopped combing her hair, set down Shara's mirror and comb, and walked over to take Basen's hands. "Thank you." She squeezed. "Thank you. I don't think I've said so yet, which was wrong. I'm afraid I've lost sight of my manners dealing with those obnoxious women locked up with me. I don't know why Crea had to punish me so. She could've put me in my own cell."

"I'm sure she knows how social you are and wanted to give you company," Basen joked.

His mother actually was social, spending much of her time at the castle organizing dinners and other events. But if there was one thing she had no tolerance for, it was rude people with no title to use as an excuse. Crea, on the other hand, was a princess, so Juliana figured she had the right to act like she did. Basen never understood his mother's reasoning behind that, but at least now she couldn't possibly treat Crea with the same deference.

He looked forward to Juliana, Henry, and Crea being stuck within the same walls. But then he remembered his mother avoided conflict at all costs. *And she's not going to want Henry to do anything, either.* It was somewhat frustrating.

"You're welcome," Basen said. "But don't forget that Crea could've left you there to die. You can't show her any respect when you return. Doing so would be disrespecting yourself."

"She'll get what she deserves," Juliana said with a mischievous smirk that satisfied Basen greatly. He hadn't seen this side of his mother before. "However, I would be surprised if she's still at the Academy by the time I return."

"She'll run?"

"Like she does from every problem."

"I don't think she will this time. She's invested too much in this war to run back to Tenred. She'll want to make amends."

"I welcome her to try."

Now Basen was beginning to worry. Juliana had never let her emotions take control like this, and she might be at the Academy for a while before Basen could return.

"Just be careful," he said. "The politics within the Academy are complicated right now and extremely delicate. When I left, it felt as if Terren and Abith were one disagreement away from a duel, and I'm not talking about the friendly kind. Meanwhile, Crea is plotting something. I forced her to sign the decree that led to your release, but she'll protect herself from our family in some way."

"She's always plotting. I'll figure her out before we're in any danger."

"But—"

"I'll be careful," his mother assured him with a toss of her hand. "I know how to handle women like her." She went back to working the knots out of her tangled hair.

After an awkward silence, Basen said, "To answer your first question, many different things have taken me away from the Academy. I have a certain skill that has become quite useful."

"Your sword fighting—your father has finally convinced you to take it up again!"

He was shocked at the pride he heard in his mother's voice. Had she wanted him to be a knight of Tenred like Henry had? She'd always made a point to take Basen's side, saying that if he wanted to be a mage, he deserved the opportunity to train as one. He supposed he'd never asked her directly what she wanted for him. It did make sense that she would want him to learn the sword over the wand, for there was more honor that way, and she cared more about honor than most.

"No," he said, "I have a skill with bastial energy that you'll soon see."

She looked absolutely bewildered, as if he'd just told her he had become the king of Kyrro.

"How does your ability with energy lead to you being selected for these missions? There must be more experienced mages who can make fire or cast light."

"Yes, third-years, but even they can't do what I can."

"Why aren't you telling me what it is?" She smiled as she seemed to realize something. "You want to surprise me."

"And you shouldn't ruin it." He smiled back.

"Something with that akorell bracelet, I presume."

Basen laughed. "Now you're the one surprising me. How do you know what it is?" He'd been charging it with energy as much as he could on the way to the forest. Now Effie was putting all she could into it so it would be ready as soon as possible.

"I know a lot of things," she said, still holding her grin. But then she frowned. "I had Sanya's father investigated after his eldest daughter died mysteriously. I found out what the akorell stone was then."

"So you also knew about Spiro's experiments?"

Juliana's face twisted with sadness. To Basen's shock, she began to weep.

"I did. I tried to get him to stop, but he wouldn't. I told Henry to speak to his brother about it, but you know how Tegry was. Your father couldn't convince him to force

Spiro to stop. That chemist was mad. He believed he was a god."

"I complained about Sanya all the time. Why didn't you tell me what was happening to her?"

"It would've come out during one of your arguments with her. Or you might've told one of your friends. I wanted to protect Sanya, to help her. Look at how sad she was because no one could."

Basen was too shocked to figure out what he was feeling. Juliana had made it sound as if all of Sanya's sins were her father's fault. *It's only because Juliana is a parent herself. For everything wrong I did as a child, I could see a bit of shame in her as she lectured me. Even last night in the cabin, it was as if my "crass" language reflected on her. At what point do parents let their children take full responsibility for their actions? If I killed someone innocent, would my mother blame herself?* It seemed absurd. Henry had never been this way with him, and Basen doubted Spiro would feel responsible for the monster he'd created.

Sanya had told Basen her father was dead, but there was no way to know if anything she'd said was true.

Basen put his hand on his mother's shoulder. He thought about telling her of the heinous things Sanya had done but decided against it. Knowing the truth would only upset her more.

"You shouldn't blame yourself for Sanya, Mother, and you shouldn't blame yourself for anything I've done wrong. You've raised me well. Any choices I make, such as using *crass* language last night, are my choices. It's the same with Sanya."

"I know I shouldn't treat you like you're ten. It's hard, Basen, but I'm going to try. I thought about you every day and vowed not to lose you again."

He could feel his mother wanting to urge him to go back to the Academy with her. He was proud of her for not pressuring him into changing his mind.

"You won't lose me," he promised.

They filled the empty barrel they'd brought from the cabin with clear river water, secured the lid, and rolled it back, together. Upon returning, he saw the Krepps had started a fire outside the cabin's fence. What looked to be a deer carcass quickly blackened under the high flames as it hung on a spit.

From behind them, Neeko and Shara came out from the trees and took each other's hands as if startled.

"I have to get there," Basen said as he ran toward them, but the Krepps didn't seem to notice or care as they took the carcass from the spit and began to cut off steaming chunks of meat.

"These really are different from the others," Shara remarked as Basen reached them.

"I believe they come from a different tribe."

Effie rushed out of the cabin. "What did you decide?"

The rest of their party was right behind her. Everyone stopped and eagerly awaited the news. Basen noticed his mother going back into the cabin, most likely to return the comb and mirror. He fetched the barrel of water as well as a ladle he knew to be in the cabin.

He wouldn't say so in front of Neeko and Shara, but Basen wouldn't be too disappointed if they decided to stay here. Effie had made Neeko seem much more valuable than he was if all he could do was move objects and choke people.

When Basen came outside again, he could see by everyone's faces that Neeko and Shara had delivered the bad news he'd expected. Basen went back into the cabin in search of the akorell bracelet, as he didn't see it on Effie.

He found it on the single table in the small cabin. She'd encased it in sartious energy to keep it from burning the wood.

Basen offered everyone water as he returned to the group. They shared the ladle as one person drank at a time. No one said anything, and Basen didn't feel comfortable in the silence for too long.

"Is the akorell stone charged yet?" he asked Effie.

"I think it's going to take many more hours, maybe even a day."

"It's fine. It'll take me at least a day to reach the area where I can make a portal."

A female Krepp came over and pointed at the water. Basen gave her the ladle. She scooped up some water and poured it into her lipless mouth without touching the ladle. Her politeness surprised and impressed Basen. Perhaps Rickik's Krepps were crass in comparison to others of their kind.

When the Krepp left, Shara said, "I'm sorry. I know you wanted us to come with you. We do want to go to the Academy, but we're just not ready for the commitment."

"I know," Effie said. "If I were you, I might not go, either. But you should know that if you come with us you won't regret it. There's no other place like the Academy. Whether I'm there to train or to fight, I would rather be there than anywhere else."

Her words seemed to greatly affect both Neeko and Shara, who looked at each other as if expecting the other to have a change of heart. Then another Krepp came over for water and the moment seemed to be lost. As soon as the Krepp left, Basen asked the party who would be leading the group back to the Academy.

Steffen seemed surprised when he looked at Annah and Effie and found them staring back at him.

"I suppose I will," he said.

Basen handed over the map he'd brought. "Only travel along the mountain at evening as it begins to get dark. Stay in the forest during the day as much as you can so the troops on the mountain can't see you."

He wished he could make a portal back to the Academy for them, but it was already going to take at least a day to get to the small forest in Kilmar where he knew he could make a portal for himself. His week was almost up, and the last thing he wanted was to teleport to Fatholl on the last day, exactly when the Elf was expecting him.

He supposed he could bring everyone with him to Kilmar, make a portal for them there, then spend the next couple of days charging his akorell stone for another portal to the Elves. But it didn't seem worth it to arrive late and break his promise. None of their enemies expected them to be going back to the Academy from the east. *They will be safe.*

"I should be leaving," Basen concluded. He hugged his

mother. "I'll see you back at the Academy."

"I love you."

"I love you, too." He raised his eyebrows at the rest of the party. "I'm trusting all of you with my mother."

"She'll be fine," Effie said, still sounding dejected from Neeko and Shara's decision. "Be careful with Fatholl."

"Don't worry, I'll have Vithos to watch my back."

At hearing his name, the Elf came over from the Krepps. "We leave now?" His hands and chin glistened with grease.

"Yes," Basen said. "As soon as you're done with your breakfast."

"I'm done. The meat is gone. Krepps eat too fast for me to get much. I'm happy we brought food in bags." He turned to Juliana and offered his hand. "Nice to meet you, Juliana Hiller."

She turned her lips inward as she looked at his greasy fingers. With a grimace, she extended her hand and shook his. "Nice to meet you, too."

The awkward silence returned as everyone in the circle stared at each other and waited for someone to do something.

This goodbye didn't feel right. Neeko and Shara's rejection of the Academy had put everyone on edge. Effie and Steffen had come to them as friends, asking for their help, only to be denied. And why? Because the outcome of the war looked so dire for the Academy that Neeko and Shara gave up their opportunity to join. It left a bitter taste in Basen's mouth.

"I need to say something." Neeko and Shara looked as if he was about to scold them. "Relax. I don't know you well enough to judge you. I understand your choice, but there's something you're not understanding about us, about why we feel so strongly that fighting with the Academy is the right decision. My mother was in prison, and although she was as miserable as any of us would be living behind bars, she was safe there. Yet my father and I still were adamant about getting her released as soon as possible. My father and I are Hillers. Our family was more hated than the Takarys by everyone at the Academy just last year.

"But here I am now telling you the Academy is the best place not only for you, but for me and my family. It's not because the Academy is the only option we have left. I would choose it over my old life in Tenred castle, even knowing the danger it puts me in. Effie told me a little about what you were doing in Sumar, so I know you're used to fighting for what you believe in. You must know what it's like to put all your effort into something for weeks, even months, to the point where the few free moments you have to enjoy friends, laughter, and food are bliss. Once you've fought for what you believe in, it gives you an appreciation for life that nothing else can. I can't wait for this war to be over, but at the same time, I can't imagine not having fought for Kyrro.

"A friend of mine, Alabell Kerr, saw her family murdered at Tauwin Takary's command. I didn't realize it at the time, but as soon as I heard that news, I knew I wouldn't let Tauwin be king even if I had to fight to my last breath to prevent it. I agree with how you feel about risking your life in war, but we're not the ones forcing you to pick a side. It's Tauwin. By not fighting, you're risking just as much, because you're letting it be known that men like Tauwin can murder entire families and be king so long as they have the wealth to back up their greed. I'd rather not live in that world, and I don't think you would either."

His words seemed to give them second thoughts as they stared at each other again. Crim came over and noisily slurped down some water without the ladle, tilting the barrel to get a better angle and sticking most of his flat, greasy face into it.

As soon as he was done, he stood up and, with water dripping from his chin, said, "Krepps leave now. We go to Academy. Humans?"

"Yes, we're leaving as well," Steffen said.

Crim nodded, then hollered something at the Krepps. They put out the fire and began to walk.

"We have to hurry," Steffen said. "I need to be in front so they don't choose their own route back." He ran into the cabin, presumably to get his belongings together.

"So what will you do?" Effie asked the young couple.

"It's up to you," Neeko told Shara. It almost looked as if he wanted to go as he leaned toward her.

Her expression turned sad. "I don't think we're ready."

He nodded with seeming reluctance. "We're staying," he told Effie. "I'm sorry."

Steffen had already gotten in front of the Krepps. "Come on!" he yelled to their party.

Annah gave a quick curtsy. "It was nice to meet you both." She turned to Basen. "Goodbye."

"Goodbye, Annah."

Juliana embraced Basen without hurry, then walked

after the Krepps. That left Effie. She looked at Neeko imploringly.

"I don't think you want to stay," she said, then turned her hard gaze to Shara. "Honestly, I believe you'll regret it."

Shara cleared her throat. "Effie, nothing could cause me more regret than if Neeko died in this war."

Effie let out a quick breath. She forced a bitter smile as she lowered her head. "Goodbye then." She turned and pushed herself against Basen's chest for a hug that ended all too quickly. She did the same to Vithos, then ran off.

"Neeko," Basen said, "tell me something, if you don't mind."

"You don't have to go with them?"

"No. Vithos and I need to take care of something away from the Academy."

"What do you want to know?"

"Why does Effie so desperately want you to join us in this war? She went against her instructor to come here for the two of you, but mostly for you."

Neeko sucked in a breath, looking exactly how Basen had hoped, as if he wanted to prove his worth right there.

"He's a pyforial mage," Shara answered. "He might be the best in the world."

"Effie told me that, but I still don't understand. Even if he was able to teach others how to use pyforial energy, I can't imagine anyone learning the skill well enough to replace what they came to the Academy to do, at least not in time to be of much help. But Neeko, you should've seen her face when I described our earlier encounter and she realized it was you and Shara. It was as if I'd told her an entire army could've joined us if I'd simply asked. So I'm still wondering, what can you do...and what did you do to those three Krepps chasing after you?"

Shara looked at Neeko with surprise. "What three Krepps?"

He didn't answer right away, instead giving Basen a hard stare. Neeko's eyes were kind, but there was a twinkle of superiority in them, as if Basen should consider himself lucky to see what Neeko could do. Basen challenged him with the same look. *Prove yourself.* He could think of no better way to recruit the young man now that everything else had failed.

Neeko sighed, softened his expression, and then turned to Shara. "When the Krepps came to our cabin the first time while you were away, I left. Three of them came after me. I didn't know what they wanted, but as I sped up, so did they. I was never actually in danger, so I didn't tell you."

Shara nodded. "All right."

For someone supposedly worried about Neeko's safety, Shara seemed surprisingly comfortable with him facing three Krepps. Perhaps Effie was right and Neeko really was special.

"I should go," Basen said. "Forgive my earlier curiosity. If the two of you won't join us, I suppose it's better that I don't know exactly what we'll be missing. Take care."

The hostility dissolved in an instant as both of them smiled politely and said goodbye. Basen left with Vithos. He had seen something when he'd looked into Neeko's eyes, the same thing Effie must've seen during her time in

Sumar.

Basen didn't need a demonstration of Neeko's power. That look had been enough to show he could've helped them in this war far greater than just another swordsman.

CHAPTER ELEVEN

Basen supposed he could sneak back into Tenred's castle at night with Vithos. It was a shorter trip than going to Kilmar, and he could use the damaged corner of the castle to get in undetected. But he had a feeling that Fatholl would want him to teleport to Kilmar, and he needed to revisit the area to refresh his memory. He didn't want to disappoint Fatholl, especially because the Elf already would be angry at what Basen was going to tell him.

Vithos was a man of many jokes, Basen found out during their short journey. Given that he'd been raised with the dour Krepps, it came as a surprise he found humor so easily in most things. It furthered Basen's belief that the harder people fight to survive, the more they appreciate life. He hadn't taken time to consider this until he'd given his speech to Neeko and Shara. Now he was glad he had. Instead of fearing his encounter with Fatholl, he enjoyed his time with Vithos as they traveled through the forest.

He learned about what life was like for the Elf. He'd only recently escaped the Krepps while they were led by two monstrous Slugari, Doe and Haemon, and Vithos had Zoke—the Krepp who knew Cleve—to thank for it. Vithos believed that Zoke would help now if need be.

"There is also a pretty Elf who can help," Vithos told Basen. "Maybe," he added, then paused.

"Why wouldn't she?"

"We fight often. We don't like each other."

"Then why might she help?"

"We have much sex."

"You what?" Basen assumed Vithos had used the wrong word. But no, the Elf was nodding enthusiastically.

"Yes, much sex. We like the sex, but not...other time with each other."

Basen chuckled. "Well, I hope Fatholl listens to her if he doesn't listen to us."

"Fatholl hears everyone but listens to no one. You understand?"

"I figured he was like that. What about with the Krepps?"

"He treats them with care, but he doesn't like them. I can feel it."

"Can you tell when he lies?"

"Yes."

It was good to know that Fatholl couldn't change his energy like Sanya could.

Vithos eventually told Basen some shocking news: Vithos' mother and father had been queen and king of the Elves in Merejic and the most powerful psychics.

"So you have more claim to leading the Elves than Fatholl does?" Basen asked.

Vithos nodded.

Even more reason Fatholl would be cautious around him. Basen couldn't rely on Vithos to convince Fatholl to come with him, but he doubted the female Elf who'd had "much sex" with Vithos would be of much help, either.

Basen had to rely on himself. The problem was, he already was assuming so much coming into this. If Fatholl wasn't trying to get rid of the Krepps like Basen figured, then he wouldn't know what to expect, and surprise of any kind could be deadly. The worst would be if Basen was wrong about Yeso's relation to Fatholl.

Confidence was everything here. Basen could pretend to be confident quite well, but psychics could read his emotions so he had to really be confident, otherwise there was no point.

"When we speak to him," Basen said, "can you use psyche to make me seem completely sure of myself?"

Vithos' mouth twisted. "I can, but it's pointless. Fatholl will figure out I change your energy."

That meant the change had to come from within. *Remember what Henry said. You have to be stronger than the psychic.*

If his mother had still been in prison, waiting to be rescued, he could've used his need to free her to bolster his strength and resist any spell of manipulation. He needed to think of something else.

*****

Basen felt it as they came to the spot. He'd never determined what had gathered enough energy here for him to make a portal, but it had to be something alive, didn't it? There was no evidence of akorell metal around them.

The feeling was strange, like falling into a dream he'd had before. It seemed as if part of his memory was trapped, destined to live here forever. He supposed he had a similar feeling in Nick's old room, now Annah's, but Basen had attributed it to the painful loss of his friend.

Basen gulped for air. Was making portals affecting him in some way he would only find out much later?

"Are you all right?" Vithos asked. "Very nervous."

"I'm fine."

Earlier, Vithos had asked Basen if he liked making portals. It was difficult to answer because the thought had never come to mind. The more Basen pondered it, the more he realized he didn't like the process at all. It put a frightening strain on his mind and heart, only to culminate with a terrible spell of dizziness whenever he tumbled through the portal.

It's gotten easier, he reminded himself. Still, he needed to know what it was doing to him.

Sanya told me it's destroying the spiritual world every time I make one. He wouldn't forget that anytime soon, not that he knew what to make of it. These portals were necessary, and he did relish having the ability to control them. He'd always had a natural skill with bastial energy that he appreciated but he'd never been able to do anything like this. It made him wonder what else he might be capable of.

"Are you ready?" he asked Vithos.

"Very excited."

The answer seemed strange, though the Elf was somewhat strange himself. Pleasantly strange.

Basen gathered a ball of bastial energy, packed it into itself as it floated in front of him, and continued to squeeze it together until it was white as snow. He drew the energy from the akorell stone, no longer surprised by the sudden weight of it on his mind. Each time it was like witnessing a terrible accident in which he had to remember every detail, his chest filling with fire, his heart racing.

While compacting the energy, he reached deep within it until he burrowed through to the other side. He'd set his mind on the Elven village, his destination, and now the image was locked and grounded, as if someone had turned him into a statue and dropped him in the center of the village.

When Vithos began to clap enthusiastically, Basen became confused. It took a moment to realize it wasn't the thought of visiting Fatholl or the pretty Elven woman that excited Vithos but the portal itself.

Despite the strain, Basen cracked a smile. Vithos had a way of improving every situation, whether he meant to or not. The Elf let out a laugh that bordered on triumphant as he ran and jumped in. Basen calmly walked in after.

The world spit him out almost immediately. He tumbled with little sense of up or down before finally coming to a stop. Vithos was groaning yet chuckling at the same time, as if his own pain amused him.

"Feel sick," the Elf muttered with a huge grin.

As his surroundings came into focus, Basen saw many other Elves and Krepps around him. All seemed busy with their own tasks, none noticing him yet.

"Come on," he said as he hurried toward a large tree.

He and Vithos moved between its trunk and a nearby building that seemed to be a storage place for food. Noticing Elves working inside through the window, Basen knew he needed to move again.

"This way." He led Vithos around the building, but a clear lane of grass made him slow to a normal walk so as not to draw attention to himself and his companion.

"Where are we going?" Vithos asked.

"Somewhere hidden, if we can."

"Oh, yes to spy."

Vithos took the lead, guiding Basen through the village at a normal pace. They passed by many groups of Elves and Krepps, but Basen never saw the two races working together as they had the last time he'd been here. He kept his head down, like Vithos, in hopes of not being recognized.

Fortunately, it was a short trip to an Elven house that seemed to be Vithos' destination. It was identical to many of the other smaller buildings, with short walls made of brick painted white and a red sturdy roof. In fact, it looked like the homes Basen would find in any human city.

Vithos knocked and a beautiful Elf answered the door. The corner of her mouth curled at seeing Vithos, then the other corner came up to form a wide grin as she glanced at Basen.

Expecting them to speak, Basen grew confused when only silence followed. Their expressions changed from smiling, to confusion, to understanding as the female Elf nodded.

She opened the door farther and stepped aside. Basen followed Vithos in with a nervous feeling in his stomach.

"Thank you," Basen said.

"You're welcome." She had a different accent from

Vithos. His was Kreppen, rough like rocks tumbling down a hill, while hers was clearly Elvish, as smooth as a ribbon dancing in the wind.

She looked at Vithos. Her eyebrows lifted as if posing a question. He began to shake his head, then stopped and put his hand on his chin in thought. Then he nodded as he shrugged his shoulders.

Basen cleared his throat as he realized they might've been discussing whether to venture into the bedroom. The woman pointed at Basen, then looked back at Vithos with her eyebrows raised again.

Vithos put up his palm and shook his head.

The woman laughed. "Jealous?"

Vithos laughed snidely to imitate her. "No."

"Do you know about my promise to Fatholl?" Basen asked her in hopes of steering the conversation to where it needed to go.

"No. What promise?"

"He gave us Krepps and armor in exchange for my return to do some task for him. He wouldn't tell me what it was. Now that I'm back..." Basen looked at Vithos. "Can we trust her?"

Vithos squinted as he stared at the woman, tilting his head from side to side. She folded her arms, clearly insulted.

"Yes, you can trust me!"

"All right, we trust you," Vithos said. "You not tell Fatholl we're here?"

"Why?"

Basen explained, "I need to get a sense of what he has planned for me."

"Why?"

Fatholl clearly wasn't the same threatening Elf to her that he was to Basen. She wasn't the right one to go to for information. "I think we should see Zoke," Basen whispered to Vithos.

"All right, we try. But his house is farther. We might get seen."

"Wait," the woman said. "Tell me why are you afraid, *handsome* human?"

"I'm not afraid. I'm just trying to figure out what he wants."

She showed Basen a sly smile. "You are afraid, but I find out for you. Wait here." She hurried off.

"Was she lying?" Basen asked.

"No, but I don't trust her," Vithos said.

"Then why are we here?"

"Less risky than finding Zoke. He not often in his house. She might know something. He won't."

"She doesn't know anything. She just said so."

"She might *find out* something," Vithos corrected himself. "Zoke can't."

Basen supposed it was settled, then. They would wait here.

In the time that followed, Basen began to wonder why this woman was the one Vithos went to first. "Don't you have other friends here besides her? Perhaps someone else would have less reason to betray you."

"She has no reason to betray me."

"You told me she doesn't like you, and that seemed obvious from your interaction."

"She likes my body. If she betrays me, she doesn't get it anymore."

"That's not…" Basen stopped himself. Actually, he supposed it *was* relevant, and he had to admit he knew nothing about this woman. *If Vithos says she's our best option, she must be.*

A short time later, the woman returned. She looked apologetic as she entered with her hands clasped. "I tried," she said.

Basen muttered a curse as Vithos blurted out an expletive in Kreppen.

In came Fatholl behind her, not at all pleased to see Basen. A couple other Elves walked in after him and stayed close behind as their leader approached.

"Give me the akorell stone," Fatholl demanded.

CHAPTER TWELVE

Fatholl said nothing after he took the stone. The other Elves grabbed Vithos by his arms. They said something in Elvish to him, his surprise changing to disappointment. He walked out of the woman's house with them, but not before giving Basen a worried look over his shoulder.

Basen didn't have a chance to figure out what to ask Vithos before everyone, even the Elven woman, was gone.

"Wait," Basen said as he went for the door.

To his surprise, it was unlocked. He went after the Elves. "Where are you taking Vithos?" *And my akorell stone?*

"He'll be fine," Fatholl called over his shoulder.

It didn't seem so much that they were running away from Basen but that they were in a hurry and Basen and Vithos' arrival had inconvenienced them. In fact, Fatholl didn't even threaten Basen to stay in the woman's house.

"What's going on?" Basen yelled at the now distant Elves, drawing the gazes of many more.

No one answered him. He looked around for a clue, but the Elves pretended he didn't exist. He hurried after Vithos, and that finally drew the attention he'd expected earlier.

"No," one Elf said, putting out his hand. He was not part of the group escorting Vithos.

All the Elves are part of this, Basen realized as he noticed none of them appeared surprised by what was happening. Their eerie gray and green eyes, their damned perfect, creamy skin, irritatingly beautiful...was this how it felt to be a Krepp in the Academy? All of them looked at Basen as if he didn't belong, waiting for him to return to the empty house.

The woman who lived there was nowhere in sight. Perhaps she really had tried and now she and Vithos would be punished.

What did that mean for Basen? *And for my akorell stone?*

Unable to take the icy stares of the perfectly still Elves any longer, Basen returned to the house and shut the door.

He had to think quickly. Fatholl had said nothing of the akorell stone during their first meeting. He hadn't seemed to know what it was. But now, the first thing he'd done was take it.

As I was researching him, he was researching portals, Basen realized. *Now he knows I can't go anywhere without the akorell stone.*

I knew we should've tried to get to Zoke. The Krepp would've helped Basen figure out what Fatholl had planned. *It must have to do with the Krepps.* Their separation from the Elves reinforced his belief.

It's the only reason the Slugari queen was so adamant about doing whatever Fatholl wanted. She knows he means to do something to the Krepps...probably get rid of them.

Night seemed to arrive quickly, but Basen was ready for it with a new plan. He'd opened a window earlier, and now it was a matter of squeezing through as silently as possible. To his amazement, the village appeared empty.

Good, no one would see him as he crept through the darkness, shrouded by his cloak.

There was only one problem. He had no idea how to find Zoke.

*****

Basen returned to the house where he figured he'd be spending the night. A quick search around the village had only gotten him lost. Even familiar places could seem strange at night, so an unfamiliar place, and one where the inhabitants seemed to make a point of using no light once the moon was out, was impossible to explore.

The village wasn't immune to the effects of the jungle surrounding it. Basen heard many of the familiar creaks and howls like the last time he was here. They were distant, not at all a danger, but they reminded him that he was a long way from home. News of whatever happened to him here might never reach the people who cared about him.

Basen decided he'd better rest. Fatholl seemed too busy to let Basen sleep past sunup. He sighed as he made himself comfortable on the bed. Whatever Fatholl had planned, it seemed to involve Basen returning early— either today or tomorrow. *He knew I would come back now. How?*

The bed was softer than what he was given at the Academy, reminding him of his mattress in Tenred. It was when he went to bed on that mattress when he was younger that he would fantasize about adventures just like this. Well, not exactly like this. There were certainly no thoughts of being used by psychic Elves.

He wanted to give up on his plan and just do whatever Fatholl asked of him. At least he'd be more likely get out of this alive. But then this trip would have no benefit to the war, no meaning. It would've been made solely out of fear. He couldn't let that be the case, even if he was afraid. Eventually he managed to fall into a fitful sleep.

Everything was different in the morning. Basen had locked the door, simply because he saw no reason not to. But rather than the Elves forcing their way in, Basen was roused by a polite knock. Whoever was there waited patiently for Basen to dress and answer it. He was shocked to find Fatholl, alone and wearing a smug grin like he was about to show Basen a trick.

"Where are Vithos and the woman?" Basen asked.

"I had to keep them for the night. They're fine, and you'll see them soon. Come with me."

Basen didn't move. "What will you have me do?"

"Make a portal, of course."

"To where?"

"You mentioned you can teleport to a small forest in Kilmar. You might not have realized it, but I know the exact forest. It's called Regash—the Slugaren word for peace."

Basen put up his hand as he walked ahead of Fatholl. "How about waiting to describe what you want me to do until we're with Vithos?"

"Why would I lie to you?" Fatholl gestured that Basen

was going in the wrong direction.

Soon they were walking beside each other, neither speaking.

"Think about where you are, Basen," Fatholl continued. "You didn't come here because you believe I'll help you. You came here, wisely so, because you know I am capable of destruction. If you leave without making a portal, or if you make a portal to somewhere besides Regash Forest, you will regret it. I don't need to lie or manipulate you. Don't you see that now?"

Basen supposed Fatholl had a point. By coming here, he'd shown the Elf he wished to fulfill their agreement. Basen wouldn't leave without doing so. *Unless it's going to hurt the Academy.*

"Why Regash Forest?"

"I'm about to tell everyone in the village. Be patient, and you'll hear it with everyone else."

Fatholl was clearly leading him to the center of the settlement. Elves and Krepps were headed in the same direction, though only the Krepps appeared confused or worried, like Basen.

Nervousness buzzed in the air. An enormous crowd had gathered, thousands of Krepps outnumbering the Elves. A stage had been set up, a simple square of wood for Fatholl to stand upon and face everyone. He stepped up, then waited for Basen to follow.

He thinks I'm less likely to go against him in front of so many. He doesn't know me.

Basen found Vithos and the woman surrounded by a group of Elves with daggers on their belts.

Fatholl called for silence, and the crowd hushed.

"Change does not come easily to any creature if they are not ready for it," Fatholl began. "We miss what we no longer have when we feel it's been taken from us." He made a fist. "But I promise, Krepps, that although I am proposing a change, my Elves will never take anything from you."

These Krepps seemed better behaved than those with Rickik, stirring a bit yet without aggression. They appeared to understand common tongue at least well enough to know that something was coming that was likely to alter the course of their lives.

"It's time for you to build a legacy," Fatholl continued. "You came here to do that. You didn't want to be known as the Krepps who supported Tegry Hiller, this human's uncle." He pointed at Basen.

The Krepps hissed like snakes. God's mercy, Fatholl really had done his research. *And now he's turning them against me.*

"Tegry was a man without honor. A weak, coward of a king who lied to you Krepps in order to use you."

The Krepps groaned and gurgled, then hissed and screeched.

"There's been concern among you that we Elves plan to use you like Tegry wanted to do. I promise *never* to do that. What I propose instead is something that will benefit both our races."

Slowly, the Elves had begun to move away from the noisy creatures, but now that the Krepps had quieted, the Elves seemed comfortable again in proximity. *They're using psyche to control the Krepps' emotions. The Elves thought they might lose control, but now they have it again.* This could be trouble.

"It's time for you to build a legacy," Fatholl repeated, slower this time. "You were in Ovira long before anyone else. For more than a thousand years, there were just dajriks, Slugari, and Krepps. You were the strongest race then, and you are the strongest now. So take a moment to consider what your children will think when they are born in a village ruled by Elves."

The Krepps looked to each other, anger building in their yellow eyes. Basen found Zoke among them, standing beside a female. He remembered Zoke mentioning something about a sister and assumed this younger Krepp to be her. They were the only Krepps who looked concerned.

Vithos shook his head grimly. *He no longer believes my plan will work.* But Basen wasn't about to give up. He was just waiting for his opportunity.

Fatholl's speech had come as no surprise so far. It was obvious from the only conversation they'd had that the Elf wanted to rid himself of these Krepps.

"Your children might be confused," Fatholl went on, "and more so when they hear about how Krepps used to rule Ovira." He shook his fist. "Every animal feared the Krepps. *Dajriks* moved to the mountains. Slugari fled underground." He opened his hands. "I'm not saying the most fearsome creatures deserve the most respect. They don't. What I'm trying to show you is the progression of the Krepps based on your history. Your race has been separated over a disagreement in a human war. Except for Rickik and the Krepps that follow him, none of your kind fights for any stake in Ovira anymore.

"This wouldn't matter if Ovira was the same continent as when only dajriks, Slugari, and Krepps roamed the land. But now that humans are here, everything is quickly changing. Human greed—a concept we all know well—is more than just an explanation for their behavior. It's a threat to your legacy. They *are* greedy. They will come for all of Ovira eventually. Many of you must know they are currently engaged in another war." Fatholl raised his arms dramatically. "The dust hasn't even settled from the last one!"

"Human greed," the Krepps echoed in agreement.

The creatures couldn't possibly understand every word of Fatholl's speech, but with the help of psyche and the Elf's gestures, they seemed to understand enough.

"Rather than waiting for humans to take all of Ovira," Fatholl continued. "You need to establish your home. Claim what belonged to your ancestors as we Elves have done. Take all the land north of Tenred. Take everything up to Merejic. We Elves will remain in this territory because, unlike humans, we do not have greed for more than we need. In exchange for all the help you've given us, we will help you. Go with us to a forest in Kilmar and we will supply you with everything *you* need to build homes and farms like these. When the humans come for your land, which they will eventually, we will stand together."

They can't actually believe the Elves will fight with them?

But not only did these Krepps believe Fatholl, they seemed enthused by the idea. Basen caught a hint of a smirk on Fatholl's face as he leaned close to whisper, "Now watch."

The Krepps gathered at the center of the crowd. One spoke while all listened, but then Zoke seemed to object. The Krepp nearest to him grabbed his face and pushed him back.

"If you think I'm making a portal for the Krepps so they can fight us, you're mistaken," Basen whispered to Fatholl.

The Elf was slightly taller than Basen and moved close to look down at him. "You could try to run. Try," Fatholl dared. "That's your other choice."

"I have one other option. And you're not going to like it."

"Human!" one of the Krepps yelled.

Basen muttered a curse as the Krepps approached the platform. He pushed down his fear and stepped forward as confidently as he could. No matter what answer he gave them, he needed their respect for them to listen. He needed to be strong.

"It is you human, make us get to new home?"

"I can make a portal, yes. But—"

"He helps you to repay the debt of his uncle!" Fatholl interrupted.

Before Basen could say anything, the Krepps screeched their enthusiasm. They seemed to be celebrating as they grabbed each other and jumped about. There was no doubt in Basen's mind that psyche was influencing their behavior.

Fatholl was assuming too much to think Basen wouldn't go against this. Not a thousand Krepps—not even ten thousand—could pressure him into sparking a battle between them and humans.

Fatholl, as if knowing Basen's exact thoughts, put his hand on Basen's shoulder and whispered, "If you don't cooperate, they will find their own way to Kilmar...and beyond. You should agree to take them there quickly for your own benefit."

The Krepps still seemed to be deciding something as they conversed in an unorganized cluster.

"Zoke," Basen called. "What are they saying?"

The smaller Krepp appeared horrified, his long mouth slack as he drew quick breaths. "They are asking themselves why they don't just take back the land from the humans. It is their land, after all, they say."

Fatholl bellowed something in Kreppen that silenced them. But it only lasted a moment as the creatures broke into fevered screams.

"What did he say?" Basen asked Zoke.

"The Elves will stand with the Krepps no matter what they decide."

God's mercy. "*Make them believe it's their choice,*" Fatholl had told Basen the last time he was here. "*It's the only way to control Krepps.*"

CHAPTER THIRTEEN

Fatholl moved toward the other side of the platform and motioned for Basen to follow. Away from Zoke, Fatholl said, "Don't worry, Basen. Your humans will destroy them. It'll give those greedy Takarys something else to focus on besides the Academy."

Basen couldn't believe his ears. Fatholl was a diabolical Elf, but this...this was something far worse than Basen had imagined. It sickened him that Queen would go along with this with such devotion. *"Anything Fatholl asks, you do it,"* the little Slugari leader had said. *"Anything."*

"And after these thousands of Krepps are wiped clean from Ovira?" Basen asked. "You expect Tauwin to hunt down the rest of them?"

"He will see them as a threat. I've learned enough about the boy to know how he deals with threats."

"Krepps have done nothing but help you." Basen's voice shook as he spoke, devastation creeping up from his chest and taking hold of his throat. "And you repay them by attempting to decimate their race."

"You know nothing of what they've done to my kind!" Fatholl's face twisted with rage. "They are the scourge of the world. Their children don't deserve to be born."

This Elf...*god's mercy.* Basen had assumed Fatholl wanted the Krepps gone from the village, but now everything made sense. The armor for the Krepps—he'd intended to convince them to fight from the beginning. He just needed some way of doing that, and Basen was the perfect solution.

Or so he thinks.

"Basen," Zoke called to him. A couple of Elves had their hands on the Krepp, but he easily shrugged them off as he stepped up onto the platform. "Just make the portal and go now."

"I can't," Basen replied. "Fatholl has my akorell stone."

"Where?"

"I don't know, but it doesn't matter."

"Why not?"

"I'm going to say something that will put an end to this. Will you translate for me?"

"Gladly."

As Zoke screeched out something in Kreppen that broke through the clamor, Basen checked on Vithos at the side of the platform. He was still being held by a group of Elves, sure to be threatened in case Basen didn't obey Fatholl's demands.

This might not be the best idea, but it was Basen's only option.

"I will take you to where you want to go," Basen announced, waiting for Zoke to translate. "But first listen to what I have to say. Being the only human here, I have the unfortunate responsibility to speak for all of my kind."

As he searched for the right words, one thought kept creeping to the front of his mind. "Fatholl is right. Humans are greedy. *Some* of us will never settle for what we have and will always want more."

Fatholl was giving him a look that dared him to keep talking. Basen ignored it. *He can't stop me from saying whatever I want, and he knows it. If he interferes, it might turn the Krepps against him.*

When Zoke was done translating, with the other Krepps muttering in response as if they refused to believe what Basen had to say, he went on.

"Right now, a young human with more wealth than thousands of us combined has decided he wants control of Kyrro. He will kill anyone who stops him from getting it. Many have already died."

Basen remembered Rickik's reaction when he'd heard this news of Tauwin. The Krepp had been impressed, asking what weapon the young king had used. Basen could see the same reaction on the faces of some Krepps, taking this as a challenge to defeat the powerful human.

"This young man, Tauwin Takary, has personally slain only one human: an old, defenseless man who was loved by his people. Tauwin's army has killed all the others. This human has no strength by himself. He does not fight in the battles he's created."

At that, the Krepps began to spit. Others yelled something to Zoke as they pointed their claws at Basen.

"They want to know why a coward has an army," Zoke explained.

"Human greed," Basen replied. "His troops believe Tauwin will win this war, and they receive money for joining. The rest of us are fighting against his army because we don't want to live in a territory controlled by him or anyone like him. This war isn't about humans fighting for more land than we already have. It's about stopping an army from taking control.

"Fatholl has explained human greed to you in a way

that makes it seem like humans will eventually come for all of Ovira. What Fatholl doesn't know, however, and what I've come here to tell him, is that humans aren't the only ones fighting this war. They aren't the only ones who, if they win this war, will control Kyrro and have the power to seek more land to the north. Your land."

Basen took a breath as he waited for Zoke to catch up in translating. *God's mercy, I hope I'm right about this.*

"Fatholl's own *brother* came to this continent to join the coward king. He means to steal land from the humans for himself and the Elves with him."

Basen looked at Fatholl and pretended to be unafraid. The Krepps couldn't see his fear, and that's all that mattered at the moment. The news apparently shocked them so much their enormous mouths dropped open in disbelief.

"Brother?" they repeated in common tongue.

Fatholl put on a smile and walked to the front of the platform with his arms raised. "The human doesn't know what he's talking about."

"His name is Yeso," Basen announced. "Fatholl wanted his brother's help in Greenedge, but Yeso refused to help him. Instead, Yeso and many Elves joined with the coward Takarys." He lowered his voice to tell Fatholl, "I *know* you met Ulric Takary."

Fatholl put himself between Basen and the crowd, his teeth gritted as he whispered. "You think you can find out about my family and come here to threaten me? If you ever want to leave this place, you'll remain silent while I clean up the mess you're making. Then we will speak about my brother. *Privately.*"

The Elf put on his false smile again as he turned to the roaring Krepps. "This human doesn't know me or any of you Krepps. He's heard rumors..."

Fatholl's voice trailed off. Basen was ready to interrupt him and point out the Elves with knives surrounding Vithos. However, it seemed that Fatholl wasn't just searching for the right words. The news of his brother had begun to affect him.

The Krepps were dead silent. Despite how much Fatholl despised the creatures, he'd somehow earned their complete respect.

The Elf looked to be in pain. Fatholl shot a questioning look at Basen, his jaw clenched.

Basen shook his head. "It's not just rumors," he said only for Fatholl's ears. "I know Yeso is there."

Fatholl lowered his head and squinted, and Basen felt a wave of psyche crash through his mind. It almost took him to his knees, but he held onto his confidence to steady himself. *You must face him!* Basen screamed in his mind. *Don't run from your brother.*

He felt Fatholl rifle through any and all thoughts about him. Then Basen switched his thoughts to the Elves who'd attacked the Academy. He recalled the powerful image of them dashing toward him and his father, the Elves risking their lives to inflict pain. *They must be led by someone, and you know better than I do it's Yeso.*

Fatholl brushed his hand through the air at his Elves. "Ready the animals going with them. Basen will still make the portal. Bring the akorell stone."

"What of your brother?" Basen asked quietly.

"I will speak with him when the time comes."

"Waiting to speak to him will do nothing," Basen implored. "He's already there with his Elves, and they've begun to fight. If you let them continue, there's a good chance they'll kill us and take Kyrro. You plan to eradicate the Krepps. You believe they will fight against the humans, and the humans will retaliate and kill them all. You might be right. You might even be right about the humans eventually trying to take all of Ovira, once we're done fighting each other for Kyrro. You should know better than anyone that we will extend our civilization as far as possible and fight each other for land instead of aligning to overcome what's stopping our further expansion.

"I know that's what happened in Greenedge. But what do you think will happen when your Elves get in the way? If you're right about any of this, then Elves and humans will eventually be at war."

"Psyche—"

"Your numbers will never be enough, even with psyche. Chemists at the Academy are developing potions to resist psyche, no training needed. I'm sure other potions will be developed by the time the first battle comes. You can't rely on psyche."

"Stop. Talking." Fatholl muttered something in Elvish. "You're so full of words, you look as if you're about to burst if you don't shut your mouth." He started to turn back to face the Krepps as his animals arrived from the outskirts.

Basen grabbed his arm. "Humans remember our history. When we win this war with your help, we will see that the Elves are on our side."

"Let go of me."

"*Yeso's* Elves are cowards. They choose to take land from others instead of standing with you in Greenedge. You are a hypocrite to put so much effort into eradicating Krepps who have done nothing to you, yet you let your own race destroy life so selfishly."

"Let..."

Basen released his hold. "I'm not wrong."

"And that's the only reason you're still standing before me instead of crumpled into a ball." Fatholl sighed. "Yeso and the fools who follow him are a blight on this world. We spent many months in debate. Speaking with him *will* do nothing, and I'm not stupid enough to confront him expecting anything to change."

Fatholl leaned closer, lowering his voice even more. "Nor am I stupid enough to face an army of his Elves in which we would be outnumbered."

"Right. Which is why I have a plan."

CHAPTER FOURTEEN

Sanya had spoken to no one at the castle since her midnight encounter with Yeso. The Elf expected her to protect Ulric from assassination—to kill Tauwin's most trusted psychic. She'd spent the last day following the man around the castle, hoping to learn without a doubt whether he really was the king's chosen assassin.

She'd found out nothing. Not even his name. No one spoke to him when in his company, and no one spoke of him after he left. He seemed to have no family, no friends. It was almost like he didn't exist.

Almost like Sanya.

His only purpose was to notify Tauwin when someone told a lie, but his very presence behind Tauwin resulted in everyone telling the truth anyway. Sanya couldn't stomach the idea of murdering him, one ghost ending the life of another.

She was in no rush. Yeso had gone with the majority of Ulric's army to the Fjallejon Mountains, Ulric as well.

Ulric would be safe from assassination there. Rockbreak would guard him like a loyal dog, and if Sanya couldn't use psyche against the giant, no one could.

She needed to speak to Ulric, but he hadn't given her the opportunity. A note had been left for her with his signature.

"The cane of my great-grandfather is no longer sturdy enough to offer support. The temptation of using it has made it become a danger to anyone who sees it. I need

you to get rid of it before it hurts someone. You're the only one who knows where it belongs and the only one who knows how to put it back there. I'm trusting you with this task."

She knew he was speaking of the weapon. There was only one other person who knew of it—Yeso—and she doubted the Elf would write as delicately. She'd already seen one of his false notes and spoken to him enough times to understand he was much more blunt than Ulric.

Sanya now had to make some decisions that were sure to change her life.

She made her way to the dungeons and found that the tower of enormous rocks had been toppled. Someone had propped the weapon against the wall, its imposing black spheres beckoning Sanya toward them while she fought the urge to run away.

The last time she'd used this weapon, a portal had shot out and ripped the life clean out of Alex and Lori's bodies, but the portal had opened and closed too quickly for her to have any hope of controlling it. *There's no way I could discard the weapon into one.*

She needed an akorell stone, but there was only one she knew of, and she had no idea where Basen was now. He'd been making many portals since they'd last met, and the most recent one was far to the north.

He doesn't seem to be spending much time training at the Academy. Sanya supposed now that he was a portal mage, he would be used for more important tasks than hurling fireballs at enemies.

In his note, Ulric had mentioned nothing about stopping an assassination attempt. Either he wasn't aware of Yeso's threat or he was careful not to even hint at it in a letter that might be seen by others. A day wasn't enough time to determine whether Ulric was actually in danger from this psychic, and she figured Ulric would understand her delay.

Yeso's probably whispering in his ear that he can't trust me. But Sanya trusted Ulric. Their bond had become strong, while it appeared Yeso's bond with him was getting weaker.

She decided to remove a threat after all—a threat to herself. Yeso could be disposed of at the same time as the weapon. She carefully moved around the boulders until she came to the heavy staff. The cold bit her skin while the dense energy of the black spheres caused a terrible ringing in her ears. She shoved the weapon into a cloth bag as fast as she could.

Some relief came once she closed the bag, but she still felt the weapon draining her energy. She carefully dragged it out of the hidden room, using the bag's long leather strap to keep her distance. She fit the bag into a larger one of leather. It was the second largest bag she could acquire, the first being the final one she used to hold the other two. This one had an even longer and sturdier strap so, while dragging it, she could keep the weapon at an even greater distance from her body and ultimately her heart, which ached worse than her head.

It wasn't too long ago that she'd felt Basen open a portal somewhere in the Fjallejon Mountains. Knowing that Fjallejons had little control over bastial energy, it was probably akorell metal within the mountains that had allowed Basen to form the portal. *If there's enough there for him to make a portal, there's enough for me to make one to the spiritual world.* She would show Yeso what kind of mistake he'd made by threatening her.

Yes, she was liking this plan better the more she thought about it. But what would she do after she got rid of Yeso? Would his Elf army disband after he was gone? None of that mattered to her. The only thing that did was what Ulric would do with her when he found out.

She would have plenty of time to figure that out on the way there. She was taking the weapon to the mountains no matter what. Whether she would use it on Yeso before getting rid of it was the only question.

*****

The next morning, Sanya acquired a horse and carriage from the castle's stables. Many of the majestic animals had come with Ulric from Greenedge, yet there wasn't a use for all of them here. The stablehand thought her to be a Takary, so it was easy for her to point at something and receive it without question.

She'd gotten more used to her silver mask. It no longer caused her forehead to itch, and she'd taught herself to breathe through her mouth so she didn't have to hear the annoying windy sound of her breath coming in and out through her nose.

The stablehand asked if she knew how to drive a horse carriage. Although she didn't, she figured psyche would make the task simple. She nodded as she put the bagged weapon in the carriage and climbed upon the animal's back. As predicted, it was as easy as walking.

Once she was clear of the capital, she gladly removed her mask and hood and told the great animal to gallop faster. The wind stole her next breath as the land became a blur. She laughed with joy.

It would take less than a day to go around the Academy and into the Fjallejon Pathway, but she was tempted to ride east instead. She could just keep going and never return. Eventually she'd turn north and find out why Basen had made a portal to the other side of the continent. There had to be some kind of life for her there, but what? Only Elves had lived that far north, and they had abandoned their homes many years ago.

She had to ignore her curiosity. In the bouncing carriage behind her was death itself, now her responsibility. She had to get rid of it.

Yeso would want to speak with her in private when she arrived to make sure she'd killed Tauwin's psychic. It would then just be a matter of getting energy into the staff, aiming it at him, and...but what if he pained her and she dropped the weapon? He was too strong to resist, and she couldn't destroy the bastial energy in the air without making the weapon useless.

If she was able to rip the life from his body, no one would know how he died. *No one except Ulric.* He wouldn't want anyone to know of the weapon, which would be back in the spiritual world. *So he'd either keep me around and be forced to trust me, or he'd have me killed. I could sense it if his feelings turned hostile. But then what?*

Everything had become so complicated since Tauwin's plan to take Kyrro in a day had failed. Now Ulric taking over the Academy and eventually taking control of Kyrro from Tauwin was the only way she could get some semblance of the life she'd planned. It was still possible, more than possible, really. Yeso was the only one standing in her way.

And if I don't kill him, he'll ensure I'm executed or exiled. She couldn't blame him for being suspicious of her. She *was* dangerous. *Soon he'll see just how right his suspicions are.*

She took the eastern road around the Academy. The camp at Lake Kayvol was still abandoned. Tauwin would have everyone in his army working on the catapults if they weren't keeping the cities under control. From what Sanya had heard in the castle, news of the Academy coming through the cities and recruiting thousands had reached the ears of even the most secluded commoners on the edges of town. Apparently, rebellion was growing at a faster rate since those who'd gone to the Academy and then come back were being rewarded with extra food.

The citizens were angry that the Takarys would take their crops and their tax money and give them nothing in return. Sanya had heard Tauwin's excuse for this too many times. *"I'll give them the best version of Kyrro they've ever had once this is over. First, I'm taking back what belongs to me."*

No, first you're taking what belongs to them, Sanya had always wanted to say.

*****

Sanya made it to the Fjallejon Pathway with many hours of daylight left. She gave the horse a needed break, petting him where he seemed to enjoy the feeling the most at this moment, down his mane. She valued his strength and loyalty and told him this through psyche. He nuzzled her with his tremendous head, then rested it on her shoulder.

It had been a while since she'd crossed through this pathway from Tenred to Kyrro. Last she remembered, there was no flat path in the bowl-shaped passage between the mountains. Many loose rocks sitting on uneven ground had made the trip treacherous if it wasn't done with care, but now there seemed to be a path beaten down enough for her horse to trot through without her worrying about the animal twisting an ankle.

So much had changed in her lifetime. Two wars, multiple takeovers of the Fjallejon Mountains, two massive and ugly trenches stretching from Trentyre to the ocean, three different kings of Kyrro, and three of Tenred once the new ruler came to power.

All the use of energy had left the spiritual world misshapen as well. It was quickly forming pocks and scars like the body of a veteran soldier. But wasn't she as much to blame as anyone else? It wasn't as if she'd stood with the Academy to stop this greedy takeover. She was one of many who'd sided with Tauwin in order to get a better life when this was over. She and her mother were supposed to be happy by now. Instead, she was miserable and her mother was dead.

It was a boring trip through the passageway between the mountains. Gone were the days when Fjallejons stood in the way of travelers, demanding to know their business before letting them pass. A message would be sent to Kyrro's castle by pigeon if the traveler was coming from Tenred—an agreement set decades ago between men and Fjallejons. In exchange, men would leave the mountain to the smaller beings, who treated the land with more care. This agreement meant nothing anymore. The Fjallejons must despise humans by now.

How much longer will it take the Krepps and the Elves to feel the same way?

It was night by the time she'd made it through the snaking chasm between the mountains. From here, there were a few paths up the mountain now available to her and the horse, but she wouldn't risk guiding the large animal up in the darkness. Instead, she led her tired mount into Corin Forest.

The animal seemed to want to stay on his feet. It took a considerable amount of psyche to make him feel safe and relaxed enough to lie down, his sturdy legs folding beneath him. She curled up and closed her eyes. It took even more psyche to get herself to sleep, thanks to all the safli potions she'd taken to reach her mother in the spiritual world recently. With that journey now over, Sanya felt a sense of peace.

There was no resolution for the murders she'd committed at the Academy, nothing she could do to right her wrongs. *Except to turn myself in.* Her pulse quickened as she dreamt of entering the Academy. Would they shoot her on sight? Capture her? Certainly one of the two. Would they even let her speak before they strung her up by her neck? *If they gave me the chance, I could explain why I did what I did. I could tell them what I've done to help the Academy since then...*

It wasn't much, though.

She couldn't get the image out of her mind of going to the Academy and facing everyone she'd wronged. Is this what guilt was, wanting to face punishment?

She suddenly knew what to do. She would help Ulric become king and convince him to spare the lives of the people of the Academy. That meant she could follow through with her plan to eliminate Tauwin. She wanted to be the one to do it. She owed it to Kyrro.

Eventually morning came. After breakfast, she set out again with her horse. The trip up the mountain wasn't long. She noticed several archers looking down upon her, but none drew their arrows. Her horse made it obvious she was with Ulric, in case they missed her silver mask.

"Ulric is on the other side of the peak," one of the men informed her when she reached the top. "What's in the bag?"

She'd left the carriage at the bottom of the mountain and was dragging the weapon behind her. She felt none of its effects yet, though she knew it was only a matter of time before the piercing cold would get through the thick bags.

She looked at the archer for a while, catching her breath. He had to know she couldn't speak, so he must be expecting her to open the bag. He started toward it, but she stepped in front of him and shook her head.

One of the other men approached. "Let him go through." It seemed she was being mistaken for a man here, just like in the castle. "Do you need help carrying that?"

She shook her head again and hurried off.

It won't be easy to keep the weapon from being seen. She had to get into the mountains and find somewhere to hide it until she found the akorell metal.

After the short battle a few nights ago, Academy scouts must've seen the Elves going north to this mountain. At this point, everyone knew where their enemies were. The army at the Academy couldn't go anywhere without Ulric hearing of it. *Except Basen.* Ulric and Tauwin still knew nothing of his ability to make portals.

She wouldn't mind him making another to these mountains. It would be difficult to find akorell metal without a hint, though he would be a fool to come here now with most of Ulric's army present.

Rockbreak had to be here somewhere as well. He frightened Sanya more than Yeso, more than anyone she'd met. He was the only one who could defeat her in combat because of his ability to completely resist psyche. Even though they were on the same side, it didn't alleviate her worry.

Sanya walked for hours. She drew many glances of confused curiosity from the troops hiding in the mountains, thanks to her silver mask and the large bag she dragged behind her. Whenever someone approached, she used psyche to make them nervous to ask about it. Most walked on past her after that, pretending they weren't interested.

Eventually she found her way down into the lower levels of the mountains, where the air was dense. Here, she finally began to see the inhabitants bustling about. The small Fjallejons barely paid attention to her, though she could feel their anger whenever they looked over.

They seemed less curious than the humans. She could probably leave the weapon somewhere without any of them moving it. Even if one opened the bag, the threat of imminent death would overwhelm them and keep them from touching it. In Corin Forest, she'd felt animals approach and then scurry away. Every living creature knew to fear death, and death was exactly what she'd brought here.

CHAPTER FIFTEEN

Basen was surprised at how quickly Fatholl had agreed to his plan. Perhaps the Elf really was able to put his own interests aside to ensure a better future for Ovira.

Fatholl had just one demand.

"You first must teleport the Krepps and the Elves going with them to Regash Forest."

After much thought, Basen agreed. It was unlikely the Krepps would cause any immediate problems if he brought them to Kilmar because they would be closer to Tenred than to Kyrro, and it probably would take until the end of the war before their city, or village, or whatever it was they were building was done. By then, the Elves would be gone from Kilmar and their psyche would no longer affect the Krepps. But just in case, Basen needed to speak with Zoke before he made the portal.

"Can you convince them not to attack humans?" Basen asked.

"I will eventually, I'm sure. But I could use support from other smart Krepps. There aren't enough of us. Do any of the Krepps who went with Rickik show intelligence?"

"Only one," Basen said. "But he didn't come with Rickik." Basen then remembered how Zoke had smiled at hearing of Nebre writing about the last war. They used to practice common tongue together, Zoke had said. If Krepps could be friends, these two were.

At seeing Basen's expression, Zoke's long mouth

twisted into a crooked smile. "Who?"

"Nebre—he was in Tenred."

"Nebre," Zoke echoed as he formed a full smile. "He's at the Academy with Rickik?"

"Yes."

The smile left Zoke's face. "He does not belong with those Krepps. You must bring him through a portal to Regash Forest. He will help us."

"I will," Basen said. *Eventually.*

Zoke was right; Nebre didn't belong with Rickik or his mindless Krepps, but Basen couldn't ignore how valuable Nebre had been and would continue to be. He and Vithos were the only two who could get the Krepps' attention when it was needed.

This war needs to end swiftly. Then Nebre can help Zoke control these overzealous Krepps I'm taking to Kilmar.

"Basen!" Fatholl yelled. "They're ready. Get over here now."

"He's not a very patient Elf, is he?" Basen remarked.

"He's always busy and expects others to be just as busy," Zoke explained.

"They'll have to hurry into the portal once it's open," Basen told Zoke while walking toward the massive line of Krepps. "How many are there?"

"About two thousand. They are ready to run."

The Elves had organized the Krepps into a line of two each. It stretched out of the center of the village, around houses and trees, and out of sight.

How long will it take for all the Krepps to run into a portal?

If Basen couldn't keep it open long enough, he would have to make another portal for the rest after his akorell stone charged again. But he already needed to wait for it to charge to make a portal for himself, Fatholl, Vithos, and the others going with them into the heart of the Fjallejon Mountains. Elven mages would be charging the stone between the making of portals, but it would still take many hours if not a day.

Basen and Fatholl had agreed they needed to enter the mountains at night, when they had the best chance of figuring out which way was north before they were caught. But if Basen had to make a second portal for the rest of the Krepps, he would have to wait until the next night for the portal to the Fjallejon Mountains, and every day mattered.

He would keep it open as long as it took. Every Krepp needed to get through.

He'd prepared himself by gathering enormous clusters of energy over the last hour, holding each cluster together as long as he could. Basen didn't know how talented the Elven mages were, but they seemed to know enough to realize his method of training was dangerous, as the energy could slip from the grip of his mind and shoot out in a beam. They'd warned their kin to move away from him while he practiced, and the Krepps eventually got the same idea.

Most Krepps and Elves were busy anyway, collecting their belongings and herding all the animals to be taken with them.

The animals—they're going to be the hardest to get into the portal. But then he remembered the influence of hundreds of psychics. The animals would run in at full speed just like the Krepps and Elves.

"Ready?" he asked the Krepps.

"Ready!" they hollered back, then many began to laugh and screech. It was a terrifying sound that broke Basen's concentration, echoing down the line until every Krepp seemed to be uttering a deafening sound of intimidation as if they were preparing for battle.

He shot Fatholl a questioning look. *Are these Krepps ready to storm Kyrro?* Fatholl put up his hands and rolled his eyes as if to tell Basen the creatures were getting excited for nothing.

It was a good thing the Fjallejon Mountains, and all of Ulric's army, would be between these Krepps and the Academy. Basen shouldn't have to worry about them for now.

*****

Effie had stayed close to Steffen at the front as he led the group around the eastern side of the Fjallejon Mountains. They'd seen no one else, no signs of life, but they'd had the cover of trees until then.

They'd gone as far south as they could and now needed to head straight west to get to the Academy. Effie didn't have a good eye for distances, but Steffen said it was between ten and twenty miles and they might be able to reach it tomorrow.

The only thing in their way now was Lake Kayvol,

where an abandoned enemy camp made Effie nervous. With all their allies already at the Academy, it seemed unnecessary for Tauwin to keep them surrounded as he had before. There were already so many on the Fjallejon Mountains to the north, watching and waiting, and many more in the cities to the south. Basen hadn't seen a reason for their enemies to still be at Lake Kayvol, and Effie didn't, either. But she wouldn't be able to find relief until she passed the lake and got within the Academy's walls.

Basen's mother didn't talk much, though she always spoke politely whenever Annah pestered her with a question about their family history. As the only psychic, it was Annah's responsibility to keep the Krepps under control, but these creatures were calmer than Rickik's Krepps at the Academy. Crim was the only Krepp who spoke common tongue among them, but they did a fine job communicating requests directly with Steffen on the rare occasions they had them. The rest of the time, they kept to themselves.

During the first day of travel from the cabin, the Krepps picked up sticks to use as weapons. By night, they were fighting each other and seemed to be sharing instructions on the best way to use the sticks. Effie couldn't decide whether to tell them to be quiet so as not to alert enemy scouts or to let them practice in case they were caught and needed to fight. She spoke with Annah and Steffen, and the three of them decided to let the Krepps train.

Crim joined in as they fought each other the next night, borrowing a stick from one of them so he wouldn't have an unfair advantage with his sword. He won all of his duels, but as more joined in and they faced each other two on two, then three on three, he looked lost. The other teams of Krepps moved as if they could read each other's thoughts, striking at the same time when they weren't defending each others' backs.

If this wasn't impressive enough, the sticks chosen by both male and female Krepps were thick and longer than a sword. Effie couldn't imagine any human swinging one fast enough to actually strike an opponent. The creatures must've trained hard during their imprisonment. Effie looked closer at their arms during these breaks to see well-defined muscles. Although these Krepps weren't as large and imposing as the ones that had come with Rickik, they seemed just as capable.

She supposed these Krepps had given up on retrieving their dead from Tenred, as they simply looked glad to be free again. Crim said he'd explained the war to them, but Effie wondered how much of it he really understood himself.

When their group was close enough to the abandoned camp around the lake, Steffen took the spyglass with him on a short trek up part of the tail of the Fjallejon Mountains. When he came back down, he had a grim look on his face.

"There are men there," he said, ushering everyone toward the mountains for cover. "Let's not be seen."

Annah told Crim, and all the Krepps moved north with them. They didn't show the same worry that Effie felt, grinning instead as if excited by the news. They began to chatter, their excitement growing as they made fists, their long mouths twisting upward even more.

"How many did you see?" Effie asked Steffen.

"About a hundred. Not many."

"Not many?" Effie repeated.

"One hundred is a low number. They must be there only to serve as eyes for Tauwin and Ulric."

"One hundred, small amount," Crim said. "We kill all."

"No," Effie said. She knew Crim hated the word, as he made the same scowl every time he heard it, but she'd learned early that she had to be forceful with him or he wouldn't listen. "We're going around."

Basen's mother approached, her concerned look never changing. "What's happening?" She was always the last to know anything and seemed to be getting sick of it, her voice carrying more irritation each time she had to ask.

"There's a small army at the lake," Effie explained. "We're going to find a way around."

"Eff," Steffen said, "there is no way around without being seen."

Effie felt her blood go hot at what he was suggesting. No, he had to be wrong.

"We'll sneak past them during the night, then," Effie insisted. *We're not fighting. Bastial hell, we only have one mage, one psychic, and a bunch of Krepps with sticks.*

"No!" Crim protested. "Sneak during night is coward do. Battle. Glory!" He thumped his chest. "Honor."

"Honor!" repeated all the other Krepps, shaking sticks that had begun to look a lot smaller to Effie.

"We have to fight," Steffen said to Effie's surprise. "They have archers. If they catch us trying to sneak past during the night, we'll have no cover, but I doubt there are many in that camp who are as skilled as our group in close combat. One hundred isn't enough to stand up to the Academy, which means they're only there to deter us from getting to the lake for water. They probably have some way of calling for support: a flaming arrow, a carrier pigeon...their allies are close. But they won't be watching the east. No one is. We might be able to surprise them."

"We use..." Crim pointed to the side of the mountain, to where rocky slopes rolled out. "Hills."

Effie looked to Annah. Effie didn't know her well, but it was clear the psychic was easily frightened. With her large blue eyes and her small body, she sometimes looked like a startled child. Effie expected her to say something against this ridiculous plan, as she now wore the same terrified expression Effie was used to, but she didn't utter a word.

Effie gave herself a moment to consider other options. If they went far to the south, around the lake, they wouldn't be seen. They could make a wide arc around it, but that would put them close to Oakshen, which might be even more of a risk.

Bastial hell, Steffen's idea might be the best, after all. The enemy camp *was* on the western side of the lake, and there were many trees along the northern side. By using the mountain slopes for cover, they should be able to make it to the eastern side of the lake, then through the trees without being seen.

Effie sighed deeply. "Let's go. We might be able to make it by night."

"*Rrrah*," Crim hissed through his teeth with a smile.

He went to tell his Krepps the news.

"Who will be taking me?" Juliana asked with a strange lack of fear.

"Take you?" Annah asked.

"Who will be taking me around to the Academy, to avoid the battle?" Juliana specified, looking at them expectantly.

As her meaning sank in, they looked at each other in expectation. When their gazes settled on Steffen, he pursed his lips and grimaced. He turned to Juliana and took a breath before delivering the bad news.

"We can't take you around the lake because it'll be more dangerous. So you'll stay to the back and avoid the battle."

She looked as if Steffen had told her she would lead the charge.

"What if..." Juliana stopped and said no more.

Effie knew what she wanted to ask. "If the battle doesn't go in our favor, run. You'll have to find your way to the Academy later."

"Can't we signal for help?" Juliana asked.

"No. It would draw the attention of our enemies, and concealment is the only thing that could get us to the Academy."

"That young man and woman," Juliana said, "from the cabin. You spoke to them as if they were great assets in this war. We can go back for them."

Effie had secretly hoped Neeko and Shara had changed their minds and would show up one morning. It seemed she wasn't the only one with this thought, as they had taken their time during the journey in the first few days, many looking back over their shoulders.

"We can't go back for them," Effie explained. "We don't have enough food, and it's not likely for them to change their minds just because an enemy camp is in the way."

Juliana surprised Effie with a brave face. "Then I will do what I must." She looked around, then picked up a rock just smaller than her palm. She tested its weight, then clenched her teeth and swung.

"You don't have to fight," Steffen assured her.

Juliana put her other hand on top of the rock to keep it from him. "I won't stand idle and watch all of you fight for me. You agreed to help Basen by bringing me back to the Academy. If there's no safe route around the lake, it's my obligation to join you."

The Krepps started moving. They were quick and organized, staying close without getting in each other's way.

"Let's go," Steffen said, and they all hurried to catch up.

*****

Effie felt a surprising lack of fear as they moved through the sparse trees on the northern side of the lake. If they all died in battle here, it would devastate Basen. He'd formed this plan in secret and had gone against direct orders from his instructor to put it into action. If his mother and his friends were killed, he would never get over the guilt. Effie couldn't let him suffer such a fate. She was the one who'd practically demanded they go back for Neeko and Shara. This predicament was as much her fault as his, but he would blame himself.

She stayed behind Annah as the psychic skulked from tree to tree. She lingered behind cover just a moment longer than everyone else, then sprinted to catch up.

"Come on, Annah," Steffen hissed from the front of their cluster. "We need you here."

Effie could hear Annah swallow as she froze. "Coming," she said, her voice cracking.

"The camp's just ahead," Steffen whispered. "No more noise after this. Crim, tell your Krepps."

"Shut up. They know."

They'd gone over the plan on the way here. Effie's task was easy. She'd stay to the back with Juliana, as light wouldn't be necessary and fireballs would do the opposite of what they hoped to accomplish.

Steffen pointed two fingers and all the Krepps followed Crim out. Trees continued to provide cover as they came closer to the water. It was a dark night, thankfully. Fires closer to the center of camp put everything in shadow.

As Effie followed behind, she noticed there seemed to be no order to the tents except they weren't close to the moonlit water. Soft grass crunched beneath their feet, but they'd planned for this and would use it to their advantage.

The trees grew along the northern edge of the lake, a few standing in the midst of the camp. There were a few rows of the thick trunks left before the first tents, and that's where the Krepps took their spots.

At risk of being seen, Effie could watch no further as she hid behind a tree. She shut her eyes to concentrate on sounds. The Krepps stomped in place, then stopped.

Dead silence.

"Did you hear something?" an enemy asked.

"Some animal," another replied.

"Didn't sound like any animal."

"It's an ambush," said someone else. "They've snuck all the way around the lake without being seen. Shall I fetch your sword, *my lord*?"

One of them chuckled.

"My weapon stays with me at all times, as should yours," the first man replied.

"When you make officer, you can tell me where I should stick my sword. But for now, that choice belongs to your mother."

Another laugh.

Crim moved his feet to rustle the grass. A few other Krepps joined in.

There was no way all of them could stay hidden as soon as anyone approached and put light upon them, but they needed one or two of the enemies to come. They needed more swords.

"You must've heard that," the first man said.

"I did," said the second. "Whatever it is, let's eat it."

Effie heard the sound of metal as if the men had retrieved their swords. Footsteps approached. A beam of light came out.

"Stop," the second man said. "Don't scare it off."

The light went out.

They came closer, and closer still. Effie risked a look in the darkness.

The Krepps at the front pounced from behind the trees. Steffen joined them, though a bit late, as Annah raised her hands at the three men.

Crim killed one with his sword while Annah took the other two down with psyche. The Krepps used their palms to stifle the men's screams. Steffen impaled one with his sword as the Krepps stabbed the other with their jagged sticks. He fought until Crim hurried over and finished him off.

The enemy swords were quickly snatched up. One Krepp knelt for the fallen wand, then tossed it away in frustration. He found a knife on the dead mage's belt and licked his teeth as he took it.

"What was that?" someone else asked near one of the distant fires. Shadows came out from behind tents.

An enemy mage cast his light upon them.

"Krepps!" they screamed.

The creatures screeched right back as they darted toward the enemies scampering for their weapons.

"Charge them!" Steffen yelled from behind the Krepps, Annah sprinting after him.

Juliana ran past Effie as she stood still to focus on gathering energy. Effie shot her fireball well over the heads of her allies. It struck a distant tent, sending out a flaming and screaming enemy.

She hurried to catch up as the Krepps' superior speed had already brought them in contact with their enemies. The few men who'd had their swords handy were backing away as they waited for their comrades to join them. But they couldn't get away fast enough, the Krepps knocking them down with powerful swings of their heavy sticks. Other Krepps ripped the swords right out of the enemies' hands.

Effie gathered energy for her next fireball as more men poured from their tents. She shot at a cluster of silhouettes. Her fireball arced down onto a man just bringing a trumpet to his lips. The start of his blare was interrupted as he was blasted away.

Enemies late to the battle came in behind the Krepps. One already had his sword up, about to plunge it through Crim's spine as the Krepp engaged two swordsmen at once.

"Behind you, Crim!" Effie shouted, unable to gather energy quickly enough.

He didn't seem to hear, though Steffen did and dashed toward him. He was too far and wouldn't make it in time.

Annah! Where had she gone? Then Effie found her, in the heart of the battle, too far from Crim to help.

Juliana intercepted the enemy at full speed, smashing the rock against the side of his head. His feet came out from under him, then he lay still on the ground.

Juliana froze as she stared down at him. Effie had caught up by then and grabbed the soldier's sword. She put it into Juliana's hands. Basen's mother looked down at it, seeming to remember where she was. She gripped it tightly. Two enemies came straight for them, but Steffen jumped in front.

He hopped to the side to dodge their attacks. Effie shot one as Steffen sliced the other man's leg. Juliana screamed as she came toward the fallen enemies with the sword overhead. She brought it down hard into one man's chest as Steffen finished the other.

Juliana fell backward as she tried to pull her sword free. Effie helped her up, then wrenched the bloody sword out of the man's body. Juliana looked exhausted as she took it, groaning just to lift the blade upright. *The woman has no stamina after rotting in prison and then walking for days.*

"I'll keep you safe," Effie said.

Steffen was already back with the Krepps. Annah had turned her focus toward the enemies coming behind them, and in a short time there were none left but those in front.

Effie saw her first Krepp fall as they finally were outnumbered. The female Krepp took a blade to her side. She yelled something to another Krepp, who turned and lopped off the enemy's head. Effie lost the female Krepp in the crowd, only to find her later, dead.

Others began to fall. Their progression stopped completely as a horde of enemies surrounded them. Effie shot from the rear, but soon there were no more enemies for her to hit without risking burning her allies. She could only stand in the back with Juliana and watch death approach as the Krepps were cut down.

These enemy swordsmen weren't as skilled as the warriors from the Academy, but there were just so damn many. They'd shown confusion and a great lack of coordination at first, but now they'd been organized by an officer screaming orders from the back of their horde.

Effie tried to move around to the side to get a shot at

him. Juliana followed. Effie saw only swordsmen and mages, which meant she didn't have to worry about getting hit with an arrow as she had in the past. It gave her the confidence she needed to separate far from her group as she came farther around.

More swordsmen coming out of tents stopped her and sent a stab of fear into her heart.

"Hide," she told Juliana as she tried to get the older woman behind an empty tent. It was too late. They'd been seen.

Three swordsmen charged. Effie aimed her wand. They put up their arms for protection as she let loose the blinding fireball, which struck the grass just in front of them and knocked them on their backs. She grabbed Juliana's hand and pulled her toward their army, their only chance of survival. The three swordsmen were up and chasing them before Effie had gotten a good lead, and Juliana was slowing her too much.

Bastial hell, even if they did make it back in time, all of her allies were too overwhelmed to help.

"We have to fight," Effie said as she came to a stop. She aimed her wand and readied more energy, Juliana taking a lackluster fighter's stance to her side.

Their enemies were just shadows this far from the campfires. They separated from each other as Effie fired, her fireball striking only one. The explosion forced her eyes shut for a breath. Now with splotches of white clouding her vision, she searched for the two left.

Three shadows again—did she miss one of them after all? But they appeared to be fighting each other. Something flew through the air, an arrow perhaps. It cut through one shadow. Another zipped toward the other shadow, impaling him. Both arrows returned to the third shadow, as if drawn by powerful magnets.

The silhouette of a man came toward Effie. She raised her wand, straining for breath and focusing to gather the necessary energy.

His familiar voice stopped her. "Effie, it's me."

CHAPTER SIXTEEN

Basen wasn't allowed to leave the Elven woman's house. He didn't know where she was spending her day, but it wasn't here. He and Vithos had been escorted back after making a portal for all the Krepps, farm animals, and Elves to Regash Forest. He'd kept the portal open longer than he ever had before, and he eventually would allow himself to be proud that his training had paid off, but he was too worried at the moment to feel much else.

He'd freed his mother from prison, but now it seemed as if he'd become a captive himself. Fatholl seemed to be someone who needed complete control, like Tauwin, because he'd taken Basen's akorell stone once again to have it charged by his Elven mages. Basen had warned it would take a tremendous amount of energy to have it ready by tonight and that he would be of better use than three of their mages combined, but Fatholl still refused to let Basen anywhere near the stone.

Since their meeting, the only time they'd agreed on anything was over Basen's plan involving Yeso. *Quite amusing considering my plan seemed absurd to me the first time I came up with it.* But Fatholl had taken to it immediately, like an animal stalking a kill. *That's what it will seem like to Yeso, but it's the opposite. We are the hunter luring the prey.*

Basen had been right to assume that Fatholl and Yeso had become enemies. It only seemed natural given their history. Basen could see it in Fatholl's eyes when he mentioned his brother's name. Yeso was a threat to him and his ideals, so Yeso must feel the same about Fatholl.

He and Vithos mostly slept as they waited for night. There was but one bed, though it was big enough for two. Basen awoke several times to Vithos' forearms pressed against his back, the sleeping Elf curled up against him as if seeking warmth. Vithos slept quite soundly, so Basen was able to turn him around to face the other way without waking him.

Basen became confused when he awoke later to find Vithos positioned as before.

He grew up with Krepps and has only recently felt the comfort of a gentler race, Basen reminded himself. *He has many years of being unloved to make up.*

Basen felt the same about his mother, even though it had been less than a year since his exile. It was as if he needed the rest of her life to make up for the time they'd lost. *And the terrible thoughts I had about her choosing Tegry over us.*

She should reach the Academy by today or tomorrow. The thought brought him enough comfort to fall back asleep with Vithos pressed against him until someone entering the house roused Basen.

"Wake up, Vithos," he said, shaking the Elf. Given the chance, Fatholl could kill Basen and keep his akorell stone, and no one would have a chance to retaliate. Terren would never go to war with the Elves over the death of one man, not that Basen would want him to.

"I hope you slept well," Fatholl said as he came into the bedroom, "because you'll need all your strength for this."

*****

Sanya had decided she would end Yeso's life with the weapon, then throw it into a portal to the spiritual world. Getting Yeso near the akorell metal would be easy. He would want to speak privately to find out whether she'd killed Tauwin's psychic. She just needed to find the akorell metal within the mountains then get Yeso close enough to it.

She still hadn't figured out how Ulric would respond, but she expected he'd understand after she explained Yeso's threat. *He tried to force me to run or get myself caught.*

No one was going to force Sanya to do anything now that her father was dead. Ulric might lose the loyalty of the Elves with their leader gone, but Ulric didn't need them to win this war. He would forgive her.

Part of her wanted to kill Yeso in order to give the Academy the chance it deserved, but she had to be honest with herself. She wanted him dead for selfish reasons.

It had been two days since she'd arrived at the Fjallejon Mountains, and night was approaching. The tunnels inside the mountain, some vast and others annoyingly small, would no longer be lit by sconces when it was time for the Fjallejons to sleep. She didn't want to spend another day here. She had to find the akorell metal soon.

She'd stored the bags containing the weapon near where she'd been sleeping. An alcove there seemed as good as any other place, located toward the middle of the mountain. It made it easier to return after she'd been off searching. Ulric wouldn't approve of her leaving the weapon anywhere out of her sight, but she couldn't bear keeping it close to her.

The inside of the Fjallejon Mountains had very little to distinguish one part from the next. Ulric's men and Yeso's Elves kept to the upper sections, where man-sized chairs, tables, and beds had been assembled. With little to do as they waited for the siege weapons to be built to take the Academy, much of the army had been hard at work transforming the mountains into a more suitable place for them to live.

It seemed as if at least some of them planned to stay here. Sanya didn't need psyche to tell that the Fjallejons disliked the humans coming into their home, but what could they do about it? The small beings had proven time and again that they'd choose suffering over aggression if it meant avoiding conflict.

Sanya spent the rest of that day searching for the akorell metal. If she didn't find it by the end of the next day, she might need to alter her plans. Ulric and Yeso would return to the castle soon enough to seize it from Tauwin.

Where was that damn akorell metal! Sanya started back to her little alcove after another long day of searching.

She suddenly felt a portal opening not far away. Basen

had returned to the mountains. The idiot—thousands of enemies were here! She grabbed her weapon of death and ran down the dark hallways.

*****

Basen worried he'd forgotten the location of the akorell metal in the Fjallejon Mountains, but it turned out he couldn't forget this place. It was as if the battle here against Abith and his countless men was just yesterday. Pillars of warped stone were blackened or cracked. One had crumbled after Basen blasted it twice with fireballs, and the rubble remained.

As he'd predicted, no one was here. All should be sleeping now.

A few of the Elves who'd come with him had wands, like Basen, though he'd convinced Fatholl to give him a sword as well. They would be fighting together, after all, *before possibly fighting each other.* There had been no reluctance as Fatholl had ordered an Elf to fetch a sword of fine steel for Basen. But he wasn't foolish enough to take that as a sign of peace to come.

Basen had pocketed the akorell bracelet after being the last one through the portal. The disorienting travel had hit him as hard, if not harder, then the other times he'd gone through. It might have to do with the great distance he'd just covered, from Merejic to Kyrro, or perhaps the many portals were starting to take a toll on his body.

The lead Elf was a woman whose beauty was almost a distraction, especially considering the cut of her shirt showed most of her bosom. It didn't make sense to Basen until he realized she would be the one taking the role of questioner in his plan. *Psyche and beauty,* it was bound to work so long as the first troops they encountered had any interest in women.

As Basen had expected, the caverns within the mountain were black as pitch. But most of the Elves had come with lamps, their swords in their sheaths for the moment. First they needed to figure out how to get out of here, as even Basen didn't know, then they could fight.

He stayed close enough to the front to give directions to the Elven woman but far enough so that when they encountered someone, he could hide in the shadows along with the rest of their small army. He had her lead them back the way he'd come with Jackrie, or at least he tried. It didn't take long for him to feel lost, as the tunnels and caverns looked the same.

Vithos stayed toward the back, and the separation made Basen nervous. But there was a small chance someone might recognize the Elf who'd grown up with the Krepps and realize this group wasn't with Yeso. They already were taking a huge risk with this plan, so they couldn't afford more.

So much relied on the Elves who'd gone with the Krepps through the first portal. Fatholl didn't seem worried about them, though, which allowed Basen to relax a little.

Fatholl barely spoke, his hard features never changing. Basen expected nothing less severe, as Fatholl had the face of an Elf ready to kill his own brother.

The Elves soon sensed the presence of life above them as well as below.

"We need to go up," Basen said. He remembered encountering only enemies on the way down here, not Fjallejons. *And those disgusting rodents.*

After following the inclining tunnels, they finally began to sense people ahead of them. The woman at the front said something in her language and everyone stopped.

"What?" Basen asked.

"Someone is coming toward us," Fatholl explained. He put out his hand. "They're going the other way now. It might be a psychic who detected us." He transitioned into Elvish to converse with the others.

Soon they plodded on. Basen still hadn't gotten used to being here. Moments ago, he'd been in Merejic. A few days before that, he'd been in Tenred, and before that he'd been at the Academy. A surge of dizziness struck him as each location spun around in his mind. It was as if he was in all three places at once. He reached out to steady himself and grabbed Fatholl's shoulder, but it wasn't enough to keep him on his feet.

As he fell to his knees, Fatholl grabbed his arms to hold him up. "What's the matter with you? Stand up!"

Basen focused on the Fjallejon Mountains, knowing he was there now. However, all he could see was the sand of the Group One training grounds, the shelves of the castle's kitchen, and the grass of the Elven village, all swirling together fast enough to make him sick if it didn't stop.

Fatholl squeezed his arm hard. "Focus!"

The dancing shadows from everyone's moving lamps took over. Basen managed to stand.

"You will be left behind if you can't keep up," Fatholl warned.

There was no doubt in Basen's mind that Fatholl was being completely honest. The plan would go on whether or not Basen could make it. Still reeling from the spell, he held his stomach and pushed onward.

Slowly, his mind began to clear. Whatever connection he'd made to these places, it felt as if they were part of him now, more than just a memory.

Eventually their group happened upon a large cavern where many men slept in makeshift beds. Basen stayed back with the others while the beautiful woman approached the closest one.

"Excuse me," she said. "Can you help me?"

"What's wrong—oh."

Basen could almost feel the moment when the man noticed her beauty. No doubt psyche was involved as well. It was probably keeping the others asleep, as her voice did seem loud enough to wake them.

"I'm sorry to bother you, but I'm looking for Yeso." She had just a trace of an accent.

"He and your Elves are that way. Stay to the right. They aren't far. How did you get lost?"

"I just arrived with some others, but we've already confused our route. I don't want to show up in front of Yeso without knowing where I am. How do I get to the top of the mountains?"

"The top? Yeso isn't there."

"I can ask someone else if I'm bothering you."

"No, it's fine. Stay to the left instead and you'll reach the top. All other routes have been blocked to make it easier."

"Thank you."

When he didn't respond, Basen figured she'd put the man back asleep with psyche. Soon the rest of them were trailing behind the woman as she crept through the cavern. There were far more enemies sleeping here than Basen first realized, at least fifty.

The cavern stretched on for a while, one main route going up the center like a spine. These men had laid down a rug, muffling Basen's footsteps. Psyche kept all of them asleep as he carefully walked through.

Basen thought he caught a glimpse of light from the exit tunnel ahead of them, but it was gone before he could be sure. *The psychic from earlier,* he thought. Was their surprise already taken from them? No, a psychic would've woken these men if he or she wanted Basen and the Elves to be caught. So who else could it be?

They made their way through the long sleeping quarters and soon came to another tunnel. The mountain finally appeared different. Sconces on the wall and lighter air made Basen feel less like he was suffocating as he came closer to the kind of civilization he recognized. The tunnel became wider, allowing up to four people to walk side by side. Vithos suddenly appeared, surprising Basen.

"Shouldn't you be in the back?" he asked.

"Yeso's Elves will recognize anyone the same as they recognize me. But I am not the same. My psyche is strongest. I fight well, and they are close now. Be ready."

Basen drew his sword with his left hand, keeping his wand in his right. The tunnel split, and they kept to the right as instructed. He could already see within the cavern where Yeso's Elves were sleeping.

Suddenly, Basen's reflexes told him to run from something tremendously powerful coming toward him from his left. He jumped back and noticed Fatholl's Elves around him jumping as well as the same sense of danger overwhelmed them. But the only thing there was the stone wall that separated the two tunnels.

"Psychic," some of the Elves muttered.

Someone was on to them, perhaps now trying to warn them or scare them off? No, it didn't feel like psyche putting the fear of death in Basen. There was something far more real on the other side of the wall.

They had to ignore it, as Yeso's Elves ahead were beginning to stir.

"They're waking," Basen hissed back down the tunnel.

Fatholl pushed his Elves out of the way to get to the front. "Yeso!" he called.

What in god's world was he doing? Basen and the few other mages could've launched fireballs into the sleeping quarters, but now all were quickly rising and lighting lamps.

"Fatholl?" a distant voice questioned. A string of Elvish followed that roused the waking Elves quicker, all of them grabbing weapons.

Fatholl replied in their language. He sounded reluctant, not aggressive. Fatholl should've ignored the urge to speak to his brother before attacking. He was going to get all of them killed.

Now with the cavern as bright as day, Yeso hesitantly came forward wearing a look of confusion and worry. He said something softly in Elvish, as if to himself. Then he repeated it louder as he stood straighter. A third time he repeated it, opening his palms and scowling as if accusing Fatholl of something.

Fatholl's reluctance dissolved as he pointed a finger in what appeared to be fury. But Yeso began to yell before his brother could say anything.

Suddenly they were screaming at each other. Ulric's name was the only word Basen recognized. It was strange to hear Elvish at such a loud volume. Their words, usually light as a feather riding the wind, were now more like a flag thrashing from an approaching hurricane.

"What are they saying?" Basen asked Vithos. The Elf had told him he knew some Elvish but not enough to be fluent.

"Bad words for stupid, traitor, for destroyer of life. Yeso blames Fatholl for abandoning the Elves. Fatholl blames Yeso for greed."

It was quite clear there would be no agreement between these two anytime soon. With Yeso's much larger and better equipped army looking more and more hostile, Basen had only one choice of what to do.

CHAPTER SEVENTEEN

Neither brother looked ready to dishonor the other with a surprise attack, so Basen had to be the one to do it. Part of Penny's instruction had involved gathering energy quickly, and he made use of this practice by readying his fireball in the span of a breath. He could kill Yeso right here and avoid relying so much on chance for their plan to work.

Fatholl would be livid, as he'd insisted he be the one to kill his brother. But Fatholl had opened his mouth to start an argument rather than attack with psyche as he'd said he would.

Basen pulled out a fine stream of sartious dust from his wand, moving it into the burning ball of energy. It caught fire as he directed it at Yeso.

The Elf dropped flat on the ground, the fireball exploding amid the Elves behind him. Basen cursed.

Fatholl tried to grab Basen, but he was ready for Fatholl to throw him to the wolves and spun away. *Damn Fatholl.* He'd ruined everything.

Screams rang out on both sides, half of all the Elves dropping like Yeso. Now back a few rows and untouched by psyche, Basen took a moment to launch another fireball. It exploded into a heap of charging Elves. He hoped they were part of the group who'd broken the Academy's wall a few days ago.

Basen backed away, expecting the rest of his temporary allies to follow. But most were down and seemed unable to get up. He raised his wand for another fireball when he caught sight of Yeso raising his arm. An intense pain akin to being struck by lightning made Basen curl up before he hit the ground. It tore through him with more force, and screaming did nothing to help.

Someone grabbed him by his shirt collar. He could do nothing to focus, nothing to resist the spell or even move.

But whoever had him by his collar dragged him away from the fray. He regained some strength in his legs the farther he went from the psyche spell. Soon it stopped completely, though it had taken a lot out of him as he struggled to stand.

"We run now," Vithos said, still holding onto Basen.

He found his footing and hurried toward what now would be the front of their army. He couldn't take another spell like that, and frankly he cared just as little about Fatholl's Elves as they did about him.

Damn, Fatholl has to live, Basen grudgingly reminded himself. He went back to find the Elf on his knees, his outstretched hand aimed at nearly a mirror image of himself. Both he and Yeso groaned in pain as Elves crawled around them to get to each other. No one could get up or even get their hands around a bow or wand. Fresh to the scene, Basen hadn't yet been targeted and hurried to gather more energy.

He almost lost his grip on his wand as another terrible spell of pain took him down and sapped his strength.

"We have to get out of here!" he yelled through the agony. "More will come!"

But his words had no effect as everyone seemed to be disabling each other with psyche. It was a testament to the power of Fatholl's Elves, as he had only about a fourth as many as Yeso.

Suddenly the spells stopped and everyone's screams ceased. A scent came to the air, bitter and tart. Basen recognized it immediately.

Sanya.

She must be the psychic they'd sensed earlier. Now she'd broken the bastial energy in the air as she had when she'd killed Nick...and then again when she'd killed Alex. Who did she plan to kill now?

Basen raced down the short tunnel, hearing both armies of Elves behind him as he quickly made it to the front. He took a sharp turn and expected to see Sanya in front of him, but the tunnel was too dark.

Fatholl's Elves were close behind, with Yeso's behind them. Had Sanya done this to save Basen and his group from certain death? It seemed likely, as she'd done nothing earlier to alert Yeso's Elves about the ambush.

Soon the odor was gone and Basen could feel his grasp on bastial energy returning. Screams of agony rang out behind him, but he didn't slow. Fatholl's Elves had known they might not make it out of these mountains.

Vithos was quicker than most and soon caught up to Basen.

"Do you sense anyone ahead of us?" Basen asked.

"We go too fast," Vithos replied.

There was only one route to follow. Planks of wood barred the entrances to every other tunnel. It wasn't long before Basen caught sight of someone running ahead of him. The figure was cloaked in loose robes of black and dragging an enormous satchel. Basen noticed a mask when the person glanced back.

Sanya? Whatever she'd gotten herself into here, Basen didn't care to know. The only thing that did matter was how whatever she had planned would affect his group.

Effie had told Basen about her encounter with Sanya and a woman claiming to be Sanya's mother. There was no chance Sanya could still be angry with Basen for opening portals if she'd brought her mother back from the dead. But Cleve and Reela had heard from Sanya that her mother and Alex were now at peace after some horrendous event in the dungeons of Kyrro's castle. None of it made much sense to Basen, and he hadn't had time to consider any of it, but now, with Sanya leading the way, he regretted not finding out more about it.

Basen gained on her but separated from Vithos and the other Elves in the process. The tunnels through the mountain were mostly straight, giving a strong runner like him the advantage. The ground began to incline soon enough. It wouldn't be long before they reached the top.

Ahead of him, the cloaked figure made a turn. Basen came to the same turn but stopped when he noticed a plank of wood nailed across the entrance to this tunnel. It wasn't the way to the top. Sanya didn't want to be caught, or she had something else in mind.

Basen chose the other route instead. But as he came through the short tunnel and into a vast cavern filled with sleeping men, he realized Sanya wasn't just trying to avoid him; she wanted to avoid everyone.

The men awoke and began to shout to each other that something was happening.

"What is it?" someone asked Basen. "An attack?

"The Academy is trying to pass through the pathway," he announced. "Get to the top!"

Hundreds rushed to grab their swords and bows.

"Hurry," Basen said, knowing Fatholl's Elves wouldn't be far behind.

Bustling and screaming at each other to move, they exited the cavern quickly. Basen stayed at the back of their ranks. He looked over his shoulder to find Vithos and the Fatholl's Elves coming in. He waved for them to follow.

The mountain peak turned out to be close, and soon Basen was relieved to feel the fresh air on his damp forehead. He didn't know where Sanya had gone. Why had she helped them escape? Effie had mentioned something about Sanya telling Reela she would assist the Academy, but both Basen and Effie believed Sanya was just saying whatever she could to keep herself alive.

Fortunately, the peak of the southern end of the mountain was not like the northern side. Countless pillars of rock coming up from the ground provided cover for Basen to slink away without being noticed. As Vithos and Fatholl's Elves reached the top, Basen called out to them.

Eventually all of them were running north while their human enemies went south, soon hidden behind the tall spikes of the mountaintop. But where were Yeso's Elves? Basen continued to jog as he turned back to watch the opening in the ground.

"Where are they?" he asked Vithos.

"I heard them fighting. Not far."

Yeso was the first to emerge, his face twisted by aggression. He started after Fatholl's Elves but then checked behind him. Yeso could've shouted for human reinforcements, but he didn't. Whatever the reason, Basen was thankful.

Fatholl had brought the Elves with the greatest stamina for this task, but already most of them had begun to slow more than Basen would've liked. It would be daylight before they got down the slope on the other side. Basen stayed a good distance ahead of everyone.

Before long, he reached the flat plains of the northern side. The first light of the sun came up over the eastern ridge, painting the clouds red. The Elvish shouting behind him was almost like the caws of morning birds.

Basen had a swig from the water skin he'd brought, then checked over his shoulder yet again. Yeso's Elves didn't appear to be as fit as Fatholl's, struggling to keep up. Their determination was admirable, though it would soon prove to be foolish.

There were many more entrances down into the mountains, but Basen worried less and less about an army coming out of one to stop him the closer they got to the northern edge.

"Basen." Sanya, with her mask removed, peered out from behind a jutting pillar. "Don't tell anyone I'm here. There's something you need to know."

He stopped and realized there was nowhere he could run to find cover, while she had plenty of protection in case they exchanged fireballs. He wasn't sure she could even cast one, though she certainly could kill him with psyche.

"What?"

"I noticed your Elves are lacking bows and arrows."

We knew we'd be running a long distance. "And?"

"What do you plan to do here?"

He looked behind him. He was far ahead, but he didn't like standing idle.

"Helping our side in this war."

She stomped her foot, showing the same anger he'd seen countless times in Tenred castle.

"Don't be vague! I'm trying to help you."

"Why?"

She looked even more perturbed as she gritted her teeth. "Just tell me! You don't have much time."

"Yeso is going to die." He wasn't sure why he was confiding in Sanya of all people, but he knew to trust his gut. "Still going to help us?"

"Yes," she said. "First by telling you that some of Ulric's troops now know about your escape and will try to block your way down the slope. You won't be able to beat one of them. The largest one—he'll stand out. Don't try to fight your way past him. Just run around him because he doesn't like to."

"Doesn't like to what?"

"Run!" She shook her fist and disappeared behind the pillar.

Basen didn't know why, but he believed her.

As Sanya had warned, enemy troops began to pour out of an opening ahead of him. Among them was a giant of a man. With a torso as thick and strong as the trunk of a tree, he would've made Cleve look like a small boy if the two stood next to each other. He wielded a massive battle axe of orange and red bastial steel that looked too heavy for most men to lift with two hands, though he gripped it with one. In his other was a tall shield of the same precious metal, no doubt strong enough to block a fireball.

He let out a roar like a beast, then put on a sick grin. "Battle!" he yelled to the morning sky above, as if making an announcement to grab the attention of the heavens.

CHAPTER EIGHTEEN

"Who you speak to?" Vithos asked as he came up to Basen, huffing for breath.

"Sanya. She told us we can't beat him." Basen pointed toward the group of men forming ranks.

"Them?" Vithos asked.

"No, just him," Basen specified as he kept his finger aimed at the giant. There were about twenty others that looked like Fjallejons next to him. They didn't share his fervor for battle, holding up their weapons with nervous, inexperienced hands, none wielding a bow.

Making matters worse, Yeso's small army of Elves was closing in from behind with Fatholl and the others. There would be no time for this glorious "battle" that the giant had announced to the heavens.

There was only one option, and it was the opposite of what Sanya had said. They would have to fight through the giant, and quickly.

The moment Basen drew his wand, they began to charge. "Don't waste psyche on the big one," Basen advised Vithos as they took their places shoulder to shoulder. "It won't work."

"How you know?"

"I'm trusting Sanya." Basen launched his first fireball, happy to see that his aim was true. It plummeted quickly upon his enemies, all of them scattering except for one. The giant actually moved toward it, catching it with his enormous shield. The force of it knocked him back, his massive boots sliding across the mountaintop. It came no closer to knocking him over than if Basen had sneezed on him.

Basen muttered a curse as he put away his wand and drew his blade. "How many of them can you pain at once?" he asked Vithos.

"Half," Vithos replied to Basen's shock. "They look weak. But I want hurt the big one."

"Don't try to hurt the big one," Basen urged.

"I will."

Basen dashed at a sharp angle to the side and called for Vithos to follow. Half of the humans chased after them, showing their flank to Basen's allies. The giant gave Basen a passing glance as he crossed by, ready to protect himself from a fireball if needed. Basen didn't have time to cast one.

"Now, Vithos," he said as he charged the oncoming enemies.

Vithos screamed and slapped his hands together. The men groaned and gasped as the spell hit them. Half of them tumbled, tripping the others who'd managed to stay on their feet. Basen cut whatever flesh was in front of him, landing a few deadly blows. It wasn't his priority. He just needed to maim as many as he could before they could get up.

"Fatholl!" Basen shouted without taking time to look. "The giant cannot be hurt. Run past him!" Basen circled around while the men he hadn't had a chance to cut began to stand. Now with the mountain slope—the exit— behind him, he had a clear view of the terrible collision between Fatholl's Elves and their enemies.

His advice to Fatholl was ignored, as many of the Elves had their hands directed at the giant. Their faces contorted with strain at first, then morphed into confusion, and then concern. Fatholl showed complete shock just before ducking under a surprisingly nimble swing from the giant's massive battle axe.

Half of the other men had split to pursue Basen and Vithos. There were ten, as those Basen had cut remained on the ground licking their wounds. That still left five for him, and he hadn't been trained to defend himself against more than one opponent.

He took his wand with his free hand as he backed away. The sight of it stopped all but two of them, and he hit them both with a single fireball.

Once they were on the ground nursing their burns, the other three seemed uncertain whether to give chase.

One soon did, yelling, "Come on!"

The others followed close behind. Basen was about to shoot the man in front but noticed one of the three approaching from the side, much faster than the other two. Basen aimed as he gathered energy. The man turned his shoulder inward and cursed loudly, but neither reaction protected him from the enormous force of heat that lifted the man off the ground. He rolled away and left a trail of smoke.

The other two screamed in aggression. Drained, Basen didn't have the stamina to run from them. If he were to cast another fireball, it would be from his knees. He poured the last of his strength into getting his sword up and deflecting the first attack. He ducked under the second one, then stabbed his nearest enemy in the leg.

It was enough to take the man down. Basen barely got his sword up in time to block the third attack. His assailant tried to kick Basen while their swords were locked, but he saw it coming and grabbed the man's boot, Basen's side absorbing much of the impact. He kicked the man's other leg out from under him, then slashed the sword out of his hands. Basen brought his weapon down to stab this man in the leg as well.

"Stay down," he advised as he checked on Vithos.

Only equipped with a dagger and psyche, the Elf pained the closest man chasing him to buy time. A couple of their attackers gave up and joined the main battle led by the giant, leaving Basen and Vithos to deal with only three enemies.

Basen went for their legs as it was easier than killing them. He was stunned as he looked over to find the giant taking on three Elven swordsmen at once and making it look easy. He blocked the sword of an unseen attack with his shield while swiping his battle axe at the other two Elves. Only one Elf was quick enough to get out of the way. The other tried to block the attack, but there was too much force behind it, knocking his weapon away and cleaving off a chunk of his leg.

Spinning to keep up his momentum, the giant brought his two-sided axe up and caught another Elf in the heart. The dead Elf's body stuck to the axe, lifting off the ground as if he were as light as an empty satchel. The giant turned his weapon in the air to shake off the dead Elf, then brought the axe down.

Fatholl was nearly chopped in half as he spun out of the way. A small gray cloud of his long hair feathered to the ground. Basen was running straight for the giant without a plan. He jumped as he neared the giant's back, getting both boots up to kick him in the spine with all of his strength. Something cracked against Basen's side, dazing him before he realized he was rolling across the ground.

The shield. He'd been hit with it, and now the giant had chosen him as his next victim, practically shaking the ground as he stomped toward Basen.

"Psyche no work!" Vithos yelled.

"I told you!" Basen scrambled to his feet. "We have to run!" he announced to all, noticing Yeso's Elves almost reaching them.

Fortunately, Fatholl's Elves had made good work of the normal-size men by then, and there were only a few left standing. The Elves were forced to leave some of their own behind as they ran, Basen at the head of the pack.

"No!" the massive man shouted after them. "Return, you cowards!"

Anger reddened his face. Veins in his neck bulged. He gave chase, only to give up after a surprisingly short effort. He threw down his shield like a child having a tantrum.

Yeso's Elves, however, were quickly catching up. The mountain slope was close enough that Basen knew they could make it. Everyone would be forced to descend slowly, giving them a chance to recoup their spent energy.

It was almost steep enough for Basen to slide down on his ass, but he didn't have the luxury of time or a change of pants.

The scene was almost laughable as Elves skittered down after each other, Fatholl and Yeso continuing to yell in Elvish. Basen asked Vithos what they were saying, but all Vithos could gather was Fatholl mentioning something about a duel to settle their differences and Yeso refusing to agree. Basen wondered if Fatholl's pleas were as heartfelt as they sounded, or if he meant to follow through with Basen's plan.

Either way, Basen wasn't about to let Yeso walk out of this with his life.

It's his fault some of the Elves have joined our enemies. They need to go back from where they came from or die.

The descent was slow enough to give Basen time to ponder the exact reason behind Yeso chasing his brother all this way. Surely, he meant to kill Fatholl, but was it to protect himself or was it solely out of anger?

The ground came as a welcome relief when Basen reached the bottom. He could barely make out the blurred leaves on the trees ahead after running for this long, feeling as if he would collapse the moment he stopped. Yeso's cries of anger finally subsided. Basen turned to find that he and his Elves had halted, most of them with their hands on their knees as they fought for breath

No, just a little farther.

"This is ridiculous!" Yeso announced. "We are away from everyone here. Let's settle this like Elves."

"Fine," Fatholl spat back, motioning for his Elves to stop.

What are you doing? Get him into the forest!

"Admit you came to the mountains to kill me," Yeso said, then pointed at Basen. "This human brought you here to do it. You've decided to stand with them against me."

Fatholl took a moment to regain his breath. "As I've said, I take no side in this war...just like in Greenedge. I only do what I know to be right."

Yeso spat out an Elvish word that was probably a curse. "You think yourself to be the god of Elves ever since our exile from Meritar. It's as if you've forgotten that we trained in psyche together. *I* was the one who convinced you it needed to be done. *I* told you what could be accomplished with that kind of power."

"And yet you accomplish nothing but destruction! You are an embarrassment to all Elves."

Yeso took in a sharp breath. "I will not have this conversation with you again." With his Elves gathering behind him, Yeso started toward Fatholl.

He didn't move, nor did any of his Elves. Basen's fingers twitched as the urge to grab his wand overcame him.

No, Yeso is quick. He'll see me and dodge it again.

Besides, Fatholl would kill Basen if he tried to interfere now. *He might try to kill me anyway.* Basen wrapped his hand tightly around the warm akorell bracelet in his pocket.

"I have always been able to tell when you lie to me," Yeso said, giving Basen a quick look that warned him not to move. As Yeso's full attention returned to Fatholl, he turned his lips inward as if unable to contain the fury causing deep lines in his forehead. "So tell me the truth! You came here to kill me."

No one was watching Basen anymore. He slunk into the forest behind him.

He found some shrubbery growing around a tree, grabbed it low near the soil, and pulled it until the dirt came up. He stashed his akorell stone underneath, then reburied the roots, patting around until it looked just as he'd found it.

"Answer me!" Yeso yelled.

"You already know the truth," Fatholl said. "What you choose to do about it is what makes us who we are."

"*You* were the one who chose to come here. I didn't force you."

"You did force me," Fatholl argued, "when you joined Ulric. I should've killed you back in Greenedge for your betrayal. We lost hundreds making the continent safe again. You could've helped, but you didn't."

Yeso drew the dagger from his belt. He surprised Basen by looking straight at him. "Kill the mages first while I deal with Fatholl."

The enemy mages aimed their wands. There were too many of them. A battle of fire would result in three times the casualties on Basen's side, and he appeared to be the target for most of them.

He spun and ran for the trees. A fireball flew over his shoulder and exploded against the trunk of the nearest one. He shielded his head as best he could as he hid behind another tree.

"Vithos!" he called to the Elf. "Don't fight!"

"I don't," Vithos said from the cover of a tree somewhere to Basen's side.

Good. Basen didn't care how many Elves on each side died as long as Vithos wasn't one of them.

Another fireball blasted Basen's tree, keeping him

from peering out as screams of aggression and pain mixed together. Someone behind him yelled out in Elvish. Fatholl stopped his spell of psyche on Yeso to drop flat to the ground. He screamed something to the Elves around him, and they, too, dropped.

A hundred arrows buzzed by and found the torsos and legs of Yeso's Elves.

No Elves were left standing. Swarms of Fatholl's Elves emerged from behind the trees. Wielding daggers, they stood menacingly over their enemies, yet did not attack.

Soon Yeso was the only one left struggling. He writhed on the ground as Fatholl approached. Both had their arms outstretched toward the other, though Yeso looked as if he was trying to block a bright sun while Fatholl's fingers were crooked as if reaching to grab something. Fatholl came near enough for their hands to meet and closed his fingers tightly around Yeso's fist.

"I hate that you made me do this to you," Fatholl announced over Yeso's screams. He knelt down and drew his dagger with hesitation.

"I've always hated you," Yeso forced out behind gritted teeth, his lips red with blood. "I know you've felt it."

"You haven't always," Fatholl said sadly, then grimaced as he pushed the blade into his brother's chest.

Yeso screamed as he grabbed Fatholl's dagger-hand. But the surrounding Elves extended their arms and sapped Yeso's strength. He went limp as if falling asleep, looking oddly peaceful as his eyes shut. Fatholl took out his dagger and then pushed it in one more time. Yeso gave no reaction.

Fatholl pushed himself up. A single tear fell down his cheek before he swiped it.

Although all of Yeso's Elves were on the ground, many had fallen voluntarily in surrender and were without injury. Fatholl lifted his arms and spoke to them in Elvish. They rose hesitantly, the fear of death on each of their faces.

"Do all of you know common tongue?" Fatholl asked them.

They nodded as they eyed more archers moving out from the trees with arrows at the ready. Basen tried to back farther into the forest without being seen, but Fatholl pointed at him. "Don't move!" His eyes showed fury, but there was a hint of pain behind them.

"How many more Elves came with you?" Fatholl asked them.

"Three hundred," one answered.

The same number of Krepps we recruited from Fatholl's village. But there was no doubt in Basen's mind who would win a battle between equal numbers of each race.

"You will go back to fetch them," Fatholl said. "Then you will have two choices. You can return here before sunset and be brought to Regash Forest, where you will help Krepps build their new home. There are other Elves there, who will bring you to Merejic to live with us when we are done. Or you can return to Greenedge. I don't care if you decide to stay together, or if half of you go back while the other half join us. But if you try to do anything else, I will find you just like I found Yeso."

Basen had made it to the next row of trees, now

motioning for Vithos to follow. But as he came toward Basen, Fatholl noticed.

"I said don't—!"

Basen and Vithos ran.

CHAPTER NINETEEN

Of all the unknowns of this plan, one thing was for certain. Basen and Vithos had decided at the start of this they would flee the moment they had the chance. Unfortunately, the moment had never arrived, so Basen had to create one.

Fatholl was too powerful and too emotionless. He didn't care about the needs of others. If taking the akorell stone wasn't reason enough for killing Basen, he would come up with some other excuse.

Vithos would survive if captured, being an Elf, and there was some solace to that. But Basen needed his assistance as the two of them ran.

Basen could come back for his akorell stone later. First, he had to lose the horde of psychic Elves…who could sense him no matter where he hid. God's mercy, he could think of no worse predicament.

He was glad Vithos was fast, as it helped them get a good head start. Basen didn't chance a look behind him, focusing all of his efforts on speed. He zipped around trees, separating from Vithos by accident.

"This way!" Basen called to him.

Vithos replied with a scream. The psychics had gotten to him.

"Keep going!" Vithos yelled.

Basen turned and saw a few veer off toward a fallen Vithos. The rest came for Basen as he made a split decision to follow Vithos' advice. There was nothing

Basen could do to help his comrade against so many.

His heart jumped into his throat as he spotted more Elves in front of him. Not all of them had come through to join the battle! He stopped, and before he could figure out what to do, his body convulsed with pain.

Basen lifted his wand toward the Elf hurting him and watched the psychic's aggression turn to fear. Basen gathered energy and fired at the Elf's feet. He would avoid killing any of them if he could, for it would only anger Fatholl more.

Released from pain as the Elf somersaulted backward, Basen found a new route with no one in front of him. He would come back for the akorell stone *and* Vithos after he escaped.

He was hit again with pain so terrible he lost control of his legs. It was a reflex to go down, submit, and scream.

Fatholl's furious voice rang out. "Don't! Move!"

Through the pain, Basen was overwhelmed with the urge to look up. If it was the last thing he ever did, he would raise his head. Feeling as if he were being crushed by a bed of nails, Basen strained to bend back his neck.

Through blurred vision, he made out Sanya deeper in the forest. She was fully disguised again, a silver mask hiding her face. She held something in her outstretched hand that Basen had never seen before. It looked like a staff with orbs on either end that were as black as two holes deep enough to reach hell.

She called to him silently with psyche, then moved to hide herself behind the nearest tree. The urge to go to her intensified.

Groans slipped out of Basen's throat as he tried to

crawl away from the sound of Fatholl's approaching footsteps. He'd never known such agony, as if every muscle was slowly expanding, ripping his skin from the inside out.

Sanya wanted to help him—he just had to make it to her. He tried to keep going, but with Fatholl's psychic spell came a weakness as if Basen had aged a hundred years. His arms shook under his weight, his muscles refusing to work.

Why didn't she just alter the energy in the air? Then he could run to her...*the weapon needs bastial energy*. He had to get closer.

As he inched toward her, hands clutched him and turned him over. Fatholl still wouldn't relent, giving Basen no opportunity to fight back.

The Elf quickly searched his pockets.

"Where is the akorell stone?" Fatholl demanded as he wiped his dagger on the grass to clean off his brother's blood.

They were all paining him now, he realized, feeling not one but countless minds inside his head. But the pain wasn't any worse than if Fatholl was the only one. Perhaps Basen had reached the limit of agony he could possibly feel.

He focused to remember what his father had told him about resisting psyche.

"You must feel something stronger than the pain."

"Where is it?" Fatholl asked again as he pulled a small vial from his pocket. With care, he wiggled off the cork and poured the viscous substance onto his dagger.

Basen needed to buy time. While groaning in pain, he

asked, "Will you...let me go...if I give it to you?"

"Of course," Fatholl said.

Faintly, Basen heard muffled screaming. He managed to turn his head to locate Vithos being dragged off as he tried to yell a warning through a gag.

Fatholl is lying.

Yet what could Basen do about it? He searched for Sanya again, now unable to locate her. She had to stay back so as not to be detected with psyche, but then how was he supposed to reach her?

At least Yeso is dead and his Elves will no longer fight in this war. Basen had done his part. His mother was free as well, probably back at the Academy already.

The pain was beginning to anger him as he writhed helplessly. How cruel could one Elf be? *He must know the torture he's putting me through, yet he doesn't care.*

Fatholl appeared to have finished coating his blade in what had to be poison. He held it away from himself as it dripped.

Basen tried to think of his mother needing him, but she was free now. His father was safe back at the Academy as well.

The Academy—he'd never felt a deeper connection to any other place. But the thought of returning wasn't enough to override this agony. He screamed as his thoughts broke apart.

Basen noticed something being dragged down his arm. He blinked to clear his blurred vision and saw Fatholl opening up his skin with the poisoned dagger, though Basen was already in too much pain to feel more.

"You don't have long," Fatholl said. "I brought the

antidote, and you'll have it once you tell me where the stone is. Then this pain can stop." He put his hand flat against Basen's chest. "Your heart can't take it much longer. It'll give out, if the poison doesn't kill you first."

Anger came over him again, but Basen felt so utterly weak he could do nothing about it. Yes, he could tell them where the akorell stone was, but if they were going to kill him anyway, he didn't want them to have it.

He thought of his mother and father awaiting his return day after day. Eventually, Juliana would lead a search party. It might be a while, but they would come across his body. His mother would weep for days, weeks, maybe even months.

This didn't bring Basen the strength he needed. He tried to grab the hand pushing against his chest, but Fatholl simply brushed his arm aside as if Basen were as feeble as a fevered man.

If he didn't figure a way through this spell, he would die. Fear came over him, but it did nothing to stop the spell. He screamed, just wanting the agony to be over.

"It's buried," he said, unable to hold the words back any longer.

"Where?"

"Give me the antidote...and I'll show you."

"Tell me where first," Fatholl demanded.

"I can't...talk...like this."

"You will! Get the words out."

The bastard. Basen shut his eyes and put himself back at the Academy. A piece of it lived inside him now, and it was easy to visit even through the pain. He went back to the training grounds for Group One mages, where Effie was smiling at him in welcome.

Behind her, he could see Alabell. She'd been furious he'd left without telling her, but she was so overjoyed at his return, and so gentle by nature, that her anger evaporated. She smiled and...

Basen could feel his strength returning, the pain fading as the image of Alabell became clearer. She was beautiful beyond words, often making his breath catch in his throat whenever he saw her. She was a healer, a bringer of life in a world of death. A rose in a graveyard.

The only time he truly felt at peace was by her side, and peace was what he needed most during this gruesome time of war.

Fatholl yelped as Basen suddenly kicked him in the face and jumped up. He ran toward where he'd last seen Sanya.

The spell of pain never subsided, but it was now at the back of his mind like the endless, annoying barking of a faraway dog. He could feel all the psychics trying to take him down, but he kept his mind strong as he focused on Alabell within the Academy. He put himself there so vividly, he barely noticed the trees in front of him.

His right arm bumped into a branch and a new surge of pain ran up his body. This was not psyche, he noticed, as he looked down at his arm. His skin had turned red around the open wound and had swollen so much his arm looked twice its usual size.

Suddenly remembering he lacked a plan, Basen lost his focus. The Academy slipped from his mind, Alabell gone with it. Pain burned every inch of his body as if he'd been thrown into a fire.

He stumbled for a while as he screamed, somehow maintaining his balance enough to stay up. But then he lost it and fell without feeling himself hit the ground. He strained to look up. Sanya emerged, her staff glowing as she pointed it over Basen. A great fear came over him, as if staring death in the face.

"Get out of the way!" she urged him.

He put his last strength into rolling to the side.

The sight he beheld was one he knew would stay with him for the rest of his life. Her staff glowed and shook as if about to explode. A great *whoosh* of air came out so violently it threw Basen farther from the path of destruction. As the rushing air came back the other way in a clap, a red sphere as big as the giant they'd faced on top of the mountain tunneled down the forest lane, appearing to bend branches, trunks, and even the ground.

Basen was a good ten yards from it, though that felt far too close as the energy stormed past him. It wasn't quite pain that he felt as the essence of his being was gently tugged from within his bones, just the utter fear of being sucked out from his body. As in a nightmare, he somehow knew this burning, rippling entity would send him to another world in which he could never return whole again.

Too quick to dodge, it caught two Elves whose eyes rolled back into their heads as their bodies went limp.

All other Elves—even the usually fearless Fatholl—had darted away from Sanya's line of sight like frightened wild cats.

"You! Don't move," Sanya ordered as she walked toward Fatholl. "If any of you try to use psyche on me or come behind me, I will do that again." She pointed to where the Elves held Vithos. "Release him."

"Do it," Fatholl called from behind a tree.

"Give Basen the antidote," Sanya demanded.

He checked his arm. It felt like air had been trapped within his skin, intense pressure making it difficult to move.

"There is no antidote," Fatholl said.

Overwhelmed by anger, Basen reached for his sword, only to realize it had been taken. His wand as well. He cursed at Fatholl as he walked toward him. The Elf's bloody nose wasn't enough punishment.

"Basen, stop," Sanya said.

What was he doing? He was about to block her path, and she wouldn't be able to follow through with her threat without killing Basen as well.

"And no more psyche on him, either," Sanya told Fatholl.

Basen's anger—it had been produced by Fatholl. *That sneaky bastard.*

"You're a psychic." Fatholl took a brave step toward Sanya. "Who are you?"

"No one to you."

"That's not true. You're the masked woman who killed two of my Elves. You should be careful about what else you plan to do."

"I plan to kill you and the rest of your Elves if you take one more step. Or if *anyone* moves again! I see you!"

The Elves closing in on her stopped.

"When you say there's no antidote…" Basen's voice trailed off.

"Because the potion isn't going to kill you," Fatholl said. "It was just to scare you. Obviously, you're too much of a fool for it to work."

"A fool? You mean for knowing you would kill me even after I gave you the stone?" The lack of surprise on Fatholl's face told Basen he was right. "It doesn't matter anymore. We won't be seeing each other again."

"Don't you want to know why you were going to die, Basen?"

"What man wouldn't?" he asked sarcastically.

"You did not follow our plan. You tried to shoot Yeso when I told you not to do *anything* but get us there and then help us escape."

"What did it matter if I shot him with a fireball or you stabbed him in the heart? He's dead either way."

Fatholl leaned back and lifted his chin as if greatly offended. "This was a matter between Elves and you never should've interfered."

"Yet that is not the reason you planned to kill me when this was done," Basen said. "You worry I'll return. You're just like Yeso, ready to kill others to protect yourself. That's what we're all doing now in this war, yet you're the only one who refuses to believe it."

Fatholl gave no reply. He turned to Sanya and announced, "We're leaving."

The Elves picked up their dead.

As they carefully walked off into the forest while eyeing Sanya's weapon, Basen yelled after them, "You don't have to worry about me returning to Merejic. Enjoy your little piece of Ovira without me, and I'll enjoy mine without you!"

Fatholl ignored him. Basen desperately needed verification the Elf would leave him alone at the Academy, but it didn't look like he would get it.

Vithos came to stand beside Basen, each of them facing Sanya. She dropped her weapon and hurried away from it. Once she'd created distance, she coughed for a while, then took a couple of deep breaths. After checking on the Elves one last time to see they were gone, she removed her mask.

Vithos pointed at her face. "I remember you from the castle." His pointed finger swung to the weapon on the ground, the grass slowly blackening around it. "That was in the room you come from, yes?"

"Yes."

"What is it?" Basen asked.

"I don't know what to call it. I didn't create it, but I am tasked with getting rid of it. I was going to use it on Yeso before removing it from this world, but I could only do that after I found the akorell metal in the Fjallejon Mountains. I felt you make a portal there a while ago, but I still couldn't locate it."

Basen crinkled his brow. "I've been wondering how my portals are affecting you."

"Not at all anymore. In fact, the last one will help me put this back in the spiritual world where it belongs."

"Back? So it came from there?"

"Yes, long before we were born. Ulric knew about it before coming to the castle—it doesn't matter," she interrupted herself.

"You're right, it doesn't. What does is why you wanted to kill Yeso and why you helped me."

"I didn't just help you. I saved your life," she corrected.

"But why? I made portals after you threatened me not to. I hope you know, Sanya, that I only did what I needed to do. I didn't want to harm your mother in any way, and I'm sorry for anything that happened to her." He was careful not to apologize for perhaps forcing Sanya to kill Nick and Alex, for he could never live with himself if he took that blame. That was on her, and it would stay that way.

She looked surprised by his kind words for her mother. "What happened to her...was not your fault. I was able to keep her together against the damage of your portals, but in the end, I was meddling where I shouldn't have."

God's mercy, she seems like a different person again. This was the Sanya he'd met at the Academy, the *human* Sanya. Could Vithos tell if she was lying? Basen gave a questioning look to the Elf.

"All truth," Vithos said.

"You're not even angry about the portals?" Basen asked Sanya. "I made them before a week was up."

"I was angry," she admitted. "But you didn't make very many. I suppose I figured you only did what you must, as you just confirmed. That's all I've done as well. Only recently have I realized that I didn't *need* to do any of it. I chose to."

Basen checked on his injured arm with a tender touch. The pain had become different, he realized. He'd endured the worst agony possible and had come so close to death. Now pain reminded him he was alive, a glorious feeling he wanted to celebrate.

"Come back to the Academy with me," he suggested

to her. "Let them decide your punishment, and you won't need to run any longer."

She shook her head. "I'm not ready."

"After you get rid of the weapon."

"No, there's a list of tasks I need to do."

He wanted her to answer for her crimes, but he understood there was little reason for her to give up on life yet. If she wouldn't go with him, then that was that.

"Why would you try to kill Yeso?" he asked, hoping to get a better sense of whether this woman was his enemy or really his ally as she'd made it seem.

"Because he wanted me dead or gone."

Basen sighed at having to give her the unfortunate news. "Sanya, there are a lot more people than Yeso who want that."

"I know."

"Do you plan to kill them all?"

"Of course not."

She didn't seem to want to say more.

"What will you do now?" she asked. "The path back through the Fjallejon Mountains isn't safe for you."

"And why is it safe for you? Who do my enemies think you are?"

"A Takary."

Basen paused. "God's mercy, you're serious."

"Ulric has put his trust in me and given me this disguise. He told people I came with him from Greenedge and cannot speak, nor can I show my face because of a fire that made me hideous."

It seemed absurd until he remembered she'd tricked everyone at the Academy without a disguise, even Basen, who had grown up with her.

"What will you do with his trust?" Basen asked, even less sure now if she was his ally.

"I will kill Tauwin."

Her quick answer made it clear this had been her plan for some time. But she was either lying to him or lying to herself.

"He would've been dead already if that's really what you want."

Her head jerked as if insulted, her hair falling over half her face. "It's not that easy. There's been no opportunity."

"So create your own."

Silence came upon them.

She brushed her hair away. If she wasn't such a monster, she might've been beautiful. Her face drew the eye, her surprisingly gentle features put together nicely. She did not look at all like the easily angered young woman he remembered who always wore a scowl.

He realized she must've spent years practicing to become this other woman, as it was not in her nature. So much work she'd put into changing herself, just to choose such a terrible path in life. *What a waste.*

He wondered if she would try to take his akorell stone. He wasn't sure he and Vithos could kill her if necessary. She was quick, after all, and could get to her weapon in the time it took Basen to cast a single fireball. It would all depend on Vithos, whether his psyche was strong enough to slow her down. If she broke the bastial energy in the air, she couldn't use the weapon, and Basen knew he could defeat her in a brawl, as neither of them had a sword.

Should he attack? What would Effie say if she knew he'd let Sanya live?

But fighting her was the last thing he wanted right now. Even if she deserved it, he couldn't bring himself to kill someone who'd just saved his life. *Her time will come later,* he told himself. *Even she seems to know that.*

"You don't have to worry about your precious stone," she said. "I don't need it."

"When did you become able to pick up on thoughts?" *And what else did you find out just now?*

"I can only feel your emotion—your fear of losing something. It has to be the akorell stone. I've been able to read feelings for years. I almost couldn't take it in the castle." Her voice quieted. "Everyone despised me. I couldn't help who I was, so all I could do was hate them in return."

Basen felt a pang of guilt. He had been part of the problem, not the solution. He remembered how his mother had wanted so desperately to help Sanya, while the thought had never crossed Basen's mind.

"I still don't understand why you helped me." It was his last attempt at deciphering whether this was an ally or enemy in front of him, as he still didn't know what to do about her.

She bit down on her lip as she looked at the black grass around her weapon.

"I don't know."

"Everyone has to choose a side in this war," Basen informed her. "You'd better make your decision quick, or it'll be made for you."

Sanya paused as if thinking, but she said nothing. She retrieved her weapon and set off without a goodbye. Basen watched her for a while, still unsure of his thoughts about her.

She stopped and looked back. "Basen."

"What?"

"Tauwin likes to watch the battles from the top of Kyrro's castle."

They stared at each other in silence.

"Thank you," Basen said.

Sanya left without another word.

CHAPTER TWENTY

After some consideration, Basen and Vithos realized their best route back to the Academy would take them to a place Basen had promised he would never return. Tenred castle. It seemed safer than the other two options. One was to go through the Fjallejon Pathway, which was likely to get Basen shot from above if he wasn't killed by Yeso's Elves going the opposite way. The second was to head north, like those Elves, to Regash Forest, where Basen could make a portal.

But that was also where he'd likely run into Fatholl again, as the Elves and Krepps would be there for a while, building. No doubt the Elves would be happy to take a moment out of their busy day to kill him.

Basen and Vithos needed to wait until the cover of night and for the akorell stone to charge, not that they minded. They each had a bit of coin they used to purchase a meal and a bath in the city of Tenred leading up to the castle.

With a few hours to spare before night, Basen spent it charging the stone in remote alleys of the city while chatting with Vithos. The swelling of his arm had gone down enough so it wasn't noticeable, and his mood couldn't have been better. He had no more obligations to scary psychic Elves. His mother and father were both safe. Basen felt as though he'd been given a second chance at life, and he liked how this one was shaping up.

He wasn't sure what he could say to Alabell, but she

needed to know the strength she'd given him. Thoughts and emotions were more powerful than he'd realized. He longed to see her and kiss her, to tell her how he felt about her.

"Good trip," Vithos said after smiling in silence for a while, his hands on his hips. He looked pleased by his thoughts as he watched the sunset sky grow ever darker.

"Good trip," Basen agreed. He touched his bandaged arm and found it to be healing quicker each moment, though he might have a long scar to remind him Fatholl was alive and probably wishing Basen wasn't.

Eventually the akorell stone was ready. It glowed so bright, Basen had to purchase a satchel so its light wouldn't give them away as they snuck into the castle through the exposed hole among the rubble. He wondered why he was not at all worried about being caught as they headed there, and soon he realized why. He felt a new power within himself. Not an ability, exactly, but confidence he could handle whatever dared to put itself in his way. His plan to kill Yeso had worked, despite flaws and surprises. That giant on the mountain, with his battle axe...Basen would never forget him.

But the most difficult challenge he'd faced was Fatholl. Basen wasn't sure he would've made it out of Corin Forest without Sanya's help. *Should I tell anyone what she did for me?*

It looked as if stonemasons had been working on the corner of the castle, as stones cut to replace the damage in the walls were lying around the openings. Basen and Vithos had to shove a few out of the way to fit through, but soon they were walking down the quiet castle halls and headed for the kitchen.

They passed a couple people using a candle to light their path, and then a guard, but no one paid any attention. Basen kept his wand up, the light making it hard for others to make out his face or Vithos' Elvish ears. Soon they were in the kitchen, and Vithos went straight for the pantry where he stole some bread and cheese for the two of them, because why not?

Afterward, Basen ripped open a portal to the Group One training grounds. He'd gotten so used to this arduous task that now it just felt like lifting something heavy. A great strain, yes, but completely manageable. He wondered if it might be possible one day to make a portal without the boost of energy from an akorell stone.

He tumbled through the portal after Vithos and onto the training grounds. As much as he'd gotten used to creating a portal, going through one was still a problem. He sat on the sand and held his stomach.

There was no crowd of Group One mages to celebrate his return. In fact, not a single person knew he was back or what he'd done. With Yeso dead, and Fatholl's threat to the rest of Yeso's Elves, they would no longer be an opponent in this war. Basen smiled through the nausea at being able to deliver this exciting news. Even Penny wouldn't be able to deny he'd made good use of his time away from training.

First he had to make sure his mother and her escorts had returned safely. "I'm going to see my father," he told Vithos.

"I'm going to see Terren," Vithos replied.

With both leaders living near each other, Basen and

Vithos could walk in the same direction. Enjoying Vithos' silent companionship, Basen felt as if he'd made at least one Elven friend, even if all others wanted to kill him.

*****

The lights were out in his father's house. Basen raised his arm to knock, then stopped himself. News of his return could wait until tomorrow, so as not to disturb Henry's sleep. He just wanted to make sure his mother was in fact there. Basen walked around to where he knew the bedroom to be of this small house. Being a residence for faculty, it was different than the student houses. It had a large living room that Henry could use as an office or to hold meetings. The bedroom was bigger as well, with a bed that fit two far easier than any of the student beds.

Basen tried to get a glimpse to ensure both his parents were there, but the curtains were drawn. He noticed Vithos hadn't yet knocked on Terren's door, so he hurried over.

"I didn't want to wake them," Basen explained.

That stopped Vithos from knocking. "You're right. We shouldn't wake Terren, too."

After he and Vithos separated, Basen decided to check on his roommate to make sure that she, Effie, Steffen, the Krepps, and of course his mother were back and safe. Otherwise, Basen wouldn't be able to sleep.

Fortunately, Annah awoke when he unlocked the front door. She looked suspicious and a bit worried as she peered down the hallway, squinting as she moved her hair out of her face.

"It's me," he said, putting light upon himself from his wand.

"Basen!"

They met halfway down the hall and hugged.

"Did everyone make it back safely?" he asked.

"Yes, except some of the Krepps fell."

"Fell? Did you have to climb part of the mountain?"

"No," she whispered, her voice carrying pain. "Fell in battle. There were troops at Lake Kayvol, a hundred or so."

"God's mercy, I'm sorry! I didn't think there would be, otherwise I wouldn't have sent you there."

"None of us thought anyone would be there, Basen. It's not your fault. We all knew the plan before we left and assumed we would return without encountering enemies."

"How many Krepps died?"

"Eight. But they were prepared to die. It was an honor for them. The other Krepps were proud of them, themselves, and us. Your mother..."

"What?"

"She fought in the battle. She mostly stayed with Effie toward the back, but I know she claimed at least one kill."

"What in god's world? I can't even imagine her yelling, so I certainly can't see her killing someone. Wait, did you say a hundred enemies?"

"Yes. We took them by surprise at night. They didn't expect us to attack from the east. But soon they overwhelmed us, and the Krepps began to fall quickly. I heard Effie thanking Neeko later for saving her and

Juliana's life. He joined us mid-battle, Basen. He—" She stopped in search of words. "I don't know how to describe what he does with swords, but it was incredible. I don't think even Effie knew what he was fully capable of, because she seemed shocked, too."

Basen held his head, suddenly dizzy. This was too much to take in. "I need to sit down, and we need some light other than from my wand."

They went to Annah's room, where he sat in the chair at her desk. She lit her bedside lamp and settled on her mattress, then proceeded to tell him everything.

"Neeko and Shara changed their minds the day after everyone left their cabin. They hurried to catch up but didn't know the shortest or the safest route to the Academy. Neeko can lift himself with pyforial energy, and that's eventually how he spotted us."

"What do you mean?" Basen asked. "Are you saying he can fly?"

"Not exactly. It takes too much out of him to keep himself in the air, so he can't stay up for long. He carried himself above the trees to look for us often, and as he and Shara caught up, he noticed enemies in our way. He and Shara—my stars." Annah put her hands over her mouth, then dropped them. "I haven't asked about your trip yet. Forgive me, I'm not quite awake yet."

"It's fine. I'd rather hear about what happened to you first anyway."

"Did you at least...do what you intended to do?"

"Yeso I did..."

She chuckled, but then swatted her hand at him. "It's not appropriate to joke about killing!" She stood and came over to hug him once more. "I'm glad you're safe. So all went well, seriously?"

"Yes...o."

They laughed together this time.

CHAPTER TWENTY-ONE

Although his arm felt fine in the morning, Basen still needed an excuse to go to the medical building instead of to class where he would have to face Penny. Effie didn't know he was back yet, so their instructor wouldn't know, either. He hoped for Effie's sake that Penny was only angry with him and not at her for leaving the Academy.

Basen slept through breakfast hours, then awoke to eat the last of the bread and cheese Vithos had taken from the pantry in Tenred castle. Then, while all mages, warriors, psychics, and chemists were training, he made his way to the medical building to surprise the person he most wanted to see.

He kept the bandage on his arm, and when he arrived, the first healer who noticed him asked about it.

"It's fine," Basen told the man. "I'm here to see Alabell Kerr. Do you know where she is?"

"That way." The healer pointed down one of the three hallways branching out from the entrance.

Basen was shocked to find her trying to communicate with a Krepp. They were huddled over drawings of Krepps with injuries. Pointing at one of the drawings, then at her arm, the Krepp seemed to be attempting to explain how to treat a wound.

"Bandage?" Alabell asked, pointing at the rolls of cloth beside them.

"No," the Krepp uttered. "Blood...*errr*..." She seemed to be thinking as she searched for the word.

"A lot of blood?"

"No. Blood good. Blood *free*."

"I don't understand? Why is blood good and free?"

Basen happily eavesdropped as he stood in the doorway.

"No. Good is *free*. *Free!*"

"Oh, *free* is Kreppen for good?"

"Yes, human."

Alabell frowned. "That might get confusing."

"What?"

"Nothing."

"What nothing?"

Alabell shook her palms. "Don't worry about it." She pointed at the image of a Kreppen arm with a long cut. "Why is blood good?" Then she lowered her voice. "*Dra lu...*um...*blu free?*"

Basen held in a laugh. It was an amazing attempt at Kreppen, sounding akin to the female Krepps Basen had heard. But that didn't stop the guttural sound from being hilarious coming from a dainty woman like Alabell.

"Blood heals. Human blood no heal?"

"No," Alabell said with some surprise. "So...*blu free*...let bleed, then dry and bandage?"

"Yes, human. Good."

Alabell took a breath as if exhausted already. Basen couldn't imagine spending all day like this, but Alabell was already pointing at the next image of an arrow in a Krepp's stomach.

Basen cleared his throat before she had a chance to ask about it. She turned and gasped.

"You're back!"

She didn't seem to notice his bandage yet as he opened his arms and she walked into them for a hug. It had been wonderful to return, but it didn't compare to this feeling of holding her close. This was where he belonged, with her. She was the kindest person he knew, and he strived to be a better man whenever he thought of her drive to assist others.

"Hug," the female Krepp commented, probably to practice her common tongue.

But something felt different in the way Alabell hugged him back. She seemed reserved, not squeezing as tightly or putting her head on his shoulder as she had in the past.

"Yes, hug," Alabell confirmed.

"Love," the Krepp commented.

A heavy silence followed. Alabell and Basen parted.

"Will you excuse us?" she asked the Krepp, then gestured toward the door with a polite turn of her hand.

"Yes. I will...execute you." The Krepp promptly left.

"I sure hope not," Basen teased.

Alabell chuckled. "That Krepp keeps calling me 'human,' did you hear?"

"Yes."

"Is it just in my mind, or does she say it as if I'm a child?"

"You probably don't want my theory."

"Oh, I do."

"I think she knows common tongue perfectly and she just enjoys creating disorder."

Alabell laughed loudly. Her mouth had a way of opening wide first before a sound came out that Basen found adorable.

"I can imagine that very well," Alabell said, then pointed at his bandaged arm. "Let me see."

He unwrapped the bandage to show her his long wound. She didn't do more than blink at the unsightly gash.

"Looks to be healing nicely. You got this early yesterday I assume?"

"Yes. Fatholl cut me with a poisoned dagger, but it wasn't lethal. My arm swelled to about the size of my leg."

"Ah, yellow poison. He intended to scare you."

"You *are* smart. Yellow poison—that's the name of it? Doesn't sound very original."

She took a quick sip of water, looking tired even though the day had just begun. "No, but that's what most chemists call it. Sit and tell me everything." She took a seat on the nearby medical bed but pointed at a chair facing her for him. He would've preferred the spot beside her, but something still seemed off about her demeanor. Perhaps she was angry with him, after all.

"I heard about your plan from your father," she said. "You don't need to explain it. The plan was risky but a good one. I'm glad to see you back here with just a cut on your arm."

He gave her a quick summary of his events starting with his trip to Tenred castle. He'd lost track of the days he was away, though it felt like a month. As he told his story, it was almost impossible to keep his eyes from roaming up and down Alabell. She had grown more beautiful to him in their time apart. Her piercing eyes were mesmerizing, and her generous curves made his blood run hot.

But she appeared somewhat indifferent as she listened, wearing a small smile that could only be described as polite.

"That's incredible," she said when he was done. "Truly incredible. We can really expect the Elves to leave. I'm proud of you."

While her words were sweet, there was barely any emotion attached to them.

"Uh, thank you."

"I can give you an ointment that will reduce the chances of a scar on your arm, unless you want one?"

"Who wants a scar?"

"Some of the warriors."

"Well, I don't." The thought of her touching him, even to rub ointment on an injury, was too pleasant to pass up.

"It's actually a potion Steffen came up with," Alabell said as she headed toward the hallway. "Stay there and I'll get it."

Basen would have to thank Steffen later, and not just for creating something to erase his scar. From what Annah had told Basen, Steffen had been the one to lead the Krepps into battle, fighting with them at the front.

Alabell returned with a silvery liquid on her fingers, her other hand cupped beneath to catch the drops.

"Caregelow?" Basen asked.

"It's part of the potion."

As she rubbed his arm gently, he felt goosebumps rise on his other arm as if it were jealous. When she seemed to be done, he took her hand.

"Alabell, I need to tell you something." Since returning

to the Academy, he'd been trying to come up with the right words but hadn't found them yet. He'd hoped that when he saw her and she smiled at him, the right words would pour out of his mouth. But she had yet to give him one of her true Alabell smiles.

She put her hand on top of his as she showed him a crushing frown. "I have to tell you something as well." She blushed. "I think you should let me speak first."

"That doesn't sound good."

She pulled her hand out of his grasp, and it felt like part of him had left with her.

"I was worried when I heard what you planned to do outside the Academy," she said. "Each day that passed, the feeling became worse."

Alabell seemed to have trouble keeping her gaze on Basen's. He could hear in her tone that this was not out of embarrassment or discomfort but something far worse. She didn't need to say the rest; Basen already knew. He could see their relationship withering away before him, yet there was nothing he could do to give it life again. His trip had caused a grievous wound that was about to bleed out.

"I missed you," she continued. "I hoped to hear news each morning, but none came. I started to feel anger toward you, blind rage I couldn't understand. Until finally, I did." She paused for what looked to be a painful breath.

I'm sorry. He opened his mouth to say the words but nothing came out.

"I lost friends in the last war," Alabell said. "And in this one, I lost my family. I think the anger at you comes from my heart trying to protect me. I can do everything in my power to save people from dying, but once they're dead, I can't...I don't know how..." She let her voice trail off as she gave him the longest gaze yet.

It appeared she was searching for something in his eyes, studying him the same way Basen had found himself studying Fatholl. He hadn't been sure whether the Elf was friend or foe, and now Alabell wasn't sure whether Basen would bring her happiness or grief.

She stood. "I'm glad you're back and you're safe. And I'm so proud of you for what you've done. But I...can't let myself open to you in *that* way. I got a glimpse of what it would be like to lose you, and I can't deal with it. I can't...let myself love you."

She finally seemed to be finished, awaiting his reply with a lean toward him.

"Well...dammit," he muttered, then stood as well.

"You're not mad?"

"I can't be mad when it makes sense." He didn't want her to see how much pain he was in. Her decision had been made, and he didn't want her to feel miserable for it. But god's mercy, those words were like a knife in his gut. *"I can't let myself love you."*

Now a hand was reaching up from his stomach and grabbing his throat. But he had to speak. She was waiting.

"I guess I'll be going." There was considerable strain in his voice that she had to notice.

"I'm so sorry." She wiped a tear from one eye, then from the other.

He nodded and chewed on his lip, at a loss for words. After a moment of awkward silence, he left. The inner hand choking his throat was stronger than ever as he stumbled out of the medical building. He went around the corner and knelt, surprised at how weak he felt.

His father had made many rules for Basen, and one was to never cry. He'd learned how to hold in his tears, as he would now. But he'd never learned how to end this debilitating feeling. That one conversation with Alabell had made his life feel pointless.

Stop being a fool, he told himself, though it was his father's voice in his head. *Just keep your head up and do your tasks. Time will heal you.*

His sarcastic voice gave reply. *Yeah...but time will also bring her into sight again.*

He wasn't sure how he was going to bear it. He'd been an idiot to assume they would end up together. He'd gotten his hopes too high.

The higher you are the worse the fall, and here I have fallen from the clouds.

CHAPTER TWENTY-TWO

Basen was thankful when the Redfield bell rang out three times. A meeting at Redfield Stadium might take his mind off Alabell, as well as delay whatever punishment Penny would give him. It wasn't that he was worried, as a demotion to a lower group number was the worst she could do. He just didn't want to see anyone right now.

Already close to the center of campus, he arrived to the stadium early and took a spot all the way at the top on the other side of the entrance, hoping none of his friends would notice him.

It took a long while for the stadium to fill with all the new people now at the Academy. They poured in through the wide entrance, most chatting with each other and even smiling. If there had been any strife between the original Academy members and those from Tenred, all signs of it were gone.

Terren entered when the stadium was about full, taking his place in the center to speak with Jack Rose. The last time Basen had seen the master chemist, he and Terren had been worried about Abith's wishes to become headmaster. But when Abith entered, neither man gave him more than a passing glance. *Either they're not suspicious of him anymore or they're good at pretending.*

Basen recognized only about a tenth of the people coming in and knew the names of no more than a third of those he recognized. It was a marvel to think that of all his allies, all fighting for the same cause, many wouldn't ever have the chance to introduce themselves to each other. He wondered what it was like for third-years, if they finally knew everyone who'd come into the school the same year they had.

Cleve entered at the same time as the other Group One warriors, with Krepps right on their tail. To Basen's amazement, they took their seats together and even looked to be communicating as they waited for the announcement to begin.

Reela came in later, glanced in Cleve's direction, and then went the opposite way to find her seat. Effie soon joined her, then waved to Steffen when he came through the open gate. The chemist went up to join the two of them.

The one person Basen did not want to see was Alabell, and she came in toward the end, still chatting with that female Krepp. He felt a pang of sadness and forced his thoughts toward another matter. Crea Hiller.

Where was she? Crea should be next to Abith, but Abith was standing with the instructors against one of the circular walls.

Henry entered the stadium with Juliana. They faced each other and said something before she turned to go up to the benches. Henry took his place with the instructors. Basen would greet them both as soon as this was over. He had the rest of the announcement to find a way to dissolve the feeling Alabell had given him that nothing mattered anymore.

Terren lifted his arms for silence.

"I have only good news to share. First, we have confirmed that your friends and family who left the

Academy with Tauwin's military commander are safe."

Basen clapped with the others, surprised the commander had kept his promise. It seemed odd that Terren would wait so long to send scouts for verification of this, but then Basen realized it wasn't that. Terren had known for a while, but if this news had come out earlier, others might've left the Academy, too.

"And secondly," Terren continued, "by now, all of you know that Ulric Takary has come from Greenedge to join Tauwin against us. Some of you also may have heard that Elves came with him, most of them strong psychics."

Nervous excitement fluttered in Basen's stomach. *This is about what I've done. Vithos must've told Terren this morning.*

"Although Ulric appears to be leading and financing these new enemies, some of whom attacked us the night after Tenred joined us, it is an Elf by the name of Yeso who led the other Elves in this troop. *Led,*" Terren emphasized. "He has been confirmed *dead*, and the Elves who followed him here, *all of them*, no longer fight against us. They've gone north and will not return."

Among the applause, people yelled out to ask how Terren knew this. The headmaster smiled as he lifted his arms again. He seemed to be searching the audience.

Please don't call me down there.

"Our portal mage, Basen Hiller, devised a plan and carried it through. It resulted in Yeso's death and all of his Elves abandoning Ulric. Basen, come down here!"

Basen muttered a curse that was lost to the sound of roaring applause. The entire audience turned toward him once he was descending the stairs, his legs shaking from nervousness. These steps had never seemed steeper. *Just don't fall, just don't fall.*

He hopped down from the short wall to enter the sandy arena. During his descent, his father had joined Terren in the middle. Henry held a cloth necklace with a bronze medallion that Basen knew would be going around his neck.

Why was he so nervous? He should be proud. Still, he wiped sweat from his brow as he walked to the center. He made a point to stand straight and smile. Somehow, acting the part actually gave him the real feeling. Now he relished the applause as his smile widened.

The cheering quieted enough for Terren to speak. "This is a medal to recognize cunning and bravery. There isn't time to tell the whole tale of what Basen did, but I'm sure it'll get around. This is the Academy, after all." The headmaster's comment elicited light laughter. "With the Elves gone, the confidence of our enemies will dwindle. This gives us new opportunities in this war, and you can trust in your leaders that we will take full advantage."

Terren put his hand on Basen's back. "With this medal comes a new title. Basen the Cunning."

"Oh, I like that," Basen said a little too loudly. Everyone in the first rows laughed as Terren presented him with a certificate of the title. The whole stadium cheered as Henry hung the medal around Basen's neck.

Basen had never seen his father so proud, smiling like a drunken fool. He found his mother in the audience, wearing the same embarrassing look. Then his eyes darted over to Alabell. God's mercy, she was beautiful as she grinned and lowered her head to acknowledge his glance. There was some pain in her smile. The same pain he could feel in his chest getting stronger each moment he looked at her. Terren said something that brought on another wave of applause. Judging by the way everyone stared at Basen, it must've been about him.

He put on a false smile as he hoped it wasn't a question. As the applause quieted, there was one man still clapping. Basen's heart sank as he saw who it was.

The older man from the workhouse clapped loudly enough for the entire stadium to hear, bringing his hands together forcefully but slowly in a sarcastic manner. Everyone stared at him.

"Is that it?" he asked in a deep voice that reverberated throughout the stadium. "Shouldn't we be giving the Hillers *more* medals? How about a medal for starting a war that no one needed? What about a title for that? Hiller, Hand of Destruction. It has a nice sound to it. Killing is all they're good for, so why shouldn't we award them for that?"

He let the silence hold after each of his ridiculous questions.

"Might as well put one around Tauwin's neck, too!" he bellowed. "The Takarys are the only ones equally vile to the Hillers, and now we're forced to choose the side of one to fight against the other! All of you from the Academy who stood against Tegry Hiller—how do you now allow his brother to hang medals upon his nephew's neck? You're rewarding the wrong people!"

Basen felt a response bubbling up, but the words hadn't formed yet. He couldn't be the only one who wanted to speak up. Yes, he could see it on *many* faces.

But they seemed just as stunned as he was. Even Terren gave no indication he would interrupt this berating anytime soon.

Could it be that they actually found truth in what this man was saying?

"My son was trained as a warrior here at the Academy," he continued. "He finished his three years, then returned to working at my bakery with nothing to show for his efforts except for a binding contract—a death contract. War came, because of the Hillers, and so he fought, and he died." The man pointed at a group of older troops from Tenred as they sat together not far from him. "My son fought against the lot of you. He died in battle, never to be awarded any medals, any *honor*."

Basen didn't know the man's name, but he'd worked alone in the workhouse. He had no wife and certainly no bakery anymore.

"Shut up!" someone yelled.

"Let him finish," Terren announced to Basen's surprise.

"Thank you, Terren. You *are* an honorable man. My son lost his life!" he shouted in the direction of the person who'd tried to quiet him. "And now I have to sit here and watch the people responsible for the war as well as those who fought against my son give awards to each other. You act as if these Hillers are heroes because they're standing against the Takarys. They were forced to pick a side, and that's *all* they've done! They did nothing in the last war! *Nothing*! How do the rest of you not see this?"

He pointed again at the nearest troops from Tenred.

"None of you are any better. Just like the Hillers, you did nothing about your king. Yet look at what Kyrro is doing when our king shows he's not fit to rule. *Civil...war!* Just like the Hillers, you join now only because you have something to gain. But the only men and women with any honor are those who've followed Terren from the beginning! From when Tegry Hiller declared war. You're making a mockery of honor by awarding *scum.*"

Finally, he seemed to be done. The man had a throat made for shouting, his voice gaining even more confidence by the end of it.

Yelling—insults by the sound of most of them—bombarded the man from every angle. But they quickly quieted when Terren raised his arms.

The headmaster motioned for guards as he spoke. "We listened to you. Now you're going to listen to us before you leave."

"May I?" Basen asked, not wanting Terren to speak on his behalf, especially when he had something he was itching say.

"Go ahead," Terren encouraged.

The man folded his arms and looked to be proud of himself. The Academy quieted completely to listen to Basen.

There had been some truth, too much truth, to the spiteful old man's words. Half the people waiting for Basen to speak looked at him dubiously, as if the medal around his neck was indeed ironic. He could see it in their eyes—he was just a Hiller again, as he was to the man from the workhouse. But the others, those who knew him, looked to him in expectation that he would put this man in his place.

The medallion felt heavy around Basen's neck, wanting to pull his head down. He forced his gaze to meet his audience, specifically the man willing to risk death to speak so *highly* of Basen's family.

Basen wanted to begin with how this man had been angry since they'd met in the workhouse, that none of that anger had been directed at Basen until later, when he'd learned who Basen was. *There's too much judgment in a name.*

"Basen?" Terren prodded with a gentle squeeze to his shoulder.

He wasn't sure why the silence of those waiting in the stadium put such little pressure on him. But now that Basen was here in front of them, and he realized no harm would come to him, he took his time to find the right words.

Too much judgment in a name.

"He gives no response because he has none to give!" the man yelled. "You can't argue with the truth, Hiller."

"You speak as if I bowed before my uncle," Basen spat.

"You are a liar if you say you did not, and the psychics here can confirm it."

"I did *not* bow to Tegry. I bowed to the crown atop his head."

"So you did bow to him, when you could've fought—"

"I did not interrupt your tirade," Basen said, "now let me respond without interruption."

The man smirked as he put up his hands in mock surrender.

"Boys don't lower their heads in deference to their

uncles, and I never did for mine. But I had to bow to the King of Tenred. Paying respect to a leader is a tradition as old as man. It's how we recognize those who give us direction, especially during times of war when unity is important.

"You speak as if people are foolish for taking orders from Henry Hiller, but there is no shame in that because his name has nothing to do with his role. Yes, he helped his king in the last war, but he did not help his brother. If you knew what kind of man Tegry was to his *own family*, you wouldn't be using the words 'brother' and 'nephew' like they mean something. They didn't then, and they don't now. You're the one holding onto the past.

"Henry's troops have followed him here to join us, and Abith's men have done the same. Together with Terren's troops, we all stand against a legion of men who strive to kill us. We must fight as one, and we can only do so by having honor. We must respect our leaders and each other. Now you try to take away that honor and respect. You speak about my family and the men from Tenred as if we're traitors, as if there's nothing we can do to redeem our past. You are the one striving to turn everyone against each other, while the *Hillers* are trying to help win this war.

"You're more toxic than a traitor, yet you speak like you're the last honorable man. There's a reason you're about to be removed from the Academy. It's the same reason that I, a Hiller, was given a medal of honor. Present. Rules. Past."

The audience erupted with applause so suddenly it shocked Basen. He grabbed the medallion and lifted it in his fist. They grew even louder.

Basen figured he would never know the name of the man who had put so much focus on the Hiller name. There was no way to know what this man would do after his exile from the Academy, but Basen didn't care as he gladly watched him escorted from the stadium. He hoped this man would take this experience as a lesson. Such focused rage doesn't always require an equal response.

CHAPTER TWENTY-THREE

Life in the Academy soon returned to what Basen had expected, with a few big changes. He was reminded of the hole in his heart every time he saw Alabell or anyone who resembled her. Fortunately, though, there were a number of things that helped fill that hole.

He was pleased during mealtime when he noticed warriors and Krepps sitting together as they had during the Redfield announcement. Nebre and Cleve had become friends, or Cleve was just intent on learning Kreppen. Whatever it was, Basen saw the large warrior sitting only with the civilized Krepp.

Zoke had told Basen he should bring Nebre to Regash Forest. Nebre was one of the few Krepps, like Zoke, who could keep the others from doing anything foolish, like getting involved in the war. But Nebre seemed just as needed here, for he was constantly asked to translate.

Nebre's father, Rickik, looked to have gained some pride in his son. Basen no longer saw Rickik dirtying Nebre's clean face, messing with his combed hair, or forcing him to change out of his cloth shirt. Instead, he let his son speak to the humans as he looked on in apparent curiosity. Basen didn't know what their relationship was like on Warrior's Field, as he couldn't imagine Nebre fighting with the same fervor as the other Krepps, but that didn't seem to matter anymore. Not even Rickik could deny how useful Nebre was.

In time, Basen would mention the request from

Nebre's old friend, but not yet. *Sorry, Zoke.*

Abith called Basen over to a table filled with troops from Tenred.

"That was some speech you gave on our behalf," Abith said.

The speech wasn't meant to benefit them, but Basen smiled anyway and said, "You're welcome."

He looked around to confirm Crea's absence. "Where is she?" Basen asked, having no need to specify who he referred to.

"Crea left," Abith said. "Did you really expect her to stay after you told Henry what she did to your mother?"

"She's Crea," Basen retorted. "She does whatever she wants, no matter the consequences to anyone else."

"I suppose that's right. She is a Hiller, after all." Abith's disarming smile showed he meant no offense with the jest. Besides, Basen couldn't deny there was truth to it.

"Have you abandoned your plan to overthrow Terren, or just put it on hold?" he asked.

"It's on hold," Abith replied. "Why don't you have a seat?" He gestured for everyone to make room so Basen could squeeze in beside him.

"Sitting at a Tenred table...I'm not ready for such a commitment," Basen commented. Joining them meant so much more than just lunch.

"Very well," Abith said. "But when you find yourself questioning the methods of your instructors, as you will, come back and speak with me."

Abith had always been a bold man, so his statement came as no surprise.

"They're not incompetent," Basen said, "as you imply."

"No, they just don't know how to handle someone of your potential." Abith made a shooing motion. "Don't hover there with your food. Either sit and allow me to explain, or get going." His friendly smile diffused the situation, though Basen didn't smile in return. He was curious to know what Abith meant about his potential but decided against staying to find out. Terren and Jack treated Abith like an enemy, so Basen couldn't be associated with him or his men.

He left to sit with Effie, Reela, and Steffen.

"I haven't had the chance to thank the two of you," Basen told Effie and Steffen. "Annah explained everything. I'm sorry you had to fight. If I had known that would happen, I would've come up with a better plan."

"There was no safer option." Steffen spoke with confidence and finality. "I'm glad we went. No thanks necessary."

Effie pointed her fork at Steffen. "What he said. We got Neeko as a result, so it was worth it." She seemed to realize her mistake as her eyes lit up. "Not to imply your mother isn't important."

As long as Juliana was here in one piece, Basen didn't care what Effie thought. "Did my mother really...kill someone?" he asked.

Effie pursed her lips, looking impressed as she remembered it with a nod. "She's a fierce woman when she needs to be."

"That's true." Just as Basen was about to take a bite of his food, someone slapped his back and knocked the fork out of his hand.

"Basen!" Vithos cried with utter joy. "Good talking in Redfield! I'm very proud of you."

"Thank you," Basen said as he retrieved his fork from the floor and wiped it on his napkin.

The Elf danced over to Reela, kissed her cheek, and settled beside her. Just then, a group of students came to stand at the end of their table. There were four of them, all women Basen had seen before but never met. They asked to hear what happened with the Elves.

Vithos seemed excited to tell the tale, ignoring his food as he gestured emphatically with his arms. "Basen took us to Merejic in a portal." He stopped to imitate the whooshing of a portal, then grabbed his stomach. "Make us sick, but necessary."

Others gathered to listen, and soon there was a small audience of students of all classes. Effie and Reela politely took their plates and left, Reela patting Basen on the back on her way to another table.

"Sorry," Basen mouthed to them.

"It's all right," Effie replied.

Steffen didn't seem as uncomfortable, though, finishing his food quickly and listening intently.

It was a relief when Basen was able to slip away later. He was quite nervous when he showed up for Penny's class. He arrived early so she wouldn't scold him in front of the other students, but she wasn't at the training grounds.

He found her inside the Group One classroom. She was leaning over her lecturing podium, making notes on her scrolls. At the sound of his approaching footsteps, she looked up and seemed surprised to see him.

Basen gave her a bashful smile.

When she smiled in return, he thought he might've been wrong about her all this time. Perhaps she wouldn't punish him for leaving without permission. They *had* awarded him a medal, after all.

She was waiting for him to speak, her smile slowly leaving her face.

"Um, sorry I left."

She drummed her fingers on the podium, showing him a confused expression.

He gave her the same look right back.

"Why are you apologizing?" she asked.

"You're right. Allow me to specify. I'm sorry if you took my leaving as an insult. I did not mean it that way."

"How else was I supposed to take it when you recruited one of my best mages—besides yourself—to go with you, and you didn't ask me first?"

It felt awkward to receive a compliment from a clearly annoyed instructor, especially in such a bitter tone.

"We haven't always agreed in the past," he said. "That gave me reason to believe you wouldn't approve of my plan."

"Imagine how different things would be if your plan hadn't worked."

"Yes, I could've been killed."

"Do you realize that, really? Because it doesn't seem as if you do. I'm concerned about you, Basen. I'm concerned about the safety of all my students, but you in particular. Your audacity...has kept me awake nights. I'm glad you went on this trip. You accomplished a lot, and, in doing so, proved what kind of young mage you are."

Her tone made it clear that wasn't a compliment.

"I spoke to Mage Trela," Penny continued. "She agrees with me that you've missed too much training to be part of Group One any longer. It isn't just their skills that allow your *former* classmates to work together so well, it's practice."

His heart dropped like a rock. "I believe I can make up for the time lost. I would be a valuable mage in any group, but more valuable in the top class where my skills will be of more use."

"Your skills will be of use wherever *you* decide to put them. You've made that clear. But we can't have you without a group. Even the troops who came from Tenred, some of them so far below others in their skill levels they wouldn't have been accepted into the Academy otherwise, have been put in groups. It's the only way to train everyone. With that being said, Trela and I agree you should join the group where you're best likely to mesh after having missed so much training. And that is Group Eight."

Basen bit his lip before replying. "I don't suppose it matters whether I agree?"

"Be happy, Basen. Jackrie is the instructor of Group Eight, which is the only reason you weren't put in an even lower group. She vouched for you, and she was the only one to do so of the instructors we spoke to. No one else wants the liability you bring because instructors are responsible for their students' lives." Penny looked back down at her scrolls, picking up her quill once again. "Everyone will be safer with you in that group, including you. It's the right decision."

*****

Basen didn't get a chance to dwell on his demotion. He had to hurry to the Group Eight training area so he wouldn't be late for Jackrie's battle lessons. He had a lot more to lose if he misbehaved further.

Jackrie introduced him, though he already recognized most of his new classmates, and soon he was casting fireballs at training dummies with the rest of them.

During the first break, he asked Jackrie how this group would be different than his last.

"We aren't likely to be the group that Terren sends to the wall unless every mage is to stand behind the parapets and cast at our enemies. We spend most of our time improving our skills rather than going through the different scenarios of attack."

Basen soon saw why this was necessary. The skill gap between him and the others set him apart from them instantly. They couldn't cast for as long, nor were their fireballs large or strong enough to fell an enemy in a single cast. None of them had enough skill with sartious energy to block a fireball, either. Basen couldn't claim that ability yet, and he might never be able to, but Effie and others in his group could.

My old group, he reminded himself. The sooner he accepted his new status, the better.

Gathering energy, forming fireballs, and aiming them

wasn't all that different from running a long distance. There was a proper form but no one style to fit everyone. It seemed that many in this group were still figuring out what suited them best.

Basen felt as if he'd already found his own style and that his time was better spent strengthening his mental endurance and physical ability to hold massive amounts of energy. He also wondered whether he should be training as a swordsman with the warriors. Much of this war had involved the sword already. It seemed prudent.

When Jackrie went to fetch a drink from the nearby water barrel, Basen took advantage of the opportunity to speak with her in private.

"You seem keen on helping everyone individually," he commented.

"Penny doesn't?"

"Not in the way you do. She demands things of each of us, but she doesn't always follow through with instruction."

"Well, that's the benefit of being in Group One. You're expected to have a better grasp on everything related to energy, so you're given more freedom and responsibility."

"That's what I was hoping to speak to you about."

"I figured," she said. "Let me tell you what you need to hear." She drank her water quickly, gazing at her students the same way a worried mother might at her children.

"I don't take attendance in my class," Jackrie said. "But everyone always comes on time. They want to be here, but more importantly, they don't have anywhere better to be. If they did, I wouldn't force them to be here. Do you understand?"

"I do. Thank you."

When dinner hours came, Basen looked for Effie while waiting in line for his food. He found Cleve sitting with Nebre, like before, and the other Group One warriors taking up the rest of table. Next he found Alabell, sitting with the same female Krepp he'd seen her with before. *What an exhausting day.* There was room on the bench across from Alabell. He wanted to be close even if it would amount to nothing. But she hadn't been clear about whether they could remain friends, and he didn't want to impose.

The dining hall was enormous, making it difficult to locate a single person. Eventually he came to the conclusion that Effie wasn't here yet and kept his eyes on the open doors instead. He had his food by the time she came in, and he stared at her until she noticed him. When she did, he gestured at the empty bench in front of him. She nodded.

There were no empty tables with all the new people here, but there were corners and middles just big enough for late arrivers to sit in small groups. He ate as he waited for Effie to get her food, his eyes drawn to Alabell. He knew he shouldn't look but couldn't help it.

Eventually Basen glanced over to find her staring back. She quickly looked down at her plate, and so did he.

Effie came to sit with him. "Penny told me. Group Eight." She moved her fork around her food. "Sorry to hear that."

"At least I'm in Jackrie's class. I need to ask you

something." He and Effie had a tendency to get sidetracked and never return to their original conversation. It was mostly enjoyable, but he didn't have time for it now. "I was speaking to Jackrie, and she's given me the hint that if I don't show up, she'll understand so long as I'm making better use of my time elsewhere."

"You'd have a better chance of strolling into Kyrro's castle than back into Penny's class."

"I figured, but I heard some of the Group Eight mages talking about a class with Neeko. Is he teaching people to use pyforial energy?"

"Why didn't you ask them?"

He tried to look charming as he gave her a wry smile. "Because I wanted to ask *you*."

"You liar. You're trying to avoid getting to know the students who might resent you for leaving them."

He nodded. "Yes, exactly that."

She chuckled. "Neeko *is* teaching...well, trying to teach. It was the reason Terren tried to recruit him earlier."

"I didn't know anyone could say no to Terren."

"Remember, Neeko's the same man who said no to you."

"Why is that so surprising?"

"Because of that speech you gave to him and Shara about the Academy! I didn't know you had such skill with words. Then you showed it wasn't just luck when you gave another speech at Redfield Stadium. The only other person I've seen speak like that without preparation, besides Terren, was...Alex."

They paused a moment. Basen missed the friendly

warrior, but Effie must feel it a thousand times worse. He didn't know much about grief, but it seemed best to give her however much time she needed to compose herself before he continued.

Eventually she looked up and asked him, "What were you going to say?"

"I plan to attend Neeko's class tomorrow. I think it'll be a better use of my time."

"Not from what Neeko told me. No one has made any progress, and he's doubting himself as an instructor."

"Perhaps he's not teaching the right people. Is it Terren who decides who goes?"

"It's open to everyone, but there hasn't been an announcement about it because Terren only wants those who're really interested to take time away from their regular training." She pointed her fork at Basen. "I thought you didn't care about pyforial energy."

"You're to blame for that! You undersold its worth. Now that I know what Neeko can do with it, I'm interested."

"Well, good luck. It took him nearly his whole life to get as proficient as he is."

"Where's his class?"

"The only place large enough. Redfield Stadium."

Basen smiled. Finally, he was excited to be back.

CHAPTER TWENTY-FOUR

Basen hadn't been completely honest with Effie. He still didn't know exactly what Neeko could do with pyforial energy besides move things and himself. But the thought of being able to lift himself into the air was enough to make Basen's imagination go wild with the possibilities. No enemy would be able to slay him except from far range.

From what Annah said, it didn't appear as if Neeko could fly around like a bird during battle, as it drained his stamina too quickly, but Basen had incredible endurance. Perhaps he could do something with the energy Neeko couldn't.

God's mercy, when did I get overconfident? It's the title. Basen the Cunning.

His ability to deliver an important speech had come as a complete surprise, but then again, he'd always been a talker among his haughty friends in Tenred. Who knew that would ever become a useful skill?

He arrived early at Redfield Stadium, but Neeko wasn't there yet. The stadium looked a bit underwhelming. A pile of rocks was pushed up against a wall. An eclectic group of men and women of all ages stood in the arena, some with swords, others with wands. Most were older, and Basen didn't recognize them as members of the Academy staff. One was much younger than the rest: the boy Basen had seen pretending to be a Redfield Champion.

As Basen approached, the boy stopped what he was doing and stood perfectly still as if stunned.

Basen extended his hand. "Hello, I'm—"

"I know who you are! Everyone knows you. I'm Micklin. It's an honor to meet you, Basen the Cunning."

All right, that title definitely doesn't fit. He let out an uncomfortable chuckle. "Just call me Basen. Have you been to this class before?"

"Yes, yesterday. I heard from Effie that pyforial mages have the potential to be the strongest type of mage."

She said that? "So you know Effie?"

"Yes, I'm staying with her, Cleve, Reela, and Steffen. I didn't know they were some of the strongest here at the Academy, like you! It's an honor to sleep in their home, as it is to meet you." He bowed...actually bowed.

"Stop that before someone sees you." Basen gestured for the boy to rise.

"Sorry. I still don't know the customs of the Academy."

"No one bows." Basen softened his words with a smile. "How did you end up staying with them?"

"I met Cleve and Reela in the capital. They recruited me." The boy stood tall and proud. But Basen couldn't imagine it was their idea to bring this child back with them.

"Effie and Reela share their room so I have one to myself," Micklin continued. "All of them are very nice, except Steffen can be strange, but don't tell him that. I like him most of all. He's a chemist, a swordsman, and an archer. Steffen the Beastslayer. He has a title, like you."

Effie and Reela share a room, not Cleve and Reela.

Had the two of them separated for good? If so, it was disappointing news. Basen had seen their devotion to each other. The ground seemed to shift under his feet at the thought of Cleve and Reela being apart.

"Yes, Steffen is a marvel. Maybe one day you'll have a title too. Micklin, the Greatest Pyforial Mage...in the World!"

The boy laughed. "That's a long title, but I'd still use it proudly so long as it was true."

Neeko and Shara arrived together a moment later. Under the morning sun, Neeko's hair was barely more blond than brown. He was of average height, with a youthful face but the physique of someone older. There were two wooden short swords in sheaths on his belt, which Basen hadn't remembered seeing when Neeko had frightened away the three Krepps. Basen was looking forward to finally finding out exactly what Neeko did to scare them.

Shara's thick curls were just as dark and long as Basen had remembered from their meeting in the forest. She seemed happy to be here as she smiled at Neeko, clearly proud of him. She took her place in the midst of the crowd as if she, too, would be learning how to manipulate pyforial energy. Or perhaps she already had a smattering of it and was here to improve her skill. Basen let his excitement turn a smile as he met Neeko's gaze.

"I see there are some new faces," Neeko announced when the crowd hushed. "Basen the Cunning, have you come here to learn pyforial energy?"

Everyone turned to him, sending blood to his cheeks.

"Please, the title isn't necessary. And yes I have."

"I see. Well, for those like Basen who are new here, let me give you a warning. I'm new at teaching others about pyforial energy, and from what I know about bastial and sartious energy, it's a more difficult concept to grasp. I see that many people didn't return to continue their lessons. Part of that might be my fault, but most of it has to do with the difficulty of manipulating the energy."

An older man raised his hand.

Neeko pointed. "Yes?"

"Some of us are only here to see a demonstration. We've heard about what you can do, and we just want to witness it."

"Oh." Neeko seemed surprised, then smiled as if happy to entertain them. "How many came here for the same reason?"

About a third of the sixty people raised a hand.

"I can't speak for everyone," the older man said, "but I don't think I have the mind, and I definitely don't have the time to train every day. I'm a stone mason, and I know some of the others here, like me, are more valuable for what we can do with our hands."

A few of the people around him chuckled.

"All right," Neeko said. "A quick demonstration. Basen, you can use both wand and sword, correct?"

"Correct."

"Then come over here. Everyone else, move back."

"I didn't bring a sword," Basen said as he walked to the front. He could tell by the serious expression on Neeko's face that this would be some sort of duel. He was glad Neeko had chosen him, as he trusted his own ability better than anyone else here and wanted to see just how difficult it would be to face a pyforial mage.

As Basen expected, Neeko drew one of his own blunt practice swords. But he pushed out his palm to stop Basen from approaching.

"I can give it to you from here." Neeko extended his arm while holding the handle of his blade, then let go. The sword floated in the air.

The audience responded with gasps and *ooohs*. Neeko lifted his arm again, then bent his thumb and fingers together to make a claw. His brow furrowed in concentration as the weapon floated over to Basen.

Many clapped and exclaimed in wonder. Neeko's mouth quirked with a hint of a smile, though he remained focused on Basen.

"Attack with whatever technique you think will work," Neeko said. "Basen the Cunning."

Basen didn't want to embarrass this mage, but he needed to find out whether Neeko could defeat him as easily as he made it seem. If Basen couldn't reach him with the blade, he would shoot Neeko with a fireball. *A small one, not with enough force to injure him.*

He knew what Neeko was planning when he didn't draw his other sword. *He's going to disarm me. Let him try.*

Basen gripped the short sword with both hands. "Are you ready, Neeko?"

"Yes."

From what Basen knew about pyforial energy, which admittedly wasn't much, Neeko had to aim it. Obviously, a moving target was more difficult to hit. So Basen charged, making sure to swing his elbows and move the weapon as much as possible. Neeko lifted his hand in the same way a psychic might before a spell. Basen switched the sword to the other side of his body, gripping so hard his knuckles turned white.

He saw it just before it hit him. The energy looked like a blanket of air. It swept in from Basen's side as fast as a sprinting man, slamming into his legs.

Basen put his hand down to keep from rolling when he fell, then he was back on his feet and running again in a heartbeat.

The energy came back from the other direction. The sand and dust from the air gave it a faint yellow color, bending the image of the wall behind it. Basen braced himself as it slammed into his side. God's mercy, it was strong, plucking him off the ground. He let go of the sword so as not to stick himself and landed on all fours like a cat.

Before he could get up, the cushiony energy pressed him down onto the warm sand. He squirmed to try to free himself, but it felt as if a thousand heavy quilts had been tossed on top of him. He flipped onto his back and pushed with all four limbs. The energy didn't feel too different from fatty flesh as he tried to rip it apart, soon discovering it was stuck together completely.

Finally he rolled out from it and was free. He grabbed the wand from the holder on his belt and turned toward Neeko while gathering bastial energy. But what Basen saw made him put up his hands and laugh. "I give up."

Neeko had taken Basen's sword and floated it between them, its tip aimed toward Basen's chest.

Neeko's arm veered and the sword swung to the side. Then Neeko bent his elbow and thrust out his arm, and the sword shot like an arrow toward a wall. Neeko let out a grunt as it stopped short. He pulled his arm toward his stomach, and the sword floated back to him. He grabbed it out of the air and returned it to his sheath.

Basen lifted his hands to clap, noticing others doing the same, but Neeko had another trick for them. He lifted both arms, then brought his elbows to his sides. He took off into the air without moving his limbs in the opposite way a bird might look while diving into the ocean for a fish.

"What in god's world?" was all Basen could mutter as Neeko soared toward the clouds. Everyone in the audience was muttering as he rose higher than the stadium...and kept going.

Basen shielded his eyes from the sun as Neeko finally slowed his ascent. He veered toward the Redfield tower, then toward the opening where Basen had taken the book to read about Fatholl. Neeko tucked in his legs and landed safely inside. He turned and waved.

Basen applauded with the rest, wondering how dangerous that was. Neeko had made it look easy, as it probably was to him now. But he had to have practiced for countless days, months, maybe even years to get to that point. Some of his trials must've threatened his life, but he had much to show for it now.

Along with the awe on people's faces, Basen noticed the same jealousy he felt. There were many people who would choose to fly if granted one wish.

Neeko floated up out of the tower in the same way

someone would lift a pup by the fur on the back of his neck, then arced down toward them. He started slow, showed a burst of speed, then slowed again before his feet touched the sand. He was huffing and sweating.

"Now teach us how to do that," Basen teased, making Neeko and most others laugh.

Unfortunately, Basen soon learned Neeko wasn't as skilled at teaching as he was at manipulating pyforial energy. After those who'd only come for a demonstration left, Neeko had everyone sit or kneel on the hard, gravelly sand.

Neeko explained that moving pyforial energy was nothing like moving the wind. "We don't know how to do that, so that comparison will only confuse you. Instead, think of turning a crank as you try to move the sand with py. You should feel your mind latch onto something, like your hand grabbing the handle of the crank. There should be some resistance as you move the py across the sand."

That was nearly all he had to offer, all of his wisdom poured into a short introduction. Whenever people asked questions, he found a different way to repeat the same information. After a couple hours, a fourth of the people had thanked Neeko and left.

All Basen could feel was bastial energy. He knew Shara was a mage, and when his back and ass needed a reprieve, he went to stand beside her. She didn't notice him, too focused on the sand as she put a finger to each temple.

"Hello," Basen said.

She tilted her head back and squinted. "Hello?"

"I'm not having any luck. As a fellow mage, I was

wondering if I could bother you for a moment."

"Yes, I need a break." She stood and stretched her back.

"All I can feel is bastial energy," Basen said. "Is it the same for you?"

"Yes. I believe it's more difficult to reach the breakthrough point with pyforial energy for mages who've specialized in other energies."

"That's disappointing. How long have you been trying to learn?"

"Since we arrived here a few days ago." She looked over at Neeko, then lowered her voice. "I'm beginning to think I would be of more use elsewhere, but so many have come and left already. I don't want to insult him."

Basen nodded. "It's too bad. I was hoping you might have some advice."

"None. Sorry."

"Thank you anyway."

Basen started off but stopped when she spoke up. "What you said at our cabin..." She glanced at Neeko again, then lowered her voice. "What you said about the Academy...made us think about our lives differently. Did you...exaggerate when you spoke of how you'll fight to your last breath to make sure Tauwin doesn't remain king?"

"Nothing I said was an exaggeration. He murdered the family of the girl I—" He caught himself. "I would fight against him or anyone like him. I should've done more to stop my uncle, and every day I'm thankful I have the chance now to fight against Tauwin. My whole family is here at the Academy now, Shara. This is the best place for them, and I believe it's the best place for you and Neeko, and anyone else who stands for justice."

Neeko joined them and asked, "Any luck?"

"I think you would hear me squeal—nay, the warriors on Warrior's Field would hear me squeal, if I was able to move py," Shara replied.

"I might not squeal *quite* as loud," Basen said, "but you would hear me as well."

Neeko chuckled. "I get it." He sighed. "I wish I knew how to teach better."

"Perhaps this is something many of us are incapable of learning," Basen said. After speaking with Shara, he'd already made the decision to leave. "I hope you don't take offense that I might not return after lunch."

"I don't," Neeko said, though the way his gaze shifted to the ground hinted at disappointment.

"Even if no one else can do anything with pyforial energy, we all know what you can do," Basen told him. "You're one of the most valuable people here. God's mercy, you helped save my mother's life. I'm indebted to you."

Neeko smiled. "It's all right."

Basen politely smiled in return, but no, it wasn't all right. He would do something for Neeko, no matter what it took.

Lunch hours began soon after that. Basen looked for his mother in the dining hall but only found his father.

"Where's Mother?"

Henry stood, grinning like a fool, and grabbed Basen's shoulder. "She's helping the kitchen staff. They're all overworked. We're proud of you. Do you know what she told me when she heard of your accomplishments? She said you're becoming more like me."

"Was that supposed to be a compliment?" Basen teased.

"Be serious," his father responded, losing the smile. "You've learned to speak and plan like a commander. These aren't lessons you've been taught. It must be in your blood."

"You mean the same blood Tegry had?"

Henry frowned. "Don't take that attitude, Basen."

His father was right. Basen wasn't sure why he was being unappreciative. His father was complimenting him, after all, even if it didn't quite sound like it.

"I'm sorry, and you're right as always. In fact, I'm thinking of starting some sword lessons, as it has become abundantly clear that the blade is *almost* as useful to me as my wand."

"I will speak with Warrior Sneary immediately." Henry glanced around, looking ready to run off. "You'll be put with the Group One warriors where you belong."

Basen groaned. *I shouldn't have mentioned anything.* "Actually, I was thinking instead that I would speak with Abith."

"I told you to stop joking."

"I'm not."

CHAPTER TWENTY-FIVE

After Henry was unsuccessful in talking Basen out of his decision to speak to Abith, he convinced Basen to at least wait until tomorrow. Henry would speak to Terren first to ensure there were no political problems with his son seeking instruction from the rebel swordsman.

Basen wouldn't tell his father he wasn't just seeking sword training. Abith had piqued his curiosity by mentioning his potential, and Basen was beginning to see that Abith was correct about the regular Academy instructors being unable to help him reach it. Basen didn't blame Jackrie or Penny. They would train him well, if he gave them the chance, and he was certain they would do everything in their power to keep him alive through battle, as they did for all their students. But recent events had made Basen believe there was more to training than perfecting his fireball and increasing his stamina.

For one, he now knew about pyforial energy. He probably would never have a grasp on it, but just the fact that it was there, and that there was at least one man who could do extraordinary things with it, made Basen believe there had to be other abilities he could attempt. He just had to create an opportunity to discover them.

Abith fought with such speed that Basen figured there was something else to his skill, and he had an idea what it was. Basen had seen a hint of it after endurance day during his first week at the Academy. Cleve—a man as large as some of the smaller male Krepps—had been the first warrior to finish the run. Reela had mentioned that Cleve used bastial energy to feed power to his limbs. She hadn't quite said it like that, but Basen couldn't think of it any other way.

Of course Abith wouldn't teach his mages how to use bastial energy to fight better with a sword. Mages were to stay out of the fray and cast fireballs in support, one of the reasons male mages were regarded with less honor than swordsmen. But there was no doubt in Basen's mind that Abith used bastial energy in the same way Cleve did, only better. Cleve wasn't a mage, after all. He didn't have the same skill over bastial energy that Abith did. *Or that I do.*

Because Basen would be running, jumping, and otherwise making a fool of himself, he wanted privacy to see what he could do with the energy. Unfortunately, there wasn't anywhere like that with sufficient space. Even outside the Academy's walls, he would be seen by the wall guards and any enemies watching from the Fjallejon Mountains.

Unfortunately, it was his best option.

He went up the ramp to get atop the northern wall. At only ten feet tall, it clearly wasn't constructed with the idea it would hold off hordes of enemies. But it was still high enough that Basen needed a way back up without bothering the guards to open the gate for him, so he brought a rope.

A wall guard eyed him suspiciously. Basen asked the man, "Can I tie this to the parapets so I can climb back up after I'm done training?"

"Why don't you train on Warrior's Field with the rest

of the swordsmen?"

"Because I'm not a warrior."

"Then what are you doing with that sword?"

This guard clearly wasn't present during the recent Redfield announcement. Basen saw no way around it, so he explained he was a mage who wanted to hone his skills with the sword in hopes of joining the warriors. It was only half true. While he might fight beside them, he didn't see himself sparring with Krepps and men like Cleve and Peter.

Basen made a mental note to ask Cleve how Peter was faring now that he'd joined forces with Tenred. Basen had gone a while without thinking of Peter, the young man he'd almost killed. Basen couldn't imagine Alabell would ever become as distant in his thoughts. Everything reminded him of her. His pulse increased whenever her image strolled unbidden through his mind.

"You should train elsewhere," the guard told him. "If it must be outside these walls, then go over to the western wall."

But this was closest to the dining hall, where Basen would return when he was done, and the Academy was enormous, the western wall a mile away.

"Why?" Basen asked. The last thing he wanted was to get in an argument with a wall guard, but walking a mile and then back seemed like a waste of time. He was eager to get started and see what he could do with bastial energy. He'd never tried moving it into his limbs before.

"I can't say." The guard pointed to the west. "But I can't allow you over this wall."

That piqued Basen's curiosity. He walked to the

western wall, staying on the northern side of the Academy. When he arrived at the northwestern corner, he had to tell the wall guard there the same tale, but this one let him jump down.

Basen looped the rope around one of the parapets and dangled the other end over the wall. He didn't need it to get down, but he would need it to climb back up.

The ground felt different outside the Academy. On this western side, there was a field of grass before the trees began, while the Fjallejon Mountains stretched out to block Basen's view of the ocean he knew to be about ten miles away.

He drew his sword, then looked up to see if the guard was watching him. As they made eye contact, the guard looked away. No doubt he would be checking on Basen.

This would be embarrassing, but Basen would make sure it was worth it. His father might take more than a day to speak to Abith, as was common when Henry didn't want to do something and thought he could get away with delaying it.

Terren had mentioned opportunities arising now that the Elves were gone, and Basen might be selected for something. It wasn't that he wished to leave the Academy again—it was here that he truly believed he could get his best training done—but he might as well prepare just in case.

Before he began, he checked around the corner of the wall. He thought he saw someone jumping down near where he'd been earlier. The man wasn't close enough for Basen to make out his features, but whoever he was, and whatever he was doing, he was the reason the guard didn't want Basen over there.

Perhaps this was another student who felt he had more to learn training on his own. No, if that was the case, the wall guard wouldn't have forced Basen to leave. This had to be an instructor if not someone higher up on the political scale.

Basen climbed back up the rope to get on top of the wall.

"Done already?" the nearby wall guard asked.

"For now."

Basen walked along the base of the wall until he came to the ramp closest to the first wall guard, then went up.

"You again." The man put up his hands for Basen to stop. "You shouldn't be up here."

Basen feigned confusion. "Why?" He came to the parapets and looked over the side.

Abith Max, a training sword in his right hand, had his fists on his hips as he smirked back up at Basen.

The guard's rough hand grabbed Basen's shoulder. "You don't listen." He pulled Basen away from the parapets, then pushed him toward the ramp. "You must leave."

"Abith, what are you doing down there?" Basen called as he backed away from the guard.

"I told you to go!" The guard drew his sword. "I will throw you off this wall if I must."

"You're going to do that with your sword out?"

The guard's mouth curled as he seemed undecided about whether to put his sword away. No doubt this was the most action he'd seen in a while.

"It's fine," Abith hollered. "Let him stay."

The guard seemed annoyed by this request. He kept his sword up as he told Abith, "I don't think you have the authority to decide that."

Why wouldn't Abith have the authority to let Basen stay with him? There were no rules about going over the wall at this exact spot, so why was this circumstance special?

"Are you seriously going to throw him off the wall?" Abith asked with a light laugh. "Just let him be."

"Fine." The guard slammed his sword back in its sheath. "But I was against this." He gave them no privacy as he stood still with his arms folded.

"Come down here, Basen," Abith requested. He appeared happy to see Basen, but he always wore that proud smile.

Basen hopped down and had the strangest feeling they were about to duel. It wouldn't matter that Basen had a real steel sword while Abith wielded a blunt one of wood. His former instructor could defeat him easily. *Abith probably could defeat two of me.*

"You impressed me with your sword fighting."

Unsure why Abith was waiting for him to respond, Basen rolled his eyes and shrugged. "I suppose you impressed me as well."

Abith laughed. "You know, Basen, you're the first mage I've met who's like me."

"A number of things can follow that observation. Not many are good, so I hope you're not about to insult us both."

Abith tilted his head down to give Basen a knowing look as he produced a wand with his other hand. "I speak of your ability to cast and cut."

"Anyone can cut." Basen sliced his sword down between them. "Anyone with fingers to grip a sword."

"But not many of them can defend themselves against me as long as you did." His smile returned as he stepped toward Basen aggressively. Basen quickly fixed his sword to defend himself. But Abith merely chuckled and stepped back. "See, it's in you. If I'd known you were this kind of fighter, our training sessions would've been different."

"And what kind of fighter is that?"

"The kind that you and I are. I watched you spar with the others when you were younger." He looked unimpressed as he flattened his mouth and shook his head. "I didn't see anything amazing, but you've improved a lot since then."

"So has Sanya, yet I don't hear you mentioning her. What are you getting at?"

"Sanya? Who in god's world is that?"

That's right, Abith hasn't met the new Sanya. Wait, they had to have met at some point in Tauwin's castle. If not, he must at least remember her as an awful child in Tenred.

"Sanya Grayhart. Haven't you heard about her?"

"Does it matter?"

"Yes, she's dangerous."

"So am I." Abith lifted his eyebrows in mockery of the situation, clearly undeterred.

"It doesn't matter. What are you doing here?"

"The same thing as you. I'm here to improve."

Basen stepped back and spread his arms. "Then let's

see how someone like you has learned to fight so well. Show me what you do to improve."

Abith put up his finger as if about to give a lesson. "For some of us, fighting isn't a skill to be learned. It's something we inherently know and just have to refine. There are many capable men who find themselves to be good with both wand and sword at an early age. They choose to train in one skill, and soon they stop improving the other. But you and I have chosen both, and now we can use one to help train the other."

It was Basen's turn to smile. He'd figured Abith must use bastial energy for something more than making fireballs, and his former instructor had all but confirmed it.

"Show me a portal," Abith blurted.

"What? Why?"

"Because I want to see it again." There was frightening determination in his raspy voice and something about his eyes that made Basen nervous. Abith looked obsessed, as if he'd dreamed of making portals every night since Basen had done so in front of him.

"I can't make one just anywhere," Basen explained. He wasn't sure he wanted to say more. If Abith learned to make portals, would it be safe for the Academy?

"Then where can you make one?"

"How about we focus on sword training instead." Basen tried to distract Abith by lifting his blade to start a duel.

Abith didn't lift his own weapon, so Basen came at him, but Abith still refused to move.

"Ha!" Basen feigned a strike at Abith's stomach.

Looking bored, Abith swiped his arm in a flash and

knocked Basen's sword out of his hand.

"Oh." Basen let his shoulders droop in disappointment as he retrieved his sword.

Abith frowned. "How am I supposed to shape you into the fighter I know you can be if you won't trust me?"

"I suppose it's too much to ask for you to trust me while I don't trust you?"

"Yes."

He snatched up his sword and pointed it at Abith. "Except I've given you no reason to distrust me, while there are plenty of reasons to distrust you."

"Interesting how you talk about distrust instead of trust."

"It's the same thing."

"No, it isn't. You speak as if I'm supposed to trust you until you give me a reason not to. But you haven't given me a reason to trust you. Don't you see the difference?"

Basen had almost forgotten how attentive Abith was to detail. Of course Basen knew what Abith was talking about. Basen had made a point to phrase it exactly as he had.

Abith's smile grew wider. "You thought I wouldn't notice. You should know by now I notice everything. I also know you're stalling about the portals."

"I—"

Abith put up his hands. "You're right—I *have* given you reasons to distrust me. It'll take time for you to trust me as you once did. In the meantime, let me assure you I'm not asking about portals in hopes of making one myself. I need to know because we are allies, and I plan to use your skill to win this war."

Basen believed Abith *did* have intentions of making portals, but that he also would use Basen's skills to win the war. Abith had already betrayed Tauwin. There was no way the young king, as foolish as he was, would take Abith back. That made Abith and Basen allies, at least against Tauwin.

"A portal can be opened only where bastial energy has been gathered many times before."

"How many times must bastial energy be gathered to make a portal?" Abith asked.

Of course he would be the only person to pose such a specific question.

"I don't know." Basen blew out a frustrated breath so Abith would know not to interrupt him with such silliness again. "A lot, but it depends on the amount. Probably hundreds of fireballs or a few massive surges of bastial energy. The portal can only lead to somewhere I've been before, where enough energy has been gathered over time. Those are the only facts I know. Everything else is theory."

"Tell me of the theory."

So Basen went on to explain portals as holes in "walls" that can't be seen. When energy is gathered in one spot over time, it weakens the wall. Before he could say more, Abith interrupted him.

"What would happen if one of these walls breaks apart from too much gathered energy?"

"I don't know. Perhaps a portal would be created until the world rebuilt the wall."

"Do you think a portal could become permanent?"

"It doesn't seem possible. A portal is a gateway that

needs stability. Whenever I've made one, I feel like I'm forcing open a door. The bigger the portal, the more difficult it is to keep it from closing. Small portals might be formed on their own from broken walls, but I would imagine they close so quickly we never see them."

He didn't want to say more, as soon the conversation would turn to akorell metal, and specifically the akorell stone Basen had in his room.

Terren's voice surprised him from above. "Basen, what are you doing here?"

"I told him to leave, headmaster," the wall guard said. "Abith argued for him to stay."

What am I doing here...? What are YOU doing here?

"Throw him the rope," the headmaster said to the guard, and the man tied one end around the parapets and tossed the other down. "Climb up, Basen."

He looked at Abith, still trying to figure out what was going on. Abith shrugged. "Better do as the headmaster says."

CHAPTER TWENTY-SIX

Basen begrudgingly climbed up. He studied Terren and caught sight of the hilt of a training sword in the headmaster's scabbard as Terren turned his hip to hide the weapon. Basen gasped, then let out a proud smile to show he knew exactly what he'd stumbled upon.

These two were enemies. Each man's safety depended on the other's death. They were only allies because Tauwin and Ulric's massive armies had joined forces, and yet Terren and Abith had come here to spar. Of course it was in private, for if anyone found out, Terren's judgment might be put into question. The instructors would certainly advise him against training with the man who meant to steal his job.

At the same time, Abith's troops would look at him with raised eyebrows. He was their leader, and they expected him to lead the Academy one day, securing their futures in the process. To see Abith training with the current headmaster was akin to him accepting his rival as an equal, maybe even a friend.

Terren cursed. "You can't tell anyone about this. Especially not your father."

Of course, Henry was always the last to trust people. He wouldn't agree with Terren's choice to be here with Abith.

"I won't," Basen said, "but first tell me why you would train with each other?"

"Shall I remove him?" the annoying wall guard asked

the headmaster.

"It's fine," Abith called up from below. "Tell him why, *headmaster*." He spoke the title in a tone of both praise and jest, as if he were teasing an old friend. *This is not the first time they've trained together,* Basen realized. *They've come here often.*

"It shouldn't be hard to believe that the challenge of facing each other is worth the ramifications of anyone finding out," Terren said as he got his long legs over the parapets and let himself down. He was about the same size as Cleve, towering over Abith as they faced each other. Terren then looked up at Basen as if trying to shoo him with his eyes.

Basen folded his arms. "I have to witness what I'm not supposed to tell anyone about."

Terren sighed. "You'd better be as good at keeping this secret as you were about your secret plot with Fatholl."

"I promise I will be."

Abith tried to poke Terren in the ass while he wasn't looking, but Terren noticed his enemy's movement out of the corner of his eye and swiped his sword behind him. Suddenly, the two men were engaged in a fierce duel.

Abith's attacks were quick and light while Terren's were slower and more powerful. Basen had been taught that quickness always beats strength, but he found himself hoping that wasn't the case as he watched Terren step away defensively.

It was concerning that neither wore a protective tunic, but Basen soon realized their skill prevented them from severe injuries. They knew how to protect themselves too well for a wooden sword to do permanent damage.

It only took a moment for Basen to see that Terren used the same techniques as Cleve. Both seemed to prefer blocking an attack rather than deflecting it, creating the opportunity to counterattack and surprise their opponents. Terren even began to sweat like Cleve, a ring of it on his chest like a necklace as his forehead glistened.

The headmaster surprised both Basen and Abith when he blocked Abith's sword with his own, then jumped toward his opponent and delivered a kick to his chest.

Abith stumbled back two steps, though his composure didn't break. He fought with more tenacity and speed as he came at Terren again. He spun around and smacked Terren in the side of his leg. Had it been a real blade, Terren would've been cut, though not deeply. Had it been his usual bastial steel sword, however, it might've sliced through to bone.

It was a clear point, but Basen had assumed the kick would've scored Terren a point as well, yet neither man stopped.

It didn't take long for Abith to score a few more strikes. He won his points with grace, never reacting with a shout or a strut. A subtle smirk never left his face, though. Basen could see by their expressions that both men knew Terren was losing.

This only seemed to make him fight harder. Terren's face took on a look of deep concentration as his mouth fell open. The only time it closed was when Abith made another strike against flesh. However, none were blows that would've led immediately to Terren's death, even if done with a bastial steel sword. He could only catch Terren's limbs, never his torso.

Eventually, Terren delivered his own strike, and it was nothing like Abith's light pokes. The headmaster had finally gotten an offensive going, forcing Abith to dodge a downward strike, then a punch aimed at his chin. Terren was able to push him off balance before Abith could counterattack, and then followed up with a fierce jab of his sword into Abith's unprotected stomach. It was hard enough to knock Abith down. He grunted in pain.

Terren appeared concerned, but Abith put his hand up. "I'm all right."

"There was someone Vithos and I fought on the mountaintop," Basen said. "Bigger than any man I've seen."

Terren and Abith looked up at him. They both seemed tired, as they should be. This was the first break in at least half an hour. Basen could think of no better time to bring up the one thing about his recent excursion that bothered him more than Fatholl still being alive.

"No psychic could harm him, not even Vithos or Fatholl. He fought with a shield and an axe, both of bastial steel. I watched him cleave an Elf and lift him off the ground as if the Elf weighed nothing. This giant practically laughed at me when I tried to shoot him with a fireball, absorbing it with his shield."

Silence followed as the two men waited for Basen to continue.

"None of the students or instructors speak of it, but we all know battle is coming soon. We will see him again."

Then, as if Basen hadn't spoken, the two of them turned to each other and began to fight once more. They poured their concentration into studying each other as they alternated between defending and attacking.

At first, Basen figured they were fighting until a victor was chosen. But as the hour came to an end and they were still scoring points as if this was a real fight, Basen realized this was not the case.

They both moved as quickly as students half their age. Even as Terren sweated through his shirt, he never lost his vigor. Meanwhile, Abith remained as quick as a cat. The only time he lost his smile was when Terren did something unexpected, like spinning and kicking Abith's sword out of his hand. Basen was amazed at the headmaster's agility, figuring he must use bastial energy in the same way Cleve and Abith did.

Eventually, Basen was able to forget about the giant atop the mountain and focus purely on this duel. He felt the itch to fight, to do what he came here to do. He knew bastial energy could help him be a better swordsman, and this was proof. He saw it work for Terren and Abith in their sudden bursts of speed and strength that couldn't otherwise be explained.

Basen eventually lost track of how many points each man scored, as it obviously mattered not to them. Finally, Terren put out his hand and stepped away from Abith.

"Enough for me."

"Very well."

Terren whistled, and the wall guard came over and tied the rope to the parapets once again. He looked in each direction before telling Terren, "It's clear."

The headmaster climbed up first, then put his sweaty hand on Basen's shoulder and looked into his eyes.

"Every man can be killed."

There was something about hearing that from Terren that put Basen's mind at ease. The headmaster hadn't shown even an inkling what to do about this threat, yet Basen still trusted him to handle it. There was comfort in that.

Terren and the wall guard left, but Abith stayed and told Basen to wait.

Basen left his own sword on the wall, then jumped down to stand in front of Abith. "Did my father speak to you?"

"No. Do you need his permission to train with me?"

"No, but it would make my life easier."

Abith grinned and patted Basen on the back. Both he and Terren seemed to be in better spirits after their session. "If that's the path you choose, then fine." Abith started to walk toward the wall, clearly having decided Basen wasn't ready to train with him.

"Wait," Basen said. "Can I use your training sword?"

Abith smirked. "Saw something you want to try for yourself, did you?"

Basen nodded and caught the sword Abith tossed to him.

"That's *my* training sword, so I expect you to treat it better than you would your own," Abith said. "Bring it back to me at Warrior's Field before dinner hours."

Finally, after everyone else had gone, even the wall guard, Basen was alone. He whispered,, "Prepare yourself, Ovira, for Basen Hiller!" He grabbed bastial energy out of the air and readied his sword for the most powerful swing he'd ever made, then moved the bastial energy into his arms, and...

"Ow!"

He cursed and flapped his arms like a fat bird too heavy to achieve flight. He hoped nobody had seen him burn himself, and he especially hoped Abith hadn't seen him toss the sword by accident. Basen picked up Abith's weapon and placed it at the base of the wall where he could find it again. Basen didn't want to risk hurling it against the wall, and it seemed as if it might take time to figure out how to do this.

One thing was for certain, pain meant he was doing it wrong. He gathered less energy this time, reminding himself that warriors like Cleve and Terren could do this, so it probably didn't take much energy. He sucked in air through his teeth as he spread the energy down his arms and felt his skin singeing. It was still too much.

Something occurred to him. Cleve and Terren probably couldn't grab bastial energy from the air because that would mean they could make light. *They have to be using the energy already within their bodies.* This energy was easier to manipulate, and there was less of it.

Basen closed his eyes and concentrated. There was probably enough energy within him to make a tiny fireball if he forced it into a ball and mixed in sartious energy from his wand. So just to be safe, he removed his wand from its sheath and set it next to Abith's sword. The last thing Basen needed was to scorch his insides. He thought of Penny and her distrust of his abilities. She'd always assumed he would hurt himself or others, and he didn't want to prove her right.

As he kept his eyes shut, the wind was all he could hear. It did nothing to disrupt the energy he felt mostly in his chest and stomach but also in his limbs. Bastial energy had a feeling similar to a feather resting on him or a soft blanket of heat when there was more of it. BE was trapped beneath his skin, no doubt doing something to keep him alive, though no one had proven the health benefits of it yet. Psychics had only confirmed it was in every living creature. Basen had felt the effects of it leaving his body when he needed every last bit of energy for fire. It had made him sick and cold, as if death was creeping closer, ready to grab him and never let go.

He took hold of the energy in his torso and tried to move it into his right arm, but all he managed to do was drag it out of his chest and press it against the skin of his arm.

Next he tried directing the energy through his shoulder and then down his arm, but when he got it there he felt no different. He hurried over to grab Abith's sword and take a test swing, but the excess energy had left his arm.

Basen put the sword back down and closed his eyes. For a while, he tested the energy in his body in various ways. He noticed it was much harder to pull bastial energy from the air into his body than it was to draw out the energy already there and then stuff it back in. It was as if the energy in his body was different than that in the air, making his body more able to accept it.

Psyche, he remembered, was the manipulation of

someone's personal bastial energy. There had to be something unique about it, a connection between it and his feelings. Perhaps even his thoughts?

Meditation...what had Nick said about it? *It's like breathing, the energy flowing in and out without effort.* Basen felt chills as everything he knew about bastial energy was connecting.

If psychics could manipulate bastial energy to make people feel real pain, then Basen should be able to manipulate his own energy to...

He forgot the world around him as he kept his eyes shut and focused.

It could've been five minutes or thirty before he opened his eyes again. He felt as if he'd just awakened from a week of sleep as he had to squint against the brightness of the evening sun, momentarily forgetting where he was but not what he was doing.

His legs were tingling as if anticipating a race. He burst into a sprint and let out a manic laugh. He ran faster and faster, feeling as if he could take flight if he jumped.

He approached a tree, its lowest branch about as high as the Academy's wall. He leapt and felt as if he were in a dream where gravity didn't exist. He soared so high he frightened himself and flailed his legs. His hand brushed against the branch before he finally sank down to earth.

He stumbled into a somersault, then rolled.

When he came to a stop, he lifted his arms and held in a shout of triumph to release it only as a guttural whisper. "Yesssss!"

Looking up at the branch, he let out a curse of surprise. It really was about as tall as the Academy's wall.

He raised his arm and extended his fingers to judge the distance that he'd jumped. It was about the length of his leg…his entire leg. He'd really jumped that high? Then he saw how far he'd run from the wall. *God's mercy.*

He had to make sure he could reproduce the same results. So he focused his mind again, keenly aware of exactly what he was doing with the energy. He readied himself much quicker this time, then broke into a sprint. The grass at his feet became a blur. He'd always been a decent sprinter, a better jumper, and an excellent distance runner, beating his friends in any contest of stamina, but never had he felt control over his body as precisely as this.

He kept running, needing to find out just how fast he could go. But even though he wasn't fatigued, his body soon slowed to the speed he was used to. He felt none of the same burst of energy in his legs.

He tried to conjure up more energy as he ran, but all he ended up doing was dragging it out of the upper half of his body and instantly draining his stamina, suddenly feeling cold and tired.

He sat right there and threw his arms around himself. It only took a few moments to feel right again, but he'd learned his lesson. These bursts of energy were just that—bursts. And now his legs felt as if he'd run a few miles. They were tight and hot, and probably would cause him pain tomorrow. Normally he wouldn't care, except injury might stop him from training further, and he had so much to explore now.

He wasn't a psychic, but it almost felt as if he was performing psyche on himself to achieve this result. The key wasn't moving energy from the air or from one part of his body into his legs, it was using the energy already there—his natural energy—to push his body to its limit.

"As humans, we're born with the idea that we're capable of extraordinary things," Basen said as he paced in circles. "Children fantasize they have powers to the point of actually convincing themselves they might. This fades with time as we get older, but only after we fail to achieve these abilities. Many people, like me, still fantasize about discovering abilities that break the rules."

Basen wasn't sure who he was talking to, exactly. He'd just felt compelled to find an explanation as to why he felt like a little boy again. There were definitely limitations to these bursts of energy, but he was confident he would find a way of pushing his body a lot further than he had today.

He jogged back to the wall, glad to be able to use the energy in his legs once again. Instead of pushing himself to the utmost speed he could achieve, he kept his slower pace to see if this energy could increase his stamina.

By the time he got to the wall, his legs already felt better than before. It was as if he'd let them rest. *This is how Cleve finished first.*

Basen could only imagine what he could accomplish once he learned how to use this energy more efficiently. He looked around for the wall guard but saw only unfamiliar men patrolling the wall.

"Excuse me," he called to one of them.

"You must be Basen," the man replied. "The other guard left with the rope. He told me I shouldn't open the gate for you, so you'll have to go around to one of the other sides."

That was no problem, for Basen wanted to jog anyway. Actually, the wall was looking rather low…

He went to grab his wand and Abith's sword, putting both in their respective sheaths. He strengthened his legs with energy as he envisioned the jump, then got a running start and leapt. He still hadn't gotten used to the feeling of flying as he propelled himself up and got his hands around the small stone blocks that made the parapets. He pulled himself up and over, then smiled at the surprised wall guard.

"Bastial hell, it's like you have Kreppen blood in you."

So this is why meditation is taught to all mages at an early age. There was no doubt it would help recoup stamina. It would take time to be able to use the energy in the same way he used his muscles, without concentrating to do so, but he was certain he'd get there eventually. When doing it correctly, it felt like flexing his mind toward a part of his body, almost like aiming his hand to grab something.

Basen cursed as he noticed the Redfield clock. Dinner hours were almost over!

He grabbed his sword, ran down the ramp to the dining hall, and hurried inside. He found Abith sitting with his usual group of followers, as if his training session with Terren had never happened.

Basen stopped short. Should he give Abith back his sword in front of everyone? Abith stopped eating when he noticed Basen holding the wooden weapon behind his leg and trudged over angrily.

"You were to meet me at Warrior's Field." He put his

arm around Basen and turned him away from the table. "You cannot return my sword here."

"I'm sorry. I didn't notice the time until it was too late."

Abith grew his usual smile. "Have something to show me, then?"

Basen mimicked his smile. "I do indeed."

"Good. Bring my sword to the northern wall at the same time tomorrow. Bring yours as well."

"So, Terren...?"

"Yes, he'll be there. I need his approval to do what I have planned for you."

CHAPTER TWENTY-SEVEN

In the morning, Basen awoke early with newfound appreciation for the sword. He dressed and practically skipped out the door. His schedule was a dream. First, a delicious breakfast, then training until lunch, then more delicious food, and then he would find out what Abith had planned for him. Abith probably expected Basen to already have some grasp over using bastial energy for bursts of strength, so Basen would do everything in his power to improve as much as possible before their meeting. Abith was a fickle man who judged people quickly. He might lose interest if Basen couldn't keep up.

By the time Basen reached the dining hall, breakfast hours had only just begun, yet the enormous room was about half full. He was headed toward the line when his heart slammed like a bell chime against his chest. Alabell walked toward him, wearing a dress of white that made her auburn hair look like a sunset. Suddenly it felt as if his tongue had rolled down into his throat. His chest tightened as he struggled for breath.

Her skin glowed as she walked beneath the beams of light streaming in through the windows. The gentle slope of her neck to her elegant shoulders led Basen's eyes down her body. Her curves were accentuated by her dress, all the way to where it fell to her knees. He drank her in and couldn't stop, completely undone by her perfection. She halted in front of him and shared her most gentle, most forgiving smile, as if telling Basen he was being rude yet excusing him for it at the same time.

"You're staring."

All sense of hunger, gone. All excitement for training, gone. All he wanted was her.

He felt nearly satisfied to stand close to her. Nearly. But he wanted more. There had to be some sort of energy yet to be discovered, for he felt it when he was near Alabell, his body aflame, every sense in tune with her. She was the only thing more powerful than the strongest psychic.

The silence had gone on too long. He had to say something. *Make her laugh.*

"It was you," he blurted.

God's mercy, he wanted to slap himself.

"What was me?"

She frowned, but he couldn't stop now. "It was you who entered my thoughts when I was in the worst pain of my life. It was you who saved me."

"Basen..." She cast her gaze down. "I can't..."

"Everything felt right when I met you. And as I got to know you...as I caught a glimpse of what it would be like to be with you, it felt like we'd been together for years. I know you, and you know me too." He shook his head. He sounded like a bumbling idiot. "I don't know how to explain it, and yet I can tell you feel the same way."

She nodded, still refusing to look up at him.

"No matter how right the rest of my life is now," he said, "it just doesn't feel right without you."

"I have to go."

He felt like a fool as she hurried off. Looking back at him, she seemed almost mesmerized. She bumped into a

Krepp, bounced off his bare chest, and fell to the floor.

Basen was there in a flash to help her up. The Krepp said nothing as he walked around them. Meanwhile, Basen couldn't take his hand off her arm, barely resisting the urge to pull her close and kiss her.

He'd met other women like Alabell who'd made his heart race, but none had *this* effect on him. He felt like they were two magnets and it went against his nature to stand so close without coming together.

His other half.

"I really do have to go," she said, her hand coming down onto his and squeezing. "That Krepp you met is waiting for me. It's why I had to eat early. There's too much for us to do, and it takes an eternity to communicate the simplest things."

"All right," Basen said, his reluctance obvious.

But Alabell didn't move. She looked down and realized she still held his hand, then carefully peeled it off like unwrapping a bandage. Basen felt as if she'd left him with an exposed wound. He needed her to return and touch him again for it to heal. She matched his gaze the whole way and was fortunate she didn't run into anyone else.

Basen looked around and remembered he was here to eat. His appetite came back slowly as he waited in line. When he got his plate of food, he looked around for someone to sit with and found Cleve beside Nebre. Basen went to join them.

Cleve actually smiled as he looked up from his food. "You've done well."

"Well, thank you, Cleve. And how are the new Krepps

faring?"

"Excellent. They fight well together, and they've been teaching the other Krepps better than we've been able to."

"They understand human customs better," Nebre added. "But my father is trying to learn more every day."

"*Lu ro*...how do I say 'happy'?" Cleve asked.

"*Heez.*"

"*Lu ro heez pa felks?*"

"No." Nebre looked at Basen in a way that made it clear an explanation was coming. "He's not happy with humans, but he's happy with the Academy."

"Your Kreppen is coming along nicely," Basen told Cleve.

"Not as quickly as I'd hoped."

"If only you could learn language by swinging a sword, you'd be a master in a week. Speaking of sword swinging, what's happened with Peter since his return?"

Cleve set down his spoon, appearing slightly perturbed. "Do you want the truth?"

"Always, Cleve."

"With Alex gone, Peter has become my best teammate." Cleve put up his hand and spoke quickly before Basen could say anything. "Peter knows how I fight better than anyone else because he's studied me in hopes of beating me."

"So the two of you fight together now?"

"They haven't been defeated in team combat," Nebre commented.

"What about solo?"

"I've lost to Rickik a few times now," Cleve replied.

"He's improving quickly here, and he's stronger than I am." At first it sounded like Cleve was making an excuse, but then Basen realized the warrior was speaking about his defeat to compliment Rickik.

"I'm glad the headache of getting them here will be worth it," Basen said. "I met Micklin recently. I heard he stays with you."

Cleve seemed focused on his meal, so Basen let him eat for a while. Only when the warrior was done did he lean back and speak about the boy.

"He complains often that he isn't useful, and I always have to convince him that he is. Just because he doesn't fight doesn't mean he has little to offer."

"Like Nebre, for example," Basen said and smiled at the Krepp.

"Thank you," Nebre replied with a silly grin of his long mouth. "But I do fight."

"Oh." It was hard to imagine.

"I train, but I'm not very good. I have been wanting to ask you if you met Zoke when you returned to Merejic?"

Basen sighed as he realized he couldn't lie to Nebre.

"I did. He wants you to go to Regash Forest to help him..." But Basen could bend the truth without guilt. "When you're done with us."

Nebre appeared confused.

"He said you're friends," Basen added.

"He said that?"

"Why wouldn't he?"

Nebre wouldn't answer, his lizard eyes focused on the table. Eventually, his head began to shake back and forth as if telling himself "no."

"Zoke smiled when he'd found out you'd written a book about the war," Cleve told Nebre.

The Krepp appeared even more confused, deep wrinkles bending the scales across his forehead.

"Whatever happened between you," Basen said, "he doesn't care about it anymore."

"He must still care because I tried to kill him. I called him a coward. I was wrong, but I never spoke to him again."

Basen couldn't believe this peaceful Krepp had tried to kill Zoke. Cleve seemed stunned as well.

"He's forgiven you," Basen said.

But Nebre shook his head. "Krepps do not forgive because we do not apologize. They accept or allow for change. I suppose, somehow, he has accepted me as friend, even though there has not been a chance for change. It's difficult to explain to humans." He put his palms flat against the table and stood. "I would like to see him. How far is Regash Forest and why does he need my help?"

Basen sighed again. This was what he'd feared. "It's in Kilmar, but I can create a portal there when you're ready. The Elves have used psyche to persuade Krepps to build a home there and perhaps one day attack us humans. Zoke is trying to maintain peace, but it will take many months for them to build their new settlement. I doubt they'll attack until it's done. Stay with us a while longer. We need you."

Nebre sat. "I will."

Basen relaxed as he leaned back and let out his breath. He was eager to finish his meal and get to training.

But soon the conversation with Cleve turned to using bastial energy in their limbs to fight, and Basen found better use of his time here.

He ended up staying in the dining hall with Cleve throughout breakfast hours.

*****

Basen was thankful when Cleve offered to skip morning battle training to help Basen get a better grasp on using bastial energy for combat. Though, Basen secretly hoped Cleve would learn something himself before the two of them were done.

They had until lunch before Basen would need to eat and then meet with Abith and Terren. He wouldn't dare break his promise to Terren to keep the sparring sessions with Abith a secret, even if Cleve was his nephew. The politics of it were too messy. But battle was coming. Everyone had to do what they must to prepare, so Basen appreciated Abith and Terren training.

Weapons of war were in construction: catapults and ballistae. Kyrro wasn't large enough for Tauwin to find anywhere to hide his, so he kept them in the open at the edge of Oakshen, where scouts of Kyrro's Allies could easily track the work. Meanwhile, Ulric's men atop the Fjallejon Mountains had a clear view of the Academy's weapons of war that Basen had heard were being built in the southeastern section of the campus, where the wide road ran between the classrooms and the farms.

Cleve brought Basen with him to Warrior's Field, where he asked Sneary for permission to train with Basen until the afternoon. Sneary hardly had to think about it before he allowed Cleve to separate from the group. They found plenty of open room on the outskirts of the grass where they wouldn't be bothered and took out their training swords. Basen still had Abith's practice sword and hoped Cleve wouldn't do anything to damage it.

"It seems strange," Basen commented, "that the use of energy to boost strength isn't taught or even discussed."

"Not as strange as the lack of discussion about learning Kreppen." Cleve warmed up his arms with a few showy swings of his sword. "There are many things a man can learn either on his own or through the help of others, yet very little of it is required to make us good fighters. Besides, most warriors do try using energy at first. They give up before they notice any benefit. Are you ready?"

"We're just going to fight? That's it?"

"We spent long enough at breakfast going over how to use the energy. It's time to practice."

Cleve came at Basen with half speed. The big warrior showed well in advance that he would be bringing his sword down in an obvious strike. Basen stepped aside and tried to teach Cleve a lesson for going too easy on him, attempting to strike Cleve's hip with a burst of speed.

But Cleve got his sword down in a flash to block Basen and kicked his ankle. As he stumbled, Cleve poked him in the arm with his wooden sword.

"That was good," Cleve said. "But you have to remember to defend yourself. That's the biggest weakness of using a new power. We strive to use it even when it isn't opportune to do so. I advise you to think first about improving your defense with bastial energy. Then focus on your offense."

"A fireball to your chest might be the only defense I can use to stop you."

Cleve looked intrigued. "I always figured mages couldn't cast while they fight. Can you?"

"I was joking, mostly. It's difficult to cast while moving. The bastial energy for a fireball has to be gathered into a single point for it to become hot enough to burn the sartious energy that's fed into it from our wands. I can't imagine anyone doing that while engaged in melee combat."

Cleve nodded. "Again." He rushed Basen this time.

He felt his arms go hot as he flexed muscles with the newfound strength from bastial energy. Cleve unleashed a combination of four attacks that had certainly been practiced hundreds of times, the precision of his longsword like the needle of a master sewer.

But Basen's strength held up. He moved his sword faster than he ever had before to block each strike. Cleve stepped in and tried to punch Basen in the stomach. Unable to focus energy into his legs to get out of the way fast enough, he used his hands to block the attack. He caught Cleve's fist and pulled it past his turned body, then extended his foot to trip his opponent.

Cleve stumbled only a bit, recovering before Basen could hope to counterattack.

"God's mercy," Basen complained, shaking his hands. His palms felt on fire. Why had he thought he could catch

Cleve's punch? He'd even been stupid enough to drop his weapon.

"That's not how you block a punch," Cleve said with a snicker. "Although I must admit I've never seen that method before. Were you never taught how?"

"No. There was no punching or kicking among swordsmen in Tenred."

"Why?"

"That's a good question. It's too bad I don't have the answer." He picked up Abith's sword and flicked off a blade of grass. "So how do I block your boulder fists?"

"Boulder fists, hmm?" Cleve grinned as he looked at his hands. "Not by catching them. Let me show you. Try to punch me."

"No thank you. That sounds like the beginning of the explanation as to why I'm in the medical building."

"How else are you going to learn?"

"I have ears. You can explain it."

"Fine. You have to use your forearms to block me above the elbow. Make sure it's done on the inside of my arm so you have leverage, which will give you options for counterattack."

"All right, you'll have to show me."

"I thought all you needed were your ears," Cleve groused.

When it came time for lunch, Basen had many new bruises.

He hadn't realized that his defense was atrocious. He was excellent at stopping Cleve's sword from doing damage, but as soon as Cleve added his hands or feet into the mix, Basen would be taken down instantly or he would soon regret it. Cleve had hit him in the cheek at one point, and even though it was done at half strength, Basen reeled and needed a few minutes before the pain no longer distracted him too much to focus. He was glad he would never face Cleve in a real fight.

Basen was surprised to find his mother in the dining hall. Of course the first thing she noticed was his bruised cheek, her hands reaching toward it as if her touch could heal him.

He leaned away. "It doesn't help to touch."

"How did you get it?"

"Training. I'm fine, Mother. You don't need to worry. How are you?"

"Busy and happy; this is a wonderful place. It's a shame we need to fight in this war."

"We?"

"Not me, personally. You must know I wasn't speaking about going into..." She paused before adding, "Battle."

"Well, I don't know anymore. I heard what you did at the lake."

"I did what I had to. I don't regret it."

"I'm impressed."

"No, I'm impressed, Basen. Why aren't you wearing your medal?"

He chuckled at the ridiculous image of that. "Because I'm not insane."

"I hope that means you won't do anything that dangerous again. I know you felt you had to go to those Elves, and I did agree with everything you told me of your plan, but you made it sound far less dangerous than I'm hearing from the stories people are telling! Just because you got away with it once doesn't mean you're invincible. Do you understand?"

"Yes, of course. All men can die."

He was glad to see that prison hadn't changed his mother, and neither had killing someone.

"Are you staying with Father now?"

"Yes."

"So everything's...fine between the two of you?"

"Yes."

Just like before, Juliana and Henry wouldn't say much about their relationship. They had always treated Basen as the glue keeping them together. He figured it had to do with his older brother he'd never met, Lexand, who'd died at sixteen thanks to a poor decision by the late king of Kyrro. Now at seventeen, Basen had outlived him, fulfilling his role as Lexand's replacement.

It made him thankful but also worried. Juliana and Henry were too old for more children now. If Basen died in this war, there was no doubt in his mind they would separate. As a team—as parents—they'd shared the goal of raising their son. But as they'd aged and their lifestyles had slowly changed, Basen remained their only common interest.

There was something else they would agree upon soon enough, though.

"I'm going to train with Abith Max again," Basen told his mother, knowing the first thing she would do was tell Henry so they could both scold Basen. "Only this time, we're focusing on the sword as well as manipulating energy."

"What! How has this come to be?"

"Because he's the only one who can cast and cut like I can."

"Basen...he's not the best of allies to your father or the headmaster of this Academy, but I assume you already know this?" She used her rhetorical mothering voice.

"I do."

"And are you certain this is the right decision?"

"I am."

She put her hand across her mouth as she thought for a while.

"Then fine. Thank you for telling me."

"That's it?"

"Yes."

Perhaps she had changed. Or maybe she just trusted him now.

He hoped Abith wouldn't make him regret this decision.

*****

He was early to the northern wall and had time to go over what he'd learned before Abith showed up. What Basen needed to practice the most was first focusing energy into his arms and then transitioning his focus to give his legs a boost of strength, all without delay. If he couldn't, this skill wouldn't be of much use in combat. Every good swordsman knew that footwork was just as important as swinging the weapon.

An hour later, Abith arrived. He put his hand on one of the parapets and swung his legs over in a showy and dangerous hop, doing a roll on the grass as he landed. It was more than a little ridiculous.

"So what can you do today that you couldn't do yesterday?" Abith asked as he brushed the dirt off his back.

Basen had forgotten how his former instructor would ask that same question at the beginning of every lesson. Thinking about it now brought back fond memories. He and Abith hadn't ever been friends, but Basen had always respected his skill and method of teaching.

"Would you like me to tell you or show you?" Basen asked.

"What do you think?" Abith opened his hand.

Basen returned Abith's training sword, then waited for him to attack.

Abith seemed surprised by Basen's reluctance to strike first. With a shrug, he came at Basen with twice the speed of a normal man. Basen blocked Abith's first two attacks and deflected the third with enough force to drive Abith's sword to the ground.

Basen grunted as he swung his sword up at a defenseless Abith. But he was like a fly zipping around as he ducked Basen's attack, then jumped to the side to avoid the next strike. In a calm yet impressively fast manner, Abith gave Basen a slap on the cheek.

"Ouch." Basen stopped his onslaught to clutch his injured face. "Did you have to go for the bruised cheek?"

"It wouldn't be nearly as fun otherwise. You fight quick, but not quick enough yet."

"Quick enough for what?"

"To protect yourself from everything." Abith stepped forward and raised his hand to Basen again, but he blocked the expected blow with his forearm like Cleve taught him. Shock registered on Abith's face as the two of them froze. Then Abith's left hand came up, and Basen blocked it as well.

Abith grinned, then slid his arms down to free them. "Good, but now let's see if you can find a way past *my* defenses."

Basen attacked Abith with everything he had, yet his sword never came close to touching Abith's body. Eventually, Basen stepped back and tried to recall how Terren had gotten past Abith's defenses. Power hadn't worked for the headmaster, who was incomparably stronger than Basen, so that left surprise.

Abith didn't press him, giving him plenty of time to strengthen the muscles of his legs with bastial energy. He didn't reveal his plan as he continued to hopelessly slice at Abith from left to right, up to down. Basen panted and grimaced as if about to give up.

"You can't be tiring this easily," Abith said with disappointment.

And that's when Basen charged with all the energy he could muster. Abith was unable to get his sword up in time and tried in vain to spin out of Basen's path. Basen rammed his shoulder into Abith's back, finally knocking his former instructor off his feet. Basen fell on top of him and pressed his sword against Abith's neck, pinning his sword arm with his knees.

Abith craned his neck to look at Basen. He had a little

triangle of beard beneath his lower lip that stretched as he smiled wide. Basen rolled off him and waited for a response.

Abith chuckled as he rose to his feet. "I'm impressed. You're not the same arrogant and annoyingly curious young man I once taught. I figured you wouldn't agree to do anything until I told you more about what I have planned for Terren. Yet you've said nothing; you haven't once questioned my requests."

"I don't need to ask what you have planned for Terren because I've already figured it out. You wish to start training a new class, some sort of battle mage. I'm the example of what others can be with you leading us."

"And you've gotten wiser as well." Abith leaned back and laughed. "This will suit us both very well." He offered his hand.

Basen was surprised at how little fear and reluctance he felt as he shook Abith's hand. In less than two days, he'd grown to completely trust that Abith Max was the best person to help Basen reach his potential. But there was something in Abith's smile that still looked sinister.

Be careful, Basen told himself. *There's more he wants from you than just training a new class.*

Fatholl had expected to use Basen as well, and Basen had maneuvered his way around that problem. He was confident he could do it again.

*****

Basen found Cleve sitting alone during dinner hours.

Knowing the warrior ate quickly, Basen hurried to get in line for his food, then rushed over to take a spot on the bench beside Cleve.

"Your advice and training was helpful," Basen said. "Thank you."

Cleve gave a faint smile. "You're welcome."

"I have some new questions about focusing energy, if you don't mind."

"Of course." Cleve grew a real smile. Perhaps he had wanted some company.

"Cleve!" a Kreppen voice boomed from behind. "You no beat me today!"

Basen turned to see Rickik with Nebre and some other Krepps. Rather than waiting in line for food, the group of Krepps started gathering the leftover morsels on nearby plates and bringing them over to Cleve's table.

Basen didn't get a chance to ask Cleve anything after that. The only time the Krepps stopped bragging was to grunt out laughter or argue with each other.

CHAPTER TWENTY-EIGHT

The moment Sanya returned to the castle, she was escorted to Tauwin's throne room, where she expected to be questioned and possibly killed. It had been nearly a week since she'd left for the Fjallejon Mountains. Yeso was dead, and the Elves were gone. Yet this came as little surprise to Ulric's army compared to the announcement of his assassination.

Ulric had returned a few days before Sanya, and it was during this time that he'd been killed. Tauwin had been hasty in getting the funeral going. Many of Ulric's troops didn't even know he was dead until his body was displayed in a casket. Sanya hadn't been there, so she didn't know whether his mask covered his face even in death. In the end, it didn't matter.

Sanya figured that Ulric's troops had already joined Tauwin's, because Takary coin and promises held the same allure no matter who led the army. It was what Tauwin would do with Sanya that remained a mystery.

There were just three people in his throne room when she entered: Tauwin, Kithala, and Tauwin's psychic, who might very well have been the one who'd assassinated Ulric during the night. *The one Yeso told me to kill.*

Tauwin had no beautiful woman by his side, no one yet taking Sanya's place as his queen-to-be. He was probably enjoying his bachelorhood too much to consider the benefits of joining his family with another through marriage. The overconfident king must've been certain he would win this war soon and didn't need such help.

Hector, the royal executioner, came in after Sanya.

"Shut the door," Tauwin commanded, and Hector obeyed. He stood against it with his arms resting on the blunt top of his ax.

"Have you heard the terrible news?" Tauwin asked her.

She nodded.

"I'm preparing a boat for you. It will leave in a few days to take you back to Greenedge."

No. She took a note from her pocket and held it up. Tauwin gestured for her to come closer. As he took it from her hand, he peered into her eyes. She lowered her head and turned away.

He opened her note and read it aloud. "I'm your blood. You're my king."

She hadn't known what he would say to her, so it seemed like the best message to cover all scenarios.

"You wish to *stay*?" he asked incredulously.

She nodded.

"You weren't here for his funeral, so let me tell you the same thing I told everyone else. I will find out who did this to him and remove the killer's head. You don't need to stay to ensure there will be justice. I will take care of that and send notice to Greenedge of the capture of his assassin as well as the progress of the war. All the other Takarys are following this war."

Sanya shook her head, then pointed at the marble throne room floor. She then pointed at Tauwin and the note.

"Why would you want to stay?" he asked.

She gave no response.

"Speak!" Tauwin made a fist. Soon, he would be slamming it against the armrest if she didn't obey.

"She can't," Kithala interjected. How she knew Sanya was a woman, Sanya couldn't guess.

She nodded to agree.

"She?" Tauwin asked Sanya.

Sanya nodded again.

That gave him pause to consider something, but he shrugged it away. "What could you possibly do here if you can't even speak?"

"She's a Takary," Kithala said. "If she wishes to stay, she should be able to."

"We don't even know if she's related to us," Tauwin complained. "Ulric could've lied. My psychics never tested his statement about her."

"Are you worried about the coin she requires? Because it's more expensive to send her off in a ship than to feed and shelter her."

With Ulric no longer helping finance this war, money certainly had become an issue for Tauwin.

"The ships are leaving no matter what, Mother. Putting her on one will cost nothing."

"And who will be on Ulric's ships?" Kithala asked.

"No one save a small crew to sail them out and then back again in a month."

"What is the point of that?" She was beginning to sound nervous, probably realizing her questions were irritating her son.

"If you must know everything, then I will tell you. But first you will agree that I make the final decision about her." He pointed at Sanya.

"You are the king," Kithala reminded him. "You will make the final decision about everything."

That seemed to satisfy him. "Terren Polken has scouts watching my cities. We've chased them off, but they always return. Raywhite Forest is too big and dense to keep them from spying. So I've decided to use their incessant scouting against them. Soon they will hear news of Ulric's death, and they will watch his ships leave. What else can they assume other than his troops are on those ships?"

Tauwin smiled devilishly. "They will attack in hopes of striking while we are weak and before we can recruit more citizens to strengthen our ranks. First, they will plan to destroy our siege weapons that we never wished to use against the Academy anyway. Then they will storm the capital."

Psyche confirmed that Tauwin had meant everything he said, except that he wasn't the one who'd come up with this ploy. Ulric was the strategist who'd developed this plan, sharing it with Stanmar, who'd passed it along to Tauwin. It would help demonstrate why Stanmar should be reinstated as Tauwin's commander.

"That's a good plan," Kithala said. "But I think our Takary guest should have the choice of staying here or returning to Greenedge."

"I don't trust her," Tauwin said and looked deeply into Sanya's eyes. "Something about her bothers me."

"Whatever it is, I'm sure a few honest answers will help," Kithala suggested. "Your psychic is right here."

"Fine." The young king slid his fingers together and

cleared his throat. Then he chuckled bitterly. "I don't even know what to call you."

"I heard that her name is Laree Takary."

Sanya figured that name must've come from Ulric.

"Is that really your name?" Tauwin asked.

She nodded and manipulated her energy to convince them of her honesty.

"It's true," Tauwin's psychic said.

Sanya had little confidence she could make it out of the castle alive if this went wrong, but she would put up an epic fight. Part of her longed to be caught. It had been a while since she'd had the chance to swing a sword, and she was feeling more agitated each night she went to sleep without experiencing a battle.

At first, she couldn't figure out why she rose out of bed with a pounding heart and why the thought of going to Warrior's Field calmed her. She became more panicked as she realized she would never again have that opportunity, unless she fought in the battle everyone knew was coming. But there was no side she could join for which a victory would benefit her. And if there was no point in victory, then there was no point in fighting.

"Are you loyal to me?" Tauwin asked.

She nodded.

"It's true, sire."

Tauwin put up his palm as if annoyed by his psychic. "You don't need to speak unless she lies." The monarch turned his head as he squinted at Sanya. "Why are you loyal?"

"Is it because you are a Takary?" Kithala asked, clearly trying to help "Laree" through an inquisition that would be difficult for the timid, mute girl she pretended to be.

Sanya nodded.

"Do you seek vengeance against Ulric's assassin?"

This was the first troublesome question. She had only to answer the way Tauwin wanted, but why did he care about her vengeance, or lack of it? If he'd sent Ulric's assassin, which was almost certain, her need for vengeance might pose a risk to him. Or was he so confident he wouldn't be caught that her need for vengeance would prove her loyalty to the family?

She shook her head. She didn't want Tauwin to know she was capable of hurting anyone. It would only help her cause when it came time to kill him.

He seemed satisfied by her answer, leaning back on his throne.

"Are you wearing a mask to hide your identity?"

She shook her head.

"To hide your ugliness?" Tauwin asked.

She nodded.

"Show me."

Sanya didn't move.

"Take off your mask." Tauwin wasn't demanding, but he would be soon. Sanya shifted to face Kithala.

"Tauwin," his mother said in a careful voice. "I'm sure she doesn't want to do that, which is the reason she keeps herself covered."

"If she's to stay here and overhear my sensitive plans, she'll need to show herself to me."

"You've already questioned her loyalty and her name. You would embarrass her just to satisfy your curiosity?"

"It's more than just curiosity. What if someone else

comes into the castle disguised with a silver mask and black robes and we need to identify him or her? What if she gets lost or captured? There are many situations that, if we never know Laree's face, will prove difficult for us."

Had Tauwin gotten smarter since Sanya had last been here? She could feel with psyche that it *was* only curiosity that drove his request, but without psyche, she never would've known.

"You're right," Kithala agreed. "I'm sorry, Laree, but please remove your hood and mask for a moment."

Sanya glanced at Hector. He stepped toward her, cocking his head to the side and taking his ax in hand.

She carefully adjusted her silver mask, making sure it wasn't stuck. She could only hope her preparation and her psyche would keep her alive.

She slowly slid the mask up to reveal a chin that looked as if it had been coated in rust and dried blood. Her flayed flesh continued up to her mouth as she lifted her mask higher, her lips turning inward. Her cheeks looked like mangled plums stomped into white dirt. She got her mask up over her head to reveal one eye. The other was closed, her eyelid painted a grotesque mix of red and white like the rest of her face. She revealed her forehead last, sliding up the mask to hide her hair beneath her hood.

The ground leaves and mixture of oil, butter, and glue wouldn't normally create such a hideous appearance. But when set in the right way, and when the audience knew what to expect, the result was unmistakable.

Tauwin made a sound of disgust. He closed his eyes and looked away as he pushed his hand down. "Put your mask back on."

"Does it hurt?" Kithala asked with a concerned expression.

Sanya nodded. Sympathy would help her cause.

Sanya was a woman of many skills, but altering the appearance of her face was not one of them. It was Ulric who'd taught her how to do this, using his own bare face as an example. After Yeso's death, she and Ulric had spent a couple days together in the Fjallejon Mountains as his plan came together.

There had been nothing ugly about his face one might want to hide. He was as handsome as any man could be in his fifties, with piercing brown eyes that radiated wisdom beyond his years. He'd given her no warning before removing his mask. He'd simply taken it off the way a man might remove his hat.

"It's finally time," he'd told a shocked Sanya. "You need to remember how I look because it will be important later."

When she'd asked him why, all he would say was that someone would die soon. This man would be wearing Ulric's clothes, have the same hairstyle, the same bronze skin tone, and be of the same height and weight. "But he's not me," Ulric had added. "Prepare a note for Tauwin that, no matter what he asks of you, will convince him you are loyal. And be ready to show him your hideous face."

She had done exactly that during her short trip back to the castle. It had been uncomfortable, her skin feeling stretched and itchy from the alteration. But now, with her mask back on and Tauwin in her pocket, she finally relaxed. She could tell from his expression he would never ask her to prove a single thing again.

CHAPTER TWENTY-NINE

Basen trained hard with Abith every hour of every day and collapsed into bed each night after the long walk back from the northern wall.

All was well, until one night when someone came into his room to kill him. *Sanya.* He fell out of bed and scrambled toward his sword.

I should've locked my door! I should've had my sword closer!

Then Annah screamed, and he realized his mistake.

"It's all right!" he told her, sitting with his hand clutched to his chest. He let his sword fall, metal clanking against the wooden floor. "God's mercy, what are you doing coming into my room at night? I thought you were Sanya."

"I just wanted to make sure—"

Someone burst through the front door of their house. "Annah!" It was Alabell. She came running down the hall. "Basen!" She fell to her knees in front of him. "Is it your chest?"

He lowered his hand. "I'm fine."

"Are you sure?" She slipped her hand under his shirt to put her palm against his chest. "It's racing."

"Because you're touching me."

She closed her eyes and put her forehead against his. "You worried me."

"I'm fine," he repeated.

She removed her hand and stood to face Annah. "Are

you all right?"

"Yes, I apologize for screaming."

"What happened?" Alabell asked.

"She came into my room," Basen said as he pushed himself up. "I went for my sword thinking it was Sanya."

"I'm sorry," Annah said. "I haven't seen you in days, so I wanted to check on you. I didn't even know if you were still living here. Have you been sleeping somewhere else?"

"If everyone's all right, I should be leaving," Alabell said abruptly.

"Stay." Basen gave her a pleading look. He needed her to hear that he wasn't spending his nights in other women's beds. "I've been here every night, Annah."

"So then you're coming home after I'm asleep and leaving in the morning before I'm up."

"I've been training." He wished he could show them the speeds he could reach, the heights he could jump, the theatrical yet effective attacks he'd learned that would surprise any enemy.

Each day, Abith had brought a new mage to train with them. By the end of the day, the mage would be sent back to his group and a new man would be selected the following day. It was really unfortunate Sanya had turned out to be a traitor, because she was the only person, man or woman, who Basen was certain could meet Abith's strict requirements.

Basen was barely keeping up with his instructor's demands. Abith had one habit in particular Basen wished he hadn't forgotten about. He expected greater achievements the more Basen accomplished, so Abith was never satisfied, only momentarily pleased. This made Basen strive harder to earn his respect.

"I can't imagine Jackrie forcing everyone in Group Eight to train after dinner hours," Annah said.

"How did you know I'd been sent to Group Eight?"

"People talk about Basen the Cunning a lot," Alabell said, sounding as if she didn't appreciate that fact. "I knew it as well."

"What are you training?" Annah asked. "And where?"

"The two of you like surprises, don't you?"

"No," they answered at the same time.

He sighed. "Very well. I've been with Abith Max."

"You're training with *him*?" Annah's voice cracked as it rose.

"Does Terren know?" Alabell asked.

"Yes and yes." Basen was too tired for more talk. He got beneath his sheets, turned on his side, and closed his eyes. "If either of you want to speak more about it, we can do so in the dining hall. I tend to eat breakfast and lunch early, and dinner even earlier. Good night."

He fell asleep and never heard them leave his room.

*****

During breakfast the next morning, Abith approached. "We won't be training today," he said as he walked by Basen's table without turning his head. "Eat as much as you can and then relax here or go back home and sleep."

Abith left before Basen could ask why.

He ate, then went home. Curiosity kept him awake for all of a minute before he fell asleep.

He awoke later to the loud ringing of the Redfield bell. It stopped after three, signifying that all were to meet at the stadium for an announcement.

Battle.

He was ready, though that didn't ease his nerves. He removed the wooden training sword from his sheath and replaced it with steel. As he walked to the stadium, he felt butterflies in his stomach and ants crawling down his arms. He took a deep breath.

Having to walk to the center of campus from the student housing area made him the last to arrive. The stadium was already packed, and Terren took his place in the center. Basen hurried up the steps, looking for a seat.

"Basen," a man called out.

He looked over to see Neeko and Shara moving over to create a spot for him. Basen sat and thanked them. He noticed Shara staring at his sword. She looked up at him with worried eyes.

"It's time?"

"I think so," Basen said.

She grabbed Neeko's hand.

As Terren raised his arms for silence, Basen checked his comrades around him. It seemed that most people had come to the same conclusion as he had, their faces hard with determination, their eyes staring at Terren as they waited for the inevitable news.

But what the headmaster said first shocked the stadium.

"Three days ago, Ulric Takary was assassinated."

Gasps and murmurs interrupted him, so he raised his arms again. "Allow me to finish before you start speaking amongst each other."

A hush fell over the stadium.

"We became aware of the news yesterday, but we weren't able to confirm it until later. This morning our scouts noticed that Ulric's ships from Greenedge are now gone. Tauwin must've convinced them to wait until night before leaving in hopes we wouldn't notice his army shrinking to half its size."

People began to clap and cheer, and Basen joined them.

"Tauwin's army still outnumbers ours, we believe, but not by much," Terren said to answer the question shouted at him by several students.

The cheering resumed. Terren let it go on for a little while, then lifted his arms once again.

"We have to act fast, now. Needing to recruit more, Tauwin will put pressure on the citizens of Kyrro. He might starve them, threaten to kill them, or bribe them into taking up arms against us. We need to attack before that, while his army is weak. It's the only way to avoid battle coming to the Academy, which will surely destroy much of this beloved place. So today, we march to the capital."

Terren paused as if expecting a reaction, but there was none.

"I admire all of your courage," he continued. "I will lead the charge, but Tauwin will most likely be prepared for us. That is why we have no intention of storming the capital. We will fight to draw out his army while he watches the battle from atop his stolen castle. We will fight with aggression and fury, but also with strategy that will keep us protected from harm.

"Most of our enemies have come from Greenedge to usurp our cities. But they will return with their tails between their legs because, by the end of this day, Tauwin will be dead."

Confusion spread as students murmured, "How will he die?"

But Basen already knew, because he would be the assassin.

*****

Outside the stadium, every student—now soldier—gathered around their instructors, now officers. Henry's seasoned troops stood before him in organized ranks, making everyone else look sloppy.

The older troops from Tenred stood out. Having no instructors, they flocked to Abith and seemed the most nervous of any group. Meanwhile, the many staff and citizens who wouldn't be fighting formed an unorganized circle around those who would. The onlookers appeared surprisingly happy, no doubt assuming this battle would finally put an end to their worries.

Basen didn't know where to go.

Fortunately, neither did Neeko and Shara. They kept him company as they formed their own small circle between the many large clusters.

"Any luck teaching your pyforial skills to others?" Basen asked Neeko.

"A few people have been able to move the sand."

Basen mistakenly showed his surprise.

"You didn't think they would," Neeko muttered.

"Sorry, but no. How much longer until they can fight with pyforial energy?"

Neeko and Shara chuckled.

"Um, probably months," Neeko replied.

The two of you should've come here long ago.

Eventually, Terren came over to them. "Shara, there's a place for you among the mages who will stay at the back of our ranks with little risk of injury."

Neeko shook his head. "We agreed she wouldn't be fighting."

"I wanted to let her know in case she changed her mind. It will be safe, Shara. These are the mages of the lower group numbers. If the enemy reaches them, we'll be in retreat anyway."

"I'll stay at the Academy," Shara said in a meek voice.

"All right," Terren said with a smile. "That's fine." He looked around at his army. "I wish I could give everyone the same choice." He gave a pointed look at Neeko. "We need you now."

"I'm ready. Tell me what I'm to do."

Basen was disappointed when he realized the headmaster had come over here only for Neeko. He figured his training with Abith would mean the two of them would go after Tauwin while everyone else distracted the enemy army. Basen imagined storming the castle with Abith and a psychic to protect them, confident they could get through any of Tauwin's troops.

Except one. The giant.

Basen hoped that beast had already left with the others of Ulric's army.

"A small group will sneak into the capital from the south as the rest of us attack from the north," Terren explained. "It can't be more than a few people, otherwise your chances of being seen are too high. If Tauwin figures out the real threat to his life is coming from the other way, he'll call back his troops to defend the castle, and we'll have a very messy battle in which a victory is not guaranteed."

Terren was looking between Basen and Neeko now, giving Basen hope. The headmaster seemed to notice someone behind Basen, and Basen turned his head to find Effie. Was she going instead of him? She was a more well-rounded mage, possessing skill with sartious energy. But Basen still felt he was the best person to go after Tauwin, besides Abith.

"I'm just waiting to speak to them," Effie told Terren.

The headmaster leaned down again to Neeko's eye level. "Are you sure you can kill him when the opportunity comes?"

"I'm sure. I've heard what he's done, so there will be no guilt."

But this was the reason Basen wanted to claim the kill. Tauwin had murdered Alabell's family and tried to have her killed as well. Every time Basen thought of it, the rest of the war faded to the background. She'd almost died because of Tauwin. *And this pretend king would gladly slit her throat if he got the chance.*

"You'll be coming in through Oakshen," Terren said.

"Why Oakshen?" Basen asked, prickles going down his spine.

"Because you can't make a portal straight to the capital, isn't that right?"

"Yes." He felt relief wash over him. He would have his chance. "Please tell me I'm going to the capital with Neeko instead of just taking him to Oakshen."

"Abith Max will be leading the two of you all the way there."

"Good. And that will take Abith out of the battle, so you don't have to worry about him stabbing you in the back."

Terren pushed out his palm. "If you don't trust Abith, this isn't going to work."

"Oh, I trust him enough when we share the goal of killing Tauwin. It's what he plans for you when this battle is over that I worry about."

"I know, but I'll handle him when the time comes."

"What about the promise we made to Rickik?" Basen asked. "Tauwin's bastial steel sword."

"Don't let that concern you now. Just focus on getting Neeko close enough to the castle so he can rise up and slay Tauwin by surprise."

So this was still just about Neeko. But Basen couldn't dwell on his disappointment. Killing Tauwin, no matter who did the deed, was all that mattered now.

"Abith will meet you here soon. Good luck." Terren shook their hands and left.

Effie took his spot and hugged Basen. "Be careful."

Being careful goes against our plan. She should be

telling me to be audacious.

"I will," he said simply.

She tilted her head. "Can I speak to Neeko and Shara alone?"

A little confused, Basen shrugged and gave them privacy as they talked for a few minutes.

Abith finished addressing his men, who joined the enormous group of warriors and quickly became lost among them. The Krepps began to cluck and screech with excitement, and Basen soon saw why.

The other inhabitants of the Academy pushed wheelbarrows toward them filled with weapons and armor. Basen recognized all the plated chest pieces that had come from the Elves. Fatholl had intended them as his last gift to the Krepps before they left Merejic.

It was strangely fitting that everyone had gotten what they wanted so far, even though everything had gone wrong. Rickik's Krepps would fight, as they were born to do. The other Krepps were building their own home, which was their original reason for going to Merejic. Everyone loyal to Kyrro had joined to stand against Tauwin, including those from Tenred who saw this as an opportunity in the same way Tauwin's mercenary troops did. Everyone would get their chance for honor and could even earn a stake in the Academy.

Abith was one of the few mysteries left. How he planned to become headmaster was lost on Basen. After training so often with Terren, could Abith really bring himself to kill the man when this was done? There was no way Basen and the others would let Abith get away with it, and he had to know that and have something else planned.

Eventually Effie left Neeko and Shara. The couple hugged before Neeko separated to join Basen.

"What did Effie tell you?" Basen asked.

"She didn't want me to say."

Basen looked at Effie, who glanced at him over her shoulder. *I thought we trusted each other.*

He could think of only one thing it could be. She'd heard of his encounter with Sanya, how he'd made no effort to kill her.

She does trust me, except when it comes to taking vengeance for Alex.

"She wants you to kill Sanya," Basen said.

Neeko looked surprised. "You won't try to stop me, will you? I met Alex—I'm not sure if you knew that."

"I didn't."

"He helped me even though he didn't know me."

"That's the kind of person he is."

They fell silent to respect the dead.

"No, I won't try to stop you." But Basen wasn't sure he could help Neeko if needed. Sanya had saved Basen's life, and she was the reason they might be able to kill Tauwin before the end of the day. She'd done terrible things out of stupidity and deserved to be punished, but Basen didn't want to be the one to take her miserable life.

CHAPTER THIRTY

It was fortunate that Worender Training Center in Oakshen was empty. If anyone had seen Abith, Neeko, and Basen teleport in, they might've made a big enough scene for Tauwin's city guards to find out. Abith had never told or heard anything from Tauwin about portals after Basen used one to escape the Fjallejon Mountains. However, some of Abith's old troops could've told someone, who then told Tauwin. When Basen had asked how likely this was, Abith shrugged and said, "Not very. Most of the men I was given were poor excuses for soldiers. They probably fled the army after abandoning the mountain."

As Basen made his way west with Abith and Neeko beside him, they encountered dirty and hungry people who looked to have no home. Tauwin obviously had taken enough coin from the citizenry to make them destitute. No wonder so many had found their way to Trentyre, joining Basen's father in the rebellion.

Terren was leading the Academy's army toward the capital from the north. It was about four miles, the same distance as it was from Basen's location in Oakshen. But Basen's party had to get to the castle before their army engaged in combat or many would die. They would have to kill Tauwin swiftly and then spread the word in hopes of bringing a quick end to the battle.

Ideally, Basen could sever Tauwin's head and run with it through the crowded streets of the capital. How would he carry it? By the hair? As satisfying as it would be to kill this king, the idea of such a spectacle was disgusting. Basen supposed he would have to figure out the logistics after the deed was done.

It didn't take long before people began to notice Basen's party. They wore no armor, each donning plain pants and shirts that would give them the most mobility. Basen had even left his cloak behind, as it would only draw more attention. But now he was beginning to wonder if it would even matter. The three of them carried swords, Neeko with two on his belt. Everyone looked at them and wondered who they were if they weren't Tauwin's guards.

Most of those loyal to Tauwin were on the northern side of the city, with the weapons of war. None of these people knew of the battle about to rock Kyrro. If they did, they might revolt.

"Why aren't we telling them?" Basen wondered aloud. "Some might want to join the fight."

"While others will see this as a chance for a reward and snitch on us," Abith replied. "Yes, some might want to help, but we don't need their help, and we certainly don't need the risk of Tauwin becoming aware of us."

"People will snitch no matter what," Basen argued. "Look at the way they regard us. They know we aren't citizens of Oakshen strolling around the streets for fun."

"He's right," Neeko agreed. "If they help, they might distract our enemies enough to at least delay the transport of the catapults."

"That doesn't matter," Abith said, picking up his pace. "Go faster. We'll reach the forest soon enough."

"Delaying their catapults will help our comrades," Basen said, unsure why he had to remind Abith of something so obvious. For every moment that Terren was able to use the Academy's catapults and ballistae without worry of retaliation, it increased their chances of staying alive. "Our mages and archers are bound to be more skilled than theirs. Imagine our enemies' disadvantage if they have to fight without their weapons of war."

Abith stopped and shot them an angry look. "You trust Terren, don't you?"

"Of course," Basen replied.

"Terren didn't send us here to cause a riot or delay the catapults from getting to him. Our task is to kill Tauwin, and it's more important than anything else we could hope to do." Abith broke into a jog. "Keep up and keep quiet if all you have to offer are alternatives to Terren's plan."

They headed toward the forest in silence. It was painfully clear that Abith didn't care how many people died.

We have to be careful. He might not protect us if doing so slows him from getting to Tauwin.

*****

Cleve marched beside Terren at the front. They'd met no resistance so far, already halfway to the capital. They kept to the west, where there were fewer trees of Raywhite Forest to obscure their approach. This took away the element of surprise, but that didn't matter. Tauwin had troops watching the Academy from the Fjallejon Mountains. No doubt they'd already sent him word of the impending attack.

"Every time we march toward battle," Terren said, "I think of it as the last time we'll need to. I'm finally realizing how wrong I've been." He looked ahead, his mouth now a flat line. "This world we live and die in...is forgiving to some, like us. We Polkens have never been known as scholars, yet we thrive here because of our ability to fight and strategize. Without that, I don't know where we would be."

"What are you saying?" It was unlike his uncle to be so vague.

Terren sighed. "I'm tired of this, Cleve. I was never like Abith. I never aspired to lead the Academy, but it's what I had to do. And I'm damn good at it."

"You are, so why are you talking like this?"

Terren looked at Cleve's face as if he hadn't seen it in years. "There's more to life than fighting. I know it doesn't seem that way right now, but there is." He looked ahead for a while before speaking again. "You haven't been sitting with Reela or Effie when I've seen you in the dining hall. What happened?"

"Reela and I...had a disagreement." *She protected a murderer.*

"How long has this disagreement come between you two?"

"A while." This didn't seem the time or place to discuss it, but Cleve wasn't about to tell Terren to be quiet.

"More than a day?"

"More than a week." *Closer to a month.*

Terren's eyes bulged. "You can't let a disagreement split you apart. Do you still love her?"

"Terren, please." Cleve felt uncomfortable. Never had his uncle pressed him this way.

Terren paused and rubbed his chin. Hoping his uncle was considering dropping the topic, Cleve decided to push him toward that decision.

"Leave it alone."

But Terren shook his head. "I can't. Go speak with her. There's still time."

Cleve kept walking beside Terren.

"At least tell her you love her."

"We'll just argue."

Cleve had tried making amends with Reela, but the topic of Sanya always came up. Reela was steadfast in her beliefs. "We aren't Death," she'd told him several times. "We don't choose who lives and dies, unless we *must* defend ourselves."

She wanted Cleve to apologize, but she was the one who was wrong.

She won't accept that sometimes people need to die in order to save others.

Cleve had asked her, "What would you do if you had the chance to kill Tauwin? If he lives, he'll continue this war until thousands die."

"You mean if he cannot be captured?" Reela had asked.

"Yes. You only have one chance to stop him, and it means killing him." *Like with Sanya. We might've missed our only chance.* Cleve couldn't let go of his anger at Reela for stopping him. Even Effie agreed with him, and she was Reela's closest friend.

"I don't know, Cleve. I might kill him, but I might not."

Every time he remembered the conversation, he felt more anger building on top of the layers of rage he'd buried deep within himself. Reela hadn't known Alex like he had. If Effie had been murdered instead, Reela...

No, she still wouldn't advocate killing Sanya! Reela's as stubborn as a mule.

Cleve didn't care how much Sanya had helped the Academy. Yes, they were finally in a good position, and she had a lot to do with that, but she'd also caused considerable misery. No amount of good deeds would make up for her atrocities.

The thing that bothered Cleve most was his jealousy of Reela. This righteous path she'd chosen had allowed her to let go of her anger. He knew Reela was trying to help him find peace, but the only thing that would bring Cleve comfort was for Sanya to admit her crimes in front of all the people she'd wronged and then be beheaded as punishment.

And if Cleve couldn't make that happen, he would kill her when he had the chance. At least he wanted to. Because of Reela, now he wasn't sure he could.

"Go, Cleve," Terren urged again. "If you can't make amends, just tell her you love her."

Thinking about this had surfaced his rage. He gritted his teeth and spat out, "Stop! Why do you care so much?"

Terren sighed again, his eyes wet as if he might cry. What the bastial hell was wrong with him? They were marching to battle!

"Jackrie's sick," Terren said, his voice quivering.

Cleve cursed inwardly. He hadn't known the extent of Terren's relationship with the younger mage instructor but had seen enough to know they were close. They would sit with barely an inch between them while eating, smiling at each other as if they shared a secret. On one occasion, Cleve had dropped by unannounced at Terren's house and found Jackrie there.

"How sick?" Cleve asked, though he already knew the answer. He could tell by the terrible sadness on his uncle's face.

"I don't think she has more than a few months."

"Bastial hell, I'm sorry." Cleve's rage drained out of him. "There's no cure?"

"None. She has lumps. Opening her up to remove them would kill her anyway." He sucked in a sharp breath, suddenly looking stronger. "You think Reela's wrong about something, but it sounds like you've never considered the possibility that you might be wrong."

"Because I'm not. She refuses to accept that sometimes it's necessary to kill others."

Terren took his time before answering. "You should think about which one of you has a better attitude about life and death, war and justice, friendship and love."

Terren had a point. Reela was a happier person, always smiling, holding a more positive perspective on life.

"Think of a warrior who lost his good arm in battle and now can only use his left," Terren continued. "He tries to learn the sword again, but he becomes impatient with losing to the same swordsmen he used to beat. He can either wallow in his despair and give up, or he can find solace in still having one arm and learn to fight all over again. I know Reela well by now. Not only would she choose the latter, she would be disappointed in anyone who wouldn't. She expects more out of people than you do, and that gives her a bright outlook toward the future."

"So?"

"So, it's easy to look at reality and say, 'This is right because this is what happens.' That's what we tend to do, Cleve. We face reality with a readiness to fight. There is pride in that, and the world needs people like us. But the world needs people like Reela as well. She dreams of a better reality, and she has the courage to say, 'This is wrong. This is not what we should be doing.' You speak about her as if she's wrong, but maybe she's just dreaming of something good that you don't think is possible." Terren swallowed. "I know because Jackrie's the same way."

Terren was too modest. He always spoke as if his only worth was in swinging his sword at whatever was in front of him, yet whenever Cleve had a problem like this, Terren's advice was perfect. Reela was a dreamer. Cleve couldn't stay angry at her for that.

"I'll be right back," he said. "And thank you."

There were no hills between the capital and the Academy, only mounds that rose and fell fluidly. He and Terren had just climbed to the top of one of those inclines when Cleve turned to look for Reela and was blessed with a view of their entire army. The Group One warriors made up the middle of the first rank, Krepps mixed among them.

The creatures had learned to fight with each other and with humans, but Cleve was unsure how well they would protect his kind during the chaos. If he had to choose between a human and a Krepp, he would save a human. The only exception would be Nebre. In that case, Cleve's choice would be impossible.

The rest of the warriors of the next highest skill made up the first few rows. It was comforting to recognize all of them. His best allies would be at his back and sides. Behind them were Reela, Vithos, Annah, and a few of the other psychics who'd proven their ability in battle already. Unlike the warriors, the psychics were spread out among the army. They were too strong and too few to waste by grouping them together. The less skilled psychics, however, were in the back with chemists who had little to no battle experience. They would be safer back there, and hopefully some would feel brave enough to come forward and engage their enemies.

If Tauwin's troops found a way to reach the Academy's forces at the back, this could spell doom for the whole army. The formation would have to be broken, and even a good leader like Terren would have no hope of reorganizing everyone. This was the only way they could lose. Unfortunately, being outnumbered as they were, this was too likely a possibility for Cleve to feel at ease.

Many of the mages were in back with the archers, but Effie and the others at the top of their class were closer to the front, guarding the flanks. Their fireballs would drive their enemies to the middle like a funnel of fire.

There were some archers, like Cleve and Peter, who

had brought both a bow and a sword. Terren could move them to a different position to focus on shooting instead of charging. It all depended on the enemy's formation.

Tauwin's troops weren't very skilled, but it seemed as if his officers and commanders knew as much about battle as Terren did. They would use their numbers as an advantage.

When Cleve reached Reela, she smiled as if she knew he was there to make amends.

"I understand now," Cleve said. "You believe in a world you want to live in, where people don't need to kill each other."

"And where people can forgive each other," she added, nodding.

"I'm not sure if I'll ever be in this dream world with you. My dreams are chaos, and I'm the only one who can make them right. I need to force peace—with my sword or bow—or it never happens."

"It's one of the things I admire and respect about you." She took his hands. Her green eyes, as bright as sartious energy, twinkled with sadness. "But I can't be with you if you don't admire me and respect me in the same way."

"I lost sight of what was important, and I didn't allow myself to understand your viewpoint."

"We don't always have to agree," Reela said.

"Good, because I'm not sure if I can when it comes to Sanya."

She laughed, then leaned into him for a hug. The rest of their army walked around them, Cleve paying them no mind. He'd longed for this closeness for weeks, never forgetting how complete it made him feel.

"I'm sorry," he said when they finally parted. "I have to return to the front. I love you."

"I love you, too."

Cleve caught sight of Jackrie leading her group of mages along the edge of their rectangular formation. He'd spent much time with her during their attempt to reach Tenred castle, yet he'd never seen the expression now on her face. She looked savage and surly, as if she would kill any enemy who tried to reach her group and would lash out at any ally who attempted to hold her back.

CHAPTER THIRTY-ONE

The capital was surrounded by a tall yet thin wooden wall. There were but a few guards patrolling the southern side. Each had bows, and although they might not have been skilled enough to shoot a moving target, Basen didn't want to test them by trying to break through one of the doors. Alternatively, if any of the guards fled instead of shooting, they could alert everyone in the castle, and all hope of surprising Tauwin would be lost.

Instead, when the wall was clear, Neeko swooped up over it and disappeared. A moment later, the door swung open.

Basen and Abith ran through the door, and Basen closed it behind them. They waited for the footsteps of the patrolling guard to pass by overhead, then ran into the cover of the crude shanties on the outskirts of the city. Just as in Oakshen, they wouldn't blend in here. Fortunately, most of these shacks seemed to be empty, their inhabitants probably hard at work somewhere in the city.

Basen jogged with Abith and Neeko toward the center of town, staying on the streets that had the fewest people. Neeko and Abith both had good endurance, neither showing signs of fatigue after their four-mile journey from Oakshen. However, Basen doubted they could match his stamina, especially now that he'd discovered how to use his grasp over bastial energy to increase his strength and endurance. He felt as if he could jog for days.

A feeling like a swarm of flies trying to escape his stomach hit him as they neared the center of town. Shops and homes were bigger here, painted and decorated to give the city a more opulent feeling than Oakshen, but the people looked none the richer. Most were thin and wore clothes too big for them. Not one of them smiled. Some even appeared afraid as they noticed the three strangers' swords, as if Basen and his companions had come to punish them for something.

Basen could see the castle was not far ahead. The white Takary flag of sky blue wings was annoyingly gorgeous as it shimmered in the light breeze. For the first time that day, Basen noticed the wonderful weather. The sky was as clear as a pristine lake, the pleasant warmth of the sun perfectly contrasting with the cool wind. This was not a day for battle. This was a day to celebrate life. Tauwin would pay for putting everyone in this dire situation on such a beautiful day.

But Basen had to face the reality that all might not go as planned. *And if we don't kill him, he'll be more cautious in the future. It will be more difficult to reach him.*

He had an idea. "Wait," he told Abith and Neeko.

"We're almost there," Abith complained.

"It'll only take a moment, and it'll be worth it."

"Explain," Abith demanded.

"It's faster if we just do it." Basen hurried toward the nearest person on the street and showed him a friendly smile.

"Excuse me. Where is the nearest training center?" Basen asked.

"Oh, so that's what the three of you are doing. Talk of battle is on everyone's lips. I thought—"

"Just tell us," Abith interrupted. "We're in a hurry."

"That way." The man pointed, regaining his worried frown. "Just follow the street."

They hurried to the west.

Neeko asked, "What are we doing?"

"In case this doesn't work," Basen said.

It didn't take long for the training center to come into view.

Abith was smirking again. "This is actually a good idea."

"I still don't understand," Neeko said. "Why go to a training center?"

Basen had already explained to Neeko the way portals worked. It was Neeko's inexperience with training centers that led to his confusion.

"Mages have been going to training centers for years," Basen explained. "They've cast thousands of fireballs here."

"Oh, I see. You're familiarizing yourself here so it's easier to make a portal if we need to escape."

"Actually, no. We won't be able to escape by portal." Basen showed him the akorell bracelet that was barely glowing. "This won't be charged until tomorrow."

"Then what did you mean when you said, 'In case this doesn't work'?"

"In case we have to return to kill Tauwin at a later time."

When they entered the training center, Basen walked around the training dummies until he came to that familiar feeling of heaviness in the air. It would take only a few moments to sear the image of this location into his mind. But Neeko kept distracting him with a look as if he pitied Basen.

"What is it?"

"Nothing," Neeko answered.

"I'm trying to memorize this place, but your face keeps distracting me. Just satisfy my curiosity so we can move on. What?"

"You and Abith don't seem to realize something."

Abith clicked his tongue and folded his arms. "And what's that?"

"If I don't kill Tauwin cleanly by surprise, we'll have two hells of a fight to deal with. So how do you expect us to escape with our lives unless we can take a portal out?"

Abith and Basen were to finish Tauwin if Neeko couldn't. Then they would escape. If all of them failed, Abith would give the order to run. He and Basen could outrun anyone, and Neeko could lose any pursuer with his ability to take flight, even if it didn't last long.

Basen didn't see the problem.

"What's so bad about the plan?"

"You'll really leave with Tauwin still alive?" Neeko asked.

"If we have to," Basen said. "Hence the portal I'm learning to make here."

"If Tauwin lives, our army will be chased back to the Academy, which will be destroyed. The war will end today anyway, win or lose."

"Did Terren tell you that?"

"No."

"Then it's not true," Basen insisted.

"We're losing time here, boys," Abith said. "Basen, focus to get this done. Neeko, trust the plan."

But Basen couldn't focus. He was too busy trying to read Neeko's expression.

He's still not completely invested in this war.

"Neeko, if we protect each other, we'll get through this alive. And if you can't kill Tauwin, I will."

Neeko nodded as he rolled his hand through the air. "I'm with you; let's go."

*****

Cleve got his first glimpse of Tauwin's army in its entirety as his enemies stood in front of the walls of the capital. There were thousands, but how many exactly? Their numbers would determine the battle strategy. Cleve had seen an army this size before, when they'd faced the Krepps and the forces allegiant to Basen's uncle, but Cleve had more allies to fight with him then. It seemed now they would be outnumbered at least two to one.

It was almost as if Ulric's army hadn't gone after all. Could Terren be wrong?

There was another issue. Tauwin's army positioned itself in front of the city rather than taking cover behind the walls. *Why aren't they using the walls to their advantage?*

Either they'd anticipated the walls collapsing from the catapults neatly positioned behind the first ten rows of swordsmen and psychics for protection, or there was some other advantage they hoped to claim by engaging out here on the open land. The only other cover was the forest to the east. But Terren had made sure to keep clear of the trees, where their enemies could be hiding.

"Halt!" Terren raised his fist as he turned to face his army.

No doubt, Terren needed to wait for their scouts to return. They'd been sent to look for traps. Most had gone toward the forest, as it seemed to be the only place from where a sneak attack could come. Cleve put his hand over his eyes as he peered that way, gaining some shade from the bright midday sun.

Something didn't feel right.

Where are their horses?

"The scouts should've returned by now," Terren muttered.

A terrible chill went down Cleve's spine. "They're going to charge on horseback from the forest!"

"Shit, get back into line, Cleve!" Terren cupped his hands around his mouth. "Flanking attack from the forest!"

"Shift the lines!" Warrior Sneary yelled to his swordsmen.

"Shift the lines!" Mage Trela echoed.

The deep tenor of a horn rumbled out from the forest. It was too late. They were already coming, and only unarmored mages stood in their way.

The horses charged from the trees, men in full armor on their backs, steel so bright it reflected the sun like a mirror.

"Horses scare easily!" Cleve shouted to his uncle. "Even first-year psychics can force them the other way."

But Terren was too busy shouting orders to hear him. "Archers and mages, fire! Shields—"

Another horn sounded from the south. Here came the infantry. Cleve cursed as he quickly loaded an arrow onto his bow. He found himself, like many others, unable to figure out where to go as he was stuck between the two charging hordes.

"Shields, keep those on foot from getting through. Archers, fire dammit!"

But Terren wasn't the only one shouting orders. All of his officers were screaming in their attempt to organize.

Cleve took a breath to compose himself, then found a target among the cavaliers. He shot. His arrow didn't penetrate the steel breastplate of his enemy, but the force of it was enough to knock him off his horse.

"Fire!" Terren yelled.

Other arrows flew, taking many more horsemen off their mounts. But their armored horses kept charging. A storm of fireballs felled many more, but there were still hundreds. So much steel and speed. There was no way to stop them all.

Cleve got a few more arrows off before checking the infantry on his other side. Terren had organized the shield bearers to intercept their enemies on foot. The line would hold decently, but their flank was still horribly exposed.

Mages dove on top of each other to escape the path of charging horses, but that didn't stop the students behind them from getting rammed or trampled. Cleve's arrows could do more harm than good if he were to shoot at the cavaliers creating tears through the rows of his allies, so he threw down his short bow and ran behind the shield bearers. It was time for his bastial steel sword to earn him more kills. He could only hope his allies would defend themselves against the horsemen.

The infantry collided with Cleve's shield bearers, men shrieking as steel and bronze cracked. All of Tauwin's plated armor had gone to the cavaliers now creating chaos somewhere behind Cleve, leaving the attackers in front of him in light leather like he wore.

He'd lost track of his partner, Peter, during the havoc. *It doesn't matter.* So long as Cleve wasn't attacked from behind, he would kill every man who came close enough to his blade.

The line of shield bearers was supposed to hold no matter what, while mages, archers, and psychics were to work in harmony with the shields and swords of the front swordsmen, but everything had gone to hell. Their enemies were surprisingly brave, breaking through the shield bearers and charging straight into the second row, where Cleve and the Krepps awaited.

Cleve found his first victim as the two of them locked gazes. Cleve held his ground and let him come. He blocked his enemy's attack, then focused on the next enemy as he swiftly ran his blade through the man's— Cleve was blocked! He took a punch to his stomach that made him keel over. *They're well-trained!* These weren't like the men he'd faced earlier in this war. *Ulric's bastards!* Unlike Tauwin's mercenaries, these men had been in battle before.

Cleve took his only option to defend himself from

this vulnerable position, diving into his enemy to tackle him. Unfortunately, this put them both on the ground. As Cleve tried to get up, someone tripped over him. Cleve tried to roll, but one of his arms was pinned. Before driving his sword through this person's back, Cleve checked to see if the man wore the blue armor of Kyrro's Allies or the white of the Takarys' army.

Blue, and it was not a man on Cleve's arm but a Krepp.

"*Shazara!*" Cleve yelled, but soon realized the Krepp's movements were only because of the squirming enemy beneath his legs. This Krepp was already dead, as were so many others.

Cleve sensed movement from another angle and kicked before he had time to look. His boot took the wind out of the enemy he'd first faced. The attacker stumbled backward. A sword came out through his chest as his head whipped back, then he fell forward to reveal Peter coming toward Cleve.

Peter threw the dead Krepp off Cleve's shoulder and helped him up.

"Watch out!" Cleve yelled, unable to get to the enemy advancing on Peter's back.

But Rickik was there, jumping and burying his blade deep into the man's shoulder.

Cleve caught sight of Effie running into the fray. She held a glowing ball of sartious energy as she moved her small body around Krepps and humans. Cleve knew exactly what she was doing, but he couldn't get there to help her. He, Peter, and Rickik were instantly overwhelmed by a flood of charging swordsmen.

They held their ground to make quick work of anyone

trying to go through them, but they could do nothing to stop all the others who went around.

"Effie!" Cleve yelled. If she fell, or even tripped, that mixture of sartious and bastial energy would explode among allies and enemies, and she certainly would die.

But then he noticed the green ball fly overhead. It didn't go far, but it was well enough into the ranks of the enemies that none of his allies would fall victim to the explosion.

Erupting fire and the tearing of earth mixed together in a gruesome and satisfying sound as bodies flung out. Cleve had just a moment to check behind him to see what kind of damage the cavaliers had done.

His army was in total disarray, horsemen still barreling through the ranks. His side's psychics, chemists, mages, and the other warriors fought with no pattern or efficiency, merely trying to survive. In just that short glimpse, he saw many of his allies falling, his enemies continuing to push through and circle behind him.

CHAPTER THIRTY-TWO

Sanya had told Basen that Tauwin liked to watch the battles from atop the castle, but "liked" wasn't a strong enough description. He stood at the edge of the parapets, drooling as he peered through his spyglass.

"They've engaged!" Tauwin announced, sucking in his spit. "The Academy is losing its formation!"

The power-hungry king seemed to assume this marked the end of a long struggle and that Kyrro finally would be his. But Sanya knew better. This would be the end of a long struggle—for Ulric.

Sanya had to resist the urge to grab Tauwin by the legs and throw him off the tower. Without a weapon, she couldn't fend off his attacking psychic, his mother, and his two guards, but she might be able to take one of the guard's swords and kill them all if she waited for the right moment.

Kithala and Tauwin's psychic made this complicated, however. Kithala certainly would get in the way, and Sanya didn't want to kill her. Meanwhile, the psychic was powerful enough to debilitate Sanya if she didn't break the bastial energy in the air. But if she did, she would be facing multiple people without the benefit of her best weapon.

If she could take Tauwin's bastial steel sword instead of one of the guard's, she would have the best chance. Yes, that was how she'd kill him.

It seemed prudent to wait until the guards were less

vigilant. Both appeared nervous from the way Tauwin stood so close to the edge, positioning themselves on either side of the young king so they were close enough to grab him if he started to fall.

His mother was on the other side of one guard, with the psychic on the opposite end. Sanya stood behind them, but she didn't go unnoticed. The guards, Kithala, and even Tauwin's psychic kept glancing at her as if wondering what she was doing.

Waiting for my chance. She was being too obvious. She stepped forward to stand with them, but on the far corner of the tower. Part of her worried it had been a mistake to tell Basen that Tauwin would be up here, as the Academy might have a plan to slay him, getting in her way. But part of her was hopeful they would come, as she wasn't sure she could do it on her own and escape. She was the only one looking around the other sides of the castle for signs of an attack.

Earlier, she'd given Tauwin a note requesting permission to watch the battle with him. He'd given it a cursory look before handing it back to her and saying, "Fine." But now, he seemed excited she was there. "Laree, you can't see anything without a spyglass. Mother, give her a turn so she can see what we're accomplishing."

One might think Tauwin had empathy for the girl Sanya was pretending to be, but she knew he was just acting like a child showing off a new toy. Tauwin didn't merely see Kyrro within his grasp. He thought it was already his.

Looking through Kithala's spyglass, Sanya couldn't distinguish from this distance who was from the Academy and who wasn't. But she could see it was utter chaos. This was certainly bad for the Academy, as their only hope had been to avoid a full-on brawl like this one.

Stanmar had led the charge of horsemen, though his full suit of armor made him look no different than Ulric's well-trained cavaliers. Tauwin figured the men responsible for ambushing the Academy were loyal to him now, and Sanya supposed that was true. They did, after all, believe Ulric to be dead. This meant Tauwin was the only one who would give them the future they'd come here to claim.

Many were still on horseback, breaking up the last of the Academy's organized ranks. Terren's side had many mages, while Tauwin and Ulric did not. But the Academy's mages were probably stuck in close combat, unable to fire upon their enemies. The only advantage the Academy might still have was its powerful psychics. They likely were the only reason the battle hadn't ended in a few moments after the initial charge.

Sanya couldn't discern how she felt about the prospect of a slaughter. It wasn't pity, more like a longing to be there, to fight with them to the death. She'd never realized how much she would miss combat once she fled the Academy.

She would have to kill Tauwin before the battle ended, before he descended down into the castle where Sanya could become trapped as soon as she showed her true loyalty. Here, she could kill the witnesses and escape to Ulric before anyone knew what had happened. But damn, Kithala was a complication. Sanya liked her.

She gave back the spyglass and took her place behind

everyone again. It was almost time to act. She looked around the sides one last time for signs of the Academy.

Suddenly, a shadow came over her. Sanya started to turn when something struck her in the back and sent her hard onto the stone floor.

What in god's world? It was as if someone had descended from the sky and kicked her. She scrambled to see who she was up against, thinking someone loyal to Tauwin had figured her out. But she didn't recognize this young man with blond hair holding two swords.

He couldn't have come up from the hatch leading down to the castle, for it was bolted shut. Had he really come from the sky?

His swords began to float in front of him as everyone turned. Tauwin screamed out a jumble of words, "Wha-how? Kill him!" His guards ran toward the man, who couldn't have been older than Sanya. He flicked his hand and a sword impaled each guard. They fell, but one grabbed onto the sword buried in him as if trying to staunch his bleeding. The attacker pulled back his hands and the sword came out of the other man and floated back to its owner. But the second sword was stuck, dragging the guard toward the attacker and forcing out grunts from both their throats.

"Stop him!" Tauwin yelled as he tried to get to the hatch.

As Sanya regained her feet, Tauwin's psychic lifted his arm and unleashed a spell. The attacker screamed as he dropped to his knees.

But the blond young man must've had some training resisting psyche, for he was able to get back onto his feet and send one sword floating once more. Everyone but Sanya and Tauwin moved toward him, the two injured guards as slow as snails, Kithala and the psychic quick as cats. Tauwin had his hands on the latch but fumbled with it. He watched in horror as the floating sword turned toward him. The psychic screamed and the attacker and his weapon fell once again. Kithala jumped on top of him. The two guards seemed to have given up, letting their agony take control as they cried out.

Sanya finally recovered from her shock. This person was here to kill Tauwin, and she would help. The psychic ran toward the attacker with his dagger out, Kithala holding the attacker down while her son escaped and closed the hatch after him. Sanya pushed Kithala off, then kicked the psychic in the shin to knock him down.

Kithala scrambled over to the latch as the psychic screamed at Sanya, "What are you doing?"

She stood between him and the fallen attacker, refusing to answer. The psychic's aggressive expression twisted into fear as he realized he would now have to face them both.

The psychic ran and practically jumped down the open hatch. "Tauwin!" he yelled. "Where are you?"

With only the dying guards left, Sanya pulled down her hood and lifted up her mask. "You ruined my chance at killing him. Who are you?" She pulled the young man to his feet.

"It's you, Sanya!" one of the dying guards grumbled.

Something changed in the young man's face.

He knows me.

He jumped back and lifted his arm. Unsure where the

sword was at that moment, Sanya's best chance of defending herself was to attack him with psyche. She floored him with a spell.

"You must be from the Academy," she said, thinking aloud as to what to do now.

He squirmed and screamed, but nothing intelligible came out of his mouth.

"I don't have time to deal with you," she said, not wanting to kill someone of such power by stabbing him while he was disabled. If they were to duel, it would be on her terms, and it would be epic. She regretted not giving Alex more of a battle when she had the chance, cheating with psyche instead.

She hurried over to one of the fallen guards and pulled the sword out of his stomach. It was shorter than the guards' swords, easier to run with.

"Save me and I'll make sure you get away," the guard grunted. "Wait! I'll make sure…"

But Sanya was already down the ladder. She didn't bother to close the hatch behind her. The blond man wouldn't chase them into the castle.

It took but a moment to figure out where Tauwin must've headed. The stables. A horse was the only way he could flee from someone who could fly.

Was that really what he could do? Sanya ached to find out. He hadn't used bastial energy or she would've felt it. And she knew enough about sartious to tell it wasn't that. *A new energy.* She wanted to learn it. *Just another reason I shouldn't have left the Academy.*

She encountered no one but the usual inhabitants of the castle, but their shocked expressions showed that

Tauwin had definitely gone past them. Many of these men and women appeared to recognize Sanya as she rushed down the halls and stairs, yet nobody tried to stop her.

Her long robes impeded her process, so she paused to cut away the bottom half with the attacker's bloody short sword. She had on flexible leather that ended at her knees. Longing to feel freer, she threw down her silver mask and cut away the last of her robes, leaving her in just a sleeveless shirt to go with her shorts.

She could hear Tauwin on the floor below her and peered over the railing. He'd gathered at least a hundred soldiers to protect him. A few were archers, dammit, although at least there were no mages she could see.

"Send out the flare!" Tauwin yelled at someone Sanya couldn't see from her vantage point.

She leaned back so as not to expose herself, but someone was staring. He was a mere boy and seemed frozen in fear. His clothing told Sanya he wasn't a child-servant but probably the offspring of a soldier or someone more important.

She gritted her teeth at him. "Run away and say nothing or I'll kill you."

He let out a frightened squeak as he fled.

"The flare!" Tauwin yelled again, starting down the last set of stairs. "The castle is under attack."

Little did he know that the man in charge of the flare was one of the few who knew Ulric to still be alive. Tauwin would find no help there.

Sanya cursed as she noticed the royal psychic trailing the descending army. This was not a battle she could win alone.

She kept her distance as she followed them out of the castle. It was no surprise to see them run down the main road and straight for the stables. She cursed again. *Tauwin might live to see another day.*

Sanya closed the heavy castle door behind her, hoping Tauwin's exit meant this was the last time he stepped foot inside. She could command the horses with psyche and prevent his escape, so long as she wasn't seen. Unfortunately, there was nowhere to hide down this wide road. She could only hurry and hope none of the guards turned and recognized her.

The stables had only two walls and a roof, not including the stalls for the horses. There were only a few of the animals left, the most timid of the bunch most likely, for the strongest had gone to battle. Rockbreak and an unmasked Ulric stood in front of the last of the horses. Tauwin tried to maneuver around Rockbreak, but the giant shifted to block his path.

"Move," Tauwin commanded.

"He's not going to," Ulric said.

Tauwin gasped and stumbled backward. "That voice...it's you! No, you died."

"That wasn't me."

It was the distraction Sanya needed to take cover around the side of the castle.

"Move your enormous idiot!" Tauwin yelled. "I don't care right now how you're alive. I'm under attack."

"By who? Look around. I see no one."

"There was someone who can control swords without touching them. I think he came from the sky."

Ulric let out a harsh laugh. "That's absurd. You will stand here and have a conversation with me. You owe that to me after what you did."

"What are you talking about?"

"You asked me when we met why I wear a mask. Now you know. The greed of your family was not lost on me when I decided to assist your father. You both come from a long line of men who care about nothing but power."

"Ulric, what the bastial hell are you saying? Do you think I had something to do with your supposed assassination?"

Sanya noticed a small crowd gathering on the streets branching out from this one. She was too conspicuous here, so she moved around the buildings to blend in among the spectators. She was confident Ulric would keep Tauwin and his guards busy, but what she didn't know was what Ulric would do next. Their plan had fallen apart thanks to the surprise atop the castle. *Does Ulric expect me to kill Tauwin here, while he's protected? That's impossible.*

Perhaps Ulric was buying time to change the plan. She used psyche to urge the crowd closer until she was in range of Tauwin's energy.

"I know it was you," Ulric said. "I'm just surprised it took you this long."

"Ulric, I had nothing to do with the assassination. I'm telling you the truth!"

Sanya was shocked to find Tauwin was being honest. But if he hadn't tried to kill Ulric, who had?

Sanya noticed movement from a nearby hill. There were three people at its peak, one with a spyglass, but they were too far away to be a threat. Tauwin's attacker was one of them, while the spyglass blocked the middle one's face. The third was older. She didn't recognize him, though he did look familiar.

The one in the middle let down the spyglass, and Sanya clearly saw Basen's face. No doubt they were here to kill Tauwin. They must know that if he got on horseback, even these crowded streets wouldn't impede him enough and he could escape to his army just outside the city. The three men quickly made their way down the hill. Sanya figured the blond had told the other two about her by now, but she couldn't be as much of a priority as Tauwin, could she?

"I'm getting one of my horses," the king announced. "You can have one as well and come with me, Ulric. Question me in front of one of your psychics, and you'll see the truth." Tauwin stepped toward one of the horses, but Rockbreak's movements had Tauwin retreating.

"You will not." Ulric untied the lead from one of the horses and boosted himself onto its back. "You will stay here and die for your crimes. Go, Rockbreak."

"With pleasure." The giant drew his enormous bastial steel sword, its multitude of oranges and reds giving it the appearance of a living flame. He beheaded two of Tauwin's men before anyone else had a chance to move.

Tauwin fell backward and screamed, "Kill him!"

Rockbreak slashed his sword across the chests of two more soldiers, then spun and slashed three more. Swordsmen swarmed him, but his plated breastplate and pauldrons deflected the attacks his sword didn't.

"Make room!" shouted one of the few archers.

Rockbreak lifted his massive plated arm to protect his head as arrows glanced off him. One struck a horse but did not stick. It was still enough to frighten the animal into rearing up and trying to break free. The other horses became just as scared and the entire stables began to shake, the power of these frantic beasts matching Rockbreak's.

At the back, Tauwin and his psychic hopped around frantically with their hands up as if hoping to do something yet having no idea what.

"No more arrows!" Tauwin yelled. "Just kill him with your swords!"

The horses began to break free.

"Get one." Tauwin pushed his psychic toward the escaping animals.

The psychic lifted his hand, and one horse careened over.

"No!" Rockbreak yelled. "You fight me and die!"

He tried to reach Tauwin before the king could jump up onto an unsaddled horse, but the horde of swordsmen got in Rockbreak's way. They batted at his armor, one getting through to the giant's side. He backhanded the swordsman and seemed to gain power in his fury as he swept two full-sized men out of the way with his other arm.

Sanya couldn't let Tauwin escape. She broke out from the crowd just as he leaned down to pull his mother onto the horse.

That gave Sanya time to get there and pain the animal. Its legs buckled as it shrieked, then it reared up, sending Tauwin and his mother sliding off.

"Get it under control or I'll have you killed!" Tauwin yelled at his psychic.

"Sire, it's *her!*" The psychic pointed at Sanya in disbelief.

"Kill her! Kill her!" Tauwin's face was dangerously red.

The psychic took out his dagger and ran toward Sanya. She struck him down with pain before he had a chance to do the same to her. He screamed and coiled on the ground, but what she didn't expect was his strength even through his agony. The spell hit her suddenly as if she'd run into an invisible wall.

She somehow managed to frighten the horse while keeping the psychic on the ground. Tauwin and his mother chased after the beast, quickly reaching the edge of Sanya's range. She didn't have time for this damn psychic. She broke the bastial energy in the air and rose up.

The psychic jumped up as well and shook his arm as he clawed in her direction. "What?" he muttered to himself. Sanya sprinted toward Tauwin and his mother.

"Stop her!" Tauwin yelled to his men.

Five of them blocked Sanya's path. Had there still been bastial energy to work with, she could've pained them all, but the energy wouldn't be available to her for some time.

She was forced to back away from them as she tried to figure out what to do. She turned and ran her blade through the psychic before he could stab her in the back. She barely pulled it out in time to deflect the first attack of the five swordsmen. They circled her, forcing her even farther from Tauwin. He'd gotten on the horse by then.

His mother was holding onto his leg.

"Let go," he told her as he shook her off. "They're coming for me, not you!"

Sanya had only a moment to look over her shoulder in the direction Tauwin was pointing to find Basen and the two others rushing toward the king. The blond one took flight to sail over the guards in his way.

Tauwin kicked the horse and rode north. The galloping beast was quick, faster than the flying man. Kithala ran after them but had no chance of catching up.

"Help her, Abith!" Basen yelled, pointing at Sanya. He leapt higher than Sanya thought possible, landing on the shoulders of a guard and soaring even higher. He came down on the other side of them and bolted down the street like an arrow.

"Who are you?" Abith asked as he took to Sanya's side and made quick work of the first guard to challenge him.

"A friend," she answered.

They'd never formally met, but Sanya remembered him now. He was the mage instructor of the most skilled casters, like Basen. What he was doing with a sword—a bastial steel sword at that—she had no idea. But god's mercy, was he skilled. He took on the first four guards as more began to swarm from behind, kicking the dead psychic's body out of their way.

Rockbreak, covered in sweat, showed no signs of fatigue as he fought at least a dozen others. His armor was dented and breaking apart, blood streaming down one of his legs. But a sea of bodies lay around him.

Every attacker seemed to underestimate Sanya,

making reckless moves to get at her and leaving themselves open. But she couldn't take advantage for long as more veered away from Rockbreak to surround her and Abith.

Soon there were too many. She took a cut along her leg and rolled forward to avoid being sliced in half but lost her sword in the process. Someone grabbed her in a hold too strong for her to free herself.

"Cut her open," the gruff voice said from behind as two men closed in and pulled out daggers.

The man's tight grip on her loosened as his head rolled down her face. She fell backward to avoid the daggers, then popped up and jumped away as Abith moved to defend her. But there were so many more still behind her. She ducked and weaved, barely jumping out of the way of an enemy sword that impaled his comrade's shoulder.

Shooting pain in her leg slowed her. Sanya couldn't move fast enough and soon took another cut, this one to her arm. She needed to make it through the next few moments. The bastial energy was forming back together.

Rockbreak screamed aggressively from somewhere beside her, and Abith yelped in pain. Both of the skilled fighters were being cut down as she, too, was overwhelmed.

Finally, the familiar feeling of the energy returned. She let out a roar as she pained everyone around her. Unable to pick out Abith's energy, she felled him as well.

Rockbreak was completely unaffected. But to Sanya's horror, he stopped killing their enemies.

"No." He pointed at her. "Let them fight."

"Idiot," Abith grunted as he surprisingly fought off her spell to regain his feet. He groaned as he stabbed one man, and another, then a third. "Kill them."

"Let them fight!" Rockbreak roared. "Or I kill you instead!"

Abith killed five more as the giant started toward Sanya.

She couldn't keep up the spell any longer even if she dared to challenge him. Tiring, she fell to her knees.

Her attackers rose up, but many began to flee. At seeing some run, the others gave up as well.

"No. No!" Rockbreak yelled, bloody and sweaty, his massive chest heaving with each quick breath. "Fight me!"

"Are you safe here?" Abith asked Sanya as he helped her up.

"Yes. Go."

He sprinted north. Rockbreak stomped over and pushed her back to the ground. "I want to *kill* you!" he roared. "I told you not to stop them from fighting. You're lucky Ulric wants you to live." He started south, in the direction Ulric had gone. "Come on."

She limped after him, the frightened crowds parting to make more than enough room.

CHAPTER THIRTY-THREE

Fueled by adrenaline and bastial energy, Basen felt completely uninhibited by fatigue. The speed of his sprint was one he'd never been able to sustain for more than a minute, but now he felt as if nothing could stop him from getting to Tauwin.

Once they reached the open land of Kyrro, Basen would have no hope of catching up to Tauwin and his horse. But here, with the streets crowded with curious people, Basen had the advantage. It didn't take long before Neeko descended to run beside him.

"I can't catch him," Neeko huffed, instantly lagging behind.

"I will," Basen called back.

The wall around the capital was fast approaching.

"Move out of the way of your king!" Tauwin yelled at a group of people in front of him.

They obliged, but some threw stones at him. None hit its mark. Tauwin stuck out his foot and kicked a young man who tried to grab him. A woman threw a handful of sand into his face. He yelled out but didn't fall.

"Move!" Tauwin screamed at the next group, learning his lesson not to state who he was. But these people must've heard him from before or recognized him, because they threw even more rocks at him.

One boy had good enough aim to strike Tauwin in the arm.

"I will have you killed!" he screamed at the child. "I

will remember you!"

The boy turned and ran, while many sprinted after Tauwin. But the moment Basen stormed past them at a speed they'd surely never seen before, they stopped. Some yelled out in surprise while others cheered. It caused Tauwin to turn for a look.

"Bastial hell!" Tauwin kicked his horse harder, and the animal sped up.

Soon, he reached the wall. "Open the door!" he yelled, then cursed. Basen saw why as he came closer. There was no one there.

Tauwin slowed his horse and then jumped off. He hurried toward the plank of wood keeping the door shut, holding the reins of his horse in one hand.

Basen's chest was burning from the strain he put on his body. But he would unleash an agony ten times worse on Tauwin. Basen pulled out his wand and slowed to concentrate.

As Tauwin finally pulled the door open, Basen shot a fireball toward him without taking time to aim. It exploded against the wall and scared the horse. The animal shook free from Tauwin's grasp and darted off. Tauwin started after it as he yelled out another curse but soon gave up and ran out the door.

Basen almost stopped when he went through after the king, horrified by the sight. Tauwin's cheering army was returning and damn close already! The battle had to be over, as the Academy's army was retreating. What had to be hundreds of bodies lay between the two armies.

"Kill him!" Tauwin yelled to his troops. "Kill the man chasing me!"

They charged.

Basen put everything he had into this final sprint. He would not turn and flee, even though thousands would soon be upon him. His vision blurred, each breath like inhaling fire. A shadow fell over him as Neeko soared by at an even faster speed. *Go, Neeko.* Basen didn't care who claimed the kill anymore.

"Shoot them!" Tauwin yelled.

His archers and mages unleashed arrows and fireballs. Basen veered left then right to avoid the balls of flame. The arrows were much too swift, however. He could only hope one wouldn't find its mark. The grass caught fire on either side of him. Tauwin nearly took an arrow himself as they flew around him.

"Stop!" Tauwin screamed.

"There's one in the sky," someone yelled. The mages and archers shifted their aim up at Neeko.

He quickly descended toward Tauwin as the mages unleashed a barrage of fireballs. One hit directly, sending Neeko rolling backward into a patch of burning grass. Basen rushed to him as the flames intensified.

Neeko had rolled out of the fire by the time Basen got there, but his clothes were still burning. Basen jumped on top of him to smother them, burning himself in the process.

"Go," a charred Neeko grunted when there was only smoke left. He began crawling in the opposite direction. "Get him."

Arrows and fireballs continued to rain down around them.

Tauwin was almost to his army. Basen ran through the

hailstorm of death and drew his wand. He had to slow to gather the necessary energy for a fireball, but it was his only chance. He shot and struck Tauwin's feet. Basen sprinted so fast he couldn't find the coordination to draw his sword as he neared the fallen king.

He jumped on top of the bastard as Tauwin tried to get up. Tauwin thrashed around and managed to free his bastial steel sword. He cut the top of Basen's arm, forcing him to let go.

Fortunately it was Basen's right, and he took out his sword with his left. Tauwin's army was seconds away. Tauwin managed to stand as Basen swung at his head.

Tauwin got his weapon in the way, but Basen's strength was too much, knocking the sword clean out of the monarch's hand. With one more swipe of Basen's sword, Tauwin's head tumbled off.

Basen threw down his blade as he faced too many swordsmen to have any hope of winning. Countless archers and mages were coming through the ranks from behind them, raising their weapons at Basen, too.

"It's done," he told them and lifted his hands, blood dripping down his right arm. "No one will pay you anymore. There's no reason to keep fighting."

He noticed them glancing at Tauwin's severed head. No, it was the bastial steel sword lying beside it that caught their attention.

They ran for the weapon. A brawl broke out among them. Half yelled for them to stop while the other half joined the fight. Basen turned and ran. Bastial steel was more valuable than gold, but there probably were still some among them who would rather kill him for what he'd done.

He wasn't surprised when a couple of arrows flew over his head. He looked back and was relieved to find others stopping those archers.

It *was* finally over.

Neeko was hobbling toward the capital wall when Basen caught up and tried to help him, but his touch made Neeko scream.

"Sorry," Basen said. "How can I help?"

"Lean down."

Basen did, and Neeko put his arm over his shoulder.

"You got him," Neeko said, smiling through his pain.

"I did."

"This was worth it."

His shirt was in pieces, the burns worse on his chest and back. His neck and chin were brown and already blistering, his eyebrows gone. He stumbled a bit as they made it to the wall. Basen was relieved to find Abith running toward them and pushing through a crowd.

"Tauwin's dead," Neeko told him.

"We need to get him to the Academy," Basen said, reminding everyone of their new priority.

"Past all of *them*?" Abith pointed at the army behind Basen.

"They might not kill us."

"Not worth the risk," Neeko said, then groaned as he lost his footing.

He fell and looked to have no energy left to move. The crowd quickly gathered around them.

"Did you kill Tauwin?" some asked.

"Yes," Basen answered. "And now Neeko needs help.

Is anyone a healer?"

No one answered.

Basen didn't know much about burns, but Neeko obviously was in dire condition.

"I can try," someone volunteered. "My house is close."

"Help us bring him there," Basen told the crowd. "Gently."

CHAPTER THIRTY-FOUR

Alabell had spent the entire day treating the injured. Her work began shortly after the battle started in the morning, and she'd hardly had a chance to sit since then. Now it was night, and she still hadn't found time to eat.

She remained in the medical building, overseeing the largest room there. It fit about a hundred people comfortably, so of course there were about three hundred there now. Fortunately, many of the injured had fallen asleep. The combined doses of potions in their bodies probably equaled the total number of doses given during a normal year at the Academy.

Alabell noticed a change in the room when Terren entered. People sat up in bed. Healers stood up straight and tried to hide their fatigue.

"You healers are doing a fine job," he announced.

He seemed to be heading toward Steffen. Alabell cut in front of the headmaster on his way there. "Any news?"

"None," Terren said with disappointment. "I've sent out a search party."

My stars, what are the chances he's still alive?

"How many more are injured and will need a bed?" she asked.

"None. Everyone who survived the battle is back at the Academy."

Terren seemed too tired to realize he'd just implied that Basen, Neeko, and Abith were dead. Her stomach clenched.

Terren left to speak with Steffen, who was busy treating Effie. She'd been hit by a charging horse but had managed to escape serious injury. Later, however, she'd burned herself while casting a complex spell, and then she'd been stabbed in the back. Still, she fared better than many others.

Alabell had treated more people than she could count, yet there were even more, like Cleve and Peter, who'd been cut on an arm or a leg and whose injuries weren't grievous enough to kill them, so they'd come and gone quickly.

Reela, Annah, and Vithos had survived the battle without injury and taken turns visiting Effie. Steffen had a gash on his arm that he'd bandaged himself and then gotten right back to treating others.

A few of the Krepps had died in battle, none that Alabell knew by name. Rickik and Nebre had both taken deep cuts. A bunch of uninjured Krepps had come in with them, and all proceeded to cluck and shout until Alabell yelled at them to quiet down. From the Kreppen she understood, it seemed they'd been bragging about their number of kills.

Alabell was thankful for the people who'd come from Oakshen and Kyrro City to volunteer. They'd helped save lives by simply watching over the most serious cases and notifying the healers if anyone needed immediate attention. Effie's younger sister, Gabby, was as skilled as many of the healers already at the Academy. Unfortunately for the other patients, she never left Effie's side.

Alabell walked past Terren, Effie, and Gabby to attend

to a restless young man who was drunk on the caregelow he'd been given. As she reminded him of his earlier promise to stay in bed and sleep, she overheard Terren speaking with Steffen.

"How many now?"

"Twenty-nine," Steffen answered.

The number who've died after coming in here, Alabell realized.

Some wounds were too severe for caregelow to fix, like a punctured lung, a sliced open stomach, or a broken skull. Alabell wished there was something she could give those people to send them to their permanent rest sooner, so they wouldn't suffer until the inevitable end. Other injuries required treatments besides caregelow, like broken bones, and thank the stars for that or they would've run out of the argent liquid already.

Even if she hadn't been so busy keeping people alive, Alabell doubted she'd be able to sleep. Pushing Basen away hadn't helped to alleviate this terrible dread she'd known would come.

All these people need help, yet the person I want to save the most I cannot. It was too late to pretend that Basen was just a friend. She realized that now, her heart aching as if slowly being torn in two. It felt as if everything was in slow motion, so many dying, the war all but lost, their world crumbling.

The hole that had opened beneath her feet would swallow her as soon as she stopped working and shut her eyes.

She stayed on her aching feet through the night, refusing to cry as more of her Academy brothers and sisters died. Others were depending on her strength, and she wouldn't let them down.

Basen's mother was part of a team that brought breakfast to the medical building in the morning. Alabell thanked her and was about to ask if she'd heard anything about Basen when she noticed Juliana's grief-stricken expression.

Alabell didn't know how to ask as a building devastation overwhelmed the little bit of appetite enticed by the sweet aroma of food.

"Is...?" No other words came out.

"I don't know yet," Juliana replied.

"I have hope," Alabell lied.

Truthfully, she'd lost hope when Basen had hatched his plan to manipulate Fatholl and take on Yeso's Elves. Even if he lived through that, she'd figured he surely would fall by the end of the war. Part of her hated Terren for requiring too much of Basen. Another part of her hated Basen for being too careless with his life. But she knew both men had no choice. Her only option had been to suppress her feelings for him. But her detachment hadn't been a clean break. She felt as if the two of them were a painting with a rip down its center. She could still see the beauty it held if it became whole.

It wasn't long after Juliana left that Shara ran in screaming, "We need caregelow!" She glanced around the crowded room. "And a bed!"

"What is it?" Alabell asked.

Shara rushed over to her. "Hurry!"

"There are no free beds. Who needs help?"

"I'll stand," a warrior volunteered, gingerly removing

himself from the bed. His legs were cut and bandaged, but he would live.

"In here!" Shara yelled over her shoulder. She grabbed Alabell's white coat. "The caregelow?"

"I have it ready." She pulled a vial from her pocket as she watched the doorway, praying to a god she didn't believe in to let it be Basen. She didn't care if he was an inch from death. She would save him.

Abith and Basen rushed in, carrying Neeko between them.

"Oh my stars," Alabell whispered and ran toward them. Prickles swam over her skin as tears pooled in her eyes. Basen was alive. She was so filled with emotion, she couldn't quite tell what she was feeling.

She forced herself to focus on Neeko as they set him on the free bed, a sheet wrapped around him.

"What happened?" Alabell asked.

They carefully removed the sheet, leaving him shirtless. Much of his torso had been burned. He was barely conscious, his mouth clenched in obvious agony. She then noticed the burns on his chin and his lack of eyebrows.

"He was hit with a fireball while he was flying and fell into more fire," Basen said.

"When?" Alabell asked. "This isn't fresh."

"Yesterday evening," Basen answered.

"It doesn't matter!" Shara protested. "Just give him the caregelow."

"I'm trying to figure out exactly what happened to him first," Alabell told her. "These burns are bad, but they don't appear immediately fatal." *Yet he looks close to death.*

Neeko moaned and turned his head. Shara grabbed his hand. "Try to relax."

Abith and Basen looked exhausted, both panting, but Alabell needed answers from them.

"What happened after he was burned?" she asked.

"A healer in the capital tried to treat him," Abith explained. "But he continued to get worse."

"The healer didn't know what to do," Basen added. "He tried everything he could think of. We brought Neeko here during the night after the last of Ulric's army left."

Alabell realized what the problem was. "The healer put him in cold water, didn't he?"

Basen nodded.

Shara grabbed the caregelow from Alabell's pocket. "Neeko." She held it to his mouth. "Drink this."

"Stop!" Alabell yelped louder than she meant and snatched the potion back. "That will slow his heart and kill him. That healer did more harm than good by putting him in cold water. Get me half of the blankets in that pile there, Shara."

Once Alabell had the blankets, she put them beneath Neeko's feet to raise his legs.

"Now the other half," Alabell instructed.

She covered Neeko except for his face. A few other healers had come over to help. Alabell told one, "Get me a quicken potion."

"Will he live?" Shara asked as the healer ran off.

"Yes. But he doesn't have sufficient blood flow right now."

The healer returned with the potion, and Alabell gave

it to a confused Neeko.

"Immersing him in cold put him into shock and kept his heart from beating as hard as it must to recover from this kind of trauma. We'll improve his circulation and then give him sustenance."

"You mean feed him?" Shara asked.

"In time. Burns like these take away much of his energy, and we need to restore it once his body is stronger. In the meantime, there are potions that can help. Eventually, we can give him the caregelow to prevent infection and heal his skin completely. Don't worry, Shara. I promise you he'll live. We'll even take away those nasty scars."

"I don't care about those as long as he lives. Thank you!" She threw her arms around Alabell and squeezed a grunt out of her.

"You're welcome," Alabell squeaked.

Terren approached, a look of horror on his face. His gaze was stuck on Neeko who looked dead, his face almost as white as the blankets covering him.

"He'll be fine," Alabell assured the headmaster.

"Good! That's very good!" He looked to Basen and Abith. "What happened with Tauwin?"

Abith smiled and turned to Basen. "Why don't you tell him? You were the one who did it."

Basen grinned. "The bastard's dead, Terren."

Dead? He's finally dead? "Are you certain?" Alabell asked.

"I don't think even the best healers in the world can reattach a severed head."

Finally, Tauwin had gotten what he deserved for what

he'd done to her family. She felt sparks of joy, but mixed in was sadness that brought tears to her eyes. Her mother was still gone, and Alabell would never stop missing her.

Terren laughed and grabbed Basen's shoulder. Then he turned and announced to everyone, "Tauwin is dead!"

The healers and the injured all cheered as Terren slapped Basen's back, nearly knocking the wind out of him.

"Well done! I'm calling a Redfield meeting right now. You can tell me everything that happened as we go to the stadium."

Basen smiled politely. "Actually, I'd like to stay with Neeko."

"Let's go, Terren," Abith said. "I'll tell you that and more. There's a lot we need to speak about."

They left amid continued cheers.

Neeko awoke and sat up. "What happened?" His cheeks already had regained some color.

"Lie down," Alabell told him with a gentle smile. "Try to relax. I know it might not be easy with the potion we just gave you, but you must try."

"You'll be better soon," Shara comforted.

"Shara!" he whispered with surprise. "Two hells, I'm at the Academy?"

"Yes." Her dark eyes looked up at Alabell. "Does this mean the war is over?"

"I'm...not sure. Basen?"

She was surprised to find him staring as if he hadn't heard her question. He stepped toward her, and she moved into his arms instinctually.

He leaned down and their lips came together. Heat

spread over her body, a wonderful mixture of excitement and pleasure. It intensified as the moment drew on, blocking out all the other activity in the room.

As passion built, she felt as if they'd been reunited after years apart. This bliss was...right. Contentment warmed her like Basen's embrace.

When their kiss finally ended, Basen appeared confused as he leaned back to look at her.

"Did you ask me something?"

She giggled and kissed him again.

CHAPTER THIRTY-FIVE

Rockbreak brought Sanya to Ulric, and the three of them set off for the castle together. Sanya limped the whole way, yet Ulric didn't offer her an ounce of sympathy. Rockbreak seemed in worse condition as blood dripped from numerous wounds, yet he showed no signs of pain.

The streets were filled with curious lookers. Rockbreak drew their attention, probably cluing them in that the unmasked man at his side was Ulric.

They don't know who I am. But Sanya could tell by their stares that they wanted to.

The man in charge of sending out the flare when the castle came under attack was one of the few who knew about Ulric's plan for Tauwin to die today. The man met them a few streets from the castle and informed them of the good news. Tauwin was dead and the battle had been won. The Academy had retreated. Sanya figured Basen and that flying man had gotten to Tauwin before he'd reached the safety of his army.

She would've liked to have witnessed his last breath.

"How many were killed on either side?" Ulric asked the man.

"I don't know yet, but it's safe to enter the castle now. Everyone else is on the way back."

"Good. Stanmar will keep them from disbanding long enough for me to assure our troops they'll get everything promised to them. Hurry back to the castle and spread the news that I'm alive and unmasked. I want the crown and Takary robe ready when I enter."

"Yes, sire."

As the man ran off, Sanya asked, "What about Cheot? The councilman is loyal to Tauwin."

"He'll work for me because Tauwin's dead. The only person who'll mourn the deposed king is his mother."

Ulric seemed even more confident than before, bordering on arrogant. He wore a smirk that didn't sit well with Sanya. He looked as if he thought he was innocent of any wrongdoing, but Tauwin had been truthful when he'd sworn no involvement in the faked assassination. She would get to the bottom of this.

And then what? No longer needing her mask and robes, she finally should feel free. Only Cheot would want her dead for causing the disappearance of his daughter, Bliss, and Sanya could handle him easily. Still, this didn't feel right.

When they returned to the castle, Ulric was greeted with applause and cheers from the castle staff. A crown was placed upon his head before a white cloak embroidered with blue wings was thrown over his shoulders. Everyone bowed to him, including Sanya. This was the third time these workers had seen a new king crowned, but they celebrated as if Ulric would be the best of all.

They know nothing about him. Sanya wasn't sure she did, either. He'd been like a father to her not long ago, but now he looked like a stranger. She'd felt none of his usual warmth during their walk back.

She gladly took her leave to eat, receive treatment for her wounds, and change her clothing. She felt too exposed and needed to at least cover her arms and legs.

The men returning from the battle flooded into the castle's great hall. Ulric stood on the second floor landing to address them as their new king. Many had served him already, but they'd thought him to be dead. Their relief was palpable when they heard his familiar voice.

"Tauwin died today as planned. He was a greedy liar who would've rather seen Kyrro destroyed than let it fall into someone else's hands."

Sanya watched from the floor above, making sure she was close enough to detect Ulric's energy.

"You fought well, all of you!" he continued. "Today, you have proven that no one can stand against you! The war will soon be won!"

The men cheered.

"In the meantime, you will earn the same coin as usual, and your loyalty will be rewarded with a salary for the rest of your lives. Now celebrate as we prepare a feast!"

Men slammed their boots and the ends of their swords against the stone floor, cheering so loudly that half the city must've heard them.

There goes the last chance for the Academy to recruit anyone else. Sanya wondered if anyone she knew had died in the battle. She could stomach the thought of Effie being killed, though it brought her no joy. But when she imagined Cleve on the receiving end of a sword—the person who'd taught her how to beat the best swordsmen of the Academy—it brought on such a fury that she hurt her hands gripping the railing. She had to admit it now: She hated herself.

Sanya wanted to fight. Of course Ulric would let her join the final battle against the Academy, but what joy could she get out of killing more of her former schoolmates?

"We thought you died!" some men yelled up to Ulric. "What happened? Who died in your place?"

The enormous hall quieted as those assembled waited for an answer.

"I figured Tauwin would eventually send an assassin after me," Ulric replied, "likely before what he figured would be the final battle." He paused as he seemed to be searching for the right words.

He knows he can't get away with lying.

"I took measures to protect myself, and it's unfortunate Tauwin forced me to do that. Had he been a more honorable man, we could've ruled Kyrro together." Ulric lifted his hands. "But don't blame those loyal to Tauwin. This is not their fault. And if anyone locates Kithala Takary, please escort her to the castle without harm. I need to speak with her."

So his mother is missing. It was highly unlikely that Basen or anyone from the Academy would've killed her. But there was nothing left for her in this castle. Sanya might never see her again.

"Food will be ready soon. Eat and enjoy!" Ulric concluded.

As the crowd cheered again, he left his spot and came up the stairs toward Sanya.

"We need to talk," she told the new king.

"It'll have to wait."

"It can't."

He let out a sharp breath as he reached her floor. "Fine, in your apartment."

Once they were inside, she closed the door after them.

He folded his arms. "I'm very busy right now, Sanya. What's so important?"

"I know Tauwin wasn't responsible for the death of that masked man who was supposed to be you."

"Why do you think that?"

Ulric was a good actor, appearing genuinely shocked. But she felt his energy and knew he was beginning to worry.

"Be honest with me," she implored. "If time is short, let's not play games."

He scowled. "Being smart can be dangerous, Sanya. Sometimes intelligent people think of things they shouldn't."

He didn't scare her. "It was you. You killed an innocent man."

"Careful." His mouth tightened. "You wouldn't want me to think your loyalty is faltering. Have you forgotten that you came to me to reclaim your life here in the castle? You're about to have it! Do you really want to give that up?"

Sanya hung her head. "No, that would be foolish. I'm just curious what really happened."

"I'll tell you if you agree to *leave* it alone from now on!" he snapped, pointing a finger as if to lecture her.

"Fine," she said, pretending to be defeated.

"One man had a son he loved very much. As the boy grew older, he made a terrible mistake that resulted in the death of a woman of some importance. The son was arrested and condemned to prison for life. However, his father made a deal to free him. He understood the sacrifice that would be expected of him in return, and he accepted it."

God's mercy, Ulric was more dangerous than Tauwin. The young king's emotions and actions had been predictable, but Ulric was sneaky and just as incapable of empathy. He was no better than Sanya.

"You think you're better than me?" Ulric asked as if reading her mind. "I know you had something to do with Yeso's death. You find a way to get rid of anyone threatening you, just like I do, Sanya! I don't blame you. On the contrary, I see something special in you. I need people like you I can trust. You must decide now if you'll be one of them. Will you?"

"Yes."

"Good." He headed toward the door. "Most people would've apologized by now for failing to kill Tauwin as they promised they would."

She'd already told him what happened, and he blamed her for that? How could she have predicted a flying man would swoop down and kick her in the back?

"I apologize," she said without conviction.

He paused with his hand on the doorknob. "Did anyone call you Laree?"

"Yes."

"Don't you want to know where it came from?"

"I do."

"You do, *what*? You will address me formally from now on."

"I do, *sire*."

"My wife, who is still in Greenedge, was pregnant years ago. We had a baby girl who took one breath in this world before passing on to the next. I loved her more than words can describe. We'd picked a name before she was born. Laree."

He fled the room before giving Sanya a chance to respond. She waited a moment, then closed the door after him.

He was a liar.

He'd lied to his troops about Tauwin attempting to assassinate him, and he'd lied to Sanya about a child he never had. He was trying to manipulate everyone. The name was probably the first that came to his mind.

At the beginning, Sanya had expected to marry Tauwin and become queen of Kyrro. He'd thought he would win the war in a single day, and she would've disposed of him after earning the trust of everyone she needed on her side. But all she'd done was make enemies.

Everything seemed to turn in her favor when Ulric arrived. She'd seen in him a powerful ally and friend. And she might very well get the life in the castle she'd wanted if she stayed to support him. But for this to work, the Academy would have to be taken or destroyed.

Terren would have to die in addition to anyone loyal to Alex or Nick who might seek vengeance against her. If Sanya helped Ulric win the war, he would gladly dispatch her enemies, for they were his enemies as well. But that thought twisted her stomach with guilt. She'd never felt this way until recently and couldn't imagine suffering from it for the rest of her life, which was a certainty if she took the easy path before her.

She could run from Kyrro. It wouldn't be difficult to get a horse and travel to the far reaches of Ovira where she'd never be found. She could live like she had during that brief time in Raywhite Forest with her loyal bear, Muskie. Or she could convince Ulric to send her to Greenedge on ship.

Alternatively, she could steal the money to hire her own crew to take her there. Her many skills would give her a nearly endless variety of paths to choose from once she arrived. If she was going to abandon this life in the castle, Greenedge seemed the place she'd be most happy.

As that thought entered her mind, she realized it wasn't true. The one place she'd felt she truly belonged, even though her time there had been short, was the Academy.

It's the only place I really want to be. If I seek a life elsewhere, who knows the atrocities I might commit to stay alive. Do I really want to steal, manipulate, even kill again, only to suffer the consequences later?

The Academy was the one place she had a chance to become the woman she wanted to be. But she must face her punishment first.

It might very well be death, but she was willing to try her luck.

If the Academy somehow won the war without her help, and she turned herself in afterward, they might dismiss her motives as merely a willingness to be taken alive rather than killed during her inevitable capture. By going now, she could warn them the war was not over with Tauwin's death. She could promise more information if they let her live.

No, she was done with lies. She would keep any promises she made from now on.

She gathered her few belongings and limped out of the castle without anyone seeming to care.

END OF BOOK FOUR

New Releases

Please consider leaving a review on Amazon. They are extremely important. Thank you.

The next book will be the final of the series.

Author Information

Thank you so much for reading. I hope you enjoyed what turned out to be one of my favorites of the series.

If you want to discuss the series with me or just want to say hello, look me up on Facebook or email me at brian@btnarro.com. Or feel free to start a forum discussion on my author profile page.

Come visit my website at www.btnarro.com and chat with me. I post updates about my progress with the series and provide insight about the creative process.

I'm hoping to have the next one finished by November or December, 2016. I have some big ideas for this final book of the series, so I'm excited to start writing it. Hopefully you will be just as excited to read it.

80774260R00234

Made in the USA
Middletown, DE
16 July 2018